HOST *FOR THE*
HOLIDAYS

HOST FOR THE HOLIDAYS

A CHRISTMAS ESCAPE NOVEL

MARTHA KEYES

PARADIGM
PRESS

To Paris—my first international love

Christmas Escape Bingo

Read all seven books in the series to get a Christmas romance blackout!

Broken elevator	Sleigh ride through the mountains	Allergic reaction	Snowstorm Power outage	A walk down main street
Candlelit house tour	Define the boundaries chat (multiple answers)	Ice Skating on a frozen pond	Mint hot Chocolate	"Highway to Hell" ringtone
Boat ride	"Fresh" chocolate milk	FREE SPACE	Reindeer Attack	Miniature Christmas Tree
Hot chocolate at a Christmas market	Trip to Ikea	Burning hot chocolate	Home Alone movie night (multiple answers)	Listening to Bing Crosby
An angry dachshund	Blanket fort	Snowy Beach	Mandalorian pajamas	Snowmobile ride through the mountains

ONE

MADI

JUST ADDED TO THE TIPPITY TOP OF THE LIST OF Utterly and Completely Worthless Things: getting an "A" in every term of high school French. *Je m'appelle Madi* and *Comment allez-vous?* just aren't cutting it as I speak with the employee at the lost luggage office in the Paris airport.

Would it have been so hard for Madame Wilson to teach us something useful like, "Hey, I've watched that carrousel spin around more times than a teacup at Disneyland, and my perfectly packed bag is nowhere to be seen"? Not once has this woman asked me a question that would necessitate an answer like, "I like to play soccer." I probably should have listened to my friend Siena and downloaded one of those language learning apps for a refresher before leaving home.

Having said that, I strongly suspect this woman speaks perfectly good English, but she's purposely trying to make it hard for me. Admittedly, making it hard for me is pretty easy at the moment. I just escaped eleven hours in a tight space with a herd of strangers, hovering miles above solid ground. Everything about that is contrary to my natural habitat.

After fifteen minutes, I walk away with an assurance that my bags will be delivered to my vacation rental when they arrive at the

1

airport, though when that will be, I have no idea. Thankfully, the taxi driver who approaches me just outside seems a bit less inclined to hate me than the lost luggage lady. Thank heaven for that, since it's negative seven hundred degrees outside, and my oversized cardigan and leggings have not equipped me for December in Paris.

The driver looks at the address of the Airbnb my boyfriend, Josh, booked for me and tells me in a thick French accent that it will be no problem to get me there. Grunting a bit under the weight, he chucks my carry-on into his trunk and opens the door for me to get in.

I sit down on the leather seat and take in a breath full of the gloriously heated air. It also happens to be saturated with cigarette smoke, and I try to stifle a cough. Siena warned me that the French still smoke like it's the 1960s.

She also warned me that French men are flirtatious—sometimes aggressively so. My taxi driver does not seem to fit that second stereotype, however, unless communicating in grunts is considered "aggressive flirtation" here. Either way, I'm not complaining. In the lead-up to this trip, I heard enough jokes about *Taken* to last me a lifetime.

I set my backpack full of camera gear next to me, clenching my hand around the strap as I realize how fortunate it is that *this* didn't get lost. Not only is it thousands of dollars of equipment, it's my passport into the future. The hopeful future, at least.

I pull out my phone from the bag's side pocket. It's still super early morning back home, but I promised Siena I'd text her when I arrived.

Madi: I made it!!! I'm actually in Paris! Hope you're sleeping cuz at least that'll make one of us. *GIF of woman propping open her eyelids with paperclips*

I cringe thinking of how much an international phone plan is costing me for these two and a half weeks in Paris, but when I told

Siena I wasn't going to get one at all, she insisted, offering to pay for it herself.

"I can't be cut off from my other half for three weeks," she said. "I need to know the second you have the ring on your finger."

Don't be fooled. Siena's not crazy about my boyfriend (slight understatement). But she tries to be supportive, and *I* try to believe her icy heart will melt once Josh proves he's taking things to the next level with some hard evidence. Nothing is harder than diamond, right?

My mom and my brother, Jack, will embrace him with open arms at that point, too. I'm counting on it.

Okay, so Jack is more likely to embrace Josh's face with an open fist. He *really* doesn't like Josh. Protective Older Brother Syndrome and all that nonsense. But since Jack has a history of dating and discarding my friends, who then discard *me*, I don't lose too much sleep over his opinion.

I glance down at my ring finger with a little hiccup of nerves —or maybe that's just the airplane food making itself heard. All I know is that this finger has been bare as a baby's bottom my entire life, and it finally looks like that might change. In Paris, of all places!

When he invited me to tag along on this business trip, Josh hinted pretty heavily at a perfect Paris proposal (see how amazingly alliterative that is?). I'm trying to balance my hope for that long-awaited event against the other times I've let my expectations get away from me, only to be disappointed. A woman's heart has only so many cracks and crevices to cram those kinds of experiences in before all of it pops out like a package of Pillsbury biscuits (those things are terrifying).

But Josh has had a really crazy year at work, and I know from past experience that he can pull through when it counts. So even though I got to a point last month where I was ready to go our separate ways, he helped remind me of all we've done and experienced together over the past two years—and convinced me that there was no place better than Paris to recharge us and start fresh. Not that I needed much convincing to do Christmas in the City of Love.

I swipe to unlock my screen and go to my recent calls, tapping on *Josh-wah*. No, he doesn't really spell it like that, but it's the nickname for him I stole from Rachel on *Friends*. His phone rings a few times and goes to voicemail.

I'm used to it. Josh can be tricky to get a hold of—like I said, he's a busy guy—but he *always* calls me back. His flight got in earlier this morning, so he's probably sleeping. The thought makes my eyes droop a bit with jetlagged jealousy.

Or maybe he's *not* sleeping. This is a work trip for him, so he flew on the company dime. Business class. I saw what that section of the plane looks like. The seats are like the Batmobiles of chairs, transforming into a luscious sleep space where you can extend your leg until your knee actually straightens. Magic.

"Hey!" I say to the machine. "It's me! I made it! I'm in a taxi on my way to the Airbnb right now. Took a while since the airline lost my luggage. I may have to borrow some clothes from you. Anyway, thank you so much for taking care of the Airbnb for me. Honestly, I can't wait to climb in bed and take a nap, but I'll keep my phone ringer volume up in case you call."

I catch my reflection in the rearview mirror, and my eyes balloon. Maybe a shower first. No wonder the woman at lost luggage kept looking at my hair. It looks like I put it in a ponytail then stuck it in a greasy tumble dryer.

I run my free hand through it to try to calm the mess a bit.

"Anyway," I say, "call me when you get this! Can't wait to see you. In Paris!" I barely smother a squeal. The glance the taxi driver sends at me through the rearview mirror tells me I'm as basic as tourists come.

The traffic in this city is like nothing I've ever seen, but the movie-worthy building façades lining the busy streets offer plenty of distraction from the many near-fender benders. I'm wishing I had those paperclips from the GIF I sent Siena, because blinking is my worst enemy. You might think black, wrought-iron balconies, creamy buildings, and gray rooftops would get old after a while, but you'd be wrong. Add in the Christmas lights and the wreaths and garlands hanging up all over the city, and . . . *contented sigh.*

Finally, the taxi turns onto a one-way street and stops about halfway down. The driver slings his arm over the seatback to look at me. "This is it," he says in that thick accent.

I'm not entirely sure what *this* is, since we're surrounded by tall buildings, and the only doors I can see are massive, arched ones that look like the entrance to places well out of my price range.

I smile. Good thing Josh is the one paying for this place. He felt so bad the hotel he's staying in was booked full, so he must have sprung for a ritzy rental for me. Having a kitchen works better for me, anyway. I can't afford to be eating out every meal.

I smile at the taxi driver and open my door despite not being sure where exactly I'm supposed to go. A blast of freezing air reminds me again that it's December, and I'm not in California anymore. Also, my real coat is in my bag that, according to the lady at the airport, is apparently in Morocco on its own vacation.

The driver steps out of the car, rolls his shoulders, lights a cigarette—priorities, people—then pops the trunk. He hefts my suitcase out and looks at me. "One hundred euros."

TWO

MADI

My stomach plummets. "One hundred?" I figured I'd be paying a third of that, tops. Maybe I should have done more research? Or maybe I shouldn't have made it so obvious that I'm new to this travel gig.

He nods, pulling out the cigarette in his mouth and blowing a puff of smoke straight at me. With his other hand, he keeps hold of the suitcase handle like my carry-on is full of cocaine and he's not handing it over until I show him the dough. I want to fight him on this, but that taxi trunk looks mighty roomy, and, as much as I love Josh, he is no Liam Neeson.

I pull the credit card out of my purse, my stomach twisting in knots, and hand it over to him, wondering how close to my credit limit this will put me. Little known fact: credit card companies don't love giving credit to people with unstable jobs. I can't really blame them.

The driver runs the card in a handheld machine, waits, then shakes his head.

"Declined?" I squeak.

"Declined," he says, imitating my accent in a way I find entirely unnecessary. Do I really sound like that?

"Can you try it again?" I ask.

He barely suppresses an eye roll, then swipes it again. "Declined," he says in that same attempted American accent.

I take the card back and rifle through my purse, pulling out the precious euros I got at the bank and choosing two fifties. I hand them to him, hoping it's not evident by my face that I'm not at all accustomed to throwing this much money around for a car ride.

He releases my hostage carry-on and, euros in hand, gets in the car with his glowing cigarette, slamming the door and zooming off faster than I can say a weak *Merci*.

I try to shake off the dent just put into my already tight budget. Since graduation a couple years ago, I've been living from paycheck to paycheck, hoping that business will pick up at some point. Turns out, majoring in photography does not guarantee you'll become the next Annie Liebowitz. Go figure.

I'm hoping to put those days behind me, though. Josh has promised to put me in touch with the director of marketing at his company, Dan Vincent. This could be huge for my career. And by *huge for my career*, I mean it could actually *be* a career, which my current situation does not at all qualify as. This is a sort of last shot I'm giving my dream before surrendering and getting a desk job.

Product photography might not be exactly what I was hoping to do when I set out, but this is the real world. I can either starve while pursuing my passion of portrait photography, or I can do a Ross Geller-worthy pivot to a different type of photography and eat three square meals. Compromises must be made; pivots must be embraced.

Blowing air into my freezing hands, I turn to the building next to me. It has a big, blue number five over the massive set of doors. Yesterday, Josh sent me screenshots of the check-in instructions in case my internet didn't work. He's the one who booked the Airbnb, since I didn't have the app or any guest review history. Checking his messages, I verify that it's the right building, then read the instructions the host sent him. Apparently, a neighbor will be giving me the keys.

There's a big pad of buttons next to the door, and I follow the instructions and press the bottom one. After a bit of ringing, someone answers over the microphone in French.

I wince. Anyone who thinks you need to speak the same language as someone to understand what they're saying is full of it. The guy answering is irritated in all languages.

"Um," I say, dusting the cobwebs off my high school French, "*Bonjour. Je m'appelle—*"

Beep. A loud click follows the beep. It sounds like it came from the door, but I have no idea what it means. Did he just dead-bolt it to keep me from getting in?

"Hello?" I say into the microphone on the button pad. Dead silence.

I hesitate, wondering if I should press the button again, but I don't really feel like being yelled at, even if I have no idea what's being said—my mind is all too ready to fill in the blanks. Instead, I give the door a little push, and, miraculously, it gives way.

I step through, yanking my bag over the door ledge and pulling it along through the dark archway. My suitcase wheels make a racket, but since it's cobblestone, the sound has a bit of charm to it. At least, that's what I tell myself as my hand vibrates like I'm shooting a machine gun.

I emerge into a courtyard and look around. My heart soars, floating upwards like Mary Poppins with her umbrella. Cream stone walls rise above me on all sides, punctuated by white-framed, curtained windows, green potted plants, and a few festive wreaths. My hands itch to take out my camera because I'm surrounded by the essence of Paris. At least, as much as one can know the essence of Paris after a smoky taxi ride from the airport.

My mouth stretches in a gleeful grin, and all my travel troubles are immediately forgotten. I get to stay here—in this beautiful, swanky building—for almost three weeks!

"*Excusez-moi.*"

I whirl around and find a middle-aged man walking toward me. He starts going off in a language I'm positive is not French, because it sounds nothing like what I learned in high school. He's definitely not telling me he likes to play soccer or asking me where the library is.

Just generally, he does not look thrilled to see me.

"*Bonjour*," I say with a courageous attempt at a smile. I don't want to brag, but my accent is pretty good. Or so Madame Wilson told me.

The man is unimpressed. "I have been waiting for you for an hour," he replies in heavily accented English.

"Oh," I say. "I am *so* sorry! The airline lost my baggage, and it took—"

He holds up a ring of keys that look a lot like the massive, rusted ones I almost bought at Hobby Lobby for my entry table. "Through there. Top floor." He points toward a set of French doors I must have passed in the dark archway. He holds up one key. "This is for the door from the street." He holds up the next one. "This one is for the door to the building." And one more. "This one is for the apartment." He hands them to me, nods, then turns.

Mouth still open with apologies on the tip of my tongue, I watch as he walks away, leaving via the big doors I just came through. I'm starting to think Siena was playing a sick joke on me when she told me French men are flirtatious. So far, they just hate me.

By the time I manage to open the building door and take the stairs up to the top—that's right, there's no elevator, and I'm on the fifth floor—I'm breathing like I just completed a triathlon. But I'm not over the finish line yet. The three medieval keys in my hand weigh a metric ton (look how French I already am, using the metric system!), and I still have to remember which one goes to this particular door. I am woefully inexperienced at recognizing the subtle differences in ancient key design.

After five minutes of finagling, I'm ready to give up. Apparently, I will spend my nights on this apartment landing because I'm not smart enough for Parisian doors.

I give it another go, determined to take a shower and a nap before I see Josh. The struggle continues, though, and this nightmare door is like the wind that turned my Mary Poppins umbrella inside out so I can't float anymore.

I might lose my mind. I just want to get inside, for the love of Pete.

Why does Paris hate me so much? I've been trying to stay upbeat, but it feels like the universe is telling me to get out of Dodge. I'm not someone to cuss, but plenty of four-letter words are pinging around my brain when my phone starts vibrating.

I scramble to take the phone from the side pocket of my backpack and hurry to answer. "Josh!"

"Hey, Mads."

I let out a relieved sigh. The familiar sound of his voice is exactly what I need. Everything is going to be okay. I'm in Paris. With my boyfriend. Soon to be fiancé.

"Sorry I missed your call," he says. There's chatter in the background like he's in a crowded place. "Everyone went to the hotel café after we arrived, and it was pretty loud, so I didn't hear my phone ring."

"No worries," I say. "I can't believe we're both here!" Well, not *here* here. But he knows what I mean.

"I know, right? So sorry about your luggage."

"It's okay." I toss away his sympathy as if I have no need of clothes. I packed my carry-on full of my toiletries, shoes, and boots so I could stay under the checked luggage weight limit. In retrospect, perhaps that wasn't the best idea.

I'm feeling rejuvenated by Josh's voice, so I balance the phone between my ear and my shoulder, sticking the key back in the lock. "You won't believe what a crazy day it's been, though. The lady at the lost luggage place looked like she was trying to shoot me with eye lasers—"

"Mads," he says, "I'm so sorry, but I've gotta run. It looks like we're going to have a little impromptu meeting. But I'll call you right after."

"Oh, okay," I say, trying not to betray that I'm deflating like a balloon. "I'll talk to you later."

"Love you."

The phone clicks, and, mercifully, so does the door. It squeaks loudly as it opens.

Victory! Who knew the hardest part of traveling to Paris would be unlocking my apartment? I'm assuming the hotel Josh is staying at doesn't have this sort of key, but honestly, nothing is as I expected so far, so I'm going to go ahead and refrain from placing any bets. Especially because I'm a hundred euros poorer than I was a half-hour ago.

I pull my suitcase inside and shut the squeaky door, feeling accomplished. Triathletes ain't got nothin' on me. I look around, taking stock of my new digs, wondering if I should have hired MTV *Cribs* to come film me.

But no. I definitely shouldn't have, and not just because the *Cribs* crewmembers are probably old enough to be retired by now.

Let's just say, this place used all its wow factor on the curb appeal.

The apartment is . . . small. And bare. The courtyard gave me *Downton Abbey* expectations; reality looks more like my freshman dorm. There isn't a single thing on the walls, which, honestly, could really use some pictures to cover up the places where the paint has peeled off. There's a couch up against the window with a scraggly blanket thrown over it, a small coffee table, and a galley kitchen to my right. More like half of a galley kitchen. Or half of a half of a galley kitchen. Also, is that a washing machine in there?

I take in a breath. Okay, so the place isn't winning any interior design awards, and Chip and Joanna Gaines would definitely not dub it an "open-concept floor plan," but if this is what Josh chose, I'm sure it was the best option. I'd choose location over luxury anyway.

My phone tells me it's almost 2 o'clock in the afternoon. I

blink, realizing how heavy and weird my eyelids feel. I eye the blanket on the couch, which is trying to cast a sleep spell over me. It takes every ounce of my willpower not to run over, drape it over my body, and lie down.

I'm haunted by the view of myself in the taxi rearview mirror, though, so a shower must come first. Once I'm clean and have an hour or so of rest, I will be ready to take on Paris and leave all the travel drama behind.

THREE

MADI

NOTHING IS EASY HERE. FIGURING OUT HOW TO TURN on the shower was like Unlocking the Door 2.0, but there were no dungeon keys, just dials, buttons, and a mysterious, dangling pull string. Whose idea was it to put an electric device in the same cage —an accurate description of this tiny shower—as a steady stream of water?

At least I'm free of the airplane and travel grime, even if the host only provided men's body wash and shampoo. In my rush to shower, I didn't realize until I was sopping wet that I forgot my toiletries in my carry-on. Having no conditioner means my hair will be a giant knot to comb through.

Bracing myself for electrocution, I press the button to turn off the water and reach past the shower curtain for a towel.

A loud grating noise makes me pause. That sounds way too close to be coming from anywhere but the apartment. It happens again, and I realize what it is. After how long I spent trying the key in the lock, I'd know the sound anywhere.

Sure enough, the squeak of the front door reaches me easily in the bathroom. I freeze with my hand on the towel, my heartrate kicking up to *Taken*-appropriate levels.

Footsteps approach. I might faint any second.

I tug the towel from the rack—if I'm going to be murdered, I'll at least be halfway decent when I do it—and wrap it under my armpits. My hands are almost useless, they're shaking so badly, but I manage to secure the towel in place.

There's an imperative knock on the bathroom door, followed by a question in a foreign language.

Oh gosh! It's a man. I reach out of the curtain, fumbling for my phone sitting on the small porcelain sink basin. The man in my life closest to a Liam Neeson figure is Siena's dad, and I'm praying he's awake. My wet butterfingers can't grasp the phone, though, and it clatters to the floor, tumbling toward the door.

The man repeats his question, louder and more urgent this time. Ugh. How is it possible to take three years of a language and not be able to recognize whether that's what's being spoken?! Why it matters which language he's speaking, I couldn't tell you.

I look around and grab the only weapon within arm's reach: a shampoo bottle. I pull the shower curtain closed just as the door opens, and I do the only thing a person can possibly do in this scenario: scream.

The unintelligible speaking begins again, and I'm pretty sure it's French. If I die today, someone please inform Madame Wilson of my small linguistic victory.

For a second, I'm torn between the need to stay in my fortress, which is a .00005-inch-thick shower curtain, and to face my assailant. I'll have to either squirt the shampoo in his eyes or throw the bottle at his head, and for either scenario, I'll need to see what I'm doing.

The second option seems best. Somehow I don't imagine a bit of eye stinging will deter this guy. Anyone who can unlock the apartment door that quickly is a foe to be reckoned with.

I cock my arm back and rip open the shower curtain, hurtling the shampoo bottle toward the door.

The man's got lightning-quick reflexes, and he ducks, avoiding my assault like a black-ops ninja. Whatever that is. The important thing is this is *not* his first rodeo, not that the bottle would have hit him anyway. I'm a photographer, people, not Jason Bourne.

He straightens again, hands up, looking at me like I'm a lunatic. *Me*, the lunatic! Can you believe this guy?! Also, at the risk of betraying how sheltered my life has been, I was not aware that cold-blooded killers were so young and attractive. The man has an impressive jaw covered in the perfect length of 5 o'clock shadow. Or 2:45 shadow, I guess, based on when I last checked my phone. Maybe that's the perfect length?

"Stay away," I say, holding the shower curtain up to me in case my towel decides to abandon me. I reach behind me for the body wash, keeping my eyes on the man. Geez. He's *really* young—like mid-twenties. How did he get caught up in this life?

He's got his hand up to protect his face, but he's averting his gaze rather than looking at me. For some reason, it almost seems like he's doing it to give me privacy, but more likely, he's trying to shield his eyes in case I execute Plan B and squirt them with shower gel.

"I'm not going to hurt you," he says.

Either my French abilities are way better than I gave myself or Madame Wilson credit for, or the man is speaking English. Safe to say it's the latter option. But I mustn't be lulled into a false sense of security.

"Here," he says. "I'll close the door so you can change." True to his word, he shuts it.

Unexpected move for a man trying to kill me? A bit, yes. I'm beginning to second guess myself, but I keep hold of the body wash bottle just in case.

Changing into something more secure than this small bath towel—seriously, it barely covers the essential areas—is tempting, but the idea of him charging back in while I'm mid-change keeps me in place.

"There should be a key in the cabinet," he says from behind the door, as though he can read my thoughts.

I step out of the shower, keeping an eye on the door as I open the cabinet. Sure enough, there's a key there. I insert it into the keyhole, praying that these doors lock more easily than they unlock.

I let out a large sigh when clicks tells me I've succeeded.

"I just want to talk," he says from the other side. If it weren't for the tiniest hint of a French accent, I might have thought he was American.

With a tug on the handle to ensure it really is locked, I pick up my clothes—worn, wrinkly clothes—and set them on the counter. "Why are you here, and what do you want from me?"

"I just want to know how you got into this apartment." He sounds like he's trying to talk down a crazy person.

"With the keys," I say. Does he think I Spiderman'd up the façade and slipped through a window? It was hard enough getting in the normal way.

"Wait," he says. "Are you Josh?"

My hand goes to my sopping wet hair, and I glance in the mirror. Do I look like a man? Do most French men wrap a towel under their armpits to cover their pecs after showering?

"No, Josh is my boyfriend." Realization dawns on me. "Are you the host?"

"Yes," he says. "But the booking was only for one person."

"Yeah. Me. Madi." I clasp my bra, then reach for my shirt. "Josh isn't staying here. He just made the booking for me." I don't understand why this guy cares so much. I looked in the bedroom, and there's a bed big enough for two there.

I pull on my leggings and cringe. No one should ever have to put on yesterleggings. They're like the clothing equivalent of soggy cereal—formless and droopy. But since my other clothes are partying it up in Morocco, I'm stuck with them.

"We weren't expecting you, you know," the host says. "Or anyone. The second part of the payment never went through. We've been trying to get a hold of . . . your boyfriend, but we haven't had any luck, so we figured no one was coming. That's why I was so surprised to hear someone in the bathroom when I got here."

I pause with a droopy sock in my hand. "Oh my gosh. I'm *so* sorry." Here I thought this guy was the criminal, but it's me. I have no right to be here.

"Go ahead and finish up," he replies. "We'll talk when you come out." His footsteps fade away.

I'm basically dressed, but I look in the small, round mirror on the wall and comb through my long, brown hair with my fingers. Without my usual conditioner it's like trying to comb through a crocheted blanket. I've looked better, that's for sure, but now is not the time to worry about that. This guy wants his money (I'm sensing a trend here in Paris), and for all I know, he's out there holding my suitcase hostage like the taxi driver did.

I pick up my phone from the floor—no notifications from Josh yet—and open the door, stepping out. The Airbnb host is sitting on the couch with an open folder on the coffee table in front of him. He's looking over it with a pair of thick-rimmed glasses on and a red pen in hand. It's a very non-murdery picture. If I'd seen this view of him, I probably wouldn't have felt the desire to summon Mr. Neeson.

I head to the bedroom, glad the guy is occupied enough that I can manage to drag the comb through my hair before talking money. Maybe Josh will call by the time I brush through the tangles.

"That's my room," he calls over to me.

I stop in the doorway, hesitating for a second. Is that an informational comment? "Yeah," I say with a laugh, cuz *why is he making this weird?* I turn to him and smile. "I promise I'll give it back when I leave."

He stands up, pulling off the glasses and setting them on the coffee table. "No. I mean, you aren't sleeping in that room."

Sheesh. This guy is a kill-joy. Is money all he cares about? I swipe to unlock my phone and press *Josh-wah*'s name. "I'll call Josh and have him try the payment again."

"That's not—"

"Hold on," I say as it starts ringing. I turn away, and he stops talking. If it's as loud at Josh's hotel as it was earlier, I'll need all my focus to hear.

But it goes to voicemail. I clench my eyes shut. Why can't Josh just answer his phone every once in a while? I try him three more times, sending my host reassuring smiles over my shoulder. They get less convincing with every unanswered ring.

So I shoot Josh a text in case he's still in the meeting and can't take calls, and then I watch for those three dots to tell me he's responding.

Nope. Nothing.

"Why don't we try my credit card?" I'm not particularly hopeful, since my hundred-euro payment didn't go through less than an hour ago, but I need to do *something*.

"Sure," the guy says, pulling out his phone.

I open the Airbnb app and navigate to the payment section, inputting my credit card details. My eyes bulge at the sum listed: over three hundred euros. And that's only part of the total. You'd think for that much, you'd get some conditioner and a couple of throw pillows.

"Is there a problem?"

"No," I hurry to say. After chucking a shampoo bottle at this guy's head, I'm thinking he won't need much motivation to send me packing. I press the submit button. "There." Josh will pay me back. In fact, we'll be sharing finances soon enough. I'm just praying the engagement doesn't last as long as the dating phase has.

The guy looks down at his phone and swipes to refresh the app. He looks up at me and shakes his head. "It didn't work."

I look down at my phone and, sure enough, a message pops up telling me the payment declined.

Panic starts to set in. I can't get a hold of Josh, I have no baggage, Paris refuses to acknowledge my American credit, and I am currently trespassing on private property.

"Lemme try on my computer," I say.

He cocks an eyebrow at me. He's as skeptical as I am that it'll do anything different, but I'm desperate, and I'm secretly hoping Josh will call back while I stall. I grab my laptop out of my backpack and, after inputting the longest, most convoluted WiFi password in the history of *homo sapiens*—the guy has to read it to me three times—I try the payment online.

The host stands in front of me, waiting for his money, probably ready to chuck my carry-on and precious camera gear out the window and onto those cobblestones the second it declines.

I can already see on my end that the payment failed. You know what else failed? Whatever physiological mechanism keeps me from tearing up. My eyes are filling, and I'm about to water this laptop keyboard. I blink like a madwoman to get rid of the tears.

"It didn't work," I say, shutting the laptop far too enthusiastically for someone who is about to be homeless in Paris. "I think my credit card company thinks it's fraud." Or maybe they just know I can't pay them three hundred euros plus 24% interest. "But Josh should call any minute."

My host isn't fooled by my brittle optimism. He's looking at my shiny eyes, taking stock of me. He nods. "I can show you around the apartment while we wait."

I'm pretty sure I've seen it all—it's not very big—but I agree to this without hesitation. Anything to delay my eviction.

He shows me the living area, which might as well be an IKEA display, since I'm fairly certain every single thing is from there, but it's all worn down. We head to the kitchen after. It's barely big enough for the two of us, but he doesn't seem to mind as he shows me where to find the crockery and utensils. It doesn't take long—there aren't many of them. The fridge is hotel-room size with a freezer that might fit a frozen pizza or two if it wasn't overgrown with freezer burn.

"And this is the washer," he says, pointing to the machine I noticed earlier.

"Cool. And the dryer?"

He raises a brow. "There is no dryer."

I chuckle. This guy is actually pretty funny.

But he's deadpan, and my smile fades. "Wait, what?"

He jerks his head toward the bedroom, and we make our way over there. "You dry your clothes on one of these." He opens the window to reveal a contraption I've never seen before. It looks a bit like a dish-drying rack that got zapped by the machine on *Honey, I Blew Up the Kid*. It's like an upside-down pyramid of clotheslines. He gives it a gentle spin. "This one is mine, though. Yours is outside of your window."

This guy is weirdly possessive of things that he's agreed to rent out to guests. "My window?"

"I'll show you."

He leads me out of the bedroom. Just to the left, there's an opening I hadn't even noticed before. It leads to a dark, narrow staircase from my nightmares.

I'm starting to get *Taken* vibes again, but after the shampoo incident, I'm too scared to do anything but follow him up. Every step whines like the melting witch in *The Wizard of Oz*.

Finally, we emerge into the light—there's no door to this room. I look around the space. There's a red curtain running along one wall and another, much smaller one just beside it. It must be some sort of anteroom, but I don't see a door anywhere that leads to my actual room.

The guy pulls aside the big red curtain like P.T. Barnum. "This is where you'll be sleeping."

I stare. And stare. And my eyes fill with tears. Again.

FOUR

RÉMY

THE AMERICAN IS COMPLETELY SILENT AS SHE LOOKS AT her room, and I can't really blame her. I came this morning to check out the place before heading in to work, and even though I only had time to glance into this room, I admit, it is not a pretty sight. It makes me grateful that I'm sleeping in André's room rather than this one.

André is a good friend, so when his mom suddenly got sick, I stepped in to help out with his newly acquired Airbnb, since his first guest was due to arrive in just a few days. I got a text while I was at work today, though, telling me not to expect the guest anymore because of a lack of both response and payment. I almost felt relieved for the guest, even if I was slightly disappointed on my own account. I was kind of looking forward to meeting Josh and speaking English with him.

But here I am, showing the room to this young, American woman, who is *not* named Josh. Her brown hair is still wet, and it falls down almost to her elbows, leaving wet marks on her shoulders and back. She's fresh from the shower, which means the sprinkling of freckles across her nose and cheeks is visible, as are a pair of soft pink lips.

These are the things that escaped my notice initially. I was too distracted trying to protect myself from projectile toiletries.

Anyway, to put it briefly, she's beautiful. But she also looks like I just asked her to make dinner from the contents of the garbage. I don't really understand her surprise. There are pictures of the room on Airbnb.

"It used to be a maid's room," I say, hoping that might help take the look of horror off her face. There's nothing romantic to *me* about a tiny space like this, but Americans are strange creatures. They love anything old and on the verge of breaking down, as long as it's in Europe.

"I don't really like small spaces," she says in a bare whisper. Her gaze moves to the ladder. "Or heights."

"Oh." I wasn't expecting that, but I can see why it's a problem. The bed can only be accessed by a ladder. Underneath is a small dresser for clothes and a little desk that folds out from the wall. The ceiling slopes, making it impossible to sit up in bed— we're on the top floor of the building, just under the roof, after all. I'm not even sure how you're supposed to get situated in bed, to be honest. Army crawl, maybe?

In any case, we're pushing it having the two of us in here. It's *that* small. If she's got claustrophobia and a fear of heights, this place might have been constructed by *Fear Factor* specifically for her.

"Could I just have the other room?" she asks with a smile full of clenched teeth.

I give her a look. She's pulling off the just-out-of-the-shower look pretty dang well, frankly, but just because she's pretty doesn't mean I should throw out the rules. Right? I'm here to ensure she has a good stay in the room she rented, and her review (five stars, as I promised André) will not be accurate or helpful to future guests if she stays in the room *I'm* supposed to sleep in.

"I'll pay extra," she adds.

I chuckle slightly. "You haven't even paid what you owe for *this*."

"Right," she says, biting her lip. "But I *will*."

"Sorry," I say with a sympathetic grimace, "that room downstairs is where I sleep." I feel for this girl, but no way am I giving up that bed for this one—or sharing the double bed with her, if that was in her head somewhere. Probably not, seeing as she has a boyfriend.

"Wait," she says, looking at me intently. "I thought I rented the apartment."

I stare at her for a few seconds. "You rented a *room* in the apartment. This room, specifically. The rest of the space is shared."

The silence stretches on for a good ten seconds. "Right."

Is it just me, or does she look like she might be about to cry? And why do I feel like a huge jerk for telling her what she should have known from the Airbnb listing? I'm not sure how far my responsibilities to this guest extend, but I can't say drying tears was one I anticipated.

When I came in the room this morning, I hadn't really noticed the second small curtain. I'm sincerely hoping it's hiding something that will help my guest feel better about this space. Whatever's behind it, it'll be better if I keep my reaction positive —help her make the best of things. I've got to if a 5-star review is in my future.

Crossing my fingers for closet space, I pull back the curtain.

Toilet. It's a toilet.

I nearly burst into laughter because, living in a city as old as Paris, you see a lot of quirky spaces, but this one is on a whole different level. The red curtain is so close to the toilet that there's no room for someone to actually sit down on it without a wall of fabric brushing against their face. It would have been better to just forgo the attempt at privacy altogether. I assume this was one of the things André intended to address before his mom got sick.

Madi doesn't even talk. She just stares. I'm kind of worried she might pass out, and there just isn't space here for that sort of thing.

25

"Um," she says in a weak voice, "I'm going to try to call Josh again. Can I have a minute?"

"Yeah," I say. "I'll just be downstairs." I have a mountain of papers to grade. Part of me hopes she decides she doesn't want to stay here after all. André would still split the nonrefundable part of the rental with me, and then I could spend the upcoming Christmas break here in peace. Much as I love my mom, my own space sounds pretty amazing after living with her since my landlord ended my rental contract two months ago.

But that's not going to help André. He bought the property from the last Airbnb owner and was planning to spend the past week getting it ready. But now he's in New York with his mom. Canceling the booking would have been a black mark on his brand new record, so I stepped in. He's my best friend, and he's really counting on this place being a success. Getting excellent reviews is key to getting more visibility and more bookings, and Madi's stay—assuming she does, indeed, end up paying—would be the first one.

I sit down on the couch to get back to grading. Besides the fact that there are no doors separating this space from the room upstairs, the walls and ceiling here are paper thin, and I can hear every step Madi takes. She's pacing, so there are a lot of them.

A few minutes later, she comes down the stairs, looking at me apologetically—and like she's still fighting off tears. "The signal isn't strong enough up there."

I grimace sympathetically. "These walls were not made with Wi-Fi and cell signal in mind. You're welcome to use my room, though."

She smiles—a valiant but not entirely successful attempt—and thanks me, then disappears into my room.

The ironic thing is that, even though Wi-Fi and cell signal don't do well here, noise carries. Which means, even though the door is closed, I can hear almost every word she says once she makes her call.

I try to focus on grading the papers, but even my students'

atrocious English isn't enough to distract me from the fact that Madi is sniffing as she talks.

And every snippet I catch tugs a bit more on my sympathy strings. Apart from twenty-four straight hours of travel and her luggage getting lost, she obviously got ripped off by a taxi driver. André's neighbor apparently didn't give her a warm welcome when he handed off the keys, which, technically, never should have been handed off, but that's beside the point.

Add onto that the failed payment, the fact that her boyfriend is not responding to her calls or texts, our encounter in the bathroom, and her thinking my room was hers . . . I feel for her. I already have a soft spot for Americans, a result of my dad being an American and my mom's prejudice against them (yes, they're divorced, and yes, the two things are related).

Besides, she's not whining about it; she sounds like she's trying to make the best of things, but I can hear her sniffling.

"Siena?" she says. "Siena? Are you there?"

There's silence. And then a little sob.

I hesitate, my heart twinging.

This girl needs a win today, and I am the only person who can give that to her.

I lay down my red pen and head for my room, trying an ineffective combination of shuffling my feet and stomping so that Madi knows I'm coming. I knock on the door, and there's some scrambling within before her footsteps approach and the door opens.

It's obvious she tried to do a bit of damage control before answering my knock, but there's just no way she can hide the pink cheeks, the lashes clumped together, or the tear drops on her shirt.

"I'm so sorry," she says, and the genuineness in her voice softens me even more toward her. "I'm still trying to get a hold of Josh. He's in a meeting, and—"

"The payment went through," I say. "You're all set."

Her eyes widen. "It did?"

I nod, hoping she's not a human lie detector. I'm pretty sure she's not. She seems more of the gullible type.

She puts a hand on her chest and breathes a huge sigh of relief. "Thank heaven." Her eyes flit back to mine. "Was it *my* card?"

There's no mistaking the anxiety in her expression. I get the sense she's stressed about money. "The first one."

Based on the way she sighs with relief, I made the right choice spending Josh's money. Which, technically, I didn't. It's *my* money I've just spent. I can't ask André to eat the three hundred euros. He's already worried about finances. I'll have to go into the app and pay the balance with my own card so it accepts the booking. Otherwise, Madi won't even be able to leave a review.

It's kind of a headache, and it's a chunk of money I wasn't planning on spending. But hey, if it helps André and simultaneously lightens the load this girl is carrying, I'll take the hit and hope for karma—preferably in the form of the job I'm hoping to get. André's uncle is the headmaster at the elite high school with an open position, so the karma I'm hoping for is very specific.

"Thanks for being so patient," the girl says, her voice full of relief and gratitude.

I'm not sure I've ever seen a more beautiful smile than the one she gives me now. Maybe it's the way her eyes are glistening from the crying, or maybe it's something else.

Doesn't matter, really. But if I can keep a smile on that face, I can get André that coveted 5-star review.

I think of the ladder and the bed upstairs and grimace. That room might make my goal like swimming upstream.

FIVE

RÉMY

AFTER SEEING WHERE MADI WILL BE SLEEPING, I FEEL A bit selfish looking around the relative spaciousness of my room—and the way I can actually sit up in bed. I'm living like a king in here as I unpack my bags, with plenty of drawers and a closet.

I don't really know how long I'll be staying here. André's family just found out a few days ago that his mom has cancer, and now they have to wait and see how she responds to treatments.

I get all my clothes hung up in the closet. It looks like a store display for blazers, dress shirts, and slacks. I set my toiletries in the bathroom, eying the shampoo bottle, which Madi kindly set back in the shower after trying to knock me out with it.

Once I'm settled, I sit back down on the couch in the living room, rub my eyes, and put on my glasses. I've got just a couple days before Christmas break begins, and I do not plan to spend any of my time off grading. It will be three glorious weeks of relaxation.

Madi is upstairs, and as I correct one of my students' spelling of the word *laugh*, I realize that I will always know exactly where she is. It's inevitable, given how the floor creaks with every single step. I'm just hoping she doesn't plan on keeping me up with late

29

night calls to her boyfriend, since I would be able to hear that pretty well, too.

I get up for a drink of water, taking stock of what André has available for us to use. After my mom's kitchen, it looks like Old Mother Hubbard's house. I grab a cup and fill it with water, taking a drink just as Madi's footsteps sound on the staircase. I have a weird urge to run a hand through my hair. But I don't, because I'm not *that* guy—the one who tries to impress a girl with a boyfriend.

She appears in the space that opens up into the living and kitchen area, looking around. Her hair is dry now, but it doesn't look like she's styled it in any way or put on any makeup. Once she spots me, she comes over, looking really beautiful but a bit self-conscious. "Hey. We didn't really start things off on a great foot earlier. I feel like I owe you an apology."

I smile. "For throwing a full bottle of shampoo at my head?"

"Hey, it was *not* full. But yes. I'm sorry about that. I had one too many people mention *Taken* before I left, and I didn't know anyone else would be staying here."

I wave my hand, dismissing the attempted knockout and reaching for the scrubber to clean my cup. "You're safe here. I gave up my career as an assassin a couple years ago."

There's silence, and I steal a glance at her while rinsing my cup. She's staring at me, not sure whether to take me seriously. The look of relief that passes over her face when she sees my expression is hilarious—but also mildly offensive. I thought that joke would be a home run, not a tense moment.

"You're teasing," she says with a laugh.

"Glad you picked up on that," I say with a smile. "Contrary to what Hollywood tells you, we aren't all out for young American tourists." I set the cup on the rack and dry my hands with the nearest towel. "There are far too many of you."

She laughs again, showing that straight, white smile that I thought was nothing but a Hollywood fiction.

"We are a force to be reckoned with, aren't we?" she says,

entirely unoffended by my dig at her fellow countrymen. "Well, anyway, I was thinking . . . if we're going to be roommates for the next three weeks, I should probably know your name."

"It's Rémy Scott," I say, folding my arms and turning toward her.

Her brows rise and her eyes light up. "Rémy. Like the mouse on *Ratatouille?*"

I give a reluctant nod, not thrilled that she's associated me with vermin. "Technically, I came first."

"Fair enough." She straightens her shoulders and puts out a hand. "Nice to meet you, Rémy Scott. I'm Madi."

I look at her outstretched hand and smile slightly—in my life, handshakes are reserved for the work environment, which makes this feel very businessy. I take her hand with mine and give it a single, firm shake just as her expression falters.

"What?" she asks, her gaze scanning my face.

I shrug. "Nothing."

"Am I a bad handshaker?" Her eyes widen slightly. "Oh my gosh, was it limp and cold?"

I chuckle. "Your handshake is just fine."

She tilts her head to the side, dissatisfied with my answer. "Rémy, I feel like I just walked out of the bathroom with toilet paper stuck to my shoe and you're smiling instead of telling me about it. I did something weird, and I don't want to do it again. Is shaking hands not a thing here? Should we have hugged?"

I smile. "Your stars and stripes are showing."

She pulls her lips between her teeth to stop a smile. "Okay. No hugging. No shaking hands."

"We don't do hugs. We *do* shake hands. It's just a bit more formal as a greeting." I make my way toward the homework on the coffee table. "It reminded me of being at work for a second. That's all. You didn't do anything wrong." I shoot her a reassuring look over my shoulder as she follows me from the kitchen.

"What's the *informal* way of greeting, then? What do roommates do?"

31

"*Les bises*," I say as I bend over and tidy the stack of papers.

There's silence, and I glance up. She's looking at me blankly, waiting for me to expound.

I straighten. "They're kisses on the cheeks."

"The face cheeks," she clarifies.

I cover my smile with a hand. "Yes. The face cheeks. We may seem crazy to you, but we're not *that* crazy."

She lifts her shoulders. "Hey, I'm trying to keep an open mind! Nothing here has been what I've expected so far. All right, so kisses on the cheeks." She smiles slightly. "You guys just go right for the gold, don't you?"

I raise my brows. "Kisses on the cheek are the gold?"

She levels me with an unamused expression. "You know what I mean. It's just a little . . . intimate."

"More intimate than pressing your entire body up against a stranger when you meet?"

She bites her lip, unsuccessfully trying to stop a smile. "Okay, I take your point." Her eyes thin, her expression becoming thoughtful. "You know, I think I vaguely remember talking about this in my French classes. But we definitely didn't practice it, and I get why. It's a bit too thrilling for teenagers to get that close at school." She straightens, like she's getting serious again. "Okay. Let's try this again, roommate. I'm Madison Allred. Madi for short. Nice to meet you, Rémy Scott. Or *enchanté*. Right?"

I nod, smiling as I watch her grab her right hand, like she's trying to control the irrepressible impulse to put it out for a handshake again. Instead, she leans toward me slightly.

I hesitate a moment, then say, "*Enchanté.*"

I've done this countless times in my life—*les bises*. It's a reflexive thing at this point that I don't give a second thought, but this time is different. Maybe it's because I know this isn't normal for Madi and I can't help but wonder just how strange it feels to her. Or maybe it's because she doesn't just press her cheek up to mine like people usually do. She actually kisses one of my cheeks, then the other. Either way, her lips are soft, and she smells subtle but sweet, a fragrance I can't pinpoint, and I want to linger to figure out just what it is.

But I don't. Because, like I said, I'm not that kind of guy, and I'm also not a bloodhound.

"Was that wrong?" she asks nervously as she pulls back.

"No," I say with a reassuring smile.

It *was* wrong. Of course, you'll get the odd person who actually plants a full-lip-kiss on your cheek, but generally, it's cheek-to-cheek, and often it's so abrupt and mechanical, there's nothing soft about it. But that's probably my bad. I did say *kisses on the cheek,* after all.

Apparently I'm channeling the polite American half of me right now and leaving behind the directness my mom ingrained in me growing up. But I don't want to embarrass her, and Madi will figure it out from watching other people. We're going for that 5-star review, and embarrassing the guest is not conducive to that.

A gurgling sounds, and Madi's hands fly to her stomach.

"You should eat," I say. Even though it's only 4:30, the light is starting to dim. It gets dark so early at this time of year. "I could tell you some nice restaurants nearby if you'd like."

"Thanks, but I was planning on going to a grocery store." She looks around the room. "Do you have a city guide or something? My friend said that would probably be a good way of going about deciding what to see and where to buy food and all that."

I clench my teeth together, wishing André had given me a clearer picture of what guests would be expecting. I've really tried to keep my questions to a minimum because he has a lot more to worry about than the minutiae of things back here. "Sorry. I don't think André had time to put one together. He's the one who owns this place. I'm just helping him out while he's out of the country."

"Oh," she says, trying to keep her upbeat tone. "No biggie. Could you tell me how to get to the Eiffel Tower from here, then?"

I smile.

"Predictable, I know, but Siena said to go at night to see it at its best."

"Yeah, if you take the metro from Saint Paul, it'll take you all the way there. Technically –"

"The metro?"

"The subway," I clarify. "Underground train."

She gives a little nod.

I continue, "Technically, Rambuteau station is closer than Saint Paul, but if you just turn left on Rue des Francs Bourgeois and then right on Rue Pavée, you'll save yourself a train change at Châtelet, which can be . . . hectic if it's your first time."

The way she looks at me tells me I might as well be speaking French to her.

After a second of silence, she waves a hand and smiles. "Josh will figure it out, I'm sure."

Right, Josh. I hadn't realized he was in Paris, too. So this is a romantic couple's trip . . . where the couple is staying in entirely different places. Hey, to each his own. But if I were this Josh guy, I would want Madi as close as I could manage.

My phone vibrates, and I pull it out of my pocket.

André: Hey, did you ever hear from the guy?

I forced André to delete the app from his phone to make sure he's not worrying about things while he's gone. Clearly, that's not totally working.

Me: Yes. He arrived. Except it's not a he. It's a she. How's your mom?

André: Not great, but not terrible. She's glad I'm here, but I can tell she's stressed. We all are. Her insurance is fighting us. They don't want to pay for some parts of her treatment, but it will bankrupt all of us to pay it ourselves. The healthcare system here is crazy complicated.

André: So did she pay the rest of the booking, then?

I glance over at Madi. She's pulled out her phone. Probably texting her boyfriend. I'm not about to tell André I let her off the hook—not when he's stressed about money already. What kind of sucker pays hundreds of euros to save a stranger some tears—and one with a boyfriend, no less?

Me. I do that. But what's a few hundred euros when André's going through all of this? Besides, based on how he talked about things, he seems more concerned with the reviews than with making money on the first bookings. It's an investment.

Me: Yep! It's all taken care of. Working on that 5-star review. *wink face* Give your mom my love, and don't worry about things here. I've got you covered.

André: Thanks, Rémy. I owe you bigtime.

Madi is still on her phone, a little smile on her face that makes me wish it wouldn't be certifiably insane to peek at her phone screen. The same stomach growling from a couple of minutes ago cuts through the silence. Her fingers still, and her gaze flicks up to me.

With a sheepish grin, she turns off her phone. "Is there a grocery store nearby? I better feed this thing before your neighbors call and complain about the noise."

"Yeah, there's a Monoprix on Rue Saint-Antoine. It's just a five- or six-minute walk. Just take a left at the bottom of the street, then a right on Sévigné, then . . ." There's that look again. It's like when I said Monoprix, her eyes started to glaze over and she mentally checked out. "You know what? I've got a few things to get at the store, too. How about I just come with you?"

SIX

RÉMY

MADI IS SHIVERING AS WE WALK TO THE STORE. IT'S getting dark out, and we can see our breath as we walk down the street at a brisk pace. She's not dressed for December, but she declined my coat when I offered it. The only other option I have is to put my arm around her, and while there's admittedly some appeal in that, there's also potential for me to end up with a red hand mark across my cheek, so I keep my hands in my pockets.

"So how do you speak such good English?" she asks. Since turning down my coat, it's like she's trying to keep her teeth from chattering so that she doesn't seem too obviously cold. Technically, it's working, but it seems like repressing it is having the effect of sending the rest of her body into violent trembling.

"I grew up speaking it. My dad is American."

She turns her head to look at me, her eyebrows sky-high. "Well, *that's* unexpected."

"Why?" I start turning at the street corner, and since she's not anticipating it, we bump into each other.

"Oops, sorry," she says. "I just don't get the vibe that you're terribly fond of us Yanks."

I don't answer right away. I hadn't realized I was giving off that vibe, and it bothers me a bit to hear that I am. I've always hated how much my mom complains about Americans. I guess she's rubbed off on me more than I thought if Madi thinks I don't like them after knowing me all of two hours.

"Not just you," she clarifies. "Siena warned me that French people love to hate Americans."

I chuckle. "Whoever Siena is, she's right."

"She's my best friend. So your dad is American. What about your mom?"

"French. Through and through."

"Oooh," she says. "That's gotta be interesting."

"A little too interesting," I say. "They're divorced." It still feels weird saying that, even though it's been years—ten, to be precise.

Madi is horrified. Her shivering disappears, and she stops walking. "I am so sorry, Rémy! No wonder you guys hate us. Always sticking our feet in our mouths."

"No," I say, eager to put her back at ease. "You're right. The cultural difference was . . . a lot."

Her mouth twists to the side, like she wants to say something more but she's keeping it in.

I turn to keep up our progress.

"So what do you teach?" she asks, skipping to keep up. I look over at her, and she smiles. "I saw your red pen. Dead giveaway."

I love that she thinks she's a supersleuth. There's something ridiculously endearing about her now that she's stopped chucking toiletries at me. "I teach what you guys call high school English."

She stops again, staring at me. At this rate, we'll make it to Monoprix by bedtime.

"*You* teach high school English?" she says.

I frown, not sure if I should be offended. "Yeah. Why?"

She faces forward again and starts walking. "If foreign languages at my high school were taught by people like *you*, a lot fewer people would have skipped class, that's for sure."

I glance at her from the corner of my eye. That was a compliment, I'm pretty sure. I'm also pretty sure it shouldn't make me feel like I just won some kind of prize.

"Oh, hold on," she says as she pulls out her phone. It's lit up and vibrating, with a big contact picture of a guy smiling. He's got sandy blond hair and a straight, pearly white smile. The name *Josh-wah* is written underneath.

She puts the phone to her ear. "Hey, hon. Yeah, everything is fine. Sorry, I should have texted you to let you know things got taken care of."

She's clearly talking about the payment issue. Why did I not just wait? The woman has a boyfriend, for Pete's sake. It makes a million times more sense for him to foot the bill than for me to. But what am I supposed to do now? *Oh, I was just kidding about that. The payment* didn't *go through.* Yeah, no. That's a straight shot down 2-star lane.

We stop at the street we have to cross to get to the store, waiting for it to be safe to walk. The time comes, and I start walking, but Madi's not paying attention. My impulse is to usher her forward with a hand on her back, but I resist, maybe because I feel like her boyfriend might punch me through the phone.

Do I wave a hand in front of her face? Snap? Pull her by the arm? I settle for tapping her on the shoulder, which I don't think I've ever done in my twenty-six years on earth.

She glances up at me and immediately understands, skipping forward and into the street.

"No, it's fine," she responds into the phone. "I'll just grab something from the store and see you after you get done with dinner. I can ask the host to help me let me in." She glances at me, clenching her teeth like she's worried she's overpromised.

I give her a reassuring nod and stop, since we're in front of Monoprix now.

"Have fun at dinner," she says into the phone. "Oh, can you bring me some sweats or something? I have no clothes to sleep in, and I need to wash the ones I'm wearing. Stat. I think it's a crime to smell like this in Paris, so for all of our sakes, please don't forget. Okay, thanks. Love you. Bye."

I put out my hand to invite her to go into the store ahead of me.

"Sorry about that," she says as I grab a shopping basket. "My boyfriend is here for work, and all his coworkers are going out to some fancy place by the hotel for dinner. He doesn't feel like he can skip out." She looks around at the products nearest us and halts, her eyes scanning everything in the vicinity. "Oh, gosh. Thank heaven you're here. I have no idea what I'm looking at."

For the next ten minutes, I walk around the store with her and translate, slipping a few things I think I'll need into the basket. It doesn't escape me that Madi's boyfriend is eating at a really nice restaurant while she's choosing between prepackaged cheeses. Could he not have invited her along? I'd have thought most couples would be eager to have the Parisian dining experience together.

Whatever. It's not my business.

"That should be enough," she says. "I can come back for more tomorrow when my stomach isn't staging a revolt—and when my credit card is actually working." She crosses her fingers.

I look at the stuff she's put in the basket. Prepackaged sandwich cheese, a loaf of sliced bread, and orange juice.

She's watching me take stock. "What?"

I just chuckle, shaking my head.

"My stars and stripes are showing again?"

"You might as well be waving a flag." I reach over to the baguettes set up in baskets along the bakery wall next to us, pressing on the packaging to make sure I choose one that feels just right. I stick one in the basket and make my way to the cheese refrigerator, choosing a decent Camembert.

When we get to the checkout, Madi pulls out her euros. She mentioned her credit card is currently being declined, and I know from her phone call with Siena that her taxi driver robbed her of the small supply of euros she has.

I tap my card on the credit card machine, and it beeps.

Euros in hand, Madi looks up at me.

"Save those for later," I say.

She's about to argue with me, and I don't want to give her the wrong idea about why I paid. This 5-star review is a tightrope—doing enough to keep her happy without being over the top.

"Most places prefer electronic payment these days," I explain as I bag our purchases. "You'll want to save your cash for souvenirs or something."

She can't hide her relief as she slips the euros back in her purse. "Thank you. I'll pay you back, I promise. Just need to call my credit card company so I know I'm not gonna be stranded in Paris forever."

Someone whose boyfriend is in Paris at the same time as her shouldn't be worrying about that, right? The guy has *rich* written all over his tan face. At least, it looked like it from my two-second view of his contact icon.

Apparently I'll have a better view of him tonight when he comes over. I'm more curious than I should be what kind of guy gets a girl like Madison Allred.

SEVEN

MADI

DESPITE HAVING THOUGHT RÉMY WAS A psychopathic, soulless human trying to attack me when we first met, it turns out he's an incredibly decent guy. He's been nothing but nice to me so far. Especially in comparison with luggage lady, taxi jerk, and key guy. And I didn't even throw shampoo at their heads.

I pull out our grocery store haul from the bag, setting stuff down on the itty bit of counter space not taken up by the sink, dish rack, and stove. I hold up the baguette and wheel of cheese Rémy grabbed at the end of our visit to Monoprix. I assume they were his not-so-subtle way of showing me what bread and cheese French people deem appropriate.

"Where do you want these?" I ask.

"I bought them for you," he says, sticking the orange juice in the small fridge.

I glance over at him, unsure what to make of his response. But he's busy putting away groceries. "My Americanness offends you deeply, doesn't it?" I open the wheel-shaped cheese package with genuine curiosity.

In his hand, he's holding the flat pack of sandwich cheese I chose. I have no idea what kind it is, but it's orange, which makes me trust it. I intended to make a grilled cheese sandwich with it, and only now do I realize I forgot to buy butter.

Rémy holds the package over the garbage can for a second.

My mouth opens, and I stare, waiting for him to drop it, daring him to do it.

He meets my eyes briefly with a twinkle of mischief in his own before putting it in the fridge. "No, it doesn't offend me. But just so you know, cheese should not be this color."

My nose wrinkles, and I touch a finger to the white wheel of Camembert in front of me. "According to you, it should be furry and soft and smelly? Like a pet." I stroke it lovingly.

He chuckles, giving me a full view of his smile. Rémy is a very attractive man. He's got dark hair that's cut short on the sides and longer on the top. It's styled so that it waves back from his forehead, the comb marks still just visible. I'm wondering how Josh will feel about Rémy when he comes over in a while. Though, Josh isn't really the jealous type. He's a very confident man, which is what attracted me to him initially. It's also what makes him very good at his job.

Rémy starts boiling some water in the kettle, and I'm glad he's distracted because I'm genuinely concerned about trying this cheese. I don't want to offend him if I can't control my facial expression when I do. Better to get it over with while he's focused on something else. If I eat the cheese and the bread simultaneously, maybe the bread will mask the taste of the furball.

I take a deep breath and grab the cheese in one hand and the baguette in the other, opening my mouth.

Rémy shouts something in French, rushing over and grabbing one of my wrists.

I stare at him, wondering if the cheese really *is* a living animal and he's worried I'm about to kill it. That's the only thing I can think of to justify the look on his face like he just stopped Armageddon.

We stare at each other for a second.

"Were you really about to bite into a wheel of Camembert?" he asks.

I show a smile full of clenched teeth, but I'm still holding the cheese and baguette—caught red-handed. "I plead the Fifth?"

He gives me a funny look. He has no clue what I'm talking about. My American humor is so wasted right now.

"The Fifth Amendment," I explain. "It means I can't be forced to testify against myself." I glance at his hand holding my wrist, and my heart skips a little, especially because he's close enough I can smell his cologne. Men as attractive as Rémy should be legally barred from using anything that smells good. The government should give them bottles with scents like *Men's Locker Room* or *Dairy Farm*—or Camembert. "We also have *habeas corpus*, which means you can't detain me without taking me before a judge to plead my case."

He lets go of my wrist, his mouth curling up at one edge as he steps back and rolls up his sleeves. "We have that too. But when it comes to how people treat cheese, all bets are off." He turns around and grabs two knives and a cutting board. "Allow me to show you how to *properly* eat a baguette and Camembert." He sets the baguette on the cutting board and starts slicing through it. The muscles in his forearms distract me momentarily. Is cutting a baguette an exercise I should be implementing in my workout routine? All signs point to *yes*.

With a separate knife, he cuts into the cheese like it's a pie, then expertly spreads some on the piece of baguette. It's much creamier than I had anticipated given its fuzzy exterior.

He hands the piece of baguette to me. "*Bon appétit,* Stars and Stripes."

I'm trying to act cool, like it's no biggie at all, but inside I'm wondering, given its rough start, whether this roommate relationship can withstand me throwing up all over Rémy's freshly cut baguette and sacred cheese.

But there's no avoiding it. I hold up the bread like it's a glass of champagne and take a hearty bite. I chew for a few seconds, trying to understand the things happening in my mouth. The texture of the bread is like nothing I've ever experienced. It's soft and dense, while the crust has just enough crunch for contrast.

The first thing I feel is anger that I've been deprived of this my entire life. Who dared give me anything else and call it bread? How have American bread companies not been sued for false advertising? What we have there is a distant cousin at best; it's closer to cotton.

And the cheese . . . it might smell like a zoo, but it melts on my tongue, and even though I'm not sure how to feel about the taste yet, I think it's something I could get used to. Though, to be fair, I'd eat *anything* if it was served on this baguette.

Rémy's watching my reaction, and he smiles, standing up like his work is finished here.

One of the fifty stars from my American flag just dropped onto the kitchen floor. And I'm not even mad about it. I just want more baguette.

EIGHT

MADI

Josh is late. Like, really late. I freshened up an hour ago—as much as a woman wearing the same clothes for thirty-six hours can freshen up—and I'm still waiting. But there's only so much you can do in a room made for Alice in Wonderland after she's shrunk, so I head down to the living room.

Rémy is there, but he's changed into sweats and is leaning forward on the couch, writing in a lined notebook. He's a perfect combination of work and relaxation.

He looks up, and his eyes do a quick scan of me, lingering for a second on my lipstick. Is it shouting *I'm American!*? Is there some smudged on my cheek? It was difficult to see what I was doing with the dinky little lamp that's the only light source in my room.

"You're working, and I'm interrupting," I say.

"Yes. But no. I'm just switching around a few things in my lesson plans. Besides, you're welcome to hang out here whenever you want, Madi. You rented the room, but you also have access to the common areas, you know."

I let out a little sigh of relief. I might go crazy in that tiny room if I have to spend all my time there when I'm not out and about. Hopefully my time here will be minimal, though, because I'll be out experiencing Paris.

"Have a seat," he says. "It's been a long day. You must be tired."

"Strangely, I'm not." I sit down on the other end of the couch, close enough not to make it seem like I think he has cooties but far enough not to make it weird. *Stop worrying about how close you're sitting, Madi.* "I was tired on the taxi ride, but I'm too excited about getting out to see the city, I think. Though I didn't really imagine going to see the Eiffel Tower in this."

I look down at the outfit I selected specifically for flying: yoga pants with wool socks pulled up like leg warmers over my calves, a loose t-shirt, and a baggy cardigan. Apparently this is the outfit that will be memorialized in photo format of my first visit to the Eiffel Tower. Maybe I can convince Josh to make a return trip when I'm more put together.

"You don't happen to have a change of women's clothes lying around, do you?"

Rémy laughs softly. "You look beautiful."

A loud beep sounds, making me startle and, thankfully, distracting me from what Rémy said. He thinks I'm beautiful? Like *this*?

"Your boyfriend," Rémy says with a little smile at my reaction to the loud sound. "That's him calling you to let him in."

I put a hand over my thumping heart. "Sounds more like he's trying to scare me to death."

Rémy tells me how to buzz Josh in using a wall-mounted phone by the apartment door. I follow his instructions carefully, like I might set off a bomb if I press the wrong button—or summon the key neighbor. Paris is a dangerous place for Madi Allred.

Once it's done, I step back and let out a breath. "Now we just wait ten minutes for him to get up all the flights of stairs."

"There's an elevator, you know."

I stare at Rémy. "You're joking, right?"

"I am not."

I stare more. "Then why didn't we use it when we went to the store?"

He shrugs. "I don't generally use elevators going downstairs unless I've got something heavy to carry, and when we got back, you went straight for the stairs. I just figured you were impatient. The elevator isn't the quickest thing in the world."

I narrow my eyes at him, wondering if maybe these excuses are masking some scheme to force Americans to exercise more by denying them modern conveniences.

There's a knock on the door. Josh. I hurry over and open it. Josh looks back at me, handsome as ever, with his sandy blond hair, muscular physique, and wide smile.

I smother him in a hug. He smells familiar. Like home. And home is *really* nice after the day I've had.

It takes him a second to recover from my unexpected clobbering, but he wraps his arms around me like he's missed me just as much. "Well, hello to you too!" We pull back, and he lays a quick peck on my lips, then glances behind me.

I follow his gaze. "Josh, this is Rémy." We step inside, and I close the door behind us. "He's the host, and he stays here." Why do I feel a bit nervous telling him that?

Josh walks over and puts out a hand. "Hey, man."

I glance at Rémy, thinking of our conversation about greetings. Do French men kiss each other on the cheeks? I don't see Josh going for that, so it's a relief when Rémy shakes his hand. I can't help smiling at the thought of it, though.

"Lemme just grab my camera." I walk past the two of them, mildly curious what they'll talk about while I run upstairs. I doubt they have much in common. Josh is an all-American business guy, while Rémy is . . . I'm not sure what he is, but it's different.

"Mads," Josh says.

I stop and turn my head, waiting.

His mouth twists to the side in a weird, pleading sort of

grimace. "I'm *super* tired. It's been a really long day, and I'm jetlagged. Would it be okay if we chill here tonight?"

"Oh," I say, trying to keep the tsunami of disappointment from coming through in my voice. "Yeah. Yeah, sure."

Rémy's watching me, and when I meet his eye, there's a short pause before he says, "We have Netflix if you want."

Josh lets out a relieved sigh and makes his way over to the couch, plopping down in the middle. "Thanks, man. That's exactly what I need after the day I had."

It is pretty much the opposite of what I was hoping for, and I try to push down that niggling voice I get when Josh does something like this. It sounds exactly like my brother, Jack, actually, and it says stuff like, *See? Nothing's changed. He'll let you down again and again.*

I thrust it aside because Jack doesn't know what he's talking about. He never really gave Josh a chance—probably because he was immediately threatened by Josh's confidence. Guys are weird like that.

It's probably better to hold off on the Eiffel Tower anyway. I can't decide whether I want my first time seeing it to be when he proposes, or if it'll be just as magical the second time. With any luck, my bags will come tomorrow and I can wear fresh clothes. Maybe we can get an earlier start, too. I'm itching to explore the city. Once we're both well-rested, though.

"Maybe you can find something you wanna watch while I change into the clothes you brought," I say.

Josh's face screws up, and he rubs his forehead. "Shoot. The sweats. I completely forgot."

Why do I suddenly feel like I'm going to cry? What grown woman springs a leak when her boyfriend admits he didn't bring sweats for her?

"I'm so sorry, Mads. My brain is like a sieve after all the people's names I've had to remember today. They've hired on a ton of people since last year."

I wave off the apology, forcing a smile. "It's all good." It's really *not* all good. If I was alone in this apartment, I would just walk around naked or wrapped in a towel while my clothes are in the washer and dryer, but guess what? I'm *not* alone in this apartment. And we don't even have a dryer.

I had every intention of chronicling my series of mishaps to Josh on our way to the Eiffel Tower, but he's already starting a show, and I get the feeling he's too tired to really appreciate it all. Who knew hobnobbing with work friends after a full night of sleep on an airplane would be so exhausting? Not me, that's for sure. On the plane, I was busy guarding my elbows from the food carts. And now I sleep in a maid's room. Livin' the dream here, people.

Josh falls asleep after half an hour of *Parks and Rec*, his head tipping over onto my shoulder. He really *is* tired, and I feel a little guilty for giving him a hard time, even if it was just in my mind. He's here for work, and I'm sure he's got a lot on his plate.

I haven't told Josh this, but I don't even like the show that much, so I turn it off after an hour. I sit in silence for a few minutes, debating whether I should wake him or not as my own exhaustion starts to set in. I want to sleep, but I selfishly want it to be on a comfortable bed. Or *a* bed, at least.

Rémy is in his room and has been since we started Netflix. I thought of inviting him to join us, but that felt strange for some reason. Would he sit next to Josh? That feels weird. Next to me? Also weird.

I check my phone. It's almost 11, so he might be asleep already. That makes me the lone wolf here.

I rouse Josh gently, and he mumbles an apology for falling asleep, then checks his phone. He yawns, stretching his arms above his head. "I should get back to the hotel," he says in a drowsy voice. "Early start tomorrow morning."

Rémy emerges from his bedroom with a teacup and saucer in hand just as we're getting up from the couch. Not asleep, then. Something about a dainty teacup being held by a man in sweats amuses me. He heads into the kitchen to the sink, and I realize Josh is talking to me.

"They're completely overhauling the way we handle it, Mads," he says through another yawn, "which means my schedule is going to be a lot busier than I thought. Meyers wants us doing brainstorming during lunch *and* dinner."

The vision I had of eating together at Parisian cafés while Josh is on his lunch break and then dining in dimly lit restaurants under the glow of the Eiffel Tower after he's off for the night evaporates.

"But don't worry," he says, taking my hand and lacing his fingers through mine. "We'll still have plenty of time for things afterward. I'll come over after dinner every night. And then we have this weekend."

All I can do is nod. This is a week-long training, which means he's going to be busy until the 21st. What am I supposed to do until then?

It's happening, Madi.

I wave the voice away as well as I can . . . again. This time, it sounds a bit more like Siena. She doesn't outright criticize Josh very often, but her face says it all whenever I break and vent my frustrations to her. It usually ends up as a bizarre combination of me complaining about Josh and then defending him. And I always do defend him.

Sometimes, I just wish I didn't have to defend him quite so often.

Josh looks to Rémy. "Hey, man, I want Madi to have an amazing time in Paris, so if you're ever free and want to take her around, that'd be awesome. It'd give me some peace of mind, and I'm happy to pay you—anything to make sure she has a good time."

Rémy glances at me, but I'm too embarrassed to mold my face into any recognizable expression, so I look away. Josh is actually asking Rémy to take me around like some kind of travel babysitter. My cheeks could heat all of Paris right now, which is saying something because it's below freezing.

I've got to give Rémy an out. "That's not neces—"

"Sure," Rémy says over me. "I've got some time in my schedule."

"Thanks, man," Josh says, pulling a card out of his phone wallet.

Rémy holds up a hand. "No need to pay me. I'm happy to help."

I don't know if he's just being nice or trying to help me save face, but I can't bring myself to look at him to try to figure it out.

I see Josh to the door, and as I shut the door behind him, I can't help but wonder if my coming to Paris like this was a massive mistake. Nothing is going according to my plan, and I don't like that thought at all, because I am counting on those plans for my future—both romantically and professionally.

"Do you want me to show you how to work the washing machine?" Rémy asks from the kitchen.

I take in a breath and turn. "That's okay. I have nothing to change into right now. There isn't a clothing store nearby that opens at, say, the crack of dawn, is there?"

He laughs. "No. Crack of dawn opening times are not a French value."

I pull a disappointed face. "You guys probably don't stampede over each other once a year for sales on Instant Pots and giant TVs, either, do you?" I click my tongue. "Such a shame."

I like the smile he gives me for poking fun at my country. I love where I'm from, but that doesn't mean I can't see some of the ridiculous things we do.

"I've got some extra clothes you could wear while you wash those," he says, indicating what I'm wearing.

"Really?" I sound like a woman treading water in the middle of the ocean who's just been offered a lifebuoy.

He smiles at my reaction. "Yes, really." He leaves the kitchen and disappears into his room.

Maybe I should have hesitated about wearing a stranger's clothes, but at this point, I am *that* desperate. If there was a fire nearby, I'd consider burning the ones I'm wearing. Am I being dramatic? Yes. Am I being serious? Also yes.

Rémy comes over and hands me a pile of folded sweats.

"Thank you *so* much," I say.

"It's no problem at all."

I glance at the washer, wondering how long it'll be until a cycle finishes and whether I'm willing to stay awake until then to hang the clothes up to dry. "Maybe you can teach me how to use the washer in the morning?"

"Sure. I have to leave around eight-thirty for work, so anytime before that."

"Oh, I'll definitely be up by then." I never sleep past seven.

He raises a brow. "You've never had jet lag before, have you?"

"No, but I'm *super* tired."

The way he smiles at me tells me he has serious doubts on the matter. "Netflix is here for you if the jet lag hits unexpectedly. And don't worry about waking me up if you come down. I'm a deep sleeper."

I DO *NOT* SLEEP through the night. I'm wide awake at 2 a.m., and it takes me an entire minute to remember where I am. I toss and turn, determined to vanquish jet lag if it's the last thing I do. But after an hour, I raise my white flag and head downstairs, hoping a documentary will lull me back to sleep.

Using my phone as a flashlight, I head over to the couch. There's a teacup and saucer sitting on the coffee table. Next to it is a torn piece of paper and a tea bag.

For the jet lag, the note says.

I smile and take the things with me to heat water in the kettle. Once the tea is steeping, I head back to the couch and pick up the remote. It has a note next to it too.

L'Histoire du Fromage. Look it up on Netflix.

It's been a long time since I took French classes, but I haven't forgotten enough that I fail to recognize Rémy is suggesting I watch a documentary about the history of cheese.

That ought to put me out right quick.

NINE
MADI

I WAKE UP TO THE SOUND OF A DOOR CLOSING. IT's dark, and a quick search with my hands tells me I fell asleep on a couch. The TV is still on, and there's a message displayed. It's not in English, but I'd know that humiliating text anywhere: *Are you still watching?* There's an empty cup of herbal tea on the coffee table in front of me and a piece of paper beside it.

And then I remember. I'm in Paris. Josh came over last night. I'm wearing Rémy's sweats. And I watched an entire episode about the early history of cheese. At 3 a.m. Yes, it's a multi-episode documentary. And yes, it was in French, so I had to read subtitles. It was surprisingly engrossing.

I check my phone. It's just shy of 7 a.m., and I have a bundle of texts from Siena. Her texting motto is *Why say something in one text when you can say it in ten?*

I wish she was here with me right now. She would appreciate everything that's happened. She wants to hear all about the follow-up to our teary (on my end) conversation, and she's sent me a calendar appointment for a FaceTime together this afternoon. I love her.

When Rémy comes out, he's already dressed for work in a navy blazer, a crisp white button-up shirt with the top two buttons undone, and gray slacks. His hair still looks wet, but it might just be whatever product he uses to style it. Either way, I'm worried about the fragile hearts of the high school girls in his class. They were not made for this sort of onslaught on their wild hormones.

I, on the other hand, have bedhead and bad breath, and the waistband of the sweats I'm wearing has shifted so that the crotch seam is somewhere on my hip. This is a good thing. Rémy is my host, not someone I'm trying to impress. Besides, Josh has seen me worse than this, and he still loves me. I'm so lucky.

I think my need to impress Rémy is just wanting to make a good impression on behalf of all Americans. It's like our nation's reputation is on my shoulders. I'm the U.S. ambassador to France.

Yikes.

"Rough night?" His eyes go to the TV.

I pick up the remote and turn it off. "Despite what Netflix is implying, I only made it through one episode."

He doesn't believe me. "It's okay to be fascinated by cheese. In fact, it's more than okay."

I shoot him a look. "How did you know I'd be up in the night?"

"My dad made a lot of business trips to Chicago when I was younger, so he watched a lot of TV in the middle of the night. I would sneak out of my room and watch with him sometimes."

The image of Rémy sleeping on his dad's lap in front of the flickering TV lights presents itself to me. It's a tender image, especially since I have so few memories of my own dad.

"Want me to show you how the washing machine works?"

I nod and get up from my makeshift bed. The moment he turns away, I yank the sweats into the right place on my waist. "Sorry I fell asleep on the couch. I know I've only paid for servant quarter accommodation."

He laughs and crouches down by the washer. "I don't mind if you sleep on the couch if it's more comfortable."

It is, but I still don't feel like I can do that.

The washing machine is the most complicated machine I've ever operated, which is saying something after that electric shower, but I'm more concerned with shoving my clothes inside before Rémy can smell them than I am with trying to understand all the settings.

"It's supposed to be sunny and pretty warm today," he says as he shuts the washer door, "so you should be able to hang them outside your window when the cycle finishes." He stands up, and I follow suit just as a loud beep sounds.

I jump, just like I did last time—full on, hand-over-the-heart fright jump.

Rémy smiles. "You'll get used to it." He goes over to the doorbell phone and answers in French. What follows is an incomprehensible exchange that has me staring at Rémy's mouth, because how in the world can he manage to make all those beautiful but unintelligible sounds look so effortless? It's like the baguette situation all over again. How dare anybody call anything a language that doesn't sound like what Rémy's speaking? The rest of us are grunting like cavemen in comparison.

"Good news," he says, buzzing the guy in. "It's your suitcase."

And just like that, he flips to perfect English. He is a modern world wonder.

And then his words click.

"My suitcase!" I say, as though my entire life has been leading up to this reunion.

"He said he'll leave it in the courtyard. Apparently they don't deliver right to apartment doors because a lot of buildings here don't have elevators."

"So they lose bags and then force the owners to lug them up the stairs? Super sweet."

"We aren't known here for our customer service." Rémy jerks his head toward the door. "Come on. I'll show you the elevator."

Once we're outside the apartment door, we walk toward the stairs. Rémy stops just in front of a bunch of black iron bars and presses a lone silver button amidst the tangle of metal.

I stop mid-step as some banging noises echo in the stairwell. Things start clicking in my brain, and I look at Rémy. "That? *That* is an elevator shaft?"

"*Bienvenue à Paris*," he says, clearly enjoying my reaction.

I watch as the cable inside the shaft moves. It takes almost two minutes for the elevator to reach us, during which time Rémy just leans against the bars like he's got all the time in the world. The elevator stops with a *clang*.

"You won't be able to open this outside door until the elevator is level with the floor." He opens the iron-gated door, inside of which stands a similar door. Using his back to keep open the first one, he opens the second one and puts out a hand to invite me to go in.

I shake my head, backing up slowly like the cage might swallow me if my movements are too sudden. "No no no no. That is not an elevator. That is a deathbox."

"I promise it will not kill you."

I make my way to the stairs. "I will walk, thank you very much."

Rémy chuckles and starts following me.

I stop, putting a hand on the wall. "You don't have to come."

One of his brows quirks. "You're going to carry your suitcase all the way up here yourself?"

"No," I say, lifting my chin. "I will send it up the elevator while I come up the stairs."

"You're sending your suitcase in the death trap? And here I thought you cared about it."

"Hey, I saw how the baggage handlers throw suitcases around at the airport. That thing"—I point to the elevator—"can't do anything to my bag that hasn't already been done to it."

Rémy gives a smiling nod and turns back toward the apartment door, making me kind of wish I hadn't said anything and had just let him come.

I make my way down the small, winding staircase that leads to the ground floor. As promised, the delivery man has left my suitcase in the courtyard. I pull it across the cobbles and back into the entryway, where I press the elevator button and wait, watching the cable and listening to the clanking. I can see the bottom of the elevator about two floors up when there's a big clang, and it stops. Probably for someone to get on.

But it doesn't budge, even after two minutes. I press the button again. Nothing. The elevator is protesting, and I can't say I blame it. It looks like it was made at the same time as my keys to Rémy's apartment were. It deserves to be spruced up. And by spruced up, I mean destroyed and replaced with a contraption from the modern age.

I sigh and look down at my massive suitcase. I should have listened to Josh when he told me to pack light.

I have no other option but to lug the thing—all fifty pounds of it—up the stairs. The thought makes me want to cry, but it can't be helped, so I grab my suitcase by the handles and heave it up two stairs at a time. By the time I reach the landing of the next floor, I'm wondering if Rémy will just let me wear these sweats for the next three weeks. Anything so that I don't have to bring this thing up another four flights of stairs. Yes, four flights, because here, the "first" floor is the one above street level. *Sob*.

I gather my strength, wishing I had at least eaten some baguette and cheese before attempting this, and start hefting it up the next set of stairs. Between the suitcase and me, we take up the entire stairwell.

I've managed to get it up five more stairs when the dreaded noise starts: someone is coming down. I'm hoping they're a skilled hurdler because otherwise, the only option is to go back where I came from or for them to wait while I make my way up the rest of the stairs to the next level.

"Need some help?"

I look up and find Rémy looking down at me. He's shed his blazer and rolled up the sleeves of his dress shirt.

I wipe the hair that's escaped my ponytail and is sticking to my sweaty forehead, pushing it away from my face. "The elevator decided to stage a protest halfway down the shaft."

"Yeah, they do that. We Parisians love a good transportation strike. Let me take that for you."

I'm too tired, too grateful to object. All that baguette cutting serves Rémy well as he carries my suitcase up the stairs. After two sets, I offer to change places with him.

He's breathing hard, but he rejects my offer. He's going to arrive sweaty to work today because of me.

"You're a saint," I tell him as we reach the 5th floor. "How much are you regretting telling your friend you'd help him out with hosting?"

He sets down the suitcase and looks at me for a second.

I put my hand up before he can talk. "Don't answer that. For the moment, I feel like at least one French person doesn't hate me, and I'd like to keep it that way."

He laughs. "I don't regret it at all."

I don't regret it, either. Rémy has been very nice to me. I don't know if I could have handled this experience if I'd had a host like the taxi driver. I don't see Rémy blowing smoke into my face anytime soon. Bless him.

I grimace. "Even though Josh asked you to take me around? I'm sorry about that. You *really* don't have to."

"And what if I want to?"

I don't really have an answer for that because what grown, working man wants to play free tour guide to a stranger? Our initial meeting must not have been quite as bad as I thought if he likes me enough to want to spend more time with me.

"Today is my short teaching day, so I should be home by one," he says. "There's a free museum nearby that's about the history of Paris if you want to go when I get back."

Is my face betraying how badly I'm dying to get out in the city but also how terrified I am of doing it alone? Because it sure seems like it is.

His dark brows rise slightly as he waits for my response. It's a gentle invitation, and somehow, I know I could say no without offending him.

But why would I say no?

"You don't have to decide n—"

"Yes," I hurry to say. "Yes, I want to go."

He smiles. "I'll be back here by one, then. If you need anything while I'm at work, you can just call or text me." He hands me a piece of paper. "Here's my number. Make sure you include that +33, or it won't work."

ONCE RÉMY IS GONE, I spend way too much time on the phone with my credit card company, sorting out what they think is fraudulent activity but what is actually me trying to survive in a foreign country that doesn't seem thrilled that I'm here.

It's only after that's all figured out that I remember my laundry downstairs. I take it out of the machine, then go upstairs again. I've gone up and down way too many stairs today.

I dump an armful of wet clothes on the small table under the bed and move to the window where the laundry rack stands. It's small, and, just like everything in Paris, it fights me. And it wins. I have no idea how to open this window. I suspect I need a key to do it, because the handle has a keyhole on it, and the handle won't turn.

I run downstairs, hoping to find that the window there is different, but it's not. It won't budge. After debating for a minute, I grab Rémy's number from where I set it on the coffee table and carefully type in the numbers.

Madi: Hey Rémy. It's Madi, your local incompetent American tourist. I've made it my mission to single-handedly reinforce all the worst stereotypes about my people.

I bite my top lip, wondering how long it will take him to

respond. He *is* at work, after all, and when Josh is at work, it often takes him hours to text back.

The three dots pop up right away, though.

Rémy: You might have to stay longer than three weeks to tackle that list. *wink emoji*

I smile. This guy's got jokes.

Madi: You talk a lot of trash about us for someone who's half-American. *tongue sticking out emoji*
Madi: Anyway, I'm having a bit of an issue here . . . I can't figure out how to open my window to hang my laundry.

Rémy: You have to press the silver keyhole with your thumb, then turn the handle and push.

Madi: Press it?! Who would think to do that? Aren't keyholes meant for actual keys? Or did your country run out of the enormous, rusty ones?

Rémy: *window emoji* *thumb emoji* *French flag emoji*

Madi: *window emoji* *key emoji* *American flag emoji*

Rémy: See you soon, Madi

Smiling and still somewhat suspicious, I hurry back upstairs to test Rémy's theory. It works. What devilry is this? It's intentionally misleading to put a place for a key that's actually meant to be pushed. Where I come from, we call that false advertising.

The window doesn't open very wide, which makes reaching the laundry lines tricky, to say the least. I sling my clean yoga pants, shirt, bra, and undies on the lines as carefully as I can manage with cold fingers. It's sunny, like Rémy said it would be, but the courtyard is still in morning shadows, so it's also chilly.

Once that's done, I submit to the growlings of my stomach and feed it orange juice, baguette, and more Camembert. Cutting that baguette myself only makes me appreciate even more how easy Rémy made it look. It is *not* easy. That delicious crust is a castle wall, letting through only the bravest of souls to the heavenly interior. But I'm a brave soul now that I have tasted what's on offer.

After eating half the baguette like any proper American would, I check my phone and scramble up from the chair at the table. It's a quarter after twelve, which means Rémy will be here pretty soon, and I haven't showered. After the last couple of days, I need a nice, hot, uninterrupted one.

Plus, I'm determined to show Rémy that I can be more than a travel-worn, sloppy American.

TEN

RÉMY

I'M EARLY. I PROBABLY COULD HAVE SPENT ANOTHER half an hour at the school preparing for tomorrow, but I was feeling a bit anxious to get home, despite how short the day was. Wednesdays the students' classes end at lunchtime. I only teach once, which means I can choose whether to spend the afternoon grading and working on lesson plans or—if I'm feeling irresponsible—to call it a day.

Today I choose the latter. Whether that's because the Christmas holiday is so close I can taste it or because of the prospect of going to the museum with Madi, I don't know. I'm going to go with the former, because Madi is a woman with a boyfriend—a boyfriend who asked me to take her around, though, and I'm a man of my word.

I set down my shoulder bag on the entry table just as I hear the water turn on in the bathroom. Apparently, Madi is just hopping in the shower. I might as well make some lunch while I'm waiting—maybe for the both of us in case Madi hasn't already eaten.

I step into the kitchen and note the baguette bag on the counter, much smaller than it was when I left this morning. Curious, I open the fridge and pull out the Camembert, smiling when

I see that there's less of it too. Why is it so satisfying to know Madi chose those things over the bread and cheese (I use the terms loosely) she bought?

Using the veggies, mozzarella, and balsamic vinegar I bought, I rustle up a salad, then put my efforts to making two croque-monsieurs with the sliced bread, cheese, and some of my ham. As they're cooking on the stove, I glance up at the closed bathroom door. Is Madi going for the longest shower in history? It has to have been almost half an hour, and the water is still going.

I load up two plates with the food and am just slipping the second croque-monsieur in place when there's a little shriek, and the water turns off.

I dash from the kitchen toward the bathroom. "Everything okay, Madi?"

"Rémy?!" she responds. "Um . . . help?"

I burst through the door and find Madi holding the shower curtain to cover herself. Her hair is matted to her head, sopping wet. She's looking at the floor with wide eyes, and I follow her gaze.

The tile is covered in water, creeping toward me in the doorway with each second.

I swear in French and grab the towel hanging on the wall, throwing it over the water like a picnic blanket. Praying there are a couple of extra towels, I turn toward the small, nearby closet.

There are two towels inside, which is a miracle because there is really nothing else in there.

"I'm so sorry," Madi says as I emerge back into the bathroom. She looks like she just accidentally launched a missile. "Can I help? I—"

"No," I blurt out, seeing her try to crouch down while still keeping the curtain in place. I'm doing a decent job of seeing her as a friend, but testing those limits is not a wise idea. "I can manage." I get down on my hands and knees, wiping at the water with the three towels I have to work with. "Just try not to throw any shampoo bottles at my head."

She groans. "Paris hates me."

I glance up at her as she pushes a portion of her hair over her bare shoulder to keep it from dripping onto the already wet floor. I can tell it's killing her not to be able to help.

I give her a reassuring smile before refocusing myself on my task. "Paris just isn't used to women who shower for thirty minutes."

"I don't! At least, not usually. It just felt so good after the last couple days, and the water was so warm, it almost felt like I was back in California." She looks at the base of the shower. The lip to contain the water is only a couple inches high, and since it's just a shower curtain on two sides, it's easy for water to escape even if you're being careful. "I'm not used to having to worry about water getting out, so I didn't even notice when . . ."

"Don't worry about it." I gather up the towels into my arms.

"I promise I'm not usually this much of a damsel in distress. I'm a functioning adult who contributes to society. Or I have every intention of doing so, at least."

Now that my work is done, I have nowhere to look but at Madi—the slope of her shoulder, the glistening water on her skin, the hollow of her clavicle. If only there was a tattoo on her forehead that said *I'm taken*.

"Then you will have no trouble getting dressed," I say, turning away. "Lunch is on the table."

"I was busy flooding your shower while you were making me lunch? Ugh. France: 5, America: 0."

I laugh and close the door behind me.

⸺

BY THE TIME we leave for the museum, Madi has adjusted the score to 6-to-0.

"You have ruined the perfectly good American grilled cheese for me forever," she says as we make our way down the flights of stairs together. "If in three weeks I go home hating the USA, I'm blaming you."

Go home. Right. Madi is very temporary, and that's a good reminder for me. I could get used to having her as a roommate and a friend, but this is just Christmas vacation for her. Christmas vacation with her boyfriend.

Speaking of which, I've only seen a bit of Josh, but I'm not impressed so far. I steal a glance over at Madi.

She looks amazing. That's no surprise, of course, because she looked amazing even with matted, wet hair and mascara smudged below her eyes. Now, she's wearing ankle boots, jeans, and a cream cable-knit sweater. Her hair isn't wet anymore, but it's got a wave to it since she let it air dry. I like it.

And I like Madi. She's sweet. She's fun. I'm lucky she's the guest I'm hosting. It could definitely be worse.

She's got a camera hanging at her hip, which I know now is not just a larger-than-average tourist tool. Madi is an actual photographer. As we walk to Musée Carnavalet, she's all wide-eyed wonder, taking in everything around us. It's so strange to see the city I've lived in all my life through such fresh eyes. Buildings I've passed dozens and dozens of times without even noticing are like epiphanies for her. It makes me excited for the museum.

I chose it for three main reasons: it's close, it's not a place she and Josh are likely planning to go, and it's free. I would have been happy to pay for Madi, but she's feeling guilty enough about my taking her around.

I haven't been to Musée Carnavalet since we came as a class when I was eleven. Whether it's because I'm at a better age to appreciate it or because of Madi's curiosity, I find myself as interested as she is. Not that I can match her level of enthusiasm. She's so intentional about her photos, and it's kind of fascinating to watch her scope out the space. She is completely wowed by the architecture and spends a full five minutes trying to capture the area just inside the entrance.

"I'm weird," she says when she catches me watching her

crouch as far as she can into a corner to take a picture. "I have a thing for light, and the windows here make this space just—" She does a chef's kiss before snapping another picture.

"Can I see?" I nod at her camera. I'm curious whether it will give me a clue about what *she's* seeing.

"Um, sure," she says, getting up and walking over. "It's been a while since I've done landscape photography, so I'm out of practice. Recently, I've been doing more product photography, which is always under artificial light." She shows me the LED screen.

I look from it to the actual room, like I'm checking that they're the same. They *are*, of course, but the perspective in the camera makes it look . . . different. "That's amazing," I say, trying to figure out what it is that makes it so striking.

"Sometimes doing weird things pays off," she says with a laugh. "I'm a bit neurotic about light and lines. It's part of the gig, I guess."

Madi has a lot of questions for me about what we see as we make our way through the museum. I answer as best I can, wishing I'd paid better attention to all my history classes when I was younger so that I could satiate her curiosity better.

"Oh my gosh." She stares through the warped windowpanes that provide a view onto the gardens, her expression yearning. "Look how beautiful that is."

"We can go out there, you know," I say.

She looks over at me, staring. "Are you serious? *We* can go out there? Don't joke with me about serious matters, Rémy."

"Gardens being those serious matters?"

"Gardens that look like they dropped out of a Chanel advertisement, yes. Can we really walk out there?"

I nod, smiling at her reaction. I might as well have just told her she can live here.

IT'S ALMOST dinnertime when we reach the door to our building. I've never spent that much time in a museum—and this museum isn't even on most tourists' radar. I've also never *enjoyed* my time in a museum that much. We went to a lot as a class when I was younger, and while we all looked forward to those days, it was for the change in routine, not for the museums themselves.

Madi checks her phone as I unlock the door leading off of the street. "Wow, it's late."

"Yeah, who knew hour-long showers ate up so much of the day?"

"Thirty-minute shower. And at least we Americans shower at *all*." She looks at me with horror. "Oh my gosh, that was so rude! You smell perfectly amazing, Rémy."

I laugh, wondering if she really *has* smelled me or is just trying to make up for the insult. "I know our reputation. And to be fair, some of it is deserved. You'll see that if you ever go on the metro during the summer."

She shows me a mouth full of clenched teeth. "I think I'll steer clear."

"You can't come to Paris and not go on the metro, Madi."

She shudders a little. "I'm not big on small spaces with a lot of people. And definitely not if we're adding body odor into the mix."

"Then prepare to walk a lot or pay for taxis."

She wrinkles her nose, and I turn the key in the doorknob.

"Elevator?" I ask, trying to keep a straight face.

"Uh-uh," she says, walking straight past it to the stairs.

"The metro isn't so bad if you know when to avoid it."

"Which I don't."

"That's why you have me."

She glances over at me and smiles. "True."

When we get to the apartment door, I unlock it and push it open.

"Geez," she says as I wait for her to go in. "You make it look so easy. Were you a medieval dungeon keeper in a past life?" A buzzing has her pulling her phone out of her pocket. "Oh, shoot! I totally forgot." She swipes and holds the phone in front of her face. "Siena! I'm so sorry. I completely spaced it until I saw you calling."

"Even after I sent you a calendar appointment?" Siena clucks her tongue. "I'm disappointed in you, my little *croissant*." For someone clearly exaggerating that last word, she actually did a decent job.

Other voices jump in.

"Hi, Madi!"

"Hey, Mads!"

"How's our favorite Parisian doing?"

"Oh gosh." Madi shoots a glance at me as I make my way toward my room to give her some privacy. "Don't let Rémy hear you call me that. I'm the furthest possible thing from Parisian, as he can tell you."

"Rémy?" one of them asks. "Who's Rémy? Oh, is that him in the background there? Hi, Rémy!"

"Hi, Rémy!"

"*Bonjour*, Rémy!"

I turn back toward Madi. She's looking at me with an apology written on her face. "Do you mind saying hi to the Sheppards real quick? They're like my family."

"There's no *like* about it!" The voice of the woman speaking makes me think she's probably the mom of the bunch. "We claim Madi as one of us."

Madi looks at me, full of hesitation.

"Of course," I say, coming over next to her.

She smiles and moves the phone so that we're both visible. Staring back at us is a jumble of strangers, three of them somewhere around my age, two of them clearly the parents. They're all smiling, a couple of arms slung around shoulders. They're a happy bunch.

"This is my host, Rémy," Madi says.

"Hello, Sheppards," I say with a little wave. "Good to meet you."

A chorus of overlapping responses comes through the mic.

"Wow, your English is amazing," Siena says.

"He's half-American," Madi explains. "Even if he doesn't claim it." She glances over at me with a little twinkle in her eyes. "Yet."

"Are you taking care of our Madi?" Mrs. Sheppard asks.

"Very well," Madi says, saving me a response to an awkward question. "He has saved my bacon multiple times already."

"How many times has your bacon needed saving?" the son asks with a laugh. "Didn't you just arrive, like, yesterday?"

Madi groans. "Don't ask. It's been humiliating. I should have forced one of you to come along with me." She looks at me. "The Sheppards are avid travelers. All the kids are named places around the world. There's Siena, Victoria, and Troy"—she points to each face as she says the name. Troy rears back like he got punched in the face when she points to him.

Madi laughs and shakes her head at him. "And these two angels over here are their parents—*my* second parents—Rick and Sue Sheppard. We're just missing Austin. Is he on tour?"

"Always," Siena says. "But we should see him Christmas Day, at least. It's so great to meet you, Rémy."

"Yes," says Rick. "Thank you for taking care of our Madi. She's special to us." He and his wife have their cheeks pressed up against each other. It's obvious they really like each other, and I feel a little pang of envy in my chest. The Sheppards have such a strong, fun dynamic that's evident even after two minutes with them.

"I miss you guys," Madi says, like she's having the same thoughts as I am.

Siena waves off her family. "Okay, you've all seen she's alive and well. Now let me have her. We have a longstanding appointment."

Her brother and sister give her a bit of grief, following behind her as she tries to walk away so that she can't get them out of the video. They're laughing as they do it, but they finally give up, Victoria yelling, "Great to see you, Madi, and good to meet you, Rémy!" just as Siena slams a door.

That's my cue to leave. "It's good to meet you, Siena." I look at Madi. "I'll just be in my room. You can stay out here, since the signal isn't great in your—"

"Servant quarters," Madi supplies teasingly. "Thanks, Rémy."

I grab my briefcase from where it is by the door and make my way to my room, trying to figure out how I feel. It's not like I know them well at all, but the Sheppard family oozes something I've never encountered in my life. It's that fun, functional family that I assumed was yet another one of Hollywood's creations. Being the only child of divorced parents, I've never had that. I'm envious of it, envious that Madi gets to be a part of it.

It's clear, too, from the Sheppards that the draw I feel to Madi is not unique. Everybody seems to love her and want a piece of her time. As long as I can content myself with having this short-term friendship with her, that's not a problem.

ELEVEN

MADI

Siena enjoyed my Paris-up-to-now tales every bit as much as I had hoped she would. Amazing how a little time and a good friend can turn tears of frustration into tears of laughter.

"So you've basically spent all of your time with Rémy?" she says, summing things up.

I glance at the door to his room. It's shut, but I'm still worried he can hear me. I walk to the stairs that lead to my quarters, as Siena insists on calling them. I'll take my chances with the weaker signal there. You never know what crazy things Siena will say.

"And he took you to a museum for *three* hours?"

"I know," I say, closing my door. "He's a good sport."

Siena gives a scoffing laugh. "What is he, a seven-year-old playing T-ball? He is a full-grown man with a job and his own place—not to mention a mighty fine face. Hey, I rhymed!"

"Real impressive," I say. "Though, technically not accurate. This isn't his apartment. He's been living with his mom."

"Madi, Madi, Madi. Sometimes you have to sacrifice accuracy for art. You should know that. But lemme get this straight. When you first met, you threw a shampoo bottle at Rémy's head. Since then, you've asked to borrow his clothing, had him buy you groceries and make lunch for you, flooded the bathroom—"

77

"I did not make him buy me groceries! And I did not ask to borrow his clothes." I open the window with ye olde thumb-over-the-lock trick and put a hand to my clothes to check if any are dry. "He was just being a nice host."

"Oh, Madi. Dear, sweet Madi." Siena takes the phone in both hands and brings her face right up close to it. It's like she's virtually taking me by the shoulders to talk some sense into me. "Airbnb hosts don't do those things. Trust me. I've stayed in a lot of Airbnbs. I never even *see* most hosts, let alone wear their clothes. Which, *again,* Rémy is gorgeous. That is information that should have been communicated immediately, young lady. Why did you withhold it?"

A lot of times, Siena talks like I don't have a boyfriend. When I call her out on it, she claims she's just stating observations, like a scientist does, and that I shouldn't be such a science hater.

"Oh yeah," she says before I can respond. She's in the kitchen now, snacking on what looks like cashews. "You were too busy chucking things at that beautiful face." She shakes her head like she'll never get me and pops another cashew into her mouth. "Still, you haven't been doing that the *whole* time you've been there. You could have said something."

"Why? Because you would have flown to Paris immediately?"

"Um, if *you're* not going to pursue that, one of us should. How does Josh feel about your overly helpful and attractive host?"

I feel like she's got that switched around. Rémy is not overly helpful, but he might be overly attractive. I shrug, then set the phone on the windowsill while I fold the dry clothes from the rack. "He was the one who asked Rémy to take me around."

"He *what*?"

I prepare myself for another assault on Josh. I also don't add that he offered to pay Rémy for his services.

"Josh is busier than he had expected," I say, hoping I don't sound defensive. Sometimes I wish Siena would just throw all her complaints about Josh straight at him.

Siena's head tilts to the side, and one of her eyebrows cocks. "Busy training Brianne?"

I shoot her an unamused glance. I should never have even told Siena about Josh's new coworker. He's helping train Brianne, and when I saw a picture of them at a work lunch pop up on social media, I felt a bit insecure. Since I was with Siena at the time . . .

My socks aren't quite dry, so I leave them on the line by themselves. I pause, then look at the pile of folded clothes. My bra is missing. I look out to the clotheslines again, but it's definitely not there.

Oh dear. Sticking my head out the window as far as it will let me, I look down. My vision goes a bit wobbly for a second because I'm basically on the roof of a six-story building. I can't see anything on the cobblestones, which means the bra didn't fall down to the courtyard—unless someone took it. Ew.

I'm just about to pull my head in when I spot it.

"Oh, gosh," I say.

"What? What is it?"

I step back, as if not being able to see the bra will magically make it move somewhere else. "My bra dropped."

"What the heck are you talking about?"

"I was drying it on the lines outside my window, but it dropped onto Rémy's lines downstairs."

Siena looks at me for a second with wide eyes, like she's trying to understand what I'm saying.

I turn the camera, angling it at my bra dangling over the laundry rack below.

Siena busts up laughing. "I'm sorry, but Paris Madi is killing me! I feel like we should be documenting this so we can sell the story to Netflix or something. Will you take me with you when you ask Rémy for your bra?"

I squeeze my eyes shut. I don't want to do that. Not even a little. A girl can only do so many embarrassing things before she turns into a puddle of humiliation and seeps into all those crevices between the cobblestones. "No, I'm not taking you with me."

"Aw, come on! You get to have *all* the fun."

I peek out the window again. "I'm not taking you because I'm not asking him for it. Maybe I'll get lucky, and the wind will blow it down into the courtyard."

Siena's laughing again, and I can't blame her. Talking about luck favoring me after the last couple of days . . . it's crazy. Given how things have been going, it's more likely the bra will blow right in through Rémy's closed window and onto his gorgeous face.

His perfectly average face, I mean. Siena's voice is infiltrating my head again.

"You are *not* helping right now," I say to her continuing laughter.

"I'm sorry, I'm sorry." She gets a hold of herself, clears her throat, and does a big body shake like a kindergartener trying to get out the wiggles. "Okay. I'm better now. How's your mom's cruise going?"

"Good," I say. "She texted me yesterday at whatever port they were in. I mean, I think she's going a little insane trying to relax, but all in all, it's been a really good thing."

"Old habits die hard."

I know Siena's talking about my mom being too used to working herself into the ground—single mom stuff—but since Siena has referred to Josh as my *habit* once or twice, I can't help but look at her to see if she's trying to say more than one thing.

But I must be paranoid, because she's not even looking at me; she's rifling through one of the cupboards. "Poor Jack all alone for Christmas. Should I invite him over for some Sheppard holiday shenanigans?"

I press my lips together and give her a death stare. She and Jack both like to tease me about this topic because they know how touchy it is. But the truth is, the two of them don't really get along, which I'm secretly glad about.

A text message from Josh pops up on the top of my screen.

Josh: Just heading to dinner with everyone. I should be to your place by nine.

I try not to sigh.

TWELVE

MADI

SIENA STRICTLY FORBADE ME FROM EATING BREAD AND cheese for all of my meals, and then she sent me fifty dollars on Venmo, demanding I not spend it on "boring groceries." I don't deserve her.

As the obedient friend I am, I ask Rémy if there's any good take-out nearby. Next thing I know, we're walking to a falafel place not far from the apartment. It's freezing now that the sun has gone down, and I'm feeling supremely fortunate to have my coat, even if it's not quite as warm as I would like.

Walking the streets of *le Marais*—that's what our neighborhood is called, according to Rémy—at night is something magical. Despite how cold it is, it's alive with people, twinkling Christmas lights, and a couple of street performers.

I buy the falafel for both of us, interrupting Rémy's protests with reminders about how he paid for my groceries. He looks like he wants to argue, but he relents, and we munch on the best falafel I've ever had—also the first falafel I've ever had—as we walk back to the apartment.

I think about Siena's long-distance obsession with Rémy as he's unlocking the doors for us. He *is* objectively attractive, and he has been far nicer to me than I deserve. But I'm not sold on whatever she was implying about the reason behind his kindness. It's entirely possible that he has a girlfriend. I've only known the guy since yesterday, for heaven's sake. In fact, I would be shocked if he *didn't* have a girlfriend.

Besides, even putting aside the fact that I *do* have a boyfriend, Rémy and I are from different continents. And, despite what you see in the movies, normal people don't upend their lives by starting relationships like that.

What am I even talking about?! Relationships? This whole train of thought is ridiculous. Things might not be ideal with Josh or even what I had hoped they would be here so far in Paris, but I know just how good things can be between us—thinking about the beginning of our relationship still gives me butterflies— and I'm not the sort of person to jump ship at the first sign of trouble.

First sign of trouble, Madi? Really?

I grit my teeth. Every relationship has things to work through, and both Josh and I are still settling in here.

The building is only mildly less freezing than outside, but I'm grateful for even a few degrees at this point. Rémy doesn't even try to persuade me to take the elevator. I'll admit, a ride upstairs would be nice right about now, with my stomach full of falafel, but I kind of need the bathroom, and getting stuck in the elevator with Rémy when I need to pee doesn't sound very fun.

"HOW WAS YOUR DAY?" I ask Josh as he takes off his coat. He doesn't bother removing his shoes, and I glance at Rémy, who's poring over tomorrow's lesson plan. He always removes his shoes when he gets home. He even has soft house slippers he wears inside. They're somehow adorable and funny to me at the same time because they remind me of my grandpa.

Rémy glances at Josh's feet briefly, but he doesn't say

anything. I can't help but hope this means Josh is planning on heading back out with me in a few minutes.

"Long," Josh replies as he makes his way to the couch and takes a seat. He goes off for a few minutes about all the shifts the company is making and the pushback he's getting from some of his subordinates.

"Sounds like a lot of drama," I say.

"Nah," he replies. "Just corporate life."

Corporate life. It's a phrase he uses a lot. I don't love it because it implies that I'm incapable of understanding because I don't have a corporate job. Or any sort of real job, I guess.

"How is Brianne's training going?"

That's my roundabout way of asking how much time they've spent together since arriving. It's pathetic, I know. But Josh lives so much of his life at work, sometimes it feels like this mysterious dimension of him I don't know.

"Good," he says. "She's picking things up really quick. She doesn't seem to thrive in the group training atmosphere, but once she's had some one-on-one time where I can actually address her questions"—he snaps—"she's got it like that."

I manage a smile. It's silly to feel jealous of a business relationship. Besides, it's not like I have any place to talk. Rémy and I have been together a lot since I got here. In fact, I haven't spent anywhere near this much time alone with a guy besides Josh since we started dating—well, aside from Siena's brothers, but they don't count.

Josh doesn't seem to mind, either. He's just more mature than I am, I've decided. He's got life figured out, while I'm still puttering around.

"Did you do anything today?" Josh asks, patting the seat next to him on the couch. It's between him and Rémy, who's putting away his work stuff into his briefcase.

"Yes," I say, taking the seat. "This museum was amazing, Josh! My dream location for a shoot."

"Awesome," Josh says. "Was it the Louvre?"

I shake my head. "It's this one really close to here called Carnavalet. And it was *free*. I took way too many pictures. What would you say, Rémy? Like, a hundred?"

Rémy laughs as he shuts his briefcase. "At least. But they were all worth it."

"Oh," Josh says, trying to sound enthusiastic.

My smile fades. *Shoot.* He *is* jealous. He didn't really mean it when he told Rémy to take me around. I must have missed the signs. This was a test, and I failed.

"A small, free museum is cool, I guess," he says. "I just thought you'd wanna go see some of the bigger Paris sites."

"I do," I say, feeling relieved but also kind of weird. "I just wanted to save those for when we can go together."

He shrugs, grabbing the remote. "Of course we'll see them together, but I've already seen them all. We can go again once all my trainings are over. You should take advantage of the time I'm at work to see as much of the city as you can, Mads. Especially if Rémy here can show you around." He smiles as he flips through the shows. "He said he doesn't mind. Right, Rémy?"

Rémy looks at me like he wants to ask me something. I'm sure I'm not hiding my feelings well. I don't wear my heart on my sleeve; I wear it on my face.

"Not at all," Rémy says, his eyes flitting to me again.

Josh smiles and puts an arm around me, relaxing down into the couch. "Awesome. That means we can relax at night together because, lemme tell ya, I'm beat after these long days at work!"

Josh starts up *Parks and Rec*, and my eyes are on the screen, but my mind is very much elsewhere.

He's doing it again.

It's Jack this time. He prides himself on "telling it to me straight." Sometimes I don't want it straight, though. Sometimes I want the swirly, cinnamon roll version of life where everyone tells me what I want to hear. I want Jack to say, "I'm sure this time will be different, and Josh will come through."

I guess that's the problem, though. Josh sold me the swirly, cinnamon roll version of Paris. Turns out, that cinnamon roll is stale, and the delicious cream cheese frosting is more like straight Crisco. At least for now. It will be better once his trainings are done, I'm sure. I guess I can safely assume no engagements will be happening until then, either.

He stays awake almost an hour this time. I'm *this* close to confronting him about my bed situation, but I don't want to make things awkward for Rémy by having the discussion in front of him. Also, I can see Josh offering to find me a new place, and I don't really *want* to leave. The bed isn't ideal, no, but at least here I've got Rémy.

In any case, I don't feel bad about waking Josh up five minutes after he falls asleep. I'm tired, and Josh's shoulder isn't really appealing to me at the moment. I warned you I'm less mature than he is, didn't I? I'm a five-year-old having a tantrum because I was promised bubble gum ice cream and got vanilla.

It's dumb and childish. I'm in Paris, for heaven's sake. I have no reason to complain. It's probably just the lingering jetlag making me moody. In the morning, I'll feel myself again.

THIRTEEN

MADI

I *DON'T* FEEL ENTIRELY MYSELF WHEN I WAKE UP IN THE morning. Maybe that's partially because *myself* would never willingly choose to sleep next to a five-foot drop. Myself would also never choose to pee behind a red curtain. This room is like some sick game show I never wanted to be on, but apparently the price was right for a toilet to be the prize behind curtain number two. No pun intended.

The first thing I do once I've climbed down my ladder is open the window.

I regret my choice as a burst of arctic wind blows at my face. I brace myself and stick my head out. Yep, sure enough, my bra is still hanging outside Rémy's window. Can I just leave it there and pretend someone else's underwear happened to float onto his laundry rack?

Even the most rose-colored glass version of Madi knows that's a hard sell. It's okay, though. Maybe I can sneak into his room while he's at work today and snatch it.

Rémy's having breakfast at the table when I get downstairs. He's already dressed for work in another blazer and button-up shirt. Siena would probably let herself admire him for a minute or two—I can hear her comparing him to a J Crew model—but I refrain.

Today is a longer day for Rémy. I know that from talking to him on the way back from getting falafel last night. He teaches class nineteen hours a week, holds office hours for his students, grades papers, tweaks lesson plans, and attends mandatory meetings for the teachers at Lycée Michel Gontier—that's the name of the high school he works at. It's just a couple metro stops away, which he loves, since before coming to stay here, he was commuting from his mom's house every day for 45 minutes each way.

He looks up at me and smiles. "Good morning." There's something about that smile of his, and it's not just that it's handsome. It's warm and friendly and just a great thing to see first thing in the morning.

I feel slightly self-conscious in my Christmas long-john-style PJs given how put together he looks, but it's cool. I ain't trippin'. See how cool I am?

"I have to leave soon," he says, "but what would you like to see later today?"

I take a seat across from him. "Listen, Rémy. You *really* don't need to take me anywhere. You are not my personal concierge. I'm sure you have other things you'd like to do in the precious hours outside of work."

"Actually," he says, setting down his fork, "I had an idea . . ."

My brow quirks up. I'm listening.

"When you first got here, you asked for a city guide."

I wave away the words. "Yeah, but that was just because Siena told me there'd be one."

"And I think there *should* be. André really wants this place to be successful, and providing some tips for travelers would be smart, especially if that's what other Airbnbs are doing."

"I mean, it certainly couldn't *hurt*." I don't want Rémy to feel bad there's not a city guide, especially when he's gone out of his way to help me. This hosting is just a favor for a friend, too, so it's not even his responsibility.

I'm also not quite sure what exactly his idea is or how it relates to me.

"I've lived in Paris my whole life," he says, "which means I've never seen it as a tourist. I don't really know what interests you guys most."

I laugh because he says it like tourists are some alien species. I put on my best Valley-girl imitation. "Insta-worthy photo locations. Duh!"

He looks torn between horror and laughter.

"So you want me to be your tourist goggles?" I touch my thumbs to my pointer fingers, turn them upside down and put them up against my face. Jack and I used to make ourselves into Batman and Catwoman like this as kids.

"I don't know," he says warily. "Does it require you walking around Paris like that?"

I nod, keeping my hands in place.

"No less embarrassing than some of the things tourists do," he says, obviously trying to push my buttons.

I drop my Batman mask. "Hey, your city relies on us, mister! Admit it. You'd miss us if we all left."

He raises his brows.

I meet his expression with my own that says, *You better believe it.* Inside, though, I'm reviewing his idea. He wants me to help him make this guide, which would entail seeing the city together.

It honestly sounds like a ton of fun—going around Paris and finding the best spots. My main hesitation is Josh, which is ironic, given that Josh was the one who suggested this.

So what's keeping me from saying yes? Quite literally nothing.

"Despite all the shade you're throwing at me and my peeps," I say, "yes, I will help you. I will be your tourist lens, no pun intended. Oh! We could even include that as part of the guide— most Insta-worthy spots in Paris."

I can actually *hear* him roll his eyes.

"What?" I say. "I don't make the tourist rules, but if you're going to be in the business of hosting tourists and doing it well, you have to cater to them."

He sighs, a little smile playing on his lips, which tells me his reluctance is at least partially teasing.

"It's really nice of you to do all this for André," I say. If Siena knew that Rémy was doing all of this out of the goodness of his heart, she'd be singing a different tune about the things he's done for me. He's just the kind of guy who goes out of his way to help people. It has nothing to do with me.

"I promised him I would," Rémy says, sitting back now that he's done eating. "He's going through a lot with his mom's illness, and he had a lot more planned before your arrival that didn't happen because of that. When he comes back, I want everything to be just right."

I look around, curious what André had planned and what would be different if he'd had time to do it all. While I wouldn't complain about a few updates to the place and a few more cups, plates, and utensils, I wouldn't trade those things if it also meant trading Rémy as my host. Arriving in Paris was hard enough as it was; without Rémy, I might have caught a taxi right back to the airport, my spirit broken by the City of Love.

"What did he want to do exactly?"

"I'm not totally sure." Rémy swings around in his chair to survey the place. The blazer stretches tight across his shoulders. I'm not looking because I have any interest in or respect for those shoulders; this is purely out of concern for the seams of the nice blazer.

"I know he planned to have updated pictures taken once he had put his mark on the place—the ones up now are from the past owner. He was also going to buy new duvets and towels, which I'll do after work today." He turns back toward me. "I could ask him everything he intended to do, but I don't want to bother him right now. He's spending all of his time at the hospital. I kind of want to surprise him and just get it all done, you know?"

I nod, looking at him—really looking at him. He's about to embark on Christmas break, and he's going to spend it fixing up someone else's Airbnb and taking around a pathetic tourist. "André's lucky to have you, Rémy. So am I."

His gaze locks on me, and my pulse kicks into gear.

I hurry to stand, then reach for his plate. "Lemme get that for you."

He hesitates, but I smile and take the plate anyway.

"Do you need help fixing up the apartment?" I ask as I start rinsing his dish and utensils. "I could take the pictures, if you want. Or help you pick out duvets. Not that I don't trust your design sense." I glance at his clothes again. He's got a style that's very put together without trying too hard. I can only imagine that he would have an equally capable interior design style.

He comes up next to me, grabs the dish towel, and puts a hand out for me to pass him the dish I just washed. A piece of that perfectly styled hair drops into his face, and I'm cursing Siena for putting my thoughts about Rémy onto the wrong track.

"You don't want to spend your time in Paris doing that kind of stuff, Madi."

I can't help but love how he says my name. It showcases his super subtle French accent. It's like he pronounces both syllables with equal emphasis.

I lift my shoulders. "Why not? Creating the city guide will get me out to see Paris, and doing this Airbnb stuff will give me a different experience of the city. Seems like a pretty great option to me. But also, you should feel free to tell me to just back off if I'm butting my head into—"

"You're not," he says. "I'd love your help. *If* you really don't mind."

"Then it's a deal. But maybe I should see those listing pictures first so I know what I need to top."

He frowns and dries his hands on the dish towel. What is it

about that gesture that's so attractive? Probably the domesticness of it, especially on the heels of drying the dishes. My mom has always said there's nothing more romantic than a man crushing the 50s housewife stereotype.

"You haven't seen them?" he asks.

I shake my head. "Josh booked it."

His eyes linger on me for a second. "Right. I can show you. I've got a few more minutes."

I'm curious to see what these pictures look like for them to have convinced Josh this would be the best option for my time in Paris. He knows I'm afraid of heights, so I'm wondering if maybe the picture of the bed was taken from an angle that didn't show the whole *Ladder 49* aspect. And maybe the photographer was skilled enough at editing that he or she made the red curtains look luxurious instead of vaguely creepy.

"Thanks," I say as he pulls his laptop out of his briefcase. "It's possible I'm not as good a photographer as whoever took the listing shots on there now, so I probably should wait to volunteer myself."

Rémy laughs as he sits down and opens his laptop. Not just a chuckle. He is genuinely laughing, and maybe it's because I wasn't expecting that response, but it does something weird to my pulse.

"What?" I say, taking a seat beside him.

He shakes his head, but he's doing a terrible job trying to mask his smile. "You'll see."

He pulls up the listing and clicks on the first picture. Slowly, he scrolls through the photos. It doesn't take long—there are only a few.

He looks over at me when he's finished, but I'm busy staring at the laptop screen because WHAT WAS THAT?

I reach over and scroll through the photos again. And then I shudder. I can't help it. Seeing those dim, blurry photos is the photography equivalent of nails on a chalkboard. My eyes feel violated.

But I have to scroll through again because I forgot to take

note of the bed picture. I pause on it. It's taken from below and, blurry as it is, it definitely shows the ladder.

I close the laptop lid. I can't even look at it anymore.

Rémy looks over at me. "Still not sure you're the more capable photographer?"

I can't even smile at that. "I can't believe he rented it after seeing *those*. No offense." Maybe it was the only thing available. Plus, I could have asked to see the listing if I had really wanted to be sure it was a good fit. I imagine Josh thought he was doing me a favor. He's always trying to persuade me to face my fears, but still . . . he could have prepared me at least.

"He was probably just being frugal."

I shake my head at Rémy's generous but weak excuse for Josh. My eyes glaze over as those pictures flash across my vision. "For all he knew based on those listing pictures, he was sending me to be Taken. With a capital t."

"You Americans and that movie," Rémy says. He stands up and goes over to put his laptop back in the bag. "Given how often it comes up, you'd think fewer of you would come to Paris."

"What can I say? We're adrenaline junkies."

He smiles as he slips the bag over his head so that the strap crosses his body, providing a totally unnecessary delineation between his pecs. "Have you changed your mind about helping with the apartment, then?"

"Are you kidding?" I put a hand over my heart. "It is my duty as both a photographer and a decent human being to make sure those pictures are forever buried in the black hole of cyberspace. The first thing we are doing when you get home today is sitting down and making an inventory of what we need to do to this place. We're gonna make it shine."

FOURTEEN

RÉMY

"I cannot believe we are shopping at IKEA in the middle of Paris." Madi looks around like she might see the Eiffel Tower pop up around the corner we're about to turn. She's got her camera slung across her chest. It hangs on her hip as she pushes the cart and follows the arrows that guide customers through the IKEA maze.

We walked here from the apartment, and I almost told Madi to leave her camera when she went to grab it. I'm glad I didn't. Even though our route here was pretty ordinary for me, Madi was wide-eyed the entire time, and she probably snapped more pictures in that twenty minutes than I have taken of Paris in the past ten years. It's weird that it doesn't bother me. Usually, when I see tourists with a camera fixed to their face or walking like zombies with their phone in front of them, I can't help an eye roll.

The way Madi does things is different, though. Maybe it's that she's not capturing these photos to brag to her friends on social media. It's like she takes so much delight in what she's seeing that she can't fully take it in. And that's when the camera comes out.

"What do you think of these?" She stops next to a set of curtains with thick, vertical black and white stripes. The cart is

97

already pretty full, but we've crossed most things off of the list I'm holding.

When I got home from work, Madi had already made an inventory, which she had me look over. I check it now, but there's no mention of a second set of curtains anywhere.

"They're nice," I say. "You want to switch out the ones we already chose?" We picked a set of curtains for the living room area a few minutes ago. Madi's got great taste. We agreed on a color scheme that's neither too masculine nor too feminine. I can't quite picture how it's all going to look once we're done, but I have a feeling it'll be a whole lot better than the way things are right now. It sure as heck can't be worse.

She runs the sample curtains between her fingers. "No, I think the ones we chose are perfect for the living room." She looks up at me with those pretty brown eyes. She bites her lip. "Since we got here, though, I've had . . . a vision."

I raise my brows. "That sounds serious."

"Oh, it is. I think the room I'm in could be really endearing instead of . . ." She pauses like she's afraid of choosing a word.

"Sinister," I offer.

She scrunches her nose and tilts her head to the side. "It really is, isn't it? That dinky lamp casts some eerie shadows on the curtains, which already give off creepy circus vibes." She looks down at the curtains in her hand. "But after seeing all the options here, I'm convinced it could be a cute little space with some adjustments."

"Like those."

She nods. "I mean, having a curtain around a toilet isn't ideal, even if it's a really cute curtain, but we have to work with what we've got, right? Either way, that dingy red velvet is not helping the situation. I think these would look great, though. They would photograph so much better, too. Add in some small air plants by the window, a new bedspread, decorative pillows, and a couple other items to make it feel more homey, and I can see people booking it for the charm alone. People love tiny things as long as they're aesthetically pleasing."

I smile at her teasingly. "Is your *chambre de bonne* growing on you, Madi?"

"Growing on me like the sketchy mold by the window," she says. Her eyes narrow. "What you said *did* mean my servant room, right?"

I chuckle. "Yes. *Chambre de bonne* means a maid's room. Why don't you grab a few things to make it look the way you've envisioned while I run over there? I still haven't found an indoor drying rack for the clothes, and the apartment really should have one."

It's true. But I also want to see if the mention of drying clothes gives me any hint whether Madi knows her bra is dangling outside of my window. I noticed it this morning as the sun came up, illuminating it from behind with a ridiculous halo.

The slight widening of Madi's eyes tells me she is indeed aware of it.

"Yeah, yeah," she hurries to say as she turns away. "Of course."

She is super embarrassed, and for some reason that cracks me up. It's not like I've never seen a bra before.

Okay, yes, I shut my blinds because my eyes keep veering toward it every time I set foot in my room, but whatever. I'm fine. And I'm not going to bring it up if it's going to embarrass her.

I make my way toward the drying racks, and my phone vibrates in my pocket.

"Hey, Mom." I answer in French because . . . well, my mom and I *never* speak English to each other. She can speak it pretty well, but she's always insisted on speaking French, even when she and my dad were still married.

In that way, I had very distinct relationships with my parents. My dad always spoke English at home—when he *was* home, that is—and Mom always spoke French. They even spoke this way to each other. Dad would say something to Mom in English, she would respond in

French. It was normal for me growing up, since it's all I knew, but I've since learned that it's a really extreme example of a bilingual household. And probably a good example of why they got divorced.

"Hello, my dear," she says. "How are you?"

I glance over at Madi. She's got the black-and-white striped curtains in one hand, and she's holding them up to a bunch of throw pillows, squinting her eyes, then shaking her head. She's completely charming.

I turn to the drying racks. "I'm good. I miss you, though." It's true for the most part. I love my mom. She can be difficult sometimes—okay, a lot of the time—but her strict demeanor is a thing for a reason. She's been through a lot, and she's had no one to rely on most of the time. I'm lucky enough to see her soft side from time to time.

"I miss you, too," she says in her matter-of-fact tone. "I'm calling about Christmas. Will you be coming for *le Réveillon*?"

I smile a little as I glance over the selection of racks, balancing the phone between my ear and shoulder. "I'll be there." I would never dream of missing Christmas Eve dinner. It's just Mom and me, but she still insists on asking me every year. If I said no, I doubt she'd show emotion, but I know her well enough to know she'd be crushed. It's a huge production every time, leaving us with leftovers long past the point they're edible.

"Rémy! I've found the perfect ones!" Madi comes up behind me, arms full of curtains and throw pillows. She freezes when she notices I'm on the phone, lifting her shoulders and clenching her teeth. "Sorry," she mouths.

"Who is that?" my mom asks. Sounds like a reasonable question, but the tone she says it in is almost accusatory.

Shoulders still up and her back hunched over like the Grinch, Madi tiptoes toward the cart, dumping her load into it.

I smile at her antics even though she can't see me. "It's Madi. She's the guest staying at André's."

"An American."

"Yeah," I say, trying to sound completely nonchalant about it.

There's a little silence. "Where are you? It's very loud."

"We're at IKEA. I told André I'd help with decorating the apartment since he had to fly out before he could do everything."

"You should be focusing on what you can do to get the position at Bellevue."

My mom is really gunning for me to apply for a position at one of the more elite public schools in Paris. It would definitely be a step up, since right now I work for a private school that's only been open for a couple of years.

"I can do both. I just have a couple more days of work, then I can focus more on the application."

"Good, because I plan on inviting the Garniers for *le Réveillon*, and it will be a great opportunity for you to show Monsieur Garnier why you're a good candidate."

I don't personally think Christmas Eve dinner is the best networking opportunity, but I'm not dumb enough to think that's the only reason she's inviting the Garnier family. My mom has been trying to make something happen between me and Élise Garnier for a few years now. She thinks she's been subtle, but she hasn't.

I haven't commented on it much until now because Élise is in Paris infrequently enough that there's never really a need. My mom also doesn't know that Élise and I kissed the last time we saw each other. Or that I don't plan to repeat the experience.

"Can I bring anything?" I ask.

"Between the Garniers and myself, we will have almost everything taken care of, but if you'll bring some of that *foie gras* you brought last time and then two baguettes, that should be plenty."

"Of course." I grab the drying rack I think will work best in the apartment, lifting it into the cart. With my phone between my shoulder and ear, though, it's an attempt bound to fail. Madi steps in to help, but the drying rack is like an accordion, and it starts to expand, which she was clearly not expecting.

I pinch my lips together to keep from laughing at the thoroughly confused expression on her face. "Hey, can I call you back later, Mom?"

"No need," she says. "I just wanted to check about dinner."

"Love you," I hurry to say before she can hang up.

"You too."

I slip the phone back into my pocket and look at Madi.

"I'm so sorry," Madi says, taking a break from the drying rack struggle. "I had no idea you were on the phone."

"It's no problem." I push the pillows to the side to make room for the rack in the cart.

She glances at me quickly, then starts fiddling with it again. It's kind of mesmerizing to watch how completely futile her efforts are.

"Girlfriend?"

I'm so entranced by the way the rack only manages to open wider and wider that it takes me a second to realize what Madi said. "Hm?"

"On the phone," she says. "Was that your girlfriend?" She's still focused on the rack, pure determination in her eyes, like she will collapse that rack and fit it into the cart if it's the last thing she does. I'd let things play out just for the enjoyment of it except that she's about to pinch her fingers. "What *is* this thing?!" she cries out.

I laugh and take it from her, pressing it together easily.

She stares at it for a second like she can't believe what just happened. "I definitely loosened it for you."

"Totally."

She looks up at me with a smile that makes my chest constrict like the drying rack. It's getting harder to pretend the time I'm spending with Madi is purely in search of a 5-star review. More than once tonight, I've had the impulse to wrap my arm around her shoulders and pull her into me while we've pushed this cart through IKEA. Does she really think I'd be spending my Friday night at IKEA with her if I had a girlfriend?

Given that she's spending Friday night at IKEA with *me*, and she *does* have a boyfriend, I guess it's not out of the realm of possibility. I wish I knew whether she had asked disinterestedly or because it matters to her for some reason. She hasn't asked me again, though, even though the conversation has taken a turn, which tells me it's probably the first scenario.

"That was my mom on the phone, by the way." I'm dumb for feeling the need to make that clear, but what's done is done. "Anyway, we should probably make our way to check out."

Josh is coming over later, and I have to remind myself of that every few minutes. Madi has a boyfriend, no matter how undeserving I think the guy is. I'm probably not deserving of her, either, to be clear—Madi is really great—but there are levels of undeserving, and I'm more and more confident that Josh is on one of the sub-sub-sub-basement levels.

But Madi having a boyfriend is only one problem, though. She lives thousands of miles away. I don't need anyone to tell me how those kind of "love stories" end up. I've lived in it myself.

We go through checkout, and I arrange for our purchases to be delivered to the apartment tomorrow because there's no way we can walk back to the apartment with everything we managed to pile into that cart.

When we get to the exit, Madi turns left outside to head back the way we came.

"Wait," I say.

She stops and turns toward me as she slips her beanie back on. The warm light from the window displays illuminates her face, and I'm struck again by how beautiful she is. I mean, she's genuinely and objectively beautiful, but it's more than that. She's . . . she's . . .

"Rémy?"

I blink. She's still waiting for me to tell her why I stopped her. "Sorry. Yeah, I was just wondering when Josh is going to be at the apartment."

"Oh. I think he said around eight. But he's always late, so eight-thirty is a safe bet."

I pull out my phone and check the time. It's almost 7:30. I slip it back into my pocket and look up at Madi again. Since getting home from work, I've been wondering why she didn't go sightseeing while I was gone. She spent the day doing the inventory. I've seen her in the city more than once now, and if anyone is going to properly appreciate the beauty of Paris, she is.

But she's *not* seeing it, and I'm not sure if that's because she's saving the special parts for Josh despite the fact that he told her not to hold off on his account.

"Why didn't you go out today?" I ask.

She adjusts her beanie. It's got the most massive pompom on the top I've ever seen, but she pulls it off somehow. "Um . . . will you think I'm crazy if I say I'm scared of your city?"

I narrow my eyes. "Is this a *Taken* thing again?"

She laughs, and it comes out in puffs of warm air in the evening chill. "No. I just . . ." Her mouth twists to the side. "Honestly? I *did* try to go out today. I walked all the way to the metro."

"But?"

She chews the inside of her lip before responding. "I went down into the station, and it was chaotic, and everyone was speaking French, and I tried to buy a ticket, but I couldn't figure out the machines, and—" She looks at me and shrugs. "I chickened out. I know it's dumb, but based on how things have gone so far for me in Paris, I didn't think I should try my luck in a place like that with so many people and the small spaces and by myself. I'd probably end up calling you to come pick me up in Sweden or something."

"That would be impressive, actually," I say with a sympathetic smile. But inside I don't feel like smiling; I feel like punching Josh. From what I've gathered, he invited Madi to come to Paris, yet he hasn't been here for her any of the times she's needed him—not for the journey here, not for the lost luggage or the scamming taxi driver, not to mention he booked her one of the tiniest, worst rooms in Paris and failed to pay for the booking. This guy should appear under the Urban Dictionary entry for #boyfriendfail.

Madi's wasting her time in Paris because Josh can't take some initiative—or some freaking caffeine—and escort her around like any decent guy would do.

I jerk my head the opposite direction of home. "Come on. I wanna show you something." I may not be able to show her the Eiffel Tower without stealing the wind from Josh's sails—if he even *has* sails—but I can show her other parts of Paris I know she'll appreciate.

Madi raises her brows, and I can see the curiosity spark in her eyes. As we start walking, I'm feeling a weird mixture of nerves and anticipation. If it wouldn't be weird and a bit reckless, I'd blindfold Madi with the scarf she's wearing. I just know the look in her eyes when she sees our destination will be worth it.

Suddenly, she stops. I do, too, wondering if she's onto me. But Madi doesn't know the city, and there's no way she knows what's one minute away from us. She's staring at something right behind me, though, so I turn around, looking for whatever has captured her attention.

"Wait, are you taking me to the metro?" she asks.

I frown for a second, then spot it: the stairs leading down to the nearest station.

"Is this your plan to force me to experience Paris properly?" Her voice is teasing, but I can't miss the wariness in her eyes.

"What? No. I wouldn't do that to you." What kind of a guy does she think I am? "You'll like this. I promise."

She relaxes a bit and smiles. "Okay, lead the way."

We start walking again, and I can't help looking at her, hoping she's not looking at the signs around us that tell her exactly what site we're near.

She looks up at the buildings to our right. "Is Paris always this magical? Or is it a Christmas thing?"

I grimace. "After Christmas, this place is just a pile of rubble."

She laughs and elbows me.

What is it about getting hit in the ribs like that that feels so dang good?

Stop, Rémy. She's got a boyfriend.

I force Josh's face into my mind. Now it's *me* who wants to throw an elbow, though, and the destination is *not* his ribs. Is my level of dislike for the guy disproportionate to what I know of him? Maybe.

"Okay, turn around." I take Madi by the shoulders, and, giving me a weird but curious look, she obeys as I guide her backwards.

"Rémy," she says, laughing a bit, "I have a hard enough time walking when I can see where I'm going."

"Don't worry. I won't let you run into anyone. Or anything." Keeping my hands on her shoulders, I guide her across the street when the light changes for us. Her eyes are fixed on me, full of trepidation and adventure. She can't stop laughing, and it's contagious.

People are looking at us, but I ignore them. I've seen way weirder things in Paris, and I know that, like me, people will just chalk it up to living in a city full of weird tourists.

We head into an arched stone passage, and Madi's eyes go big as it gets darker. She grabs my hands on her shoulders and stops. "Oh my gosh. Rémy, are you taking me into that underground tunnel with all the bones?"

I try to ignore the way it feels to have Madi's hands covering mine. I didn't wear gloves, but I can feel the warmth of her hands through hers. "The catacombs?"

"Yes! Siena told me about them. They sound terrifying."

"They're actually really cool. But no. I'm not taking you to the catacombs. Come on." I urge her to start walking backward again. "We're almost there."

We walk a bit farther, navigating the crowds of people coming the opposite direction. Madi keeps her eyes trained on me and her hands on my forearms to stabilize herself as she shuffles backward. I have to adopt a sort of penguin waddle to avoid hitting her feet with mine. Both of us are smiling as I try to help her navigate the uneven stone ground and the tourists too busy filming live

TikToks or coming up with a clever photo caption to watch where they're going.

In hindsight, I realize that this is not the most platonic idea I've ever had, but I can't find it in myself to regret it. It's impossible to regret anything that makes Madi smile or her eyes light up like this.

We come to the edge of the arched passageway, and I stop us, taking my hands from her shoulders with more regret than is strictly necessary. "Okay. Turn around."

She holds my gaze for a second like she might get a hint from my face about what she's going to see. Then, she turns.

FIFTEEN

MADI

The Louvre Pyramid is lit up from inside, its crisscrossing pattern reflecting on the pool around it like a pristine mirror. Everywhere I look is the massive complex that is the Louvre—an enormous square of perfectly symmetrical buildings with gray rooftops, a thousand windows, and ornately carved stone, all lit by a line of tall lamp posts running around the whole plaza.

It looks like something I dreamed up, not a real place.

Rémy reaches over and, using the edge of his finger, he pushes up on my chin, closing my mouth.

I smile guiltily. "Stars and stripes showing again?"

"A little." He's smiling back at me. "Not as much as those people's are, though." He jerks his head toward two girls twenty feet away from us. One is standing on top of the stone rim of the fountain. She's putting her finger out, pointing downward while her friend squats to take a picture. It's supposed to make it look like she's touching the top of the pyramid.

"Are you saying you refuse to take a picture of me like that?"

"That's exactly what I'm saying."

I can't even pretend to be mad. I'm already distracted by the fountains starting up near the pyramid. "How much is it to walk

109

around?" I'm on a tight budget, but I'm thinking it'll be worth it to spend a few euros just to take this all in.

"Zero euros."

I look at Rémy. "You're kidding me."

He shakes his head.

"Anyone can just walk around this place? Any time? For free?"

"Between 7 a.m. and 11 p.m., yes. Come on. I'll show you around."

I could see Chris Hemsworth shirtless and not be as starstruck as I am right now, walking around the *Cour Napoléon*, as Rémy informs me it's called. I can't believe places like this really exist—and that they're free.

Rémy's a great tour guide. He gives me bits of information every couple of minutes, but for the most part, he lets me do my thing, which is walking around and snapping photos when I see something I can't resist capturing. He doesn't hang around my side and make me feel rushed. In fact, he seems to be taking it all in himself, and I can't help but grab a couple of shots of him while he does it. He makes a dang good model. The lights from the lamps highlight the lines of his face—the square jaw, the full lips, the deep brow, the shadow of his stubble.

I'm admiring him as a photographer. It's perfectly normal to take note of beautiful things. Science, like Siena says. To pretend Rémy isn't one of the most attractive people I've ever met would be as unnatural as pretending this isn't the most beautiful place I've ever set foot. And of course I want to capture a beautiful person in a beautiful environment. It's decreed by whoever decides the laws for photographers, and I am a law-abiding woman.

"What's that?" I point to the enormous ferris wheel sitting outside the square we're in. It's got festive red, white, and green lights fanning out from the center. At the base is a line of small booths with Christmas lights draped from each gabled rooftop.

"It's the Tuileries Christmas Market," Rémy says.

"A Christmas market? Right here?"

He nods, his eyes twinkling as he looks at me.

"How do you have IKEA, the Louvre, and a Christmas market within a couple minutes of each other? Doesn't that violate some international zoning code? There should be a certain distance between amazing things to protect people from a dopamine overdose."

Rémy shoves his hands in his pockets, laughing.

"I know, I know," I say with a sigh. "My stars and stripes."

He shrugs a shoulder. "They're growing on me."

I cock a brow at him. "More like growing *in* you. You're half American, remember? Under that shirt of yours, you're probably wearing a Captain America suit." *Stop talking about what's under his shirt, Madi.* "You'll claim us someday. I'll make sure of it."

"Oh yeah?"

"Yup. You'll be singing *God Bless America*, waving around your own Old Glory, and snarfing down a supersize order of McDonald's fries when I'm done with you." My phone buzzes, and I pull it out, still looking at Rémy to make sure he knows I mean business. It's a text from Josh.

Josh: I'll be there in 15.

The text kills my mood like a bug zapper to a fly. "Shoot. How long does it take to get back to the apartment from here?"

"On foot? Twenty-five minutes if we hurry."

I bite my lip, looking around. I don't want to leave. I could sit here for hours admiring the view and people-watching. This is the most romantic place I've ever been—no contest. I thought I'd be sharing it with Josh. But I don't even know if I *want* to share it with him because he clearly doesn't care about that.

And the realization that this is what I've been missing, sitting in the apartment, waiting for him to take me around—or sitting next to him while he snores softly on the couch—makes me feel a flash of resentment. It's not entirely his fault, of course. It was my choice to walk back home instead of going on the metro today, but that's the thing. I didn't think I'd *be* touring Paris on my own.

But being here at the Louvre makes me determined not to waste another second. I don't want to go home with regrets. I want to experience everything that makes Paris, Paris.

I take in a deep breath. "How long would it take on the metro?" My experience there yesterday was pure chaos, but like Rémy said, I can't do Paris without the metro.

He looks at me for a second. "About half the time."

It's not a big deal if Josh has to sit outside the apartment waiting for us for a few minutes while we walk home—it's not like I haven't waited for him longer than that on a regular basis—but it's not just about Josh. I've got to get over my fear of the metro if I'm going to see this city, and better to do it now while I've got Rémy to guide me through it than trying by myself tomorrow.

"Let's take the metro."

He holds my gaze for a second, then smiles and nods. "This way."

We head back the way we came, but this time, I'm walking forward, and Rémy's hands aren't on my shoulders, which makes it a lot quicker but also a lot less fun. When we get to the arched passage, there's a couple in the middle of the exit, liplocked while one holds a cell phone out to capture their makeout session with the Louvre pyramid behind.

"Americans," Rémy says.

"Hey. How do you know they're Americans? The French are the ones known for being romantics."

The girl lowers the phone. "Let's check it out," she says to her boyfriend in a distinct American accent.

Rémy looks at me and smiles. "We *are* romantics. But we have a different definition of romance."

"That definition being . . . ?"

He shrugs. "What's between a man and a woman. Being in the moment together and forgetting everyone around you. And *that*"—he jerks his head back toward the couple—"is the opposite of romance."

I look back at them. They're going for round two, with the phone at a different angle this time. I can't help but agree with Rémy. There's not much I find romantic about choreographing camera angles to make sure your makeout video gets the most likes on social media.

I almost want to ask Rémy what he considers a romantic date in Paris and whether he's ever brought his girlfriend here. I still don't know if he has a girlfriend or not—he didn't really answer when I gave him the chance at IKEA—so I'm just going to assume he does because 1) how could he not? and 2) it's better that way.

We cross the street and reach the green, quirky sign that says *Métropolitain*. I stare at it for a second, then take in a deep breath.

"You sure?" Rémy asks.

I nod. If I'm going into the Paris metro with anybody, Rémy is the right person.

It's Friday night, and it's every bit as busy as it was when I made my failed attempt this morning. As we make our way down the stairs, people file down all around us, jostling me and making my chest feel tight.

I stop at the bottom, letting a group of tourists speaking a foreign language brush past. Rémy stands in front of me, facing me, like my own personal buffer.

"Sorry." I chuckle nervously. "Small spaces and heights." I feel dumb for making it a big deal—I know some people have legitimate and much bigger fears for better reasons, but that doesn't change the fact that it's not an experience I take pleasure in. I try for a smile. "I'm working on it. Last night, I only had *one* nightmare about falling off the bunkbed."

Rémy does not look amused. "Madi, you don't have to sleep on that bed. I didn't realize it was so uncomfortable for you."

I cock a brow at him, determined to keep this light.

"Okay, yes," he says, "it looks really uncomfortable, but I

didn't realize it was keeping you from sleeping. Does Josh not know you're afraid of heights?"

"He does. He just . . . thinks I need a little push to conquer my fears. He's always challenging himself to do more and be more in life and at work. It's how he's risen in the ranks so quickly."

Rémy frowns. It makes him look like the brooding hero of a movie I'd love to watch. "We don't have to do this, Madi. We can walk. We could even rent bikes."

I'm momentarily distracted. "Bikes?"

"Yeah, they have a system here. It's easy to use, and it'd be faster than walking."

I take in a breath. "No, it's okay. I wanna do this."

Rémy leads the way to the ticket machines. It takes him less than sixty seconds to get a ticket for me. Typical.

He seems to know just what I'm thinking as he turns to hand me mine. "I've had a lot of practice."

We make our way to the next machines—the ones that eat the ticket, then spit it back out on the other side of the gate you walk through. There are a zillion people waiting to pass, and I'm not looking forward to it being my turn. Rémy has me go first, talking me through it calmly as if we have all the time in the world rather than the world waiting behind us.

I have to take off my thick gloves to handle the little paper ticket. I should have done that while we were waiting.

I hurry to stuff the gloves into my coat pocket.

Rémy puts a hand on my arm. "Take your time. People can move to one of the other ones if they need to."

Someone waiting a few people behind me says something in French, clearly directed at me. It doesn't sound nice. Rémy responds with a few pithy words. I mean, technically, I have no idea what he said or how many words it was, but it must have been a great comeback, because the guy shuts his mouth and doesn't say anything else.

"He hates me, doesn't he?" I slip the ticket into the machine.

"He's just a jerk," Rémy replies.

I hurry through the turnstile and grab the ticket as it pops up on the other side, then wait for Rémy. He's such a pro at this that he has a card he just taps once to let him through.

With that obstacle over, Rémy leads the way toward . . . honestly, I don't even know where. I'm like a kid at a theme park, entirely reliant on him to get us where we need to go. I should probably just have a stroller, maybe even one of those leash backpacks.

In a lot of ways, though, this does feel like a theme park. The crowds are intense, and Rémy and I get separated as people criss-cross to get to their various destinations.

My muscles are tensing and my chest is tightening as I try to keep track of him amongst the chaos. I try to hurry my pace to catch up with him again, but a group of young and unusually tall adolescents cuts in front of me, and I lose him entirely.

SIXTEEN

MADI

It's not rational, feeling like I'm going to be swallowed up in this crowd and disappear or get trampled or something, but that's what my body and mind are telling me is going to happen. I can't see Rémy anywhere, and I'm trying to calm my building nerves, to remind myself that I'm an adult and, if the hooligans who just cut me off can handle this, so can I.

It's not working great, though, and my eyes search the people around me frantically, seeking familiarity.

Suddenly, the crowds part, and Rémy is right in front of me. He grabs my hand with his, and our gazes catch for a second, his apologetic and reassuring. I really *am* like a five-year-old at Disneyland, because that hand is my lifeline right now.

Rémy forges a way through the crowds and leads us down some stairs, through a hallway, and finally to an open space with an empty train track, never letting go of my hand. The crowds are much thinner here, with people spread out along the platform on both sides of the tracks, waiting for the trains to come.

We find a free space to stand, and I glance down. My heart skips a beat at the image of our hands. So far, Rémy holding my hand was just a kind gesture—a *really* kind one, of course. But there's no need for it anymore. And yet, I don't really want to let go.

I glance up at him, and he's looking at me like he knows what I'm thinking because he's thinking the same thing.

My phone buzzes in my pocket. It's like an electric shock, and I jerk my hand away, my conscience zinging.

Josh: Might be a few minutes late.

"He's gonna be a bit late," I say, looking up at Rémy as I slip my phone back into my pocket.

He nods, but the smile he gives me looks the tiniest bit forced as he sticks his hand in his pocket.

A low rumbling and the blinking zero on the countdown sign farther down the platform tells me that the train is coming. Not a moment too soon. We get lucky and snag two seats next to each other, but I'm not so sure it *is* luck because I'm aware of every inch of space—there are three of those inches—between my leg and Rémy's.

We sit in silence, though it might be because the rush of the train is so loud it's hard to talk over it unless you want everyone within ten feet to hear your conversation.

But even when we reach the next station—and the one after that—neither of us say anything. It's like those extra two seconds of holding hands is hanging over both of us, and while I'm dying of curiosity to know Rémy's thoughts, I'm not dumb enough to think that would be a good thing.

We've passed two stops when my phone vibrates.

Josh: I'm down here but no one is answering. Are you there?

Madi: So sorry! We'll be there in a few minutes.

I look at it before pressing send and change the *we* to *I*. I will be there in a few minutes.

"Is that Josh?" Rémy asks.

I nod. "He's waiting outside for us."

"I'm sorry, Madi," Rémy says as the door alarm sounds, notifying everyone that it'll be closing.

"For what?"

"Making you late."

I stare at him. "You're kidding me, right? I just saw the most amazing thing I've seen in my entire life, and you're apologizing for it?"

The doors shut, and the train is back on its way, too loud for us to carry on the discussion. I can't believe Rémy thinks I'd be mad at him for taking me to see the Louvre courtyard.

My nerves ramp up again when it's time to make our way out of the metro. We have to go through the same machines, but this time they've got glass doors that open and close instead of turnstiles. It's like an American Ninja Warrior challenge, and I'm nervous they're going to close when I'm only halfway through. But they don't.

I grab my ticket when it pops back up on the other side, and Rémy comes up alongside me as we hurry up the stairs into the chilly December night again. When we get to the top of the stairs, I feel a surge of victory. *I* am the newest American Ninja Warrior. Or Parisian Ninja Warrior.

"I survived!"

Rémy smiles. "You did."

I put my hand up, inviting a high-five, and he doesn't hesitate. The moment our hands touch, I remember our milliseconds-too-long-hand-hold. Rémy does too.

We drop our hands and start the walk back to the apartment, where Josh—my boyfriend—is waiting.

Rémy doesn't make things awkward, though. He talks through our IKEA purchases, which we agree we'll put up tomorrow after the morning delivery. I can't help but be excited about sprucing up the apartment, and Rémy seems to be jazzed about it too. He keeps talking about what André will think when he sees it.

When we get to the apartment building, we stop and look up and down the street. It's not particularly well-lit. There are a few apartments here and there with a string of lights on their street-facing windows, but for the most part, it's dark enough that I have to squint slightly as I look for Josh. There's no sign of him.

"Didn't he say he was already here?" Rémy asks.

I take out my phone, frowning. "Yeah, he did. And that was almost ten minutes ago." Did he leave? Wouldn't he have texted me? Why do I feel like I did something wrong?

My hand tingles guiltily, as if Josh somehow knows of those two nanoseconds—okay, it was more like two *normal* seconds—and decided to break up with me by way of disappearing without a word.

I scan the street again as if he'll magically appear, but he doesn't. "He must have left." I don't even know what to feel about that. Part of me is glad not to have to face him when I've got an overactive conscience, but the other part of me is worried.

Rémy scrubs a hand over his jaw, which is covered in that evening shadow I'm getting to know from seeing him every night before bed. "Madi . . ." he says, and I can hear the apology coming.

"Don't say sorry again, Rémy. He could have waited a few minutes. I do it for him all the time." It's true, and just saying it alleviates my guilt a bit—and makes me a bit angry. I feel like I'm constantly waiting for Josh, but he can't wait for me the one time I'm late?

I hoped Paris would be different—more like things were in the beginning of our relationship, when Josh planned fun dates and romantic dinners—but it hasn't been.

Rémy meets my eyes, and for the second time tonight, *something* is happening between us. The street doesn't just feel empty now; it feels private.

"Listen," I say to lift the tension, "I know you've probably been to the Louvre a hundred times, but that was just what I needed. Same with helping me in the metro." I can't quite meet his gaze just now because of *how* he helped me in the metro. I charge forward. "It helped me realize what I want out of my time here. Thanks to you, I'm basically a metro pro now."

He chuckles and pulls out his keys. "Before you know it, *you'll* be the one yelling at tourists figuring out the ticket machines."

"Hey, you told me to take my time."

"Yeah," he says as he wiggles the key into the lock, "but there *are* limits, you know." He's smiling at me in a teasing way that gets my blood pumping. He pushes open the door partially, then pauses. "And yeah, I've been to the Louvre a lot, but tonight was different."

There it goes again. My heart's going haywire as he looks at me. What does he mean by *different*?

"Is that you, Madi?"

The door opens wider, and Josh is on the other side. In the courtyard.

"Finally," he says. Seeing the confused looks on our faces, he explains, "Someone came through a few minutes ago and let me in."

"Oh." My heart is a bit shellshocked by his sudden appearance. "I thought you got sick of waiting and left."

He gives me a teasing look. "I was *about* to. It's not good form to make a man wait in the cold, you know. Hey, Rémy."

"It's my fault she's late," Rémy says after giving him a little nod. "I insisted on making a stop after IKEA."

"Just don't let it happen again, man." Josh is half-teasing, half-not, and I can't help but feel embarrassed—for him and for me.

I can swear Rémy has a comeback on his lips, but he just says, "Of course not."

"It's only 8:30," I say to Josh. "We could go out and see something, grab a dessert, maybe."

Josh makes a little grimace. I've seen it a million times, but for some reason, it bothers me in a new way tonight. "If I hadn't been standing in the cold forever already, maybe, but I kinda just wanna get inside and get warm."

Rémy leads the way to the door and unlocks it, opening it for me and Josh to pass through.

"Thanks," I say, not even responding to Josh's comment.

Rémy meets my eye with the ghost of a smile and tells me, "*Je t'en prie*," which is French for *you're welcome*. Add speaking French to the list of things attractive men shouldn't be allowed to do. Especially when they're putting a rude guy in his place at the metro station.

I make my way toward the stairs, but Josh grabs my hand. He presses the elevator button, looking at me like, *Duh. Of course we're taking this way up.*

"Oh," I say. "I usually take the stairs."

"What? Why?"

I just look at him.

"Right. Small spaces. You gotta get over that *someday*, Mads. Why not in Paris?"

I clench my teeth together. "I think I've hit my quota for facing my fears on this trip already. We took the metro here."

Josh's brows go up, and he glances at Rémy. "Really?"

Rémy nods. He's not usually this quiet, which makes me think Josh either makes him uncomfortable or he doesn't like him.

Josh pulls me into a side hug. "Way to go, Mads. Conquering your fears one by one like a champ. I knew all you needed was a push."

"Is that why you booked a place that forces me to go up a ladder to get to bed?"

Josh smiles guiltily. "I figured you could handle a few feet. Baby steps."

I know he's just trying to help me, but I'm feeling less than patient with his good intentions right now.

The elevator doors open, and he puts out a hand, inviting me to go in. All I can think of is the time the elevator stalled on the way down to this level. I'm not up for that right now.

Rémy is watching me, quiet as ever.

"I'm just gonna take the stairs," I say.

Josh's face falls, but he nods. "I'll see you up there, then."

SEVENTEEN

MADI

JOSH MAKES HIMSELF COMFORTABLE ON THE COUCH—his usual spot—and grabs the remote. We might as well be at his apartment right now. I mean, his apartment is definitely nicer than this Airbnb, but still.

This place has grown on me a bit, but it's no Eiffel Tower. If Josh proposes to me here with Netflix playing in the background, I might lose it.

Rémy retreated into his room pretty quickly after we came upstairs. In a way, I'm jealous of him. I don't know if I've ever felt this frustrated with Josh. Has he always been this way? Is it me who's different right now? Or is he being more aggravating than usual?

He picks *Parks and Rec*—again. He's never really noticed that he's the only one laughing most of the time. But at least at home, he stays awake.

I don't want to compare Josh to Rémy, but I'm finding it really hard not to. Rémy's got a job, just like Josh does. I'm sure he's tired—it can't be easy spending the better part of each day with hormonal adolescents more interested in pushing boundaries than in learning English. And yet, he's gone way out of his way to make me comfortable. This is a guy I've known a few days.

I'm not being fair, I know. Josh is here for work, and I should be more understanding of his situation. I also shouldn't let my anger simmer without letting him know what's on my mind.

When he starts to nod off during the second episode, I can't take it anymore.

I grab the remote and pause the show. "Josh."

His eyes are closed. "Hm?"

"Can we talk for a minute?"

His eyes open slowly, and he looks over at me, stifling a yawn. "Yeah, what's up?"

I don't speak right away because now that he's waiting, I'm feeling hesitant. Am I just being a big baby about all of this? Am I an overly indulged brat who just wants all the attention on her? Sometimes I've wondered if Josh thinks of me like one of his business deals. He *hates* when his clients jump ship. What if that's what makes him hold on to me, too—a phobia of failing—rather than any real desire to marry me?

My silence seems to rouse him a bit more. He sits up, sensing this is serious, then grabs my hand. "Are you mad because of the elevator thing?"

"No," I hurry to say. I mean, yes, I'm annoyed about that, but let's tackle one thing at a time, right? I sigh. "It's just . . . we talked about how things were gonna go when we came to Paris, and"—I press my lips together—"it's just not really happening that way."

He strokes my hand. "I know. I'm sorry. I've been way busier than I thought I would be."

I shake my head. "I knew you'd be busy during the day. Well, except for lunch, but I thought for sure we'd be able to spend time together once you were off."

"We *have* been."

"I mean, yes, technically we have. You put on Netflix and fall asleep next to me. That's not really what we talked about, though, Josh. I mean, tonight, I went to the Louvre courtyard, and it was amazing—better than I could have imagined. But you weren't there, and I thought we'd be sharing those places and moments together." Now that I'm expressing my feelings, they're all coming to the surface like an overflowing toilet. I can't stop them. "And then, I haven't wanted to bother you with it, but you haven't said anything about me meeting Dan Vincent yet, and you said he's leaving on the 20th, which means there's not much time left for me to talk to him. And—"

Josh puts up a hand to stop me. He sits up straighter, facing toward me more. "I know. It's been crazy, and I'm sorry I've been so flaky." He smiles at me warmly. "But it's the weekend now, which means we can do everything you want. I've got lunch set up with Dan tomorrow to discuss the potential of a job for you, and afterward, we'll go to the Eiffel Tower like you've been wanting to do. We can just look at it from the bottom so you don't have to go up to the top. And after that, we can go on a romantic boat cruise on the river with the whole city lit up and the reflection of the Eiffel Tower on the water."

My frustrations start to fizzle under his reassurances and the vision he's painting of this weekend. He *did* arrange a meeting with Dan about the job. He just didn't tell me. I should have asked him sooner and spared myself this building frustration.

I smile sheepishly, feeling like the toddler who had a tantrum again. I just needed to have a little patience. It seems like Josh has really thought through tomorrow, and that realization sets off a batch of fireworks inside me.

What if he's planning to propose? It would make sense, given that he knows how much I've been looking forward to the Eiffel Tower.

Excitement, hope, and nerves mix around inside my stomach, and I can't tell which one is going to win out, but it feels like it might be the nerves.

It's almost like now that it's within reach, I'm not ready for it.

"I'll make up for it all, Mads," he says with a little enigmatic look that has *it's going down tomorrow* written all over it. "Trust me. Does that sound good?"

I nod a bunch of times and smile. "It sounds perfect."

EIGHTEEN

RÉMY

I've stayed in my room as long as I possibly can, but my eyes are starting to droop as I try to focus on the words in the book I'm reading. I wanted to give Madi and Josh their privacy—okay, let's be honest, if it were up to me, I'd probably stand next to the TV, monitoring them to make sure no funny business happened—but usually Josh is gone by now, and I need to brush my teeth and get ready for bed.

I fiddle with my door handle to give them fair warning that I'm coming out. I don't want the image of Madi kissing that jerk emblazoned on my mind forever. He *is* a jerk, for the record. I wasn't being unreasonable before, it turns out. I don't like the way he treats Madi. It's not outright rude, but that's a pretty low bar for a boyfriend.

I open the door and glance toward the TV, which is on.

I make my way to the bathroom door, stopping as I get a small view of the couch. Josh's head is tipped to the side. That's no surprise. The guy has been asleep 75% of the time he's spent in this apartment. Closer to 90%, probably. Is Madi sitting there watching alone, then?

I walk over quietly to check.

Immediate regret. Josh's head is resting on Madi's, both of them fast asleep, their fingers laced together on Josh's leg.

Why is that picture like a gut punch? My eyes fixate on their hands, and I remember how I held Madi's just a few hours ago. And maybe I'm crazy, but I could swear she didn't want to let go. Until Josh texted her.

She let go real quickly at that point. *She* did. I knew I should, too, but the truth is, I would've kept holding her hand if she'd let me.

I'm the poster boy for pathetic right now, staring at the girl I like while she's asleep. I turn away to head to the bathroom just as my phone breaks the silence with an absurdly loud text tone.

André: Hey, Rémy. I've been meaning to check in, but time keeps getting away from me. How are things going?

I glance at Madi as she readjusts on the couch. Has a woman ever looked so angelic?

My fingers hover over the keyboard. What do I say? *Hey, things are going great, man. Just falling for your guest like a lovesick puppy, even though she's spoken for. If you get a 1-star review, it'll be because I can't keep my hands or eyes to myself. Have a good night.*

Rémy: Things are going great. I understand your wanting to check in, but you really don't need to worry about a thing over here. Just focus on spending time with your mom. I'm taking care of things, and everything is fine *thumbs up*

André: I owe you. Is the guest difficult?

I glance over at Madi again. Oh, she's difficult all right. Difficult to stop thinking about. Difficult not to wrap my arms around. Difficult to see with that guy.

Rémy: Not at all. She's as good as you could have hoped for.

And if she weren't leaving in two weeks, I'd be tempted to fight like heck to steal her away from Josh. Madi teased me about wearing a Captain America suit underneath my clothes earlier, but if I could have a superpower right now, I'd choose superspeed. That way, I could pick up Josh, chuck him through the window, and slip into his place on the couch next to Madi, sliding my fingers through hers.

That image alone is making me feel things a guy shouldn't feel for a taken woman. I pocket my phone and head to the bathroom where I brush my teeth for way longer than normal as I try to drown out the thought of Madi—and wait for Josh to leave.

This is it, my friends. Rock bottom—when you're 26 and stalling your bedtime routine to get a "good night" from some other guy's girlfriend.

But Josh is still there when I head to my room. He's awake now—probably thanks to André's text—and is looking at his phone, typing away on a text.

He glances up at me and immediately turns off his phone screen.

"'Sup," he says.

I smile—or maybe it's a grimace. "I'm just heading to bed. Good night."

Tonight, my superpower will have to be clean teeth.

MADI'S SITTING at the table, a wheel of Camembert cheese (a new one because she already ate the last one) and a fresh baguette from the boulangerie down the street in front of her. This has become her go-to breakfast, and it's amazing how much I can want a woman whose diet staple is smelly cheese.

Her hair is up in a lopsided ponytail, secured with a scrunchie and giving all the I-woke-up-like-dis vibes. She's not Beyoncé. She's better. Airbrushed celebrity sexy is overrated, but *this* . . . this is massively underrated.

I've watched a lot of American films over the course of my life in an effort to keep up and perfect my English, and all of them tell me the proper move right now is to go over and kiss Madi on the forehead. Thankfully, I have a behavior filter. I also have a passable memory, which is great because it helps me remember that I fell asleep alone in my room while Madi and Josh cuddled until late. I wonder how André would feel about instituting a curfew on his guests' guests.

"Morning, Rémy," she says with a sleepy smile.

"Good morning," I reply, filling up the kettle at the sink.

"Do you hate me for sleeping on the couch again?"

I chuckle, turning toward her and leaning against the counter while I wait for the water to boil. "I specifically told you that you can sleep there if it's better than the bed in your room."

"Well, it definitely *is* because it lacks the whole ladder scenario. And I was so tired when Josh left, I couldn't bring myself to walk up a set of wonky stairs *and* climb those rungs. Sleepiness is so fragile. *But* it's possible that after we fix up the room today, I'll be so won over by the cuteness of it all that I'll overlook the ladder and the death-drop."

"I don't think dropping five feet would kill you."

"But you don't *know* that, do you?" She gives me a look like she just hit a home run with that argument. "What time is the delivery coming?"

"Nine." I turn to pour the steaming water into my cup. I'm really looking forward to decorating this place with her. Part of that is because *she's* so excited about it. The other part is because . . . well, so far, I've enjoyed everything I've done with her.

"Perfect," she says, slicing the cheese like a pro. "That'll leave plenty of time before I have to go." She picks up the uncut baguette and prepares to spread the cheese on top.

I set down my cup and rush over, taking her by the wrist.

She looks up at me, totally and completely guilty. "I hoped you wouldn't notice."

I take the cheese knife from her. "We've talked about this."

Her brows rise. "Oooh, the teacher voice comes out."

"It's serious business."

"But, Rémy, my arms have been raised and formed in the country of pre-sliced bread. Not all of us have baguette biceps."

I pause, frowning slightly. "Baguette biceps . . . does that mean my biceps are strong from cutting baguettes or that my biceps *look* like baguettes? Because that second option is very different from the first."

The way she looks at me says *you know exactly what I meant.*

I'm torn between the desire to laugh at her ridiculousness and feeling like a million bucks because Madi has noticed my biceps. That's got to mean something, right? RIGHT?

I set down the knife on her plate, keeping my eye on her as I go grab the bread knife from the kitchen. "If you don't want to cut it, you can at least tear a piece off with your hands. It's a bit barbaric, yes, but definitely less than what you were about to do." I set to cutting the baguette, and no, I'm not flexing. That's just how my arms naturally look . . . .

She sighs as I hand her a piece. "Here I was, hoping to change your perception of Americans, but all I'm doing is making you think we're a bunch of incompetent fools."

I glance at her as I cut another piece. "You know I don't *really* think that, right? I'm just teasing you about being American. It's like *le Classique*—good old-fashioned rivalry."

She's not looking convinced. "What's *le Classique*?"

"It's the Paris and Marseille football rivalry."

"You mean soccer?" The way Madi cocks a brow makes her look very Hermione Granger. She might as well say *levi-OH-sa.*

"Football."

I hold her gaze until she breaks eye contact and looks down at her slice of baguette. "Well, if it's anything like sports rivalries in the U.S., it's *not* just good old-fashioned fun. People go crazy for their teams where I'm from. Some guys at my school actually beat up a person from our rival school so badly he went to the emergency room."

The rivalry between Paris Saint Germain and Olympique de Marseille gets every bit as insane as that and more. I grab my tea and take a seat, wondering if I've really given her the impression that I look down on Americans. On her. "Okay, yes. Not the best example I could have chosen, maybe. There are always the people who get caught up and do crazy stuff. And yes, there are French people who really are prejudiced against Americans." I neglect mentioning that my mom happens to be one of those people. "But I'm not. I promise. If anything, I have an unhealthy fascination with all things American." I suppress the desire to shift, realizing that my words could be interpreted more than one way, and that I *am* fascinated in an unhealthy way with Madi.

She's staring at me, her expression super serious for a conversation that started with her poking fun at her pre-sliced bread physique. Suddenly, her mouth draws up into a smile. "Gotcha. I knew it—you love us. You love us *SO MUCH*. Of course you do. You're one of us!"

I scoff and sit back in my chair, stirring my tea. I stepped right into her trap. "You don't play fair, Allred."

She puts up her arms in a bring-it-on gesture. "What are you gonna do about it, Scott?"

The image of tackling her onto the couch presents itself to me. But I'm not about to say that. "Watch your back. That's all." This whole conversation distracted me from something else, though. "You said you're leaving later. What are you up to?" That's casual, right? It doesn't sound like I've been waiting for the weekend, hoping I'd get to spend even more time than usual with her now that I'm done with work for the break.

She chews her bread and cheese before responding. "Josh is taking us someplace for lunch. I'm hoping to get a job doing photography for his company, so he's set up a meeting for all of us." She takes in a breath. "It's a big deal, and I'm really hoping to make a good impression because this could be huge for my career—it's kind of my last shot with photography. Trying to make it in the field has not gone as well as I had hoped." She cuts another piece of cheese, more out of distraction than anything since she still has a couple slices she hasn't eaten yet. "Anyway, after that, we'll be going to the Eiffel Tower, then on a river cruise."

She's got this jittery excitement as she says the last part. I can't believe she's been in Paris this long without seeing the Eiffel Tower. It's actually really hard to go around the city *without* seeing it. In fact, if we had just moved a little farther west in the Louvre plaza last night, she would have seen it sticking up in the distance. I specifically made sure we didn't do that, though, since I know she wants to see it with Josh.

At least he's stepping up his game today. I wish I could be there the moment Madi sees the tower start to sparkle. I doubt Josh will even appreciate it.

"That sounds amazing," I say.

"It does, doesn't it?" She says it in a weird tone. I don't know what it means, though. She takes in another deep breath, then blurts, "I think Josh might propose."

My brows shoot up as quickly as my stomach plummets. "Oh?" It's all I can get out. I'm the worst.

"Maybe I'm wrong," she says, and the words tumble out like she's too excited and nervous to keep them in, "but Josh told me he meant to propose while we were here—well, not in so many words—but then he hinted at it even more strongly last night. He knows I've been dying to see the Eiffel Tower, so it makes sense."

"Wow," I say. "That's . . . that's great, Madi. I hope to hear all about it later." And then I will gouge my ears out.

"For sure," she says, her finger tapping a hundred miles a minute on the table. "What about you? What plans do you have?"

Zero. None. I've got nothing. But I'll come up with some immediately because otherwise I'm going to be wondering all day whether Madi has a fiancé now instead of just a boyfriend. I'm not exactly sure why that distinction matters so much to me. But it does. "Just going out with some friends later on, assuming I get everything done here first." I really should be working on preparing what I'm going to say to Monsieur Garnier about the position at his school.

She smiles as she looks around at the room. "This place is going to look like it just got done by Chip and Joanna Gaines." She looks at me. "Do you know who they are?"

"*Fixer Upper*?"

Her expression is incredulous. "How can you possibly know so much American pop culture?"

"I try to keep up on things to keep my English current. Can't call myself a fluent English speaker if I don't know what *demo day* is, can I?"

She shakes her head, looking at me with the sort of admiration that makes me want to kidnap her so Josh can't make her into his fiancé.

"You speak two languages more fluently than I speak one," she says.

I can't pretend it doesn't feel amazing to hear her acknowledge all the work I've put into my English. My dad may never realize it, but at least someone does.

IT'S 11:30, and the IKEA delivery is still not here. Madi took a shower a little while ago, asking me to congratulate her when she emerged after less than ten minutes. Eight minutes and forty-eight seconds, to be exact. Apparently, she timed it. She kills me.

I hop in the shower when she's done. When I step out in my towel a few minutes later, she's standing there, hair still wet, hand on her hip, phone stopwatch in her other hand.

Her head comes up, and her gaze locks on me. It flicks down to my body, then right back up.

Shoot. I didn't come out of the bathroom in just a towel on purpose. I figured she'd be up in her room getting ready while I took the few steps to my room. But she's a competitive one, turns out.

"You gonna press stop?" I ask.

She blinks and taps her finger on the stop button. "Four minutes and thirty-one seconds," she says without looking back up at me.

Probably more like four minutes and twenty seconds given how long she was looking at me before pressing the button. But I'll let it pass because I'm magnanimous like that. "Almost half your time," I say. "Sorry, Stars and Stripes." I'm hoping a bit of teasing will diffuse the awkwardness my half-naked state has introduced here.

It works.

She presses her phone so that the screen turns off and looks up at me, eyes never veering from mine. "Well, considering you have way less than half the hair I have, I still consider it a win for me."

I chuckle. "You complain about French hygiene and then force me to neglect it if I want to win this competition?"

She wrinkles her nose. "Touché." She glances at her phone again. "Ah! I should be getting ready."

About thirty minutes later, I hear Madi coming down the stairs. I open the curtains on the living room windows that look down on the street one more time, hoping to see the IKEA delivery truck there, but no such luck.

"Okay, be completely honest. How do I look?"

Hand still on the curtains, I turn to look at her and freeze. Madi's got her hands out to showcase her outfit. She's wearing a short-sleeved, knee-length black dress that really rides the line between conservative and sexy. Her hair is down, draping over her shoulders and down to her chest in big, loose brown curls. A small strappy purse is slung over her shoulder and resting on her hip. It's a Kate Middleton look, and she pulls it off with just as much class.

"I figure I'll put my hair up after lunch into a quick French twist"—she pulls her hair back with both hands to give a sense for the idea—"because we're in France, of course." She drops the hair,

and I swallow down my feelings. "In the evening, I'll put on this"
—she pulls out a red lipstick and pulls off the cap to show me—
"to glam things up a bit." She looks at me nervously. "What do
you think?"

It takes me a second to talk. "I think," I say slowly, "that Josh
will be lucky if he can manage to think straight enough to get out
a proposal."

Madi's cheeks go a little pink, and she looks away. "Thanks,
Rémy." She slips her lipstick back into the purse and fumbles a bit
with the clasp. "I'm useless. I'm just so nervous." She puts up a
hand, and sure enough, it's shaking.

I walk over and take the purse in hand, working on the clasp.
"It's a big day. It's normal to be nervous." I do the clasp and look
up at her with a smile. I'm just going to be happy for Madi.
Clearly, she's been waiting for this day for a long time. I'm just
hoping Josh knows what he's doing. And what he's got.

She shrugs a shoulder. "No biggie. Just my entire future in the
balance."

Our gazes meet, and I'd kill to know what she's thinking
because I could swear she's not thinking of Josh right now. And as
for me? I'm thinking what her future would look like if I had any
say in the matter. I'm imagining kissing her and turning those
pink lips red without any help from the lipstick she showed me.

Beep!

The doorbell startles us both.

I turn away, feeling jumpy—and guilty for the direction of my
thoughts. "That must be the delivery."

"Oh, good!" she says, her voice a little higher than usual. "I
can still help you for a little while, then. And if you want to wait,
we can do the rest tomorrow—or after I get home tonight."

I walk over to the door with a wry smile on my face. "I don't
think you're going to be thinking about decorating an apartment
tonight."

NINETEEN

MADI

THE VOICE THAT RESPONDS TO RÉMY BELONGS TO A
woman. I was not expecting that. I mean, props to IKEA for
hiring strong women for their deliveries. I don't think we bought
anything *too* heavy, but there was a ton of small stuff in our cart.
And that laundry drying rack is something else, I tell ya. It could
swallow a person whole.

Rémy responds to the woman with even more surprise than I
feel. I stare at him for a second because it's impossible not to feel
mesmerized by the sound of him speaking French, especially given
how he could pass for being born and raised in America most of
the time.

Meanwhile, I can barely remember words in my native
language, and my skill in French is limited to telling people I like a
sport I haven't played since I was seven.

Rémy glances at me, making me wish I knew what in the
world he said to the delivery driver, then presses the button to let
her into the door from the street.

"Did IKEA send Luisa from *Encanto* to deliver our stuff?"
I ask.

Rémy's got his hands on his hips. He's not wearing his work
attire—Saturday, remember? Apparently Weekend Rémy's

outfit of choice is a t-shirt and athletic pants. The t-shirt sleeves stretch slightly around his biceps, and he hasn't shaved yet, drawing my attention to the way his facial hair follows the line of his upper lip and shadows his jaw—as if it needed any contouring. It's for the best that the girls in his classes don't see him like this.

I volunteer as tribute. I've already got a boyfriend, which acts like a shield against his attraction. In theory. Even shields have their bad days, right? Mine is busy powering up to move from girl-with-a-boyfriend status to girl-with-a-fiancé status. It's a thing. I'm banking on that.

"It's not IKEA." He rubs the back of his neck with a hand, his brow furrowed slightly.

"Oh. That girl didn't have a low enough voice to be Luisa anyway. Who was it?" None of my business, but clearly that doesn't weigh with me. Rémy just buzzed a girl into the building, and my curiosity is bursting at the seams.

"It's Élise."

Élise. I thought my own name sounded good when he said it, but Élise has the advantage there. By the way Rémy's acting, I'm getting some major there's-some-history-here vibes.

"She's a . . . friend."

Whoa. Definite history. Most assuredly not just a friend. Why is my stomach feeling so weird?

"She's André's cousin," he adds, like it's sufficient explanation for her showing up unexpectedly—based on his reaction—on a Saturday morning.

"Oh, cool," I say just as there's a knock on the door. That was fast. Apparently Élise is not afraid of the elevator in the building. That, or she just sprinted up a million stairs.

Rémy looks at me for another second like he wants to say something, but instead, he turns and opens the door.

The little mat in the entryway may as well be a red carpet. When Élise takes a step inside, everything moves in slow motion. She's wearing a boatneck Breton striped shirt and high-waisted light jeans around a tiny waist. Her dark brown hair is down in a style I can only describe as careless perfection.

Her gaze settles on me for the briefest of moments, but I might as well be a fixture of the apartment, because it skips right to Rémy. I mean, I can't *really* blame her. He's by far the most interesting and attractive part of this room. Not even our delivery from IKEA will change that.

Her lips pull up into a smile that *some* haters might describe as a little too *come, hither*, but really it's just beautiful. She greets him in French and goes in for a kiss—oh, nope, it's just the cheek kisses.

And suddenly I realize that the way I did them with Rémy was flat-out wrong. They're not actually kisses. It's just a quick pressing of cheeks against each other. No mouth-to-cheek action involved.

I'm the facepalm emoji. I totally kissed Rémy's cheeks when we first met. Classic American overenthusiasm. Stars and stripes flying high.

What happens next is a jumble of quick French that I can't catch a single word of because they're not telling each other their names or discussing where to find the library. Or maybe they are. My French is *that* bad, but French isn't the only language they're speaking . . .

Élise has a hand on Rémy's elbow. They're both smiling. The distance between them is just a fraction closer than is standard. This is a language anyone can understand.

For some reason, I had almost forgotten Rémy was from an entirely different country and culture than me. It hits me now, though. He lives his life in French. Sure, he speaks English with his students at work, but that's a deviation from the normal, an exception to the rule. I'm an even bigger deviation from the normal, and a temporary one. I'll be leaving back to the States with Josh, and Rémy will go on living his life—with his *friend* Élise. I'll become a memory that'll fade like a temporary tattoo.

The thought is strangely depressing to me.

They turn, and Rémy's got his hand out, gesturing to me. "Madi, this is Élise Garnier." He's speaking in English again, but his accent is a little more pronounced than usual—the result of moving between languages quickly, I assume.

Élise meets my eyes, and this time, she's sizing me up. It's hard to tell what she thinks because all her expressions are tempered, muted, classy. She reminds me of an Audrey Hepburn picture. This is a woman who has never snorted in laughter.

"Hello, Madi," she says with a strong French accent that only adds to her charm. She steps toward me, and I realize it's time to kiss cheeks. I make sure *not* to smooch this time, glancing at Rémy while touching my cheek to Élise's like I saw her do.

"It's good to meet you," I say, pulling back and hoping I didn't just break a dozen French culture codes with my greeting. My phone buzzes, and I pull it out.

Josh: I'm here

"That's him. I've gotta go." I look at Rémy. "I'm really sorry I'm not going to be here for the delivery. I'll help you tomorrow if you want to wait. Or even tonight, like I said."

"Don't worry about it," he says. "You have more important things to think about right now."

I twist my mouth to the side. It's true. I've got a business lunch—it sounds so much cooler than it is when I call it that—and a very big night ahead of me. But weirdly, I still care about this IKEA stuff.

"I can help him," Élise says as she steps back beside him. It's a nice offer, so why does it feel like she's sticking a flag in the ground and declaring her territory?

"Oh!" I try to sound totally cool about it, but I can't help but glance at Rémy. All I see when I do that is how good the two of them look next to each other—and how close they are standing. "Yeah, sure. That's really nice of you." It shouldn't bug me to think of her fixing up my servant quarters with the stuff Rémy and I chose for it.

Stop being weird, Madi. This isn't about me. This is about helping Rémy and André, and Élise is André's cousin. It makes perfect sense for her to pitch in.

My phone buzzes again.

Josh: You coming? I'm impatient to see you *wink emoji*

Me: Yep! On my way down.

My heart skips a beat or two. Who's putting the cover on the duvet on my temporary bed should be the last thing on my mind right now. What if Josh really does propose tonight?

I slip my camera bag on, grab my coat, pick up the folder holding the prints from my portfolio, then head out. Once I shut the door behind me, I can't help but shoot a text off to Siena before starting down the stairs.

Madi: I know you're asleep, but I just had to tell you . . .
Madi: Today might be THE DAY.

Typing those words is the weirdest thing ever, and my eyes linger on my ring finger for a second before I slip my phone into my camera bag and head down the stairs.

TWENTY

MADI

JOSH IS WAITING JUST OUTSIDE THE DOOR TO THE street, and he smiles when he catches sight of me. He's a handsome guy, and he looks pretty slick today, with a slim-fit suit, no tie, and his hair combed to the side. He looks the way I'd expect him to look if he meant to do something . . . important.

"Hey, beautiful," he says, pressing a kiss to my lips and pulling me toward him with a hand on my waist.

It's a weird moment, this kiss. I'm just feeling so nervous and jittery that I can't really enjoy it, despite the fact that Josh and I haven't done much in the way of physical affection since getting to Paris.

We make our way to the metro station, holding gloved hands. Josh is checking his phone a lot, so I ask him how work has been going. He can talk about work forever, and I find it oddly calming to my nerves to focus on something other than the big things that might happen today. It seems to calm him, too, since he leaves his phone alone while he recounts all the usual drama from his trainings.

There's a violist in the metro, playing "O, Holy Night" as Josh buys us tickets. I try to keep my cool as we head for the turnstiles.

I can't remember if the tickets have to go in a specific way, so I look at mine, trying to see if there's any indicator arrow. I don't wanna stick it in the machine only for it to pop right back out.

"Come on, babe," Josh says behind me. He turns and smiles apologetically at the girl waiting. "Sorry," he says to her.

He's just being considerate of her, I know—that's a good thing, right?—but it still bothers me as I slip the ticket into the machine and push through the turnstile.

We make our way to the platform and barely slip through the doors of the waiting train. While it moves from station to station, I flip through the portfolio in my camera bag, planning what I'll say to Dan Vincent about each photo. I chose each one carefully, knowing they're what he'll be judging me on—what will decide him on whether to give me the job or not. I've taken so many pictures over the course of my life; it's strange to think my future could be determined by just a few. Not only that, most of these pictures don't even represent my personal favorites from my work. Those would all be candid portraits, where all but two of these are product shots.

Thankfully, the restaurant Josh chose is just a couple minutes' walk from the station we get off at. It's a nice place, which makes me feel more nervous than ever. If I can't get it together, I'm going to leave sweatmarks on my portfolio folder. Can't imagine that's going to score me any points. No one wants a photographer they worry will drop her camera mid-shoot because of sweaty fingers.

I look around the restaurant, for what, I'm not sure. I have no idea what this guy looks like. But there isn't anyone sitting alone, so Dan must not be here yet.

I feel my camera bag vibrate and take out my phone while Josh is trying to communicate with the maître d'. He's speaking English to the man but interspersing it with whatever French words he happens to know, all of which are said with a distinctly American accent. The result is slightly embarrassing and, based on the expression of the maître d', also mildly offensive.

Rémy: *Bonne chance*, Madi.

I smile. For some reason, knowing Rémy thought to text me good luck while he's busy decorating the apartment with Élise makes me feel like a million bucks.

Madi: *Merci, mon ami.* How's the decorating going?

Rémy: Slowly. But it's coming together.

Slowly . . . do I want to know why it's going slowly?

The maître d' leads us to a table, so I put my phone away after noting the time: 12:40. The appointment we had with Dan was for 12:30. Maybe running late is company culture. If so, Josh is nailing it.

He immediately starts looking at the menu.

"Should we wait for Dan?" I ask.

"He'll probably be late, so we can start without him."

He already is late. "Okay."

Josh orders for both of us. I'm pretty easy to please, so it's fine. Plus, I've got bigger things to worry about than choosing between lunch options. And yet, I can't bring myself to talk about those bigger things. Instead, I keep asking Josh about work stuff. Apparently, it's my nervous tick.

It's not distracting Josh as much this time, though. His leg is bouncing up and down as he waits for our salads, and he keeps sliding his phone out of his pocket just enough to turn on the screen, like he's checking the time.

Both of us are on edge, and I'm not sure if for Josh, it's because he doesn't think this lunch is going to go well or because he's nervous about . . . later. Is he hiding an engagement ring somewhere? If so, it's definitely not in a ring box, because there's nowhere he could conceal it in the clothes he's wearing.

Finally, our waiter brings the salad, sliding the small bowls in front of us and leaving without a word.

Josh watches the guy walk off and scoffs a little. "Great customer service."

I stifle a smile, remembering Rémy saying the French aren't known for that.

I glance at the door as it opens and a man walks in. "Is that him?"

Josh follows my gaze, then turns back to me, frowning. "No. He'll come, okay? Let's just enjoy our food."

Geez. He really *is* on edge. Maybe he's nervous about proposing later. Should he be? And should that nervousness make him short with me? Seems a bit off, but what do I know? I've never been proposed to before.

I pierce some lettuce with my fork and take a bite. My nose scrunches a bit as I chew the bitter leaves.

"What is it?" Josh asks, fork hovering above his own salad.

I keep chewing and swallow. "Nothing."

"C'mon, Mads. Is it gross?"

"No. It's just . . . there's not very much dressing on it, but it's fine." If salad dressing is like makeup, I want my lettuce with the full coverage foundation and contouring treatment.

Josh gets distracted looking down at his phone. The length of time he spends looking at it and the way his eyes move tells me he's not just checking the time; he's reading something.

"Josh?"

He looks up at me, but it's like he's not even seeing me.

"Everything okay?"

He blinks. "Let's get you more dressing." He looks around for a waiter.

"No, no," I hurry to say. "It's fine." I would much rather scarf down rabbit food than have a confrontation with a French waiter.

Josh stands up. "If I'm paying for a salad for my girlfriend, I want her to like it." He drops his napkin and goes in search of the restaurant staff. He's all about the customer being right. Somehow, I don't think the waiter will share that opinion.

I shift in my seat, wishing I could just toss the lettuce into the planted pot nearest me and forget I ever ordered it—or that Josh ever did. Maybe I should see this as an endearing way for him to stand up for me, but I just feel uncomfortable. I wish he would have listened to me when I said it was fine.

Needing distraction, I take out my phone and navigate to my email, opening the one sitting at the top of my inbox. It has tickets that take us to the top of the Eiffel Tower. That's right. The ones that require you to get in an elevator that takes you up to 905.93832 feet above the ground. Josh doesn't know I bought them yet.

It was my way of saying, "I'm on board for the ride," but right now, I'm thinking of pleading temporary insanity—or telling Josh it was just a mistake. 905.93832 feet up, people! And yes, every decimal place matters.

My phone vibrates. Wait, nope. Not my phone. Josh's. It must have slipped out of his pocket when he got up because it's sitting on the edge of his seat, about to fall off. I grab it and set it in the middle of the table, feeling particularly protective at the moment of anything in danger of falling to an untimely death. Yeah, it's only a couple of feet, but to an iPhone, it's the equivalent of falling off a two-story building. Or the Eiffel Tower.

Gosh, my brain is morbid right now.

The screen on his phone is lit up from the text.

Dan Vincent: Sorry, man. I thought I could make it work. Next time, just gimme a little more notice, and I'll move around my schedule.

My heart plummets down to the pit of my stomach. 906 feet. I'm rounding up.

Dan Vincent isn't coming. Apparently, Josh didn't give him

enough notice. Is that why Josh has been acting weird? He's been nervous Dan Vincent wouldn't show? How much notice did he *give* him?

I glance up, looking for Josh, but he's still not back.

Still down in the pit of my stomach, my heart is racing, and I swipe to unlock his phone. The conversation with Dan Vincent comes up.

Josh (10:34 p.m. last night): Hey, Dan. My girlfriend is interested in helping out with our marketing photography. Any chance you could meet us for lunch at 12:30 tomorrow? We'll be at Les Deux Canards.

Dan Vincent (11:07 p.m. last night): My day tomorrow is pretty slammed, but I'll try to move things around and make it.
Dan Vincent (12:58 p.m. today): Unfortunately, looks like lunch isn't gonna happen today.

And then, one minute later, the text I already saw.

I swallow, staring and staring.

Last night. Josh gave the guy twelve hours of notice for this lunch meeting—the meeting we've been talking about for weeks. The one that was supposed to be my ticket into the future. Not only that, but he makes it sound like I'm some high schooler hoping to get some experience for my resume rather than an experienced, degree-holding photographer looking for a career.

I tap out of the conversation, hoping if I stop looking at it, it'll stop making me feel like . . . like what? What *is* this feeling?

As I set the phone down, my eyes catch the list of text messaging threads. Right under the texts with Dan is Brianne's name and the last text she sent.

Brianne (11:47 p.m. last night): You've been a great mentor *wink face*

Weirdly, my heart doesn't react. Maybe that's because it can't fall any farther. I don't even know what to do with that text. Especially combined with that emoji. And that time stamp. I think back to last night. I'm almost positive I was asleep at that point. I thought Josh was too.

It just seems late for texts between coworkers.

It's entirely possible I'm reading into it too much. Maybe Brianne is just genuinely thanking him for mentoring her. But I'm tempted to tap on the thread to see whether Josh was texting her before that—while I slept with my head on his shoulder.

I shut my eyes and set the phone down, feeling a bit sick.

I hate this feeling so much. Even more, though, I hate how familiar it has become.

Josh comes up to the table, sighing as he sits down and picks up his phone. "With 4.7 stars, you'd think this place would be able to dress a salad."

I watch to see if he realizes I was using his phone—and if he'll see the new texts from Dan. His jaw tightens, and he grimaces. He turns off his phone and sets it aside, picking up his utensils and looking up at me. His eyes grow more intent as they take in my expression. "Is something wrong?"

I don't even know what to say. Right now, *everything* feels wrong. I'm weirdly numb, though, as I meet his eye. Mostly, I just feel tired and disappointed. I don't think Josh had even texted Dan yet last night when he told me he had a meeting set up for us.

Josh sets down his hands on the table. "You're mad Dan isn't here yet. Look, Mads. I'm really sorry, but he texted me saying he can't make it. He got caught up with work today."

"I know." It's all I can say because right now, life feels surreal. "I saw the texts." I'm also seeing all sorts of moments from the last two years flash across my mind. The subtle shifts that took us from those happy first months to the last year and more where I've been waiting for things at work to die down for Josh so we can get back to normal.

But it finally hits me: *this* is normal. This rollercoaster. And I am not a rollercoaster person. At all.

Josh's eyebrows draw together, and his gaze moves to his phone on the table again. "You read my texts?"

I nod. Usually, when Josh starts to get frustrated like this, I pull back and do damage control, trying to put out the fire like I'm the one who started it.

Not today, though. Today, I'm finally seeing through the smoke.

I take in a full breath, filling my lungs. "Listen, Josh . . ." I bite the inside of my lip. "I hoped we could make this work. I really did." I hold his gaze. "But I don't think we can anymore."

He blinks. "You're breaking up with me because Dan can't make it to lunch? Sheesh, Madi. I didn't realize our relationship was contingent on my getting you a job."

I stare at him for a second, and it's like I'm seeing him for the first time. Josh is a decent guy, but he's got his priorities mixed up. Or maybe it's just that I'm not one of those priorities.

I shake my head. "It's not about the job, Josh."

"Is it about Brianne?"

My brows go up. "Should it be?"

"No," he says decisively. "I can't help that she's into me or that I got assigned to mentor her. It's part of my job, Madi."

I can't even unpack that right now. And I don't think I want to. "It's not about Brianne either. For a long time now, I feel like you've been doing the bare minimum to keep me around, Josh. Like a client you're trying to keep happy enough to stay on board." I shrug. "For some reason, I thought Paris might change that. Maybe because it wasn't always this way."

Josh looks at me, and I can see he's thinking through what I'm saying. "No. It wasn't, was it?" He sighs and shakes his head. "You're right. I haven't been handling things right." He scoots forward on his chair, his eyes imploring. "It can be like it used to be, Mads. It *can*. My trainings end in a few days, and we can see everything together—do whatever you want. I'll turn off my phone." He picks it up and holds the power button until it shuts off.

I try to picture the image he's painting, to imagine our relationship like it was in the beginning, when Josh was actively investing in us.

"And I can take your portfolio to Dan," he says. "Catch him before he flies out."

I shut my eyes. He's doing it again. Trying to fix things by making big promises. But I've believed him one too many times, had my hopes dashed one too many times.

How did I do this for the last two years? I'm exhausted on my own behalf, thinking of all the times I've pasted a smile on and said, "Sure!" in situations like this one. But even more than that, I'm so incredibly disappointed. I'm not sure how much of that disappointment is in Josh and how much is in myself for believing anything would change just because we're in Paris.

The ugly truth of the matter is I'm not a priority for Josh, and I haven't been for a long time. I've spent more of my time in Paris talking to Siena than I have to him, and that's even with a nine-hour time difference.

If our relationship is a plant, Josh sees it as a succulent; he waters it just enough to keep it from dying. But as much as I love succulents, I don't want my relationship to be treated like one.

The other ugly truth is that Josh will keep doing this if I let him. He will drop the ball, and then, when he sees my disappointment, he will get a bigger ball. And then he will drop that ball too.

And I'm just . . . I'm done.

I shake my head slowly. "I'm sorry, Josh. But I can't do this anymore." I look at him one more time, grab my portfolio and camera bag, and I walk out.

TWENTY-ONE

RÉMY

My fingers are itching to take my phone out of my pocket. Instead of bowing to their unrelenting pressure, I refold one of the towels in the bathroom. It looks worse after I get my hands on it because IKEA did the first fold, and evidently, I'm not as good as they are.

Élise comes in, tilting her head to the side as she surveys the bathroom. It looks *so* much better than it did before. Fresh towels, plush bathroom rugs, a new soap dispenser and shower curtain. Once we get some pictures in the gold frames on the wall—Madi's, I hope—it will look amazing.

"What made you decide on black, white, and gold?" Élise is clearly not on board with the choice.

"We just thought it would look good, I guess."

She nods, but I can tell she wants to say more. Before she can, I hand her some stuff to take into my room. This—keeping Élise busy, preferably in another room—has become my way of keeping things at bay. And by *things*, I mean history.

Last time I saw her, we kissed. It was a mistake on my part. For a few years, we traded off liking each other, but we could never seem to get the timing right for both of us to be interested and available at the same time. After *lycée*, she moved away to attend the university in Caen while I stayed in Paris to study and then work.

When she came home briefly over this past summer, we hung out right before she left back to school, and, even though I didn't feel particularly interested in dating her at that point, I was so frustrated with the back and forth that I figured my feelings might return if I just acted like I was already feeling them.

They didn't. And now I've gotten myself into an awkward and delicate situation because, aside from the fact that we're friends, Élise's dad is over the teaching position at Lycée Bellevue. If I mess things up with her, it can cause . . . problems.

So rather than trying to sort out that big mess, I keep the conversation focused on everything but that: André's mom, Élise's studies, the air-speed velocity of an unladen swallow.

Okay, not that last one, but I'm really stretching myself trying to keep control of the conversation, and so far, I've been successful. I can't keep this up forever, but I could use some more time to figure out exactly what to say to her that will be 1) kind 2) true and 3) clear. Being around Madi has clarified a lot of things for me about what I want in a woman. I can't have *her*, but I can hope there's someone else out there exactly like her. Preferably down to the very last detail. Right?

I take another look at the bathroom, wishing she was here to see the progress, then I make my way out, spotting Élise still in my room. She's opening the blinds, and she glances over at me.

"It's so dark in here," she says. "It's not healthy, you know."

I rush in with impressive speed. "You don't have to do that."

She stops, giving me a quizzical look. I can't help a glance behind her to the drying rack, where Madi's bra is dangling. Yeah, I still haven't said anything to her about it. It probably has freezer burn at this point.

Élise is smart, though. She follows the direction of my gaze, stares at the bra for a second, then looks back at me. It's like her eyebrows and mouth are connected because the left side of her mouth lifts at the same time as her left brow. "Rémy," she says in a teasing voice. She starts to open the window, but I put a hand on hers to stop her.

"Just leave it," I say. For some reason, it feels like something bad will happen if that bra gets moved. Apparently, I'm superstitious now. And also creepy?

But not creepy. I've had my blinds shut for the past couple of days like the bra needs privacy or something.

"I didn't know you wore bras," she says with a mischievous smile.

I try to shrug it off, but the fact that I've still got my hand on hers to keep her from opening the window and bringing the bra in probably isn't helping my attempt at nonchalance.

"Does André know you're fraternizing with his guest?"

I take my hand off hers and start rolling the shades back down. "I'm not. It fell there from upstairs."

The way she's looking at me tells me she doesn't believe me. It also tells me that she's covering up some jealousy.

"It must be nice to have an American here to practice your English with," she says, turning away from the window. "And other things . . . ."

"It's not like that," I say, following her out of the room. If she makes André think I'm helping him get a 5-star review by seducing his guest, he's going to be . . . disappointed. And stressed out. I don't particularly want Élise thinking it, either. Or her dad. "I mean, yes, it's nice to have someone to speak English with, but, whatever else you're thinking, that stuff is not happening." Élise has always teased me a bit about my English. She doesn't understand why it's always been so important to me to speak it as well as I can or why I have more English books than French ones in my bookcases at home.

"If that's true, your mom will be relieved." She turns toward me suddenly, forcing me to stop to avoid running into her.

I frown. "What do you mean?"

"She told me about Madi."

I stare at her for a few seconds, my brain working. "Did she send you here?" Élise doesn't usually show up out of nowhere like she did today.

She only smiles. "She knew you had an American here. She said she called last night and the two of you were shopping together." She shrugs, like it's the most natural thing in the world for her to talk with my mom about this stuff. "She wondered if there was something going on between the two of you."

"Well, you can tell my mom"—I say it with a look that tells Élise how I feel about her acting as a spy for my own mother—"not to worry. There's nothing happening."

Élise has this way of looking at you that makes you feel see-through, like she's inspecting all the parts you least want inspected. In that way, she actually kind of reminds me of my mom.

"Just be careful, Rémy. I don't think your mom can handle losing you to an American."

Now I'm getting annoyed. Maybe it's because she's right. My mom's bias against all things American has a lot to do with feeling like her American husband abandoned her for his career and country. Either way, it's not really Élise's place to lecture me on this.

"Like I said before, there's nothing going on between Madi and me. She has a boyfriend. Soon-to-be fiancé. And she's only here for another two weeks."

"Why does it matter how long she's here if she has a soon-to-be fiancé?"

I fumble for a second over my words because she has a point. "It doesn't."

Élise takes another step toward me—a step into the bubble of space that a person only enters for a few distinct reasons.

"Then why have you been keeping me at arm's length while I've been here?"

She's looking up at me right now, her eyes full of an implicit invitation: *let's pick back up where we left off last time.* Honestly, it would make my life easier in a lot of ways if I just listened and did that. It would quiet Élise's and my mom's fears about Madi, and maybe it would help me drown out my growing feelings for Madi too.

But it's the coward's way out, and, in the long run, it only complicates things. What if Élise came to think I was using her to get the position at Bellevue? It's better to be completely upfront.

"Élise," I say, taking a gentle step back, "I want to be honest with you because I care about you. You're my friend, and you have been for a long time."

At that last word, the light in her eyes shifts, becoming less inviting and a bit more guarded. But sometimes you have to be cruel to be kind, and I don't want to lead Élise on.

My voice is soft as the next words come out. "Friends is how I want to keep things between us."

She holds my gaze for a second, then turns around, heading for the coffee table, where I've gathered all the things for Madi's room. "I'll just help you with the last things. I have to leave to go to dinner with friends soon."

I don't believe her. Earlier, she mentioned hanging around for the evening here, and it's not anywhere near dinnertime. But I also don't blame her for making up plans with friends. I did the same thing this morning with Madi.

She picks up the bedspread Madi chose for the *chambre de bonne*, and my heart does a weird, anxious flip. "You don't have to do that, Élise."

She swivels her upper body to look at me, hand still on the duvet cover. She's clearly looking for some explanation—maybe she thinks I just want her to leave.

"I told Madi she could do the decorating in her room."

That left eyebrow lifts just the slightest bit. It's the definition of tiny but mighty.

"The room she's staying in," I correct myself, suppressing the impulse to smack myself in the head.

Élise will be reporting back to my mom on all this, and it's not going to be a glowing report. I'd better call my mom soon and reassure her that her son isn't going to abandon her for the land of hot dogs and Hollywood.

When Élise leaves a few minutes later, I shut the door, head straight for my room, and let myself fall back on the bed. I rub my hands over my face and, surrendering after some seriously impressive self-control, I pull out my phone to check for a text from Madi.

Nothing.

What is wrong with me?

TWENTY-TWO

MADI

LA VILLE DE L'AMOUR.

The city of love. That's what the sign a dozen feet away from me says as I sit on a bench in a plaza I don't know the name of, sipping on a cup of hot chocolate. I have tights on, thank heaven, but I was more focused on presenting the appearance of a woman being proposed to when I chose my outfit than on selecting something appropriate for the weather.

The sign is completely non-threatening, advertising an art exhibit. But right now, it feels like a detail Alanis Morisette forgot to add to her song "Ironic": a sign advertising the City of Love after you've just broken up with your boyfriend.

Okay, so it's not as pithy or rhymy as her lyrics, but I bet she could have worked it in if she had tried.

I look at the dates of the exhibit: November 5th through December 17th. Today is December 17th. Now it's really starting to feel personal. Trust Paris to try to put a dent in my mood. But I refuse to let it. I've spent way too much time letting other people and things make stuff happen in my life. As of now, I'm in charge.

After leaving Josh at the restaurant, I walked around the nearest corner and then just kept going, with no clue where I was heading. This bench is where I ended up, and this is where I've been for the past half hour, people-watching and soaking in the city while I decide where I want to go next. The world is my oyster—or maybe my cookie pizza because I don't do oysters, and the world would be a pretty great place if it was one giant pazookie.

Either way, I've been feeling strangely keyed up since leaving Les Deux Canards. Maybe that's what's keeping the tears at bay. It's gotta be something because I really haven't wanted to cry yet, and that's not normal after ending a two-year relationship.

One of my first thoughts was to go back to the apartment so I could help Rémy finish decorating. But I don't really want to go hang out with him and Élise. Besides, I'm in Paris. I should be seeing Paris. And now I can do it without worrying that I should be saving any special moments for some later date.

Bzzz.

I pull my phone from my pocket, and the texts start rolling in. Guess this means Siena just woke up.

Siena: *GIF of Buddy the Elf jumping up and down*
Siena: My girl bout to be ENGAGED!
Siena: You haven't sent me a picture, so I'm assuming it hasn't happened yet.
Siena: If it has and you've left me hanging, I'm hopping on the next flight to Paris to end you.
Siena: *GIF of Bane from Batman saying *your punishment must be more severe**

I take in a deep breath. This will be interesting. I stick my hand in front of me, snapping a picture of it and sending it to Siena. Her reply is almost instantaneous.

Siena: . . .

Madi: That's all I've got for you

Siena: Whew! I just Googled what time it is there. 3:32 p.m.
Siena: I jumped the gun by texting you. Engagements should always happen after 5.
Siena: Preferably after 7. Anyway, sorry!

Madi: Pretend it's midnight, then, and that I just sent you the same picture.

And now she's calling me.

I answer with a smile in my voice because her impatience is so predictable.

But Siena does not celebrate when I tell her what happened. She's silent for almost ten seconds, which for Siena Sheppard is, well, worrisome.

"I'm so sorry, Mads," she says. "I'm the worst. Ugh. All those texts and GIFs I sent you. I promise I never would have—"

"It's okay," I interrupt. "It's for the best. Really. I'm fine. Better than fine."

There's a pause. "Okay, who are you, and what have you done with my Madi?"

I laugh. "I'm serious, Siena." I pause for a second. "I didn't tell you this, but I almost broke up with Josh a few weeks ago. Or, I guess I tried, but . . . he convinced me to come to Paris instead."

"Whoa." She's surprised. And maybe a little hurt?

"I should have told you. I just . . . I guess I knew deep down that I was being naïve by letting him persuade me that things would be different. And I knew you'd call me out on his crap. And my crap."

"Ugh, why are you friends with me when I'm the worst?"

"You're *not* the worst. You're the best. So best that I knew you'd tell me the truth I didn't want to hear."

We sigh at the exact same time, which makes both of us laugh for a second. But then it's right back to the elephant in the room. On the phone. Whatever.

"So now what?" she asks.

That's the million-dollar question, isn't it? What do I do now? "I don't know. Which is kind of exciting, honestly. I mean, would I be glad for a little financial cushion now that I'm on my own in this city, with no job prospects? Yeah. But who needs money, right?"

"Um . . . yeah! Sure."

I'm grinning. Siena doesn't know what to do with me right now. She's used to being the adventurous one, and I'm throwing her off, which makes me feel even better than I already do, which is pretty great given the circumstances. Siena has to choose between pulling me back down to earth, which is not her thing, and potentially being an accessory to my ruin.

It's the best thing ever. Why haven't I tried this before!?

"Money shmoney," I say.

"Okay, well, let's not get carried away, Mads. I mean, don't get me wrong—I'm loving this enthusiasm. Truly. But I'm also loving the idea of sending you some more money on Venmo so that I don't have to fly out there in a few days and spend Christmas rescuing you from homelessness on the streets of Paris."

"No no no," I hurry to say. "I was exaggerating! I'm not that desperate." I have my credit card, after all. And are you even American without a load of credit card debt to prove it?

"Okay, but promise you'll tell me if you need money?"

"Cross my heart."

Siena breathes a sigh of relief. "Gosh, it's stressful being the responsible one. I'm not cut out for it. Can we trade back?"

"Nope. I'm liking this too much. But you *can* join me in being excited about all the things I can do while I'm here in Paris."

"Oh my gosh, you're really going to stay, aren't you?"

The disbelief in her voice alone decides things for me. I'm surprising everyone today. Myself included. "I don't see why not."

She squeals a little. "Oh, I'm *liking* this new Madi! Are there any limits to this *carpe diem* spirit of yours?"

"Try me if you dare."

"If I dare? All I do is dare! I was made for dares."

"You think I don't know that? You didn't bat an eye when you got dared to belt 'God Save the Queen' at that Fourth of July barbecue sophomore year."

She snorts. "That was a great night. Thank you for proving my point. So"—I can almost see her straightening and getting serious—"there are a few ways to approach this. But most obvious direction to take your *carpe diem*-ing is toward your ridiculously hot host, who's clearly more than willing."

"Wow, you really went for the outer boundaries right away, didn't you? I'm not going to make Rémy a rebound, Siena."

"Rebound is an American concept from an American sport. French men were created for this stuff! This is where they shine—showing women who've been stuck in the drudgery of an unfulfilling relationship how to zest life like a lemon. Didn't you ever see *Eat, Pray, Love?*"

My brow wrinkles. "Didn't that take place in Italy?"

"To-may-to, to-mah-to."

"Do *not* let Rémy hear you say that. Or any French person."

"I'm not saying you have to go crazy, Mads. I'm just saying to have fun. Knowing you, you'll think you owe Josh some sort of official mourning period."

"I don't think that."

"Good."

It's not that I want to lash out at Josh and hurt him by moving on super fast. I've given the relationship enough of my time, though. Letting myself have some fun sounds pretty nice right now. And having that fun with Rémy?

Chills ripple across the skin on my arms.

"You're leaving," Siena says, "and he knows that. Both of you know it. It's a great opportunity to dip your toe back into the world of being single, of having physical contact with other humans of the opposite sex."

My mind immediately goes to the hand-hold in the metro. I still don't know what that meant, or if it meant *anything*, but I do know I was the one to break contact, which makes me second-guess my assumption that Rémy is dating Élise.

A little ding tells me I've got a calendar reminder. I pull my phone away from my ear long enough to see it's for the tickets I bought.

"Ugh," I say to Siena. "First, I've gotta see if I can find some people who can use these Eiffel Tower tickets. They're non-refundable. If I hurry, maybe I can get some money for them." Every dollar counts.

"Madison Louise Allred," Siena says in her most outraged voice. "You will do no such thing. You can*not* go to Paris and not do the Eiffel Tower."

I hadn't really thought about the fact that I could still use my ticket even if Josh and I aren't going together. But now that Siena's mentioned the idea, it feels like exactly what I should be doing—the perfect way to take life by the horns.

I shiver at my own audacity. But I've got to take advantage of this mood while it lasts. "You're right. I'm doing it."

"Atta girl! Send me a picture from the top. Hashtag *accountability*."

"I will." My heart is racing with anxious anticipation. I'm really doing it. "Thanks, Siena. You're the best."

"Love you, Mads. You've got this."

Once we've hung up, I look around me. The plaza is lined on all sides by classic, cream-colored Parisian buildings—Haussmannian, Rémy called them—and the street lamps are wound with Christmas greenery. The beauty of it makes me smile, even amidst all the uncertainty I'm feeling right now. I have no idea where I am, which is a pretty great metaphor for my life at the moment.

My phone vibrates, and I'm preparing myself for a GIF from Siena—King Kong climbing the Eiffel Tower or something—but it's not her, and my heart does a little skitter at the sight of the name.

Rémy: How did it go?

It in this context is clearly referring to the business lunch. Not that it matters. All of it went badly. But Rémy's not asking about the stuff with Josh.

Madi: Remember how I keep telling you Paris hates me?
Madi: The lunch guy never showed up.

Rémy: What?! That's ridiculous.
Rémy: I'm so sorry, Madi. I hope tonight with Josh makes up for it *smiley emoji*

I stare at his text for a minute before responding. I could tell him Josh and I broke up, but for some reason, that thought makes my stomach twist up into a pretzel. I'll just keep things vague and light.

Madi: Josh can't come tonight, but I decided I'm going to do the Eiffel Tower anyway. *nervous emoji* I just need to figure out how to get there now.

I could easily give that job to Google Maps, but I don't. Part of me doesn't want to end this text conversation with Rémy. I'm curious, especially after all Siena said, and that curiosity has me jittery.

Rémy: Where are you? I can tell you how to get there.

I look around.

Madi: By some statue.

Rémy: *laughing emoji* So helpful. What statue is it?

I get up and walk over to it, trying to make sense of the inscription, which is in French. I smile when I recognize a familiar name.

Madi: George Washington *American flag emoji*

Rémy: You're joking, right?

Madi: I never joke about the land of the free and the home of the brave. Do you know where I am just by a statue? I'm very impressed right now.

Rémy: I don't. But only because there are two George Washington statues in Paris.

Madi: Ugh. You guys are so obsessed with us.

I look around for any other evidence to give him. This is much more fun than Google Maps.

Madi: Washington is hanging out with some French guy

Rémy: . . . Le Marquis de Lafayette?

Madi: Maybe . . . *GIF of dramatic nodding head*

Rémy: *GIF of unamused dog and the word *Really?**

Madi: What?

Rémy: You are at *Place des États-Unis*—United States Plaza.

Madi: Oh my gosh. Are you serious?!

I'm grinning like a fool right now. I couldn't have planned this better.

Madi: My internal GPS brought me home.

Rémy: *GIF of a mosquito flying right into a bug zapper*

Madi: *GIF of gleaming stairway to heaven*
Madi: So where do I go for the best view of the tower?

Rémy: My favorite place is Port Debilly. You can easily walk there from where you are—it should only take fifteen minutes or so. Once you get there, take the stairs just southwest of the bridge down to the bank of the river.
Rémy: I recommend getting there at 4:50 for the best views.

Madi: That seems like an oddly specific time, but okay. Thank you!

I hesitate for a second, thinking of inviting him to come with me. But he's with Élise, and if I want to keep the momentum of this mood, being shot down is not the best way forward.

I write out a text telling him to have fun with Élise, only to delete it. It was a lame way of getting him to tell me whether they're still together right now, and whether she's the "friend" he has plans with tonight. What is wrong with me?

Nothing. Nothing is wrong with me. I'm a new woman today. Everything is right with me.

I glance at the time—4:15—then put my phone in my camera bag. Time to conquer Paris.

I'M SITTING on the banks of the Seine, my feet dangling over the cement walkway while I stare and stare and stare at the Eiffel

169

Tower. The sky behind me has turned colors as the sun sets, enveloping the tower, the bridge, the trees across the river, and the boats floating along the water in an orange glow.

What is this place?! I can't even comprehend that I'm actually sitting here right now. Are all the other people around me as paralyzed with wonder as I am?

I look to my side, then behind me. There are a few people looking at the tower from the street above, but for the most part, people are just going on with their lives.

I press the button to light up my phone screen. 4:45. I'm a bit early, not that I understand how five minutes will change this view—maybe the sunset will get even prettier? I've heard people talk about the Eiffel Tower sparkling, so maybe that's what he's talking about. I can't really picture what that will be like—a big hunk of latticed metal sparkling?

My eyes shift to my phone background. It's been the same one forever—Josh and me at the county fair last year. I'm sitting on his lap, kissing his cheek while he grins at the camera.

I open the camera app and frame the Eiffel Tower, the bridge, and the water just right, then bring my thumb to the shutter button just as the tower lights up orange.

Whoa. Chills. No wonder Rémy told me to be here at 4:50. I mean, I wouldn't really call this *sparkling*, but I guess in a metaphorical kind of way, it is. Either way, it's stunning and much more subtle than I had expected. I press the shutter button, then bring up the screen asking whether I want to make it my lock screen and home screen.

I don't even hesitate because hesitation is against the rules today. And just like that, my background is the Eiffel Tower. I stare at it, tilting my head to the side and smiling as I accustom myself to it.

Someone approaches, and I look up.

"Hey, Stars and Stripes," Rémy says.

TWENTY-THREE

RÉMY

"RÉMY!" MADI'S HAIR IS STILL DOWN, HER LIPS untouched by red lipstick. She hurries up to her feet, and her mouth breaks into a huge smile. And then she hugs me.

I'm so caught off guard, I freeze. I came here expecting Madi to be incredibly bummed. She left my apartment hoping for a job and a fiancé; she has neither at this point. I figured that, even if I couldn't give her the night she was hoping for, I could make sure it didn't suck as much as the rest of the day. It felt like a majorly pretentious thought at the time—it's pretty hard to compete with career and marriage and the Eiffel Tower—but her reaction . . .

Just as I'm about to wrap my arms around her—in a very platonic and nonchalant way, of course—she pulls back. "Oh, gosh. Sorry. That time at United States Plaza got me all mixed up. Cheek kisses, right?"

I feel like a man who's just been cheated. And I have no one to blame for it but myself since I'm the one who told Madi French people don't hug. Now I'm getting *les bises*, which is a downgrade of serious proportions.

She puts her hand on my shoulder, then stops, her eyes narrowing. "Which reminds me . . . why did you let me make a fool of myself the first time? I actually kissed your cheeks—with puckered lips, like an idiot."

Not my fault I'm looking at her lips now. *She's* the one who mentioned them.

She's looking at me like I'm in trouble, though, and I can only laugh, because Madi is in a mood. I don't know what it is, but she's full of energy and . . . different. Not just different from what I expected—different from before. And each second, I'm feeling less caught off guard and more curious, more eager to encourage it. Especially if it means she might hug me again.

Wrong of me? Maybe. But if this is how she processes the disappointments of the day, who am I to be the party pooper? I came to keep her mood up, and I plan on doing just that.

I shrug, aware of her hands still on my arms. Impulse tells me to put mine on her waist, but I shake off that one because if I followed all my impulses, I would be in major trouble. Instead, I keep my arms glued to my sides and smile. "You were already dealing with a lot that day. I figured we could discuss specifics later."

"But we *didn't* discuss specifics later."

"Why do you think I'm here?"

She raises a brow. "You came all the way here *right now* to discuss *les bises?* Well, you're too late. I'm already an expert on the cheek bumps now."

I wrinkle my nose. "Cheek bumps? Sounds like another way to say acne. But okay. Let's have it, then."

She accepts the challenge, pressing one cheek against mine, then the other, disappearing along with that perfume she's wearing way too soon. She lets her hand drop from my shoulder and raises her brows at me, as if to say, *So?*

"Not too bad," I say.

"Not too bad?" she repeats, crossing her arms. "It was perfect. So you can't have come for cheek bump lessons."

Think I can convince her to give me American hugging lessons? Too on the nose?

"What brings you here, then?"

Because I will take any excuse to spend time with you, even if it means dropping what I was holding—literally—to run to the metro so I could be here before 5.

It's clear from the way she asks that she thinks I'm just stopping here for a quick hello, though. I almost tell her I was just passing on my way to hang out with friends. But that means I'd have to find something to do for the rest of the night and that I wouldn't get to be with Madi. "I thought maybe you'd want some company." I pause. "Do you?"

She smiles, and my heart is doing a lot of things, one of which is feeling bad for Josh that he doesn't get to see what I'm seeing right now. Who knew I could feel sympathy for the guy? Oh well. His loss.

Madi sits back down like she was when I arrived, scoots over like there isn't a hundred feet of free space on either side of her, then pats the spot next to her. I take a seat, but I hesitate about just where to land, which ends up putting us an awkwardly wide distance apart.

She looks at me, one eyebrow cocked. "What, do I have the plague or something?"

I laugh and scoot closer, maybe overcompensating a bit, which leaves our arms against each other. She doesn't move away, though, so neither do I.

"This place is amazing," she says, looking at the Eiffel Tower.

"I'm glad you like it." And I really am. Though, to be fair, Madi doesn't seem hard to please. She's got an eye for beauty, ready to see it everywhere. Part of me wonders if that's her secret —she's so good at looking for the beautiful that she *becomes* it. "There are always a lot of people up on the street, but not as many come down the steps to this spot."

"Lazy Americans." She winks at me. She's killing me right now with this mood.

Our legs are dangling over the edge, and she starts swinging hers.

"Whoa," I say, putting a hand on her knee. "Careful."

She looks over at me, and I pull my hand away. I'm crossing lines all over the place.

"Don't want you falling in," I say. "I don't know if your enthusiasm for Paris could survive a swim in the Seine."

She laughs and starts swinging her legs again. "And I thought *I* was the one with the irrational fears."

"Trust me. If you read the news stories and saw the types of things that float in this river, you'd have a healthy fear of it too."

Her nose wrinkles. "Ugh. Don't tell me. Ignorance is bliss." She closes her eyes and takes in a breath. "I'm just gonna imagine that the river is home to the healthiest metropolitan coral reef system on the planet."

I laugh, taking the opportunity to look at her. It's getting darker by the minute, but the light from the Eiffel Tower, the street lamps, and the twinkle lights from the river cruise boats in front of us are enough. Once she's engaged, I'll feel worse about admiring Madi, but it would be criminal not to appreciate the beauty of this moment here.

Plus, to be completely honest, I'm losing the will to care much about Josh. My concerns are for Madi. *Someone's* should be, right?

I look down at the dark water and cringe. "Yeah, because nothing says healthy coral reef like murky green water and slimy moss."

Her eyes open, and I pull away halfheartedly to avoid the elbow she tries to jab me with.

"Actually, though, there *have* been a couple times when whales have wandered all the way down the Seine to Paris."

She stares at me with eyes open wide enough that I can see her brown irises and the reflection of the light in them. "So I'm not that far off with the reef system!"

I clench my teeth, and her face falls. "What?"

"It, um . . . didn't go well for the whales. Murky green water and slimy moss, remember?"

Just call me Dream Crusher.

A few more people have joined us on the quay. I look over my shoulder and see even more lined up above us at street level. I check the time on my phone screen, glad that it's almost time for something that *won't* shatter Madi's hopes and dreams. "So are you ready?"

She raises her brows. "Ready for . . . ?"

"It's almost 5 o'clock."

Her brows pull together. "I thought you told me to be here at 4:50."

"That was just to make sure you didn't miss it."

"*It* being . . . ?"

I just smile and wait, while she stares at me like I'm crazy but also pretty interesting. I don't mind.

The time turns from 4:59 to 5:00.

It only takes a second—the collective intake of breath behind us tips Madi off to the fact that something's happening. I don't even look at the Eiffel Tower. I don't need to. I can see it all reflected in Madi's eyes.

Her head turns, her jaw slowly opens, and she goes completely silent, grabbing me by the arm like she needs something to stabilize her. I'm not even sure if she's breathing right now.

This. This is why I came. I would have hated to miss this.

"This is so much better than Edward Cullen," she says in a reverent whisper, her eyes glued to the tower.

I want to give her this moment, but I can't let a comment like that go. "Um . . . what?"

Her eyes finally break away from the tower to look at me. "Please tell me you've seen *Twilight*."

"Nope."

She looks at me like I'm some alien creature. "But you've read the books, at least."

I chuckle.

"Rémy. This is no laughing matter. I thought you were well-versed in American pop culture. Do you know what *Twilight is*?"

"Yeah, of course. But what does it have to do with the Eiffel Tower?"

"I feel like the connection is obvious."

I just look at her.

She sighs. "In the books, you learn that vampire skin sparkles in the sunlight. It sounded okay in theory, but it's a painfully awful moment in the movies—one I'm determined you'll see, by the way. If you know demo day, you should know sparkling vampires. Anyway, when people mentioned the Eiffel Tower sparkling, I worried it might ruin it like sparkling ruined vampires." She turns her head forward, and her voice is full of awe again. "It definitely doesn't."

I look at it too, and I have to admit, it's pretty amazing. "This is my favorite time to see it sparkle." I glance at her. "Twilight."

Her mouth pulls into a huge, appreciative smile, and she looks over at me.

I'm done for. I can't blame Josh for falling in love with Madi if she's ever looked at him like that.

"Wanna come with me to the top?" she asks. "I have an extra ticket."

I raise my brows, hoping that looking surprised is covering the happy dance happening inside me right now. "To the *top* top?"

"Yup."

"I thought you were afraid of heights."

"Not tonight." She tips her head back and puts her arms out, looking up at the sky. "I'm ready to take on *all* the elevators in Paris."

I'm still thrown off by this mood she's in. It's certainly not the way most people would react after losing out on a desired job and having to postpone a proposal.

She sways a bit, and I grab her arms to stabilize her. "Whoa there. There is no elevator out of *that*." The river is a dark abyss with a sprinkling of lights across it.

She drops her arms and looks at me like she's extending me a challenge. "So are you coming?"

I meet her gaze and lean into her so our shoulders press against each other. "I'm coming."

If Josh showed up right now, he'd have to fight me for that ticket.

***

THE EIFFEL TOWER offers a couple different ticket options, and Madi's aren't the ones that have you take elevators all the way to the top. That means we'll have to walk up the 674 stairs to the second level. *Then* we take an elevator up to the top.

I nudge Madi with my elbow as we start our trek. "What happened to five o'clock Madi, ready to take on all the elevators in Paris?"

"Well, *Rémy*," she says, "five o'clock Madi didn't buy these tickets. Midnight Last Night Madi bought these tickets. Plus, my wallet preferred the economical stair/elevator combination."

We try to keep a conversation going, but it's not long before we're both huffing and puffing. I shed my scarf pretty quickly and drape my coat over my arm not long after. It does *not* feel like the middle of December when you're climbing flight after flight of stairs.

We reach another landing, and Madi grabs my arm, hanging on it and pulling me to the side to let people pass us. We've traded off demanding breaks, and each time, one of us comes up with an excuse other than being tired.

Last time I needed a rest, I insisted any trip up the Eiffel Tower wouldn't be complete without a close inspection of the steel frame.

I raise a brow, waiting to hear her reason for this stop, even though I'm not about to complain. My thighs are burning with the fire of a thousand suns.

"They seemed like they were in a hurry," Madi says breathlessly, jabbing a thumb at the people passing us.

I smile at her as they stop right next to us for a breather.

She glances at them like they've let her down, then reluctantly starts making her way to the next stairs.

"Madi, we can stop for a break, you know."

"Onward and upward," she says with effort, raising a tired fist in the air. Like me, she's shed all her outerwear, but we still have at least a few flights of stairs before we reach the second floor, and neither of us has more clothes to—properly—take off. Not that I'm thinking about that.

I'm the one to stop us on the next landing, but this time I get a text notification at the perfect time to justify it.

André: Hey, Rémy. I don't know how to say this except to just . . . say it. I wanted to make sure things are staying professional between you and the Airbnb guest.

I read the text a second time. *Thanks a lot, Élise.*

Rémy: Of course. I mean, I'm being a friend to her, but there's nothing going on. She's about to get engaged.

André: Okay, cool. I just don't want a 2-star review because you're breaking hearts. *wink face emoji*

I almost text Élise to call her out. If she's messaged André about her assumptions, there's a good chance she'll mention it to her dad. Maybe giving him a reason not to hire me wouldn't be so bad after all, though. The position at Bellevue is one I *should* want, and I know it would make my mom happy, but I really like the freedom I have at Lycée Michel Gontier, even if it's not the most elite school in Paris by a long shot.

"672, 673, 674!" Madi says in a huffing attempt at a victorious voice as she sets a foot on the final step. She turns toward me as I join her on the second floor. "We did it!" She puts up a hand for a high five, and I oblige.

After discussing things for a minute, we opt not to walk

around the observation deck so that we can save the views for the very top. We can walk around this deck on the way back down.

We barely miss the next elevator to the top, putting us right at the front of the line and giving us a minute to wait for the next one. It's actually pretty calm up here for being Christmastime in Paris, and we're the only ones in line for a couple of minutes.

When the elevator shows up, a few people start making their way toward us like they mean to join. The Eiffel Tower employee motions for us to step in, and I start to step forward, but Madi's not moving. She's staring at the elevator in a way that tells me she's realizing that *it's time.*

"Madi?" I say gently.

She turns her head to look at me, the quintessential deer in the headlights.

"You sure you wanna do this?"

She blinks. "Yeah, yeah." A nervous smile. "Of course. Sorry, I was spacing out." It takes her a second, but she walks forward and right up to the edge of the elevator. She looks around it like she's a certified elevator inspector who will know just by looking at the state of the buttons whether it's sound.

She takes in a shaky breath and steps inside, and I follow after, watching her carefully for any signs that she needs me to make a last-minute excuse on her behalf. I want her to know we can leave, but if she wants to conquer this fear, I also want to support her in that.

Other people step in behind us, and the employee starts giving us the spiel first in French, then in heavily accented English, sprinkling in a few facts about the Eiffel Tower as we wait for more people to get on. It's been a while since I've done this, and I'm more focused on Madi than on what the guide is actually saying. With each person who steps in, Madi and I are pushed farther into the corner. Is it wrong for me to want ten more people in here just so I have an excuse to be closer to her?

Stop it. Here I am, thinking about stuffing people into this elevator like sardines just so I can rub arms with Madi, while she's looking through the windows next to us and up toward the ceiling for an escape hatch.

"You up for this, Stars and Stripes?"

At my nickname for her, Madi's expression relaxes a bit. "Of course I am." She shrugs like this is something she does all the time—like she's not scared of the raised bed she sleeps in that's five feet off the ground. "I'm totally cool. What's scary about shooting a thousand feet up in a metal box with a bunch of other people?"

I pretend to consider it for a second, then shrug like I can't think of a single thing wrong with it.

The employee's trivia cuts through our exchange. " . . . when it's windy, the top of the Eiffel Tower sways seven centimeters from side to side." I look at Madi, but she's not reacting.

Right. The lady is speaking in French.

Until she's not. She starts the same information but in English this time. "The antenna was placed on the tower in 1957, increasing the height to 1,063 feet. When it's windy—"

"Wait!" I say in French. If she keeps giving these little factoids, Madi may well sprint out of this elevator, and that would be a real shame.

The lady looks at me—as does everyone else. I try for a smile and speak to her in French. "Can you save the trivia for the top? Once the two of us get off?"

TWENTY-FOUR

MADI

RÉMY AND THE ELEVATOR OPERATOR ARE TALKING BACK and forth in French, and I have no idea what's going on. Most of the other people don't either, based on the looks passing between them.

But I don't have to speak French to know that the woman is delivering news to Rémy he doesn't like. She does this little shrug that tells me she really doesn't feel bad about whatever just happened. Did she turn him down for a date? Is she insane?

"As I was saying," the woman continues in accented English, "when it is windy, the top of the Eiffel Tower sways seven centimeters."

My heart stops. I'm currently dead, 674 steps above ground. I look at Rémy, who's staring at the lady with an expression that makes me afraid for her. But not as afraid as I am for myself. Which is weird, because you'd think you couldn't feel fear if you're already dead.

"Seven centimeters," I say, feeling just as breathless as I did when we were coming up all those dang steps. "That's like, nothing, right? What, like, a quarter of an inch?" Why didn't I pay attention when we learned metric conversions in school?

"It's about three inches," says the man next to us.

"Three inches?!" I squeak out. I mean, it sounds like a small amount, but something that sticks up this far from the earth should not move. At all.

"Thanks a lot," Rémy says to the guy, and it's clear that this man is now also on his blacklist.

The guy smiles unironically. "Three inches is nothing. The Burj Khalifa in Dubai sways four to five feet in the wind."

Oddly, this little factoid does not help make me feel better.

Rémy's jaw tightens like he's trying to resist punching the guy in his trivia hole.

"This tower is basically Elastigirl," I say.

The man who so kindly converted centimeters into inches for me leans a little closer. "It's actually made out of puddle iron. Weighs 10,000 tons."

Rémy gives the guy a look, and Factoid McTriviaman shrugs, then gets back to listening to the lady talk.

I look up at Rémy. "If it's going to be tipping and bending all over the place, can it just drop me off at home right now?"

He smiles, and I'm suddenly more concerned about the safety of my heart than of my body. If he keeps this up, maybe I'll be distracted enough not to notice how high we're going—or that we'll be swaying from side to side like a palm tree.

"Madi," he says softly, "we can get off if you want. Right now. I'll tell them I need to go to the bathroom or something." He searches my eyes, and given our proximity, I'm thinking it's a good thing I was never this close to him until now. A girl could disappear in those eyes, and I would *love* to disappear right now.

"I really think you'll love the top," he says as a couple final stragglers get on the elevator, "but if it's too much, just say the word. We can watch some YouTube videos of it at home. No big deal."

It's tempting. How different can experiencing the Eiffel Tower by YouTube be, really? I'd still be with Rémy, I'm sure we'd still be having fun, and I wouldn't be making a complete fool of myself like I am here. If only I'd paid for the other stupid elevator instead of the stairs, the adrenaline from earlier wouldn't have had time to wear out.

My phone buzzes with a text from Siena.

Siena: Don't forget my picture!

Immediately after, I get a notification from Venmo. A hundred bucks with a little note: *Madi's Single-and-Ready-to-Mingle Paris Fun Fund.*

The elevator lady is about to press the button to send us up into the atmosphere, but Rémy asks her to wait.

I gather my courage, remind myself what I'm doing here, and let out a breath. "I wanna go up."

He looks at me for a second, as if he's checking whether I'm sincere.

"Really," I say with a shaky smile.

He returns his own smile, and this terror is already worth it for that. "You won't regret it." He turns back to the lady and nods at her.

And then we're off.

The feeling of the elevator going up does a number on my stomach, and then the guy next to us tells his wife to look up.

Those dumb, dumb words. They're the north pole of a magnet, and my eyes are the south pole. I lift my chin, and my gaze travels up until it finds the windows on the elevator roof.

I shut my eyes immediately and bring my head back down, but it's too late. I saw us barreling upward, and I can't unsee it. The rocket has left the launchpad, though, and there is no getting off at this point. Everywhere I look, there is iron latticework rushing by windows, reminding me that we are headed up to nearly a thousand feet above the ground. *A thousand feet.*

I look down, hoping for a safe place to direct my gaze, but the first thing I see is Rémy's hand. I don't even think twice before grabbing it. I can see him look at me from the corner of my eye, and then I realize how crazy I'm being.

It's still entirely possible that Rémy has a girlfriend—Élise being a serious contender for that position. They could be engaged. Married!

Okay, probably not married, but still. Even if *I* don't have a boyfriend anymore, I can't just go around grabbing people's hands.

I loosen my grip to let go, feeling like an idiot, but Rémy's fingers tighten around mine.

I look over at him, and he meets my gaze, giving me a small but reassuring smile that says *You've got this.*

And for the rest of the ride to the top, I'm not even thinking about how many feet high we are or how many inches to the side we're swaying. All I'm thinking about is that Rémy and I are holding hands again.

Is this what Siena meant by *just have fun*?

My heart settles in at a steady pace of a million beats per minute. Who knew holding hands was a workout? My body is full of that heady, intoxicated feeling that I haven't felt since the early days with Josh.

I need to tamp it down because Rémy is holding my hand to be nice, just like he did in the metro station. He's trying to keep me calm, which is working in some ways but having the opposite effect in other ways.

The elevator jolts a bit as it comes to a stop, and my hand tightens instinctively around his. He returns the pressure and leans into me. "We made it."

I let out a huge breath as people file out of the elevator in front of us. "Easy peasy," I say in a shaky voice, letting go of Rémy's hand reluctantly.

He shakes it out, making a face like I squeezed the life out of it. I give him a little push, and he laughs as we follow the crowd I catch a little glimpse of the windows ahead—and the tiny city lights spread out in front of them.

And then it hits me for real. We are a thousand feet up. What type of iron did the man in the elevator say this thing was made out of? Puddle iron? *Puddle* iron?! What does that even mean? Isn't it an oxymoron?

I want to be brave so badly, to keep that spirit I had earlier today, but all I can picture right now is this entire structure melting into a puddle of iron under my feet.

The crowds in front of us start to disperse, some people going left, some going right, others going up the stairs (more stairs?!). Pretty soon, there will be no heads in front of me to shield me from the view of just how tiny the city is beneath us.

"Rémy?" I say hesitantly.

He looks at me, and it's like he knows immediately what I'm about to ask. He puts out his hand again, and I take it with a guilty face. But he just smiles and jerks his head toward the windows. "Let's go see Paris."

I take in a deep breath and nod. At least if the Eiffel Tower melts into a puddle, Rémy and I will experience it together. We head toward the windows hand in hand, and somewhere between the elevator and those windows, the photographer in me gags and blindfolds the acrophobe.

The nearer we get, the more of Paris spreads out before us, lit up like the Lite Brite toy I used to play with as a kid. Headlights, street lamps, Christmas lights, river boats—they all make the city glimmer and shine in an entrancing grid.

Rémy takes me around by the hand, pointing out the landmarks—the Louvre, the Arc de Triomphe, Sacré Coeur Basilica, the opera house, Notre Dame—and I'm a kid at a candy store. A really tall candy store.

Seeing the city like this, everything within my view at once, is indescribably cool. And holding Rémy's hand has nothing to do with it. I don't think.

"The views are even better from upstairs," he says as we come back to the point we started at. "There are no windows up there." There's a definite invitation in his voice.

"No windows?" I'm imagining a waist-high railing with a thousand-foot drop, and I can feel the acrophobe tugging off the blindfold and pulling down the gag. Should've handcuffed her too. Rookie mistake.

"Don't worry. There are metal bars all over. You couldn't fall no matter how hard you tried. But we don't have to go unless you want to."

"We're going," I say definitively. I haven't even taken out my camera yet because I know I won't be able to get good shots through the windows. But it's been killing me, and I'm determined to finish off strong.

Rémy leads the way, still holding my hand, and I'm suddenly wondering if there's a way I can get my camera out and take the pictures I want with just one hand. Surely, that's a skill I should have been taught in all those photography classes I took.

Spoiler alert: I can't. I'm not a circus animal. Which means I'm going to have to let go of Rémy's hand, and I'm not sure if it's the acrophobe or plain old Madi who's reluctant.

The December wind makes its way down the stairwell as we make our way up, and I shiver a bit as we reach the top, trying not to think about what wind means for the puddle iron.

"Yeah," Rémy says, chafing my upper arm with a hand, "we should probably put our coats back on."

Or you could just keep me warm. "Yeah."

For a second, we stand looking at each other, still holding hands, a lot like we did in the metro. And then we let go and put on our coats. I'm sincerely regretting the knee-length dress and tights right now, though.

Coming upstairs was the right choice. It's cold and windy up here, but it's the difference between looking at the animals in an aquarium through the glass and actually swimming with them—with a latticework of iron bars everywhere to protect you from them, of course. I wouldn't have it any other way.

My fingers are itching for the shutter button, and I pull out my camera, walking right up to the bars and sticking the lens through. I compose my photo so that I get the Louvre, the Seine,

Musée d'Orsay, and Notre Dame in it, then press the shutter. When I pull back, Rémy is looking at me with raised brows.

"Over your fear of heights?"

I smile, walk a few feet to the side and stick my lens through for a different shot. "If there's one thing you need to know about photographers, Rémy, it's that we will do anything to get the shot. I have waded into rivers and climbed trees for the right angle."

A few feet away from us, a middle-aged woman is holding out a phone to take a picture of a middle-aged man. She's shifting her arm around as she tries to find a shot she's happy with. Given that the camera is at hip height pointed upward, not only will the man's body be blocking most of Paris, he will also be shaped like the Eiffel Tower—large on bottom, small on top. My photographer heart can't even stand it.

"Would you like me to take a photo of you together?" I ask.

She glances over at me. "Oh, *would* you? That would be wonderful! It's our 30th anniversary."

I let my camera rest against my hip and take her phone from her. "Thirty years? Congratulations! What a special place to celebrate."

I direct them to move a bit to the side so that one of the thicker bars keeping us all up here in outer space isn't blocking the view. The man wraps his arm around the lady's waist, and she puts her hand on his chest. It's tender.

I take a few different pictures, trying to give them a few options, then hand the phone back.

"Thank you *so* much!" Her gaze shifts between Rémy and me. "Would you two like one?"

I glance at Rémy, but it seems like he's waiting for me to answer. I look at the lady. She's the type to make a comment about us being a cute couple, and I'd rather not make this awkward when it's gone so well so far.

However, I *did* tell Siena I'd get a picture at the top, and I'd rather be in a picture with Rémy than have him take one of me by myself. There's a reason I'm usually behind the camera rather than in front of it.

"Yeah," I finally say, getting out my phone to give to her. "That would be great."

Rémy and I switch places with the man and woman, and I realize that, despite coaching a hundred couples how to pose in pictures over the course of being a photographer, I have no idea at all how to stand with Rémy. How *does* one stand with one's Airbnb host? Does the fact that you were just holding hands with him a few minutes ago change anything?

Just have fun. Siena's words come to mind. I don't need to overcomplicate this. It's normal for friends to be close in pictures. In fact, it would be weird for them *not* to be.

I get up next to Rémy and wrap my arm around him, trying to pretend it's the most natural thing in the world after two years of zero physical touch like this with any guy but Josh. Rémy lays his arm around my shoulders. See? Friends. Fun. Easy. Breezy.

A friend totally pays attention to how solid her guy friend's abs are at the edge of her fingertips and how her shoulder fits like a puzzle piece under his arm.

The way the lady holds the phone—namely, with both hands—tells me not to expect too much from this picture. It reminds me too much of my mom, and she is no tech wiz, believe you me. I set her default web page as Google, and she still types *google.com* into the Google search bar. She and this lady could be friends.

The lady holds the phone as far away from her as humanly possible, only to realize that she's got it in selfie mode. No clue how that happened. It was already on the camera app, facing the right way when I gave it to her.

Her husband gets involved, and all the while, my hand is on Rémy's side, and his arm is around me, keeping me right up against him. We glance at each other as the couple tries to find the button to flip the camera back around, both of us trying to control our smiles. "I should probably help them," I say.

Rémy nods, and I reluctantly leave my cozy place under his arm to show them how to flip the camera around.

"Oh!" the lady says. "I thought that was a recycle button."

"Totally understandable," I say, wondering what exactly she thinks recycling means in the context of a digital camera picture.

When I turn back around, Rémy and I share amused smiles. He puts his arm up, ready for me to take my place again, and my heart goes berserk. Maybe I've lost my ability to be a normal, friendly human, because my heart seems programmed to assume more.

I brace myself for the lady to tell us to scoot closer or say something like, *Come on! Act like you like each other.*

But I did her wrong. She's way too focused on handling the technology she's holding. She presses the shutter button, squeezing the phone with her other hand while she does it like it's a gun and she's bracing for the recoil. And then it's done, and Rémy and I have no reason to stay in our totally platonic pose.

We break away from each other, expressing our gratitude to the couple as the woman hands me my phone. I resist the urge to look at the photo immediately and see whether my suspicions are correct and I'm now the proud owner of a twenty-photo burst of Rémy and me.

The couple thanks us and, just before they turn to leave, the lady shoots Rémy a look. "She's beautiful. Inside and out. A real keeper."

There it is, folks. I guess once you've lived five decades and been married thirty years, you've earned the right to make comments like that. This lady is probably on her way to ask some poor, very unpregnant woman when her baby is due.

"She is, isn't she?" Rémy says. "Happy anniversary."

I wave, glad it's fully dark now so my red cheeks and glassy eyes aren't quite as visible. Does Rémy really think I'm beautiful? Wait. Was he confirming the *beautiful inside and out* part or the *she's a real keeper* part?

Chill. Out. Madison. He was being polite. He couldn't very well say, "Nah, she's average, and I'm sending her home in a couple weeks."

He turns to me. "Well, *she* really liked you."

"Yeah, and all it took was showing her how to recycle a photo."

TWENTY-FIVE

RÉMY

MADI SWIPES TO OPEN HER PHONE, AND I WATCH HER as she navigates to an app. The lady is absolutely right. She *is* beautiful, and she *is* a keeper, and I'm feeling insanely jealous of Josh that he's the one who actually gets to keep her. Where is he, anyway? It's hard for me to believe whatever he had to do (instead of proposing to Madi?) still has him busy.

But Madi doesn't seem to be preoccupied wondering about that. Her hand shoots up to cover her mouth, but I can see from the way her eyes crinkle at the sides that she's smiling underneath.

"What?"

She moves next to me and puts out her phone so I can see the screen. It's the picture the lady took. Madi is cut off at the side, and I'm dead center.

I stop a smile. "Ha! Look who the beautiful keeper is *now*."

Madi looks up at me with an eyebrow cocked. "Don't get too big a head now. Given the quality of her eyesight, I'm not sure how much of a compliment that is."

Her expression is so teasing and—dare I say *flirtatious?*—that I can't help but react by tickling her.

She immediately squeezes her arms to her sides to stop me,

but how am I supposed to stop when her laugh sounds like that? It must continue.

She grabs my coat with her free hand, begging for mercy amidst breathless laughter, and I reluctantly relent because Madi's efforts to get away from me have migrated us across the floor so that we'll be running into people any second. In fact, we've attracted attention, and the lady we nearly ran into is looking at us with anything but amusement on her face.

Yeah, I might have gotten a bit carried away. That's what happens when you have a lot of pent-up attraction. But Madi doesn't seem to mind, even though she notices the look the lady is giving us. She glances at me, clenching her teeth with a look that says, *Yikes*. Then, she takes out her phone and pulls up the picture again.

"She took a burst of photos," she says, "so now I have . . . yep, thirty pictures. With you in the middle of them all. Oh, nope! Look. You've migrated away from the center in some of these last ones."

The final photo is *almost* centered. The way it affects my heart to see Madi and me next to each other is wild. There is officially a digital footprint of us—or thirty footprints, I guess—and I have never liked a footprint more than I do now.

I glance over at her. She's looking at the picture with her head tilted to the side. What is she thinking? There's no way she likes it as much as I do, and it makes me sad to think she'll probably delete twenty-nine of the thirty. "Should we ask someone else to take a picture?"

"Absolutely not." She turns off the phone, leaving all of them intact. "These have so much character. They capture the moment perfectly. What would we even do with a normal photo?"

I laugh. "I just figured that, being a photographer yourself, you'd want a quality photo—one where you're not tilted and falling out of the frame."

She puts the phone back in the pocket of her camera bag. "I'm used to it. It's the irony of being a photographer. You take beau-

HOST FOR THE HOLIDAYS

tiful photos of other people, but all the photos of *you* are blurry, out of focus, and usually covering the exact thing you wanted in the picture—if you even *have* any photos of yourself."

I look at her for a second as she does up one more button on her coat. It seems like a major oversight if the only pictures of Madi in existence are the way she's described.

The lady we almost ran into brushes past us, giving us a look that tells us she hasn't forgotten our offenses.

"Should we head down?" I ask.

Madi goes wide-eyed. "I had forgotten we have to do everything in reverse."

"Good thing you're a pro now."

But the pro and I hold hands in the elevator anyway because even pros need a hand sometimes.

TWENTY-SIX

RÉMY

WE'RE WALKING ALONG THE CHAMPS DE MARS, THE long lawns that stretch 2,500 feet in front of the Eiffel Tower.

"Look any different this time?" I ask, completely enamored of the way Madi's turning around to check the view like she hasn't already done it ten times.

"It really does. A bit of distance can make all the difference."

I side-eye the two feet between us. Don't I know it.

It's dumb. I don't even know what I want with Madi. It's like I told Élise—even if Josh weren't in the equation, Madi and I live on different continents, and she's only here until the New Year. For anyone keeping tally, that's not one but *two* ticking time-bombs on our friendship. But my body and spirit are adrenaline junkies. They couldn't care less about getting blown to bits because they are attracted to her despite all that.

Maybe this is all just the issues with my dad coming out in a weird, twisted way. Madi is an American who seems to appreciate me, who wants to spend time with me, and that's more than I can say for my dad. It's been ten years since he left Paris and moved to Chicago. Since then, our relationship has dwindled to its current state: texts (initiated by me) every once in a while with surface-level responses from him.

When we reach the end of the Champs de Mars, we turn and walk a bit more so that we have a clear view of the tower in front of us.

"Would you mind if we stayed to see it sparkle again?" Madi asks.

It sparkled on our way down the stairs, but that experience was . . . well, different than seeing it from afar. A lot less awe-inspiring.

I thought Madi would be underwhelmed, but she took it in stride. "It's kind of cool seeing it from this perspective. It's good to see what it takes to make the magic a reality. Hundreds of single lights just doing their jobs. Really boring up close, but tie it all together, and it's . . ."

"Better than Edward Cullen?"

She liked that response. And I liked the smile it earned me.

I agree to stay for the next sparkling that starts in fifteen minutes because I'm not a monster—and also because I'm up for delaying the end of my time with Madi as long as possible. I imagine Josh will be coming over later, and that's a reality check I'm keeping on the edges of my consciousness.

Madi sighs as we stare at the tower. "Who'd have thought a hunk of iron could be so pretty?"

"Puddle iron," I say, imitating the voice of the guy from the elevator.

"Right. Puddle iron. That must be the key. If it was any old type of iron, no one would take a second glance." She's got her eyes on the tower like it might disappear any second. It's kind of wild how long she's spent looking at it tonight.

I survey it myself. It's such a fixture of life in Paris, I hardly notice it anymore. It really is unique and impressive, though. I pull out my phone and open the camera app. I never thought I'd be taking pictures of the Eiffel Tower like some fanny-pack-wearing tourist, but here we are.

Madi reaches over and puts a hand on mine, shifting the phone so that the photo is tilted and a third of the tower is out of the frame. "There." She smiles at me like she's the cleverest person in the world, and all I can do is stare down at her.

It makes it really hard to toe the line when Madi's the one instigating. She hasn't been the type to keep me at arm's length, but I could still sense a barrier between us.

Tonight, though, it's different. Every time I've bumped up against a wall, it's not there. That's confusing, exciting, and a bit nerve-wracking since it's only a matter of time before I get too comfortable and run straight into one like a freshly cleaned glass door.

Madi walks away suddenly, heading toward a young couple taking a selfie nearby.

"Want me to take one of the two of you?"

"Yes, *please*," says the girl in a British accent. "That would be brilliant."

I stick my hands in my pockets and watch as Madi chats with them. She's a natural at making conversation with strangers. She gives them a bit of direction on where to stand, joking with them until they look more relaxed. It's fun to watch her like this, in her natural habitat. This couple has no idea how lucky they are to have Madi do this for them, even if it's just a phone picture. They sure as heck won't get a thirty-photo burst with only one and a half of them in the frame.

Madi takes a few variations of shots for them, then hands the phone to the girl and asks if the photos are what she was hoping for.

The girl—Laura—swipes through them and smiles wide. "They're perfect."

Her boyfriend, Luke, nudges her. "I told you we should just ask somebody to take it."

"The results aren't usually this good, love."

"Madi knows what she's doing," I say, stepping forward. "She's a professional photographer."

Laura's brows go up. "Are you really?" Her gaze goes to the bag hanging at Madi's side. "I should have brought my camera after all. We really only came out for this one shot tonight before we go to dinner, but since I've totally given up on getting any decent photos of us on my DSLR—may as well hand a tourist a bomb to dismantle—I left it behind. What do you shoot?"

"Canon," Madi says. "What about you?"

"Canon as well. Only the best, of course. Which body do you have?"

I raise my brows. This conversation just got weird.

But Madi opens the flap of her bag and pulls out her chunky camera. "The 5D Mark IV."

Laura's eyes go wide. "ME TOO. Favorite lens?" She's unabashedly grilling Madi now.

"Oh, tough one." Madi's mouth twists to the side for a second. "Maybe the 85?"

"1.4?"

"*Yes.*" Madi says. "I tried the 1.2, but I like this one better."

"Oh my gosh, I've been dying to try the 1.2. How was it?"

Madi scrunches her nose. "Not as good. And for $1300 more?"

"No thanks," they say in unison.

I look at Luke, who shoots me a look like *Only you get me.* But I'm just intrigued. It's like listening to a foreign language.

"Should we give the two of you some privacy?" Luke teases them.

Laura slips her arm through Madi's. "Yes. We're photography soulmates, and I'm stealing her away from . . ." She looks at me.

"Rémy," I say, but I can't help but steal a nervous glance at Madi. How many times can people assume we're a couple before she vows never to go out in public with me again?

She meets my gaze, seeming less worried about it than I feared. "Rémy is my Airbnb host."

"Oh, wow," Laura says looking at me. "So you're from here?"

I nod.

"I never would have thought that. Your English is amazing. I assumed you were American."

"What a compliment!" Madi is looking at me with pure delight on her face. She turns back to Laura. "Hey, I don't know what time your dinner reservation is, but do you want me to take a picture of you guys on my camera? I can email it to you—the RAW file, even, in case you want to edit it yourself."

Laura doesn't answer. She just takes Madi by the shoulders, looks at her like she's about to cry, then pulls her in for a hug.

Five minutes later, I'm holding Madi's camera bag, and Madi has taken at least thirty pictures. The tower started sparkling in the middle of it, and Madi and Laura just looked at each other for a second, their expressions identical in conveying *This is happening*.

I've just been watching with a little smile on my face as Madi works her magic. And then a thought hits me. I slip her phone from the pocket of the bag strapped across my chest and open the camera app. Trying my best to channel my non-existent inner photographer, I take a couple of shots of Madi as she does her thing with Laura and Luke, the Eiffel Tower sparkling behind.

I look at the result of my efforts. It's hard to take a bad photo of Madi, and right now she's clearly in her element. I slip her phone back into the bag, hoping what I did wasn't weird. It wasn't, right? Shoot. It might have been. But it's too late to try to delete the pictures because Madi is finally finished.

"Sorry," she says. "I've just never had such an amazing combination of subjects and location."

"You're saying sorry for offering us a mini photoshoot in front of the Eiffel Tower?" Laura says incredulously. "You two are up now!" She puts out her hand for Madi's camera.

I wait for Madi to decline—that hard, glass door has to be coming sometime soon—but she doesn't. And when we take our places with the sparkling Eiffel Tower behind us, she settles right into that spot under my arm, just like before, and then she looks up at me with a smile that might actually kill me.

TWENTY-SEVEN

RÉMY

WE FINISH UP JUST AS THE EIFFEL TOWER STOPS sparkling. Madi takes down Laura's email address, and the two of them hug like old friends before we part ways.

Madi sticks her camera back in her bag hanging at my side, then helps me take it off so she can wear it again. "You know, if the whole teaching English gig doesn't work out, I'd hire you on as my assistant in a New York minute."

"It seems like you've got things pretty well under control on your own," I say. "Was the business lunch you were supposed to have today for this type of job?" If so, Josh is in the doghouse more than ever. Madi was made for this.

She shakes her head as we start walking away from the Champs de Mars. "It was for product photography for the company."

"Oh." I'm trying to imagine Madi taking pictures of basketball shoes or cakes or something. I'm sure she's good at it, but her charm seems wasted on products. "Do you enjoy that type of photography?"

Her nose scrunches. "I mean, the photos are aesthetically pleasing, which I can't argue with, and little bottles of essential oils don't check their watches when the shoot runs over. They also don't show up late. Unless there are shipping delays."

I chuckle. "But?"

"But . . ." Her mouth twists to the side. "The photos are just really . . . sterile. It's hard to convey emotion with a bottle of tea tree oil."

"Really?" I ask, feigning shock.

"Yes, *Rémy*. It is."

"So conveying emotion is what you enjoy about photography?"

Her brow furrows under the bottom of the beanie she's wearing. "Yeah, I guess so. It's kind of why I started it in the first place."

"What do you mean?" I know. I'm like a curious little kitten right now. Madi is my ball of yarn, and I need to untangle her.

She shrugs a shoulder. "My mom worked a lot growing up, and even when she *was* home, she was stressed out doing the whole single mom thing. She tried really hard not to let us see how difficult things were for her, but both my brother and I knew. Anyway, there was this one night . . . I got out of bed to get a drink, and I saw her looking at this framed photo in the living room by herself. She was smiling at it, and I remember just staring at her from the hallway because it was so rare to see her look like that."

I know what she means about watching her mom work so hard to keep life together. My mom's worked hard for me, too, and I *really* want to make her proud of me. Which is where the Bellevue position comes in. She's so excited about the position, and to get it would feel like a way to show her all her hard work has paid off.

"What was the photo?" I ask.

"One of us all before my dad died. I was just a toddler, and my brother Jack was maybe four. We were at the lake, and we all looked so happy. And just *looking* at it made my mom happy again. Anyway, I decided I wanted to try to capture more of those moments—and make them accessible in the future through photos."

I gently clear away the thickness in my throat. I hadn't realized Madi's dad wasn't around.

She looks over at me with a rueful smile as we wait to cross the street toward the metro. "I know. Silly kid dream."

"It's not silly at all. I grew up for a lot of my life without my dad around, and the motivation to make your mom happy is a powerful one."

"Yeah . . ." she says, her head still turned toward me. Our eyes meet for a second, and it's like that look Luke gave me a few minutes ago. *Only you get me.* Except this time, it's accurate.

"Anyway," she says, "these days, the only people smiling at my photos are rich executives." Her nose wrinkles. "Scratch that. They probably don't even see them. As long as the money is coming in, they couldn't care less, I'm sure. The point is my childhood vision kind of got pushed to the side in the pressure of making a living."

"Can't you make a living doing what you just did? You were amazing, Madi. Really."

Her smile is grateful but rueful. "Thanks. I've tried, though. Believe me. But I just can't seem to get things off the ground the way I need to in order for it to be an actual career. It's hard to really stand out in portrait photography these days because the market is so flooded. So when Josh told me I should get into product photography, I saw it as an opportunity to keep shooting, even if it isn't my passion."

We come to a stop right in front of the metro station, where people are filtering up and down the stairs.

Madi turns to me. "Now that digital marketing is so huge, there's an even bigger need for really good product images. I thought if I could get hired on at an actual company, I would have some stability." Her gaze moves to the people, but her eyes have a hazy look, like she's not really seeing them. "But what really happened is I spent the weeks before coming here renting product photography equipment to build a portfolio for a meeting that never happened."

I really wish I could help Madi right now, that I could give her exactly what she wants. But I'm just her Airbnb host, and I know nothing about photography. "Maybe things will still work out with Josh's company."

Her eyes flit to me. "I don't think so. But it's okay. I promised myself if it didn't work out, I'd accept that photography as a job just isn't meant to be for me. When I get home, I'm gonna look for something else. I can always do photography on the side." She smiles—her way of trying to lighten what I'm sure is killing her inside. "Anyway, shall we descend into the dark abyss?"

I hesitate for a second, and my palms start sweating. In near-freezing weather. I'm a modern medical marvel. "How would you feel about walking home?" I'm basically sprinting at that glass door right now.

She looks at me for a second. "Oh, I dunno." She makes a disappointed expression that's way too dramatic to be believable. "You know how much I love a crowded metro, Rémy."

"Oh," I say, unable to refuse the opportunity she's giving me. "Well, in that case . . ." I start heading for the stairs.

Madi grabs me by the arm. "Wait, no!"

I delay turning to face her while I try to get rid of the smile on my face, but it's like trying to wipe permanent marker from a whiteboard.

She shoots me a look that's trying hard to be annoyed and unamused by my teasing.

"You sure you're up for walking? It's over an hour from here. It would only take twenty minutes on the train." Remind me why I'm trying to convince her to take the metro? Walking was *my* idea.

"I'd rather see more of the city."

And *I'd* rather see more of Madi, so off we go.

Most of the year, it's easy to forget I live in a city people spend thousands of dollars to come see, a place that's been a Mecca of sorts for hundreds of years. But during the holidays, I've gotta admit, Paris is something else. It's called the City of Love, yes, but its real nickname is the City of Lights, and at no time of year are there more bright, glowing bulbs than in December.

We make our way past Les Invalides and the Rodin Museum because I think Madi will enjoy walking along the Seine most. The river reflects all the light like a mirror, making the views all the more impressive.

We get stopped to give directions to a couple of Italian tourists at one point, and I do my best to help them with the little Italian I remember from my high school days. It's not pretty, but after they've thanked me and continued on their way—incidentally the *opposite* direction than the one they had been heading in —Madi's staring at me.

"What?" I ask as we start walking again.

"You speak Italian too?"

"Obviously not very well."

"Rémy, I know the look on people's faces when they don't understand what someone is saying to them. Trust me. I *created* that face. They totally understood you, which means you speak Italian."

I shake my head. "I really don't. I have a very basic grasp of it."

"Like you have a *very basic grasp* of English?"

"No. I wouldn't describe my English abilities like that."

"Good, because I forget 99% of the time that it isn't your native language." She's looking out over the river toward Place de la Concorde. It stands at the bottom of the Champs-Elysées, which is always decked out for the holidays.

Her head turns toward me, a curious look in her eyes. "How do you do it? Most of the time when people speak English to me here, it takes me a second to realize they *are* speaking my language because their accent makes it sound so much like French. But it's like Laura said back there—you sound like an American."

I can't help feeling a little swell of pride to hear her say that. "A *lot* of work. A lot of time. A lot of American TV, books, and movies. It's kind of been an obsession. An unhealthy one, even."

"Oh riiiight," she says, looking up at me with a twinkle in her eye. "Your whole America obsession."

"Not America. English."

She waves a dismissive hand. "Same thing." She winks at me. "So what sparked your obsession with English? Your dad?"

"Yeah. He was a businessman, which meant he was gone a lot. He exclusively spoke English with me, and my pursuit of the language was my attempt to . . . I don't know . . . connect with him, I guess? My mom only spoke French to me *and* to my dad, and it made me so mad at her. I thought if she'd make more of an effort to speak English and if I could speak it perfectly, he'd be home more." I glance at Madi with a wry smile. "Silly kid dream."

"Not silly at all."

"Anyway, when my parents split up and my dad moved back to the States, I just kept trying harder and harder. I don't know what I was thinking—that I could fix things, maybe? Make us a family again by dazzling him with my amazing accent? Either way, I read every English book I could get my hands on—a lot of times with a flashlight at night because my mom wasn't a fan of my infatuation with it. It probably hurt her feelings to see me so into it, but I didn't get that at the time. There was a channel on my neighbor's TV where they had news and a couple of programs in English, so I went over every day to watch, imitating their tones and all that until YouTube came on the scene. My mom had no idea." I grimace. "Like I said, unhealthy."

"Well," Madi says, stopping again to lean on the stone wall that lines the river, "all that work has clearly paid off. Do you still talk with your dad?"

I rest my elbows on the wall and clasp my hands in front of me. Across from us are the Tuileries. The gardens just look like a mass of trees from here, but over their tips, I can see the sliver of light that is the ferris wheel. "Kind of. It's been a while—a couple of months. He's as busy as ever, so I try not to bother him."

"I'm sure that's not how he feels about it."

"Maybe not, but whenever I *do* reach out to him, he's not particularly communicative."

She shrugs. "Maybe there's a reason for that, and maybe it's not the one you think. You could always ask."

I don't respond right away because even though she's right and I've thought of mentioning it to my dad before, I've always been too scared to—scared of the answer. What if he just genuinely doesn't care?

But Madi's doing things that she's been scared of doing. Maybe I can follow her lead.

"Besides"—she starts walking again—"after all the work you've done, you should definitely be dazzling him with your English as much as possible."

"Dazzle him 99% of the time?" I tease.

She lets out an exasperated sound. "Ninety-nine percent is amazing, Rémy. And I probably underestimated. It's more like 99.9% of the time that I forget English isn't your native language."

"But the 0.1% you refer to . . . what is it?"

"You're joking, right?"

I shake my head. "I can't help it. I'm hardwired to want to perfect my English, and I can only do that if I know what I'm doing wrong."

"Yeah, but I said 99.9%! That's the percentage they put on antibacterial hand soap—*kills 99.9% of germs.* We all know that .1% is just to protect the company from lawsuits."

"You Americans and your lawsuits."

"Hey! Easy, mister. Suing is a national pastime in the U.S. That's not the point, though. I would kill to have anyone think my native language was something other than English even 20% of the time. Heck, I'm not even sure I could convince everyone *English* is my native language 99.9% of the time."

"Now you're just being ridiculous. But if you wanted to learn

French, I could help you. I know a bit about teaching and a bit about learning languages." Wow. Real smooth, Rémy. She'll see through the excuse to spend more time with her from a hundred miles. And right now she's only a foot away.

"Really? You'd teach me French?"

I nod, which is my way of trying to seem nonchalant about it. It occurs to me that I might regret my offer once Josh has officially proposed to Madi. But that's a problem for future Rémy. Tonight, my motto is *Pretend life is what you wish it was.* Seems totally wise.

"I think you're overestimating my abilities as a student," she says.

"I think you're *underestimating* mine as a teacher."

She smiles. "Fair enough."

We pass Musée d'Orsay, the Louvre, and the Conciergerie when my stomach starts growling. In my super debonair way, I left the apartment in the middle of preparing myself an early dinner—a partially cut cucumber, undressed arugula leaves in a bowl, and chopped tomato waiting patiently to be added. I'm not even sure I closed the fridge properly.

Like I said, super debonair.

But being with Madi has successfully masked my hunger. Until now.

"Hey," I say, stopping at the intersection, "do you want to grab something to eat?"

"Oh my gosh, yes!" The words come out in a desperate jumble that has me raising a brow. "You're asking because you've been listening to my stomach growl for the past half hour, aren't you?"

"No, but ours must be communicating because mine is growling too. Why didn't you say something before?"

"Siena told me that French women survive on red wine and cigarette smoke, so I guess I was just trying to channel my inner French woman."

"Do you smoke?"

She shakes her head. "I don't drink, either. But I've inhaled enough secondhand smoke since being here, I thought I'd probably be okay."

I chuckle. "You shouldn't believe all the stereotypes you hear about us, and you *definitely* shouldn't try to imitate them." I pause, making a quick decision. "Come on, I know just where to go."

TWENTY-EIGHT

RÉMY

I LEAD US OVER THE BRIDGE AND INTO THE THRIVING area of Les Halles. It's a Saturday night, which means it's full of locals, tourists, street performers, music—the whole bit. Madi follows me with wandering eyes until I come to a stop. It takes her a second to realize that I've stopped because we've reached our destination.

She looks around, her brow furrowed. But there's only one restaurant nearby.

"Finger Lickin' Chicken?" she says incredulously.

I smile.

She elbows me in a way that I, personally, would classify as flirtatious and very not-about-to-be-engaged-to-another-man. But I may be biased.

"After lecturing me about not believing all the stereotypes I hear, you bring me to eat at *Finger Lickin' Chicken*? I'm offended. And not just because it's a stereotype. Because it's a completely *false* stereotype."

"Whereas French women surviving on cigarette smoke and wine is not?"

"You're missing the point again. A lot of French women *do*

drink red wine and smoke cigarettes. Americans do *not* eat at FLC. At least you could have taken me to McDonald's."

I fold my arms across my chest. "You're telling me Americans don't eat FLC?"

"Not under anything but dire circumstances, Rémy. FLC is the food of last-minute family gatherings at public parks and *shoot-everthing's-closed-but-I'm-starving* scenarios. FLC is American, yes, but it's rock bottom American. To be quite honest, I'm surprised that the country best known in the world for its culinary prowess would even authorize its presence here."

"There are a bunch of them in Paris, actually."

She presses her eyes shut and puts her hands to her temples like I'm hurting her brain. "No wonder you have such a low opinion of us."

I keep quiet, enjoying this too much.

"Why are you smiling like that? This is serious."

"I didn't bring you here because you're American, Madi. I brought you because Finger Lickin' Chicken is my favorite restaurant."

She stares at me, blinks once, then stares more. "Wow. Wow wow wow. Your love for us goes so much deeper than I suspected. You're serious right now?"

I nod. "I mean, I'm not particularly proud of it, which is why I've only ever come here alone. If my mom found out I ate here once a week, she might not recover."

Madi's eyes balloon. "Once a week?!"

"I have it at the end of the week as a kind of reward. For what it's worth, I hear it's better here than it is in the U.S."

"Well, that's not saying much, is it, Rémy?"

I shrug and look around. "We can go somewhere else if you'd ra—."

"Absolutely not. We are going to FLC." She starts walking toward the doors. "I will not be the one to discourage your love of America. Good gravy, it's crowded here!"

WHEN WE FINALLY WALK UP TO the apartment an hour later, Madi's got a hand on her stomach. She ate a *lot* of chicken. It gave me way too much satisfaction—and it gave her a sideache. Though, to be fair, that could have also been from all of our laughter.

Whatever willpower I had to resist Madi before, tonight obliterated it. I've learned so much about her today, and it's only grown the pull I feel.

But now we're almost home, and it's starting to set in what kind of an idiot I am to do this to myself. My only consolation is that Madi had a great time, too. And that was what I wanted in the first place, so there's that.

When we get inside, I see the exact moment Madi realizes how many flights of stairs we have to go up. My legs and feet are aching, so I can only assume hers are too. The thought of going up stairs is not a happy one, but I'll do it. She stands in the entry hall, staring at the staircase for about ten seconds. Then she turns around, walks over, and presses the elevator call button.

She looks at me like we're on some action movie about to storm into a room with twenty bad guys and just the two of us to fight them. "Let's do this."

The intensity of her words and the determination on her face is sapped a bit by the time the elevator clambers down to us. When I open the door for her and she sees how small it is inside, there's another moment of hesitation, but she steps in determinedly.

The elevator bounces a bit when she does, and I wait for her to change her mind.

But she just looks mildly annoyed. "More puddle iron?"

"You know, the Burj Khalifa in Dubai—"

She hits me as I step in as gently as I can. When the doors shut, it becomes apparent just how small this elevator is. It's really only a one-person machine, and the camera bag at Madi's hip takes up a serious portion of the limited space, which means we are in very close quarters as we inch our way up.

Every point of contact between us hums—her shoulder and my arm, her hip and the top of my leg. Even the breath from my nose is ruffling the hair on top of her head, so I try to stop breathing.

I consider turning around so that my back is to her, but that feels way weirder, so I focus my eyes on a spot above her head and pretend the mechanical certificate posted there says *She's got a boyfriend. Don't be weird.* I'd say it was just me imagining a tense atmosphere in here, but Madi is completely still, and the way her eyes flit up to me and then immediately away tells me she feels it too. Whatever *it* is.

All I know is we held hands in the other two elevators we went in today, and the fact that we *aren't* holding hands right now feels significant—like the other two times could be classified as a friend supporting another friend in a difficult moment, but now it would be . . . something else. Which makes me want to hold her hand more than ever.

But I'm not entirely lost to any sense of human decency. Again, *she's got a boyfriend. Don't be weird.* I definitely don't want to put Madi in an awkward place.

Finally, we come to a jolting stop, and the door opens painfully slowly. I let out a long, controlled breath as I step out.

"You did it," I say. And I did it too. She conquered a fear of 150-year-old elevators, and I, well . . . what's my accomplishment in this situation? Keeping my hands to myself? Pretty pathetic win.

I unlock the door and let Madi pass through. It's completely dark inside, but when I flip the switch, Madi stops, looking around.

"Oh my gosh," she says, walking in farther and surveying the work Élise and I did earlier. She turns to me. "It looks incredible! And it's going to photograph so well. André isn't even going to recognize the place compared to the old photos.

He'll have more booking requests than he can accept in no time."

I try to keep smiling, even though her words are a reminder of what I've been purposely ignoring: in order for André to get more guests, Madi has to leave.

It's almost 10 (where is Josh?!), and even though I'm tempted to suggest we watch *Twilight* right now and then start our French lessons immediately thereafter, I'm trying to use my brain. More time and more proximity with Madi would be, to use a word I learned last week, gratuitous.

"Well," I say, "I should probably get to bed."

"Yeah, me too." She smiles and meets my gaze. "Thanks for hanging out with me."

"Anytime." By which I mean probably never again because there's no way any man is dumb enough to let me spend that much time with his girlfriend a second time. Not even Josh could be that much of an idiot.

We both stand there for another few seconds, then I smile and turn to walk to my room. I've only taken two steps when Madi says, "Hey."

I stop way too quickly, way too willingly.

"I feel like I need to apologize," she says.

"Apologize?" My heart starts running amok. Madi is going to draw a line right now. This is the glass door moment, and my body is bracing for impact.

"I put you in a tough position back at the Eiffel Tower. By holding your hand in the elevator." She rubs her lips together. "Both times. I don't know what exactly the situation between you and Élise is, and it's none of my business, but . . . well, I shouldn't have made you feel like you had to do that to help me."

I'm speechless. I have no words. Not in English. Not in French. And definitely not in Italian. This doesn't feel like a glass door. In fact, it feels almost like the glass door just slid open a bit. If Madi feels she has to apologize, does that mean her holding my hand *wasn't* just for friendly support?

No.

That's dumb. It's called projecting.

It's entirely possible, in fact, that this is her way of kindly putting me in my place. Maybe she knows it wasn't just friendly on my end, and she doesn't want to be rude by telling me to step off, so she's reminding me of whatever she thinks I owe Élise.

"Madi," I say, rubbing my chin as I try to figure out how to handle this without putting my foot in my mouth or sliding the glass door shut. "There's nothing going on between Élise and me."

Her eyes lock on mine. "Really?"

"Really. You don't need to worry about that at all." I frown. "What made you think that, anyway?"

She shrugs. "She was being a bit . . . possessive of you or something this morning. Or maybe I was just seeing things. But it made sense to me that there might be something between the two of you. I mean, she seems pretty perfect."

The corner of my lip pulls up. "After the three minutes you spent with her?"

My comment elicits a little smile that expands the balloon in my chest because even the fact that Madi was paying attention to this stuff feels significant.

"I mean, yeah. Plus, she seemed kind of into you, so . . ." Her brows pull together. "Why *aren't* you together?"

I chew on my lip for a second. "We liked each other on and off over the years, but the timing never matched up. The point is, you don't need to worry. You didn't do anything wrong."

"Oh."

"Anyway, it should be *me* apologizing."

"Why?"

"I doubt Josh would be too excited about me holding your hand." I'm not even sure what Madi feels about it herself. She tried to take her hand back the first time, and I held it tighter to make sure she knew I was okay with it. Looking back, that was probably not what she was worried about.

"Actually . . ." Madi shifts her weight and looks down, tapping a thumb on her camera bag. "I broke up with Josh today."

For the second time in a matter of minutes, I'm fresh out of words.

Madi was supposed to come home tonight an engaged woman. Instead she's single. And she broke up with *him*. There's so much to unpack in that, so many questions it brings up.

But now is probably not the time. Especially because I'm just sitting like a fool with my mouth open.

"Anyway," she says, tossing it aside like leftovers that've been in the fridge too long, "I just don't want you to feel bad for . . . helping me. You spent your Saturday night with me, and I'm sure you could have been doing a dozen other things—including hanging out with your friends like you had planned."

"About that . . ." I say slowly. "I didn't really have plans with friends. I just felt dumb that I was going to spend my Saturday night grading homework."

"Oh," she says, looking at me like she's not sure what to make of it.

I'm trying to balance all sorts of reactions right now: relief on Madi's behalf, sympathy for what she must be feeling, and, stupidly, hope on my own behalf. Hope for what? She's single, yeah, but she's still just a temporary presence in my life.

"Are you . . . okay?" I ask.

Her brows pull together. "Weirdly, yes."

I nod, trying not to read into that. *Save it for later, Rémy.* "Okay, well, if you need anything—chocolate, a shoulder, more Finger Lickin' Chicken, whatever—you know where to find me."

She smiles. "I may take you up on that chocolate. Might need a few days before I venture to FLC again. But you've already helped by keeping me company and making sure I did the things I wanted to do. So thank you."

"Anytime." And I mean that more than she knows.

There's another little pause as we both look at each other, and

I'm trying really hard not to let everything I've been repressing over the past week play front and center in my mind. Okay, so I haven't been so great at the repressing part, but I've been trying, and that has to count for something.

"Goodnight, Rémy."

"Goodnight, Madi."

And then we go our separate ways.

And my way is to lie down on my bed and stare up at the ceiling, wondering how soon Madi will let me spend another day with her.

TWENTY-NINE

MADI

TODAY WAS *A DAY*. IT FEELS LIKE I LIVED AN ENTIRE week in the space of the last sixteen hours. I should be devastated. I should be tired.

I'm neither. I'm just . . . well, when I go down to brush my teeth and use the bathroom before calling it a night, I'm disappointed when I don't run into Rémy. That's how I am.

And that's weird. No one needs to tell me that. I just spent hours with him, and I just broke up with my boyfriend of two years. Something is seriously wrong with me.

Rémy's door stays closed as I use the bathroom, which is probably for the best. I need to process everything that's happened since I left this morning.

When I get up to my room, I see my phone light up.

Siena: *GIF of Mr. Bean sitting in a field of flowers, looking at his watch*

I chuckle. Patience was never one of Siena's fortes. She has a great memory, though, so there's that.

I glance at the ladder that leads up to my bed and grimace. But hey, after standing a thousand feet above Paris, I can handle five feet above the floor. I'm basically fearless.

I stick my phone up on my bed and climb the ladder like it's nothin'. Photography didn't work out, but maybe I should look into firefighting. I don't love the thought of putting out actual fire, but I could be good at rescuing cats stuck in trees.

I slither into my bed like a snake to keep from hitting my head on the sloped ceiling. And now it's time to throw Siena a bone. I swipe to open my phone and navigate to the photos app.

As a photographer, I spend a lot of my time super-zoomed into photos. I pay attention to all the details to make sure there's nothing to mar the big picture. If you've done a portrait session with me, I know the exact hue of your irises and the diameter of any zit on your face that day. I know if your mouth tilts when you smile and if one eye is slightly bigger than the other—the good, the bad, the ugly. But none of it is actually ugly. I love seeing humans up close like that. We are fascinating and so diverse.

The point is, right now, I'm prickling with curiosity because even though I saw the pictures the lady at the top of the Eiffel Tower took, I couldn't really *see* them because Rémy was watching me. Now I can take my time inspecting every minute detail of them as is my God-given right as a photographer.

I smile as I look at the first photo and the text in the top corner telling me there are twenty-nine others like it. I tilt my head to the side, partially because the photo itself is tilted.

Rémy and I look comfortable together. I never thought of myself as one of those heartless people who immediately moves on from a relationship, but I feel like it should have been less normal for me to take a picture alone with a guy that isn't Josh just hours after breaking up.

I zoom in on Rémy's face. Hot dang, he's attractive. It's not just how he looks, though. Looks only take you so far. It's everything else about Rémy—how thoughtful he's been, how willing he is to literally hold my hand as I push through my fears, how . . .

just how he makes me feel generally. And that smile . . . it does something to his eyes that—

Okay. Enough of that. I can do my pixel-level inspection later. Right now it's time to appease Siena. I start flipping through the photos, trying to find one that I can send to her. I'll be cropping out Rémy. No offense to him, but I don't need Siena jumping through the phone when she sees that I didn't go up alone.

It's harder than I thought it would be, though, finding a picture that I can crop decently and still make it clear that I am, indeed, at the top of the Eiffel Tower. I choose the last one, since it's the straightest and also the one where only my camera bag is cut out of the photo. Then I carefully crop it so that you can clearly see the patterned puddle iron bars beside me, but there's no way of knowing who I'm with.

I send it, then hurry to shoot her a text right after.

Madi: There you go! A thousand feet up and even smiling.

I swear the text has only been sent for ten seconds when I get a response.

It's the same picture I just sent, but it's marked up like a homework assignment. There's a red, lopsided circle around my shoulder where you can see a bit of Rémy's thumb I couldn't quite crop out. On top, again in red, it says *WHAT KIND OF CROP JOB IS THIS?!*

She knows me too well. With a sigh, I send the original, uncropped picture because I know my best friend, and if I try to fight this, I will be up all night, and I will end up sending it to her anyway. She always wins.

And now she's calling me.

As suspected, her level of enthusiasm approaches dangerous levels—dangerous to my hearing, if nothing else. She cuts out a bit because of the spotty service, but she's going on about how Rémy is the best souvenir I could possibly bring home and how the Eiffel Tower is untoppable as a first date.

I bring her back down to earth as best I can, reminding her that it was not a date, Rémy is not a souvenir—and definitely not *my* souvenir—and that she was the one who told me to *just have fun.*

"Yeah, yeah," she says in a high-pitched voice. "This is just me happy you're having fun!"

I pinch my lips together but decline to fight her on it.

"You *are* having fun, aren't you?" she asks.

I pause for a second before responding with a bit of reluctance. "Too much."

"Impossible."

"No, it's not. I just broke up with Josh, Siena. I should be sitting in a pile of disgusting, snotty tissues, blubbering into the phone to you right now. Is something wrong with me? Did a dementor suck out my soul without me knowing?"

"Um *no*, you're a woman who's spent the last two years of her life busting her butt to make a relationship work with a guy who should probably be attending Workaholics Anonymous. You've been starved for fun, Mads, and it's completely normal for you to take advantage of it. Everyone processes things differently."

I sigh. "You're right. I think deep down I've known for a while that it wasn't right with Josh. Last night, when he started talking about all the things he had planned for today"—I ignore Siena's scoff—"I should have been on cloud nine, but I felt . . . nervous, I guess? I assumed it was because it was finally happening after so long, but I don't think that was it."

"See? You have to trust your gut more, Madison. And right now your gut is telling you to keep enjoying your time in the greatest city in the world with the hottest host in the world. And to eat more pastries."

"Is it my gut or you telling me those things?"

"Both. You'll be home before you know it, and I promise—like, cross-my-heart-hope-to-die-stick-a-needle-in-my-eye promise—that you're not going to be wishing you spent more time in Paris covered in snotty tissues, crying over a man who couldn't get it together enough to see what he had. So if you're going to grieve, let the grief come on its own time. Don't try to force it. Especially not in Paris."

"How can you be so crazy and yet so wise?"

"Easy. Those two words mean the same thing. Also, Mads, you know he's going to try to fix things again, right?"

I think for a second before responding. Josh isn't one to give up easily, but I was firm with him yesterday—definitely more than I've ever been.

"Just prepare yourself for it," she says. "Like, actually prepare how you'll respond so that he doesn't suck you back in with smooth promises and apologies." She lets that sink in for a few seconds. "Okay, now to the good stuff! Tell me more about tonight."

When I hang up with Siena, I'm feeling a lot better. She's right. There's no sense in beating myself up over what I am or am not feeling. And I should be taking advantage of this time in Paris. Who knows if I'll ever come again?

Rémy's face stares back at me from my phone screen, and the thought that our friendship will become some blip on the radar of my existence tweaks my heart.

I tap out of the burst photos, feeling the fatigue start to set in. Just before I turn off my screen, a different photo in the app catches my eye. I didn't even notice it before because my eyes were so focused on finding the ones the photo recycling lady took for us.

But there are more recent photos than those—photos I don't remember taking—so I open one of them. It's me with Laura and Luke in front of me. Behind them is the Eiffel Tower, sparkling.

I swipe through three more—one of me with my camera to my eye, one of me looking at the camera screen to check my settings, and a last one with my camera at my side and a laugh on my lips. Laura and Luke are laughing, too.

Rémy must have sneaked these photos while he held my camera bag. And suddenly I'm blinking and swallowing a massive lump in my throat. It's not a huge deal. They're just iPhone photos.

But it *is* a big deal. Rémy must have really been listening when I mentioned not having good photos of myself. Not only that, but he caught me doing what I love—and in the most magical place on earth (sorry, Disney World).

I mean, no, these photos he took aren't going to win an International Photography Award, but they're a heckuva lot better than most of what I have. And it's more than that. They say it's the thought that counts, and guess what? I can't even count high enough to tell you how much the thoughts these pictures represent are worth to me.

I chew my lip for a second, then open the messaging app and choose the conversation thread with Rémy.

Madi: What are you up to tomorrow?

THIRTY

MADI

IT'S STILL DARK OUTSIDE WHEN I PULL OPEN THE theater curtains next to my bed in the morning. My phone is lying beside me, dead. That's what I get for sleeping with it next to me when it only had 3% battery. My legs and I were too tired to descend the ladder again to plug it into the only outlet in the room. Apparently French maids of yore were not in the habit of charging their electronics right next to them.

It took me a while to fall asleep; I couldn't stop thinking of how part of me was hoping Rémy would kiss me last night in the elevator.

I have no idea what time it is. It could be 3 a.m., or it could be 7 a.m., but based on how I feel, I'm thinking it's closer to the latter. I make my way down the ladder, wincing as the muscles in my legs protest, then use my hand as a charger detector since it's too dark to see things clearly.

It takes a minute for my phone to turn on once it's plugged in. 7:09. Not bad, Madi. A text rolls in. It's Siena, but it was sent almost half an hour ago based on the time stamp.

Siena: This is your friendly BFF morning reminder to just. have. fun.

Siena: *Treat yo self GIF*
Siena: Don't be weird. Don't stress.

I'm not sure if she's still awake, but given that it's Saturday night, the possibility is pretty high.

Madi: *GIF of Monica Geller saying "I'm breezy!"**

Siena: Oh dear heavens.
Siena: I was just about to go to sleep, but I'm wide awake now, imagining all the terrible things you must be about to do.

I laugh and head downstairs, wondering if my legs will ever not hurt again. Rémy's door is still closed—he probably likes to sleep in on Sundays like most of civilization. But some of us are feeling a little too antsy—I mean breezy—about the day ahead to sleep more. Rémy and I are planning to spend it together.

Not like *that*. This is for the city guide. Strictly business. But also fun.

Fun business. But no funny business.

I go to the kitchen and start making breakfast, grabbing as many slices of bread as my hand can grasp from the pre-sliced bread I bought my first night here. Not because I'm making enough French toast for Rémy, because that might be weird. It's just because I'm so breezy I can't be bothered to count the eight slices. And I'm hungry.

I've only managed to make two slices—the stove is tiny, and so is the pan—when Rémy's door opens. He's got on black sweats and a shirt that's still mussed, like his hair, from sleep. It's a very good look on him. So good that I start to smell the toast burning.

I hurry and flip it over. It's probably salvageable with enough syrup. Maybe.

"Did I wake you up with my clattering in here?" I ask.

He runs a hand through his hair as he shakes his head. "I was summoned by the smell." He comes up next to me and looks in the pan.

"It's an American classic," I say, glancing up at him to see what he thinks.

"An American classic called *French* toast."

"Ugh. Is there anything you don't know about American culture? Also, for the record, Americans just call things French when they want to make them more appealing to people—French fries, French toast, French dressing, French kissi—" I stop. A breezy stop. Not a weird one.

Okay, so it's really weird. Would have been much less weird if I had just said the whole word.

"French kissing?" Rémy supplies. "We're flattered by the thought that something labeled French is instantly more appealing to you. But French toast really *is* French. We call it *pain perdu*."

My brows draw together as I slip the piece that's done cooking onto the plate with the other two slices. "Lost bread?" I've been practicing my French on DuoLingo for a few minutes every day, and I've been surprised how much is coming back to me. *I've wronged you, Madame Wilson. You did real good.*

Rémy nods and picks up the package of sliced bread, turning it in his hand to inspect it and gently squishing it. He looks at me with a smile. "'Lost' because we make it from old, stale bread."

"Very environmentally conscious of you. But not feasible for me, since I would never even *consider* letting bread go uneaten long enough to go stale. But now that I know that French toast really *is* French, this breakfast is even better. It's France meets America. It's basically you."

Rémy reluctantly concedes during breakfast that the American version of *pain perdu* is a force to be reckoned with.

"Admit it," I say. "You have an American palette. Finger Lickin' Chicken, American French toast . . ."

"I thought you said no self-respecting American would eat FLC."

I stab another piece of toast to put on my plate. "I guess that just means you're part of the dregs of American society."

"Based on how much chicken we ate *together* last night, I'm confident that I'm in good company. Speaking of which, leave some room in your stomach. We'll be eating quite a bit today."

Rémy and I agreed while texting last night that he would decide on today's itinerary, and I feel like a kid who's been promised Disneyland. I'm not sure how much of it is the prospect of seeing more of Paris and how much has to do with the time with Rémy. The combination of those two things is something else.

We spend the morning finishing up the decorating process, most of which needs to happen in my room. It's a small space, which makes for a lot of bumping and touching and apologetic glances that end in smiles that make my breath hitch. We switch out the duvet cover and pillowcase, hang new curtains on the window, and change out the old, red velvet curtains for the black and white ones we chose.

I don't remember the last time I did something so satisfying. Once everything is in place and the bed has a couple throw pillows, the room actually looks *cute*. Better even than I had imagined it would.

"What do you think?" Rémy asks as we survey the tiny room, shoulder-to-shoulder. "Did we manage to make it *aesthetically pleasing*?"

"Heck yes, we did. Tourists will eat this up. André should absolutely put *maid's quarters* in the room description. If we can find some lurid history associated with the families who lived here, that would be the cherry on top."

Rémy chuckles. "I'll see what I can dig up."

⟋

RÉMY and I go our separate ways, taking turns in the shower and bathroom. I have no idea where he's taking us, which is very abnormal; I'm a planner. In the beginning, Josh planned our dates, and they were pretty amazing. But over time, things shifted, and I learned that, if I wanted to do anything more exciting than Netflix-and-chilling together, it was up to me to make it happen. Suffice it to say, it's been a while since I faced a whole day ahead where I have no idea what I'll be eating or seeing.

As I'm pulling my hair half-up, my phone buzzes.

Josh: Hey, Madi. Can we talk today? I'm free anytime, and I'm happy to meet you anywhere.

Wow. Siena's prediction ability is uncanny.

I take in a deep breath and finish fixing my hair, reminding myself I don't owe Josh anything. I'm already busy today. All day. And I'm looking forward to it way too much to change my plans for him. I've already decided what I want with us—or *don't* want —so there's no point anyway.

Madi: I don't think that's necessary. I just need space, Josh. I hope you can understand that.

Josh: Yeah, of course.

I let out a breath. It feels good to set a boundary like that.

I come down from my room with my camera bag over my shoulder just as Rémy emerges from his room.

"Nice timing," he says.

It's fine, Madi. He's just a normal human boy. There's no need to ogle him. It's harder than it sounds. He's wearing a double-breasted shawl-neck sweater that hugs his shoulders and chest. Who knew I could be jealous of clothing?

By now, I've realized that Rémy looks magazine-worthy no matter what he wears or how his hair is styled. But since I'm being super breezy, I will take a Doctor Seuss vow not to admire him right now. Or ever.

I would not, could not in a sweater.
I will not, shall not in cold weather.

I've been running under the assumption that we'll be walking or maybe taking the metro wherever we're going, but once we're out of the building, Rémy leads us to a set of bike racks.

He watches me as I look them over. "Don't worry. Just follow me, and I promise to keep you safe. Ring the bell if you want me to stop, whether it's for a site you want to see or because you don't feel comfortable on the bike."

I take in a deep breath and nod, my chest buzzing with excitement and nerves. But Rémy's given me every reason to trust him, so I'm going to do just that. Plus, yesterday was a great lesson in how much there is to gain living life right up against those fears of mine.

It's warm enough today that there's no ice on the ground and sunny enough to heat my back as we cruise through the chill December air. At first, I'm a bundle of nerves, but once it becomes clear that the cars are aware of us and that Rémy is going at a leisurely pace, I begin to relax more and more. We follow the main road until we take a left behind the Hôtel de Ville and a right once we pass it.

And then, it's bliss. There's a trail along the Seine, which means we don't have to worry about cars at all. All I have to do is avoid clipping the pedestrians. Rémy uses his bell liberally, though, alerting them of our approach. My mouth is stretched in a huge smile, and it's only partially voluntary, since the air rushing into my face has dried my teeth so that my lips refuse to close over them. I embrace it, knowing my cheeks will likely be as sore tomorrow as my thighs are today.

Rémy takes us past the Obelisk and up the Champs-Elysées, both of which are decked out for the holidays. We saw the line of bright red and white lights from the Eiffel Tower last night. In the light of day, it's almost as spectacular. We take a slow pace uphill, distracting ourselves from the complaints of our thighs with the shop windows, full of lavish Christmas displays.

We drop off our bikes on one of the streets that intersects with the Champs-Elysées, leaving a quarter of a mile of the street to do on foot. At the top stands the massive Arc de Triomphe in all its glory.

"What do you say?" Rémy asks as we lock the bikes up alongside the two dozen others. "Are you ready for a snack?"

"Psht. Am I ready?" I say dismissively. "Americans *invented* snacking."

"Like you invented French toast?"

"Like *we* invented, Rémy. You're American too, and you *will* acknowledge that if it's the last thing I do. But to answer your question, yes. I'm absolutely ready for a snack."

He leads us to Ladurée, a pastry shop straight out of my dreams. The windows are full of Christmas wreaths made of macarons and Christmas trees made of other decadent pastries. The overhang welcoming us inside is minty green and gold, its ornate design promising something impressive inside.

It does not overpromise. Checkered tile floors, elaborate gold and green trim lining every wall and ceiling, and a black display case with gold-leafed carvings.

As we wait in line, my eyes scan the rows of pastries. All I can think is what time they open and close and whether I can afford to eat here for every meal of every day until I leave.

When it's our turn to order, I'm relieved to discover that Rémy is taking charge, because I wouldn't have the first idea how to choose amongst all of this. Based on what the lady starts gathering up, he's ordered a variety of macarons. As I watch the woman carefully take one out with white and red swirls and a chocolatey (I hope) center, I'm salivating like I didn't eat a super-sized breakfast of French toast just a couple of hours ago.

The box holding the macarons is so pretty it feels like a crime to open it. But given that I know what's inside, I embrace a life of crime.

Rémy and I sit down on a bench outside, and he opens the box, pointing to each macaron one by one. "Peppermint chocolate, raspberry ginger, pistachio, blackcurrant violet, orange blossom, and caramel."

I take a bite of the orange blossom macaron, then offer Rémy the rest, and we continue that routine. The whole situation is a pretty great approximation of heaven—soft, chewy macaron in my mouth, an (attractive) friend at my side, the nip of Christmas air counteracted by the mild warmth of the sun on my face, and the prettiest city in the world in every direction.

I look at the sign in one of the windows of Ladurée and read it aloud in halting French. "*Les meilleurs macarons de Paris.*"

Rémy looks over at me. "You have a good accent."

"And you're a terrible liar," I quip. "Is that true, though? Best macarons in Paris?"

"The gospel truth," Rémy says. "According to Ladurée, at least. Pierre Hermé is another place that makes the same claim."

"Hmm," I say as he closes the empty box. "Sounds like we better verify for ourselves."

"I agree." The way he smiles at me makes me feel very unbreezy. In fact, I might be having a hot flash.

The next stop is the Arc de Triomphe, where Rémy insists we go to the top. I'm such a certified Parisian elevator pro now and my quads are burning so badly that I'm almost wishing there was one here, no matter how old and rickety. But the views from the top make me forget the panting, the dizziness from the spiral staircase, and the pain in my legs.

Watching the crazy traffic surrounding the arch, seeing the streets fan out in every possible direction, admiring the view down the Champs Elysées and the one of the Eiffel Tower—I will never forget it. Partially because I have my camera.

After spiraling back down the stairs, we head on foot for the opulent opera house and more macarons from Pierre Hermé. Those macarons are a completely different experience—creative flavor combinations I never would have thought to pair, like milk chocolate passion fruit—and Rémy and I agree that both stores deserve to tout themselves as having the best macarons in Paris.

After that, we're off to Galeries Lafayette, a shopping center where I stand with my jaw gaping open and my head tilted back for a full hundred and seventeen seconds. Rémy timed it. And filmed some of it.

The Christmas tree in the middle of the shopping center stands almost seventy feet high and is covered from top to bottom in lights and glittering ornaments bigger than my head. Even without the tree, though, the shopping center is a feast for the eyes. With it, I'm speechless.

So I pull out my camera. Because, when words don't suffice, I just have to hope that maybe my camera can capture some of it.

I take a couple shots and fiddle with the dials, trying to decide what will work best for the ambient lighting.

"What are you doing?" Rémy asks, watching my hands with curiosity.

"Adjusting my settings."

"What does that one do?" He points to the dial I just tweaked.

"It's called aperture. It changes how much light I let into the camera and how large the focus plane is."

His brow furrows. For once, it's me speaking another language.

Rémy loves foreign languages, though, and for the next ten minutes, he asks me question after question about how my camera works. As I explain, I stop and look at him now and again because there's no way I'm not boring him or talking over his head. Josh never really cared to learn the mechanics involved in my job.

But Rémy's genuinely interested—not just to know how it works but to actually try it himself. And that fills me up in a completely new way.

THIRTY-ONE

RÉMY

I'M DEFINITELY NO PHOTOGRAPHY PRO, BUT BY THE time we leave Galeries Lafayette, I know enough to fumble my way around the camera settings—with a little help from Madi.

Listening to her explain everything is fascinating. Aperture, ISO, shutter speed, sensor size . . . she knows so much—and that's dumbing it down for me to understand. It really is half-art, half-science, what she does. Composing the photo is all about lines and angles and perspective, adjusting the settings requires a knowledge of how all the different light elements interact and affect one another, and understanding how to work with the available light itself . . . well, that's a whole new world I hadn't really stopped to consider until today.

It really is interesting to me, but part of my interest is on Madi's behalf. Twice today, she offered to take photos for tourists. I've seen her take a ton of photos—I've even been in a few myself. She's snapped a few candid shots, always looking guilty after and telling me she prefers to have people in her photos.

I don't mind. If she has some photos of me, maybe she won't forget me when she leaves. It's small consolation, but it's something.

Every hour I spend in Madi's company makes me feel more

keenly how unfair it is that we've met under these circumstances —temporary ones. If she weren't leaving in a couple weeks, if she hadn't just broken off a near-engagement, we'd have enough time for things to settle so that I could date her the way I want to. But we don't.

If I were smart, I'd keep my distance. But I'm a world-class fool, so instead of doing that, I decide to spend every minute of today with her. The sun is starting to set, and already I'm feeling like it's gone by too fast.

My *real* fear is that Josh is going to sneak back into her life. He's been there for two years, and she would hardly be the first woman to get back with her ex-boyfriend. She doesn't seem too sad about the breakup, but people react to the loss of a relationship in different ways. I was kind of like that with my dad. When he left, I didn't let anyone know how much it hurt me.

Which makes me wonder if maybe all this time Madi's spending with me is denial—or a distraction.

Well . . . if she needs distraction, I'll give it to her in spades.

The air is starting to turn cooler as we walk in the direction of the Louvre. All the macarons we've eaten have since worn off, and both of us are feeling peckish. It's great timing for the last stop of the day I've got planned.

We stop for a few minutes at Place de la Concorde, admiring the fountains, the Obelisk, and the large ferris wheel. I lead us through one of the gates that accesses the Tuileries Garden, and even though a lot of the trees are bare, I'm hoping it will mask our destination long enough to make it more of a surprise. I choose one of the smaller paths rather than the wide one that goes straight through the center of the gardens.

"This is beautiful," Madi says, looking around us at the trees lining our path. I love that she thinks this *is* the destination.

If everything weren't so symmetrical, it would almost feel like we were in a forest. The gardens are big enough, too, that there's the illusion of privacy. That thought sends a little pulse through me, and I look at Madi.

236

She's admiring our surroundings, though, not a thought in her head like the ones in mine—how easily accessible her hand would be if I wanted to hold it, which, to be clear, I definitely *do* want; how I could stop those occasional shivers by pulling her close; how the pink on her cheeks complements the pink of her lips so perfectly, I want to kiss them both. And that's only the beginning of it.

She sighs.

"What's that for?"

She shrugs. "I just feel so bad for you, you know?"

I narrow my eyes. "What do you mean?"

"Living here. It must be so rough." She makes a sympathetic grimace as she looks at me.

I smile. "We all have our trials."

"Yeah, I guess so, but yours is pretty bad. I mean"—she stops as the trees open up briefly and gestures to a fountain to our right —"*another* fountain? Really? And surrounded by ancient statues and in the middle of a massive, perfectly symmetrical garden?" She pulls out her camera and takes some shots. "Maybe some people are into that stuff, but"—more shutter clicks. She lowers her camera, and the screen lights up with her last picture—"I just don't see it."

"I'm glad to have someone who understands the struggle." It makes me happy that Madi loves Paris. Partly because I know she associates *me* with Paris.

"You should come visit the U.S. We have fountains too, you know. We call them drinking fountains, and they're spectacular. Truly marvelous."

I bust up laughing. "Sounds like it's worth coming to see."

Madi smiles as she looks up at me. "Oh, absolutely."

Our eyes hold for a minute like both of us are trying to decide how much of this is a joke. And then my gaze goes rogue, dropping down to those pink lips. I force it away, hoping Madi didn't notice, then I turn to my left, motioning with my head for her to follow me.

We walk a bit, then cut a quick right as the trees open up again, revealing our destination: the Christmas market. White gabled shops line both sides of the path, their roofs decorated with garlands, red bows, and lights. "Silver Bells" is playing over loudspeakers as the huge, lit ferris wheel turns high above us and ice skaters glide along the rink.

All Madi's pretending to hate Paris melts before my eyes.

"Rémy," she says slowly, her eyes taking everything in. "You've ruined me. How am I supposed to ever be content with a day in my life after this?"

I don't know. I've been asking myself the same question, honestly, but for different reasons.

We walk the market, eating raclette and crepes, people-watching and talking about life. We ride the merry-go-round and even slip on ice skates for a bit. Madi is frustratingly good, though, which means she never falls into me or needs me to hold her hand as she wobbles around like a newborn deer. But both of us are laughing enough by the time our turn is over that my cheeks ache, so I forgive her skill.

On the walk home, she asks if she can slip into a shop on Rue de Rivoli.

"Do you wanna come in?" she asks.

"What, and risk someone I know seeing me? In a souvenir shop?"

"Riiiight. Your Parisian street cred."

"It's really fragile at the moment. I'll just head into the shop next door and get us some hot cocoa."

Her eyes light up. "Perfect. I'll be quick."

Madi is as good as her word, and she emerges just a few minutes later with a plastic sack partially concealed in her camera bag. I hand her a cup of cocoa, and we make the walk back to the apartment, tired but satisfied after a long, full day. The hot chocolate warms us as the temperature continues to drop.

We toss our empty cups in the bin just outside the building. When we get inside, Madi chooses the elevator over the stairs again. Given how close we were last night, and given how *being* that close affected me, I'm tempted to tell her I'm going to take the stairs. But I'm not gonna leave Madi to go up in the elevator alone. I'm not heartless.

"Who *are* you anymore?" I tease, trying to take my mind off how close I'm going to be to her in a minute. Or three minutes, based on how long it takes the elevator to come down.

"I'm a new woman," Madi says, putting out her arms and doing a little twirl. "But actually, my thighs are just really sore."

"Mine too! I was secretly hoping you'd choose the elevator."

She laughs softly, then her eyes grow more sincere. "Thank you for today. I really needed this."

I nod, unsure whether to focus on her thanks or why she needed it. Is it because she's hurting inside over Josh?

"It's not your job as my host to do the things that you've done for me."

"It's not your job as my guest to do the things *you've* done for *me*."

She shakes her head. "That's nothing. It's been a pleasure for me to help."

"Same here."

She holds my gaze, and I'm simultaneously willing her to take my meaning fully and not to read into it because I have no idea what Madi wants from me. Not a clue. Am I a good but temporary friend she'll forget as quickly as she forgets the address of this apartment? Am I her distraction to drown out the heartache she's hiding? And how much does it matter to me as long as I get to spend more time with her?

The way she's looking at me now tells me there's *something* there. I just wish I knew what it was.

The elevator bell dings, and the doors open.

She waits for me to step in first, which I do, shutting my eyes once I'm inside and taking a breath to ground myself as I feel the subtle bounce of the elevator when she steps in behind me. And even though it would be in the best interest of us both for me to stay facing the back wall of the elevator, it would also be incredibly weird, so I turn back toward her.

Her eyes are on me, curious and almost shy, and the smile that's such a fixture on her face is absent in a way that makes my heart pound. The doors close behind her, cutting us off from everything but each other.

I don't know what Madi's thinking, but I have a history of seeing what I want to see, and since there's quite literally nothing *to* see in this tiny space but her, I sense myself in serious trouble.

"I'm just gonna"—I lean forward to reach for the button that says *four*, anxious to be moving because I don't know how to be this close to Madi without wanting to do things I shouldn't do. But reaching for the button brings me closer than ever, and as I force myself to focus on that faded four and press it firmly, I can see Madi looking up at me from the corner of my eye.

I'm weak—so weak—and I look down at her. I see it there again in her eyes, that something that tells me I'm not the only one feeling something.

The elevator starts its climb upward, which means I have no reason to be this close anymore. But Madi's a magnet, and now that we're this close, I don't know how to pull away from her.

I haven't lost my reason entirely, though—not yet, at least—and I know it's not a good look to trap a girl in a small elevator and push myself onto her, so I shut my eyes, hoping that will break the connection, then I pull back.

A hand on my elbow stops me. My eyes fly open. Madi's looking at me, and before I can decide just what she's thinking, her hand pulls my arm gently toward her.

My stomach shoots into my chest, but there's no room for it there because my heart is knocking from the back of my ribs to the front, over and over and over. I look into her eyes, searching for evidence that this is what she really wants, and all the while, she's pulling, urging me toward her, so subtly I could almost persuade myself I'm imagining it.

But I'm not, and I know that because I have to adjust my

footing to keep from losing my balance and falling into her. Instead, I take one step closer, my body reacting like a metal detector just shy of gold.

Madi's hand slides up my arm, leaving chills in its wake that urge me closer toward the only other warmth in this elevator. Our faces are so close now, I can almost taste her. It's like seeing water after a trek through the Sahara, and I can't help myself now. My fingers are shaking, but I slip a hand around her waist, feeling her warm body on the palm of my hand and the cold metal of the elevator on the back of it.

She gives one more pull on my upper arm, this time less subtle, and I yield, trying to dip my toe in rather than diving in like my body and heart are telling me to do. Our lips meet, but just barely. It's the whisper of a kiss, really, just a taste, and I can feel it radiate from my lips just like I can follow a sip of hot chocolate in my mouth, down my throat, and into my stomach, warming me, paving a path for more.

Gosh, I want more.

Her hand tightens on my arm just as her lips press against mine more fully, and I'm there to give whatever she will take, to take whatever she'll give because I'm not even certain there's a bottom to the pool we're swimming in right now, but I want to dive deeper and deeper until I find out.

Her hand moves from my arm and joins with the other one in my hair, and my self-control frays like paper in a shredder. I slide my hand from her waist to the small of her back, pulling her toward me, needing all of her near me. There's no resistance there, though, no equal and opposite reaction, so I stumble back and into the bars behind me, Madi's mouth still on mine. The pain in my back only makes Madi's lips feel all the softer.

Everything I've been trying to hold in check is spilling over, and her willingness to reciprocate has me feeling things I've never felt until now. I put a hand on her cheek, afraid she'll pull away before I have the opportunity to express it all.

Clang.

The elevator comes to a rough halt, and we break apart, our gazes meeting. Somehow Madi's even more beautiful now than she was two minutes ago, her lips more red than pink, her breath coming quickly, and her eyes on me.

We don't even say anything. We just stand there, looking at each other, waiting for the doors to open behind her.

But they don't.

THIRTY-TWO

RÉMY

I LOOK AT THE LIGHT TO INDICATE WHICH FLOOR WE'VE reached. Three, it says. I put a hand on Madi's arm—not strictly necessary, but now that the touch barrier is broken, I can't help myself—and lean forward to press the button behind her to open the doors.

Nothing happens. Madi turns and presses the same button. Still nothing.

I look around at the bars that surround the top half of the elevator, and my eyes settle on an unwelcome view: the floor a few feet above our heads. We are stuck in the in-between.

"What?" Madi says, her voice urgent. My face must have given me away because she follows my gaze, and her eyes widen.

"It's fine," I say. "We're just between floors." I press the four button again. Nothing.

"Oh my gosh," she says in a whisper. "Did we break the elevator?"

I can't help but laugh because she makes it sound like we broke it by kissing. I feel the place on my back where it hit the bars behind me.

"Maybe," I say. "But it's not a big deal. We just press this." I

243

press the alarm button, determined to keep calm because this is a scene out of Madi's nightmares.

The seconds pass. And pass. And pass. Madi fidgets with one of the buttons on her coat while we wait for an answer, both of us staring at the red button. Paris is full of old elevators, and I've had to use the stairs while elevators are being repaired, but I've never actually been *in* one when it broke.

I grab Madi's hand, and her eyes flit to mine.

"It's gonna be okay," I say. "I promise." I'm no Superman, but I will pry these freaking bars apart with my bare hands if I have to. And failing that, I will do a YouTube search for how to escape an elevator.

Madi seems to relax slightly as her fingers settle between mine. I could dropkick this elevator for interrupting things, but maybe this is for the best. A literal jolt was probably the only thing that could stop me from kissing Madi like I was.

But she just broke up with Josh yesterday. As in less than thirty-six hours ago. And while part of me is happy to take being a rebound if it means more time with Madi, the other part of me knows that rebounds are not the healthy way to deal with a breakup. I don't want to take advantage of her in a vulnerable state.

Finally a man answers the call button, his voice muffled through the old microphone system. It takes a good deal of back and forth for us to understand one another, but once he's brought up to speed on the situation and our location, he promises help is on the way.

I relay the information to Madi in English, and she lets out a sigh of relief, loosening her grip on my hand a bit, which is nice since her nails were starting to dig into my skin. If she needed it, though, I would have let her go full Wolverine on my hand.

She needs more distraction, and I can think of a few options . . . but now that my mind and body have had some time to cool, more questions are starting to creep into my mind about what exactly that was for her—and what happens now.

So I don't kiss her again like I want to. But I also don't let go of her hand. Baby steps and all that.

I nod at her camera bag, forgotten at some point on the floor. Well, not forgotten, really. It takes up a significant portion of the space in here, which makes it hard to put more distance between us even if I wanted to. "What souvenirs did you find?"

Some of the anxiousness leaves her face, a glint of mischief twinkling in her eyes. She bends down—not an easy feat given the small space available—and pulls out the plastic bag from her camera bag. "Funny you should ask."

She shows me a small Eiffel Tower model a little taller than her hand. It's made of some type of faux-bronze metal, and she admires it with a tilted head. "They had one that lit up, but it was more of an Edward Cullen situation, so I went with the more classic look." She puts it back in the bag and pulls out a few things she bought for her mom, her brother, and the Sheppards. "And last but not least . . ." She rifles through the bag for a second, then pulls out another Eiffel Tower.

It's not like the first one. The top third is painted blue, the middle is white, and the bottom is red.

"It's for you," she says, handing it to me with a huge grin on her face and that same teasing glint in her eye that makes me feel simultaneously flattered and wary.

I take it hesitantly, twisting and turning the monstrosity in my hand. What exactly does she expect me to do with this?

"Don't forget the best part." She twists it in my hands, reaching underneath the base and fiddling with something. There's a soft click, and the tower lights up like a strobe.

I blink and pull away from it.

Madi's barely holding in her pride and amusement.

"So you saved Edward Cullen for me."

She nods. "I thought of you immediately. It was just too perfect."

"Mmhmm."

She laughs. "Just look. It's red, white, and blue. *And* it has stars—the whole twinkling aspect—and stripes. A great representation of your American side."

I cover my smile with a hand and hold the figurine slightly away from myself because the thing is flashing at me in a way that can't be safe for my vision. "You realize that the French flag is *also* red, white, and blue, right?"

"Yeah, but we did it better. We're red, white, and blue 2.0."

"The one who did something first is generally considered the best."

"First the worst, second the same, last the best of all the game."

I laugh, my brow furrowing. "What's that?"

"It's something we used to say in elementary school. Timeless wisdom."

"Okay, but there are other countries who did red, white, and blue *after* you, which makes you second, which, according to your own cute little jingle, makes you *also* the worst."

She glares at me teasingly. "The point is, we took your red, white, and blue, and we added pizzazz." She puts out both hands and wiggles her fingers. "We bedazzled it."

"Bedazzled?"

"It's when you add a bunch of sequins and jewels to something."

"So . . . you make it worse."

She punches me in the arm, and pain has never hurt so good. "The bedazzling of our flag has *meaning*, Rémy. The stars represent the—you know what?" She yanks the Eiffel Tower out of my hands. "You don't deserve this."

I fight her for it, though, because I actually *do* want that ugly thing. She bought it thinking of me, and that's a souvenir I can get behind. So I wrestle her, and since she has nowhere to hide in this small elevator, she doubles over, protecting the tower with her arms. I wrap mine around her from the back, tickling her until she surrenders.

My arms beg me to leave them around her, and I do. She

doesn't resist. Her hair is mussed from our struggle, and it smells like shampoo and a mixture of scents from the market. She turns in my arms so that she's facing me, and, taking the collar of my sweater, she pulls me down to her.

My eyes close, but the flashing of that dumb Eiffel Tower lingers, acting like a warning. Even the souvenir knows this isn't a smart move.

Mustering all my willpower, I pull back, rubbing my lips together in the hopes it'll stop the way they're insisting I let them have their way with Madi, with her lips, her neck. I press my eyes shut to get rid of that image and refocus myself. "Madi . . ."

"*Vous êtes là?*" The voice of the elevator technician comes from somewhere on the stairs, asking if we're here. As if we could be anywhere else.

We talk for a couple of minutes, and he gets my phone number so that he can talk to me while he's in the mechanical room. It's not long before he has me press the four button, and presto! We're on our way up again.

There's a whole lot of tension lingering in the air as I unlock the door to the apartment, and even though part of me wants to smack myself for stopping the kissing, the smarter part of me knows it was the right move.

After unlocking the apartment, I flip on the lamp we bought from IKEA. We both set down our things in silence. No part of me wants Madi to think I stopped kissing her because I *wanted* to stop kissing her, so I turn as I shrug off my coat.

"Hey, can we talk about . . . stuff?"

She smiles. "Yeah, of course." Okay, so she doesn't seem to be heartbroken over my interrupting things . . . I can't decide how to feel about that.

I lead the way over to the couch, taking a seat and angling myself toward her, my knee resting on the cushion.

"Listen," I say. "About back in the elevator . . ."

"You don't have to stress about it, Rémy. I'm sorry if I put you in a weird position."

"I mean"—I rotate my shoulders a bit to stretch my back—"those bars against my back didn't feel great, but . . ."

She smiles at my joke, and I feel a bit better. Is she apologizing because she thinks it's her fault? If only she knew how much I've been wanting to do exactly what we did.

"You just got out of a serious relationship," I say. "I don't want to take advantage of that."

"That's *not* what's happening. I promise. I know it seems weird when I say I'm okay, but it's true. Maybe I shouldn't be, but"—her thumb taps on her leg—"I think I've been expecting that breakup for a while. It's not like it was a sudden conclusion I came to. It's been building in me."

I don't even know what to say to that. I mean, I don't think she should be mourning Josh by any means. I'm genuinely happy for her to be out of that relationship because I don't think he deserves her, and I don't think he would make her happy. But I'm unclear what it means about what happened in the elevator.

"But it's not just about me," she says after a second. "I don't want you to feel like a rebound."

I smile ruefully. "I admit, the thought had crossed my mind. But, at the risk of mentioning the elephant in the room . . ."

"I'm leaving soon."

I nod, chewing on the inside of my lip and watching her. Her eyes are on me, exploring my face. I can see her brain working.

"Probably not super smart to jump into anything when it's got an expiration date," she says.

Expiration date. I hate that, the idea that Madi and I are going to expire like spoiled milk. But that doesn't mean it's not true. There *is* an expiration date on . . . whatever this is, and that date is January 2nd.

"Well, let's not make it complicated," she says, her tone turning more upbeat. "We can be friends. And business partners, since we've still got some work to do on the apartment and on the city guide for future guests." She lifts her shoulders in a careless shrug. "We just keep it light. Nothing serious."

There's nothing light about how I feel right now. I'm the one who brought up this whole subject, but now I'm having to quash an impulse to convince Madi against the "just friends" thing. She notices the delay in my response.

"Unless you'd rather not." Her voice sounds so hesitant all of a sudden. Almost embarrassed.

"No, no," I hurry to say. I can see the opportunity to spend time with Madi slipping away before my eyes, and even if it's the dumbest choice out there, I can't pass it up. I can keep it light, right? I mean, if that's what Madi wants, that's really my only choice. And given that she's leaving in two weeks, it's the smart thing to do. I just need to realign my priorities and remember what I set out to do in the first place: help out André and make sure Madi's stay at his place is a 5-star experience. "All of that sounds good to me."

"Great," Madi says, and her tone is at least half-convincing.

It's how I feel, too. Half-convinced. Which tells me that it'll probably be pretty easy to slip back into kissing her if I don't shore up this decision a bit. I may be able to keep things light with her if I stay on my A-game, but if we keep blurring the lines like we did in the elevator . . . well, I'm only human.

The silence after her *Great* says a lot, but we've already agreed on the path forward, so I change the subject.

"Sorry about the elevator breaking. The timing was—" I shake my head at the unbelievable bad luck. Not that it felt so bad being in there with her.

Not helpful.

"I told you your city hates me."

"She's just testing the limits of your love, making sure it's genuine."

"Sounds manipulative. But I love her anyway."

Why does my mind constantly want to assume that whenever Madi talks about Paris, she's also kind of talking about me? "You kept so calm in there."

"I don't know if I would say calm . . . ." Her cheeks tinge with pink.

Come on, Madi. You can't be looking at me like that if you're serious about just being friends. This is going to be . . . interesting.

I'll just think of it like a willpower Olympics. Easy. I'm running a willpower marathon. With no training.

It's a recipe for success.

THIRTY-THREE

MADI

SLEEP IS FOR THE BIRDS. THAT'S WHAT MY BODY'S decided. Or my brain, I guess. Every time I close my eyes, determined to sleep, I'm back in the elevator with Rémy, up against him with my hands in his hair and his hands gripping my waist while he kisses me senseless.

No, not senseless. It's kind of the opposite of that. It dominated *all* of my senses, which left zero bandwidth for remembering that we were stuck in a broken metal box five stories above ground.

Pro tip: if ever you find yourself in your worst nightmare, Rémy Scott will turn it straight into a daydream.

And a daydream is both how it feels and how it will remain because we've agreed to keep it light, keep it friendly. My whole Monica Geller "I'm breezy" vibe worked about as well as it did for her. Probably should have seen that coming.

Hopefully with both of us sharing the goal, though, it'll actually be achievable. It's the right decision. I shouldn't be mixing myself up in a sticky emotional situation immediately after ending things with Josh, and I *definitely* shouldn't do it when I'll be thousands of miles away soon. Even if kissing Rémy again feels like it's probably worth the emotional fallout because let me tell you, that. kiss. was. something. else.

I turn over in my bed for the twentieth time, then surrender to my body's tyranny and accept that I'm not going to sleep. I clamber down the ladder to grab my laptop and camera, which I take to the itty bitty table and chair under the bed. I can edit Laura's photos and send them to her until my mind and body calm down enough to sleep. It should occupy me enough that my thoughts don't wander to the elevator, since I can still feel the press of his chest against mine.

I touch a hand to my cheeks. Speaking of breezy, I could use a breeze about now. This whole time I've been worrying about the teenage girls in Rémy's English classes. News flash: I *am* those teenage girls. *I'm* the one everyone should be worrying about.

BUT I'm going to be an adult and keep it friendly like we decided. Because unlike a teenage girl, the prefrontal cortex of my brain is almost fully developed, which means I can plan and strategize and control my impulses. In theory.

A call comes in from Siena as I transfer yesterday's files from my camera to my laptop. *Oh dear. This will be interesting.*

I answer, trying to keep it light and sound totally normal. But Siena is a bloodhound, and she smells something's up from literally thousands of miles away, so I end up telling her about the elevator incident.

Siena isn't breezy either. Not even close. It takes me a few minutes to bring her back down to earth as she hounds me for details.

"Lemme get this straight," she says. "You, Madison Allred, who is afraid of small spaces, got trapped in a medieval elevator with the most beautiful human in France and proceeded to make out with him until help came?"

"A few things," I say. "First, I'm fairly certain they didn't have elevators in the middle ages. Second, there's no solid proof that Rémy is the most beautiful human in France, though I admit I have no evidence to the contrary. And third, we actually kissed *before* we were trapped."

"You're missing the forest for the trees, Mads. If you got trapped with *me* in an elevator, do you even *know* what would have happened?"

"Well, I definitely wouldn't have kissed you, if that's what you're getting at. But it wasn't as bad as it sounds." I shrug, as if she can see me. "Rémy's pretty good at keeping me calm."

"If you can stay calm kissing *him*, then I don't know how to relate to you anymore. It would fall under the *irreconcilable differences* category, which means divorce."

I roll my eyes, but I can't stop a smile as I tap through the pictures of Laura and Luke in my editing software. "Okay, so I wasn't calm, *per se*, but I wasn't thinking about falling to my death or the walls closing in on me. But we talked afterward, and we both agree that it wasn't smart, and we're just going to be friends."

Siena snorts like an actual pig. "Good one!"

"It *is* good."

My heart skitters, and I stop scrolling when I come to the pictures Laura took of Rémy and me. And then I stare because this is a new and rare experience, like a blue whale sighting. Laura nailed the pictures. The focus is tack-sharp, the Eiffel Tower is positioned perfectly behind us at one of the rule-of-thirds "crash points," and Rémy and I are both laughing and looking at each other.

Just friends.

I DO, in fact, manage to sleep at some point, but it's not until I've edited Laura's photos and sent them to her. When I wake up in the morning, the room is chillier than usual, and there's a lattice-work of frost on my small window. I check my phone to find a teasing text from Siena and a bunch of Instagram notifications.

Apparently, Laura already posted a few of the photos I sent her, which she tagged me in and added a bunch of hashtags to. That accounts for the sudden twenty new followers I have.

I smile. *Thank you, Laura.*

I've worn most of the clothes I brought, which means I need to do more laundry, so I take the little mesh bag full of my clothes downstairs. I really should wash my bra, but guess what? I only brought two, and the other one is still hanging outside Rémy's window. I checked.

Sigh. Guess it's time to be a big girl and bring it up.

Rémy isn't in the living room or kitchen, so I glance at the bedroom door. It's barely ajar, and my glance coincides with him pulling a t-shirt over his head, covering everything our kissing session hinted at last night. He looks straight ahead, at a mirror, I assume, and runs a hand through his hair.

Welp. That was one of the least *just friends* images I could possibly start my day with. I can hear Siena cackling right now.

I shake it off and head for the kitchen, where Rémy joins me after a few minutes. Every nerve in my body is on high alert because that's what happens when you spend every single waking minute thinking about kissing someone.

But Rémy is better at this than I am. He just smiles and says good morning like it doesn't do *things* to me just to be near him.

"I have a confession," he says.

"What's that?" I say it like my nerves aren't fraying, and I can only do that because I'm focusing on stuffing my laundry into the washer.

"I did some research last night. Turns out the tricolor French flag came *after* the American flag."

My hands stop, and I look up at him, checking if he's serious. He is, but he's also got laughing eyes.

I cluck my tongue and stand up. "These examples of the French obsession with America are really piling up. It's getting a bit pathetic."

"We simplified it, though. Made it classy. Chic."

I can't really argue with that. But I will anyway. "You say classy. I say boring." One of the legs of my pants is trying to escape the washer, so I push it back in and busy myself with the rest of the clothes so I don't have to look at him for the next part. "Hey, so, um, I think my bra fell off my rack."

I freeze.

Oh. My. Gosh. Most unfortunate word choice in history. I whirl my head around to look at Rémy as my cheeks start blistering from the raw heat they're generating.

Rémy's trying valiantly not to smile. UGH. Why does he have to know English well enough to know slang?

"I meant," I say very carefully, "that I put it on the drying rack upstairs a few days ago, but it fell down onto *your* drying rack."

He can't stop the smile anymore. "I knew what you meant. And yes, it's there. I can go grab it."

"I can do it!" I call as he turns. I don't think it's good for our newly reaffirmed friendship for me to see him holding my bra.

"I *have* seen bras before, you know. I'll help you open the window. It's a bit tricky."

"Of course it is," I say bitterly.

Rémy opens the blinds and then the window, and I admire the way his muscles aid in this process. Good friends should always notice and encourage their friends' strengths.

The gust of cold that comes in effectively puts an end to my "platonic" admiration, and I reach out and grab my bra. It's a popsicle, and it takes self-control not to throw it onto Rémy's bed to save my fingers from frostbite. There are literal icicles hanging in a few spots—some of them placed very unfortunately indeed—and based on the way Rémy's covering his mouth but his eyes are crinkled at the sides, he's noticed it too.

Looks like I'll be wearing my current bra another day while this one goes through humiliation detox. I shove the bra into the washer and start the laundry cycle.

We talk over breakfast about the day's plans, and I'm feeling a lot more relaxed now that the bra incident is behind me. Rémy isn't an awkward type of guy. I kind of wish he was. Maybe that would make it easier not to see him the way I'm seeing him now.

I suggest we do a quick French lesson, take pictures of the apartment, then head out for some more work on the guide book.

"Unless you have other plans," I say, realizing I've just scheduled out his entire day. Maybe Rémy's idea of what *just friends* looks like means spending less time together. That would make perfect sense, but I kind of hope it's not what he had in mind. Okay, I *really* hope it's not what he had in mind. "Because technically this whole guide book thing was my idea, and you don't—"

"I'm free as a bird until Christmas break ends."

I smile, unable to stop my relief and the anticipation of spending another day with him. Don't get me wrong, kissing Rémy blew my mind. But I genuinely enjoy being with him even without being liplocked.

"There's just one thing," he says.

"Yeah, sure. What's up?"

He wets his lips, and immediately my shoulder devil is whispering in my ear that maybe the one thing is that we need to kiss again just to, you know, get it entirely out of our systems.

"I think we might need to set some boundaries," he says with a little hesitation.

Poof, shoulder devil.

"Oh," I say. "Yeah, totally. For sure. Yep. Boundaries."

"Just a few lines to help us . . ."

"Stay in the lines." I'm so eloquent.

"Yeah."

"Smart," I say even as I see Siena wielding a giant eraser and watching us with an evil smile. "What sort of lines are you thinking?"

He taps a finger on the table. "Well, for one, no kissing."

I nod. That's an obvious one. And yet also somehow still disappointing to hear him say.

"Hugging should probably be a line."

I nod again. I feel like I should contribute something. "No

holding hands? I feel like that might have been where this all started for me."

"It started before that for me, but yeah . . ."

That sends a jolt through me. *It.* I want so badly to follow up on that word, to know what exactly he means by *it.* And how long *it* has been going on.

"I guess that means no metro and no elevators today," he says.

"I don't know. I'm getting better." Or maybe I'm not. Maybe without Rémy's hand, without his lips on mine, I'll be back to square one. "It's silly, I know. You'd think I'd have grown out of needing to hold someone's hand when I'm scared."

"Do people *ever* grow out of that? I think we all just figure out how to pretend we don't want a hand to hold."

I meet his gaze, unsure how to respond to that. Josh teased me a lot for the whole hand-holding thing. It wasn't rude teasing, but it still made me feel childish. But what Rémy is saying . . . it makes sense.

"Maybe you're right. I don't remember much about my dad dying except for being in the hospital a lot and holding his hand whenever I was there. And then when my mom broke the news to us that he was gone, she held my and my brother's hands. I guess it became a thing for me."

Rémy's mouth is turned down at the sides, his face thoughtful as he looks at me. "If you need my hand, Madi, you can hold it, okay? We're friends." He meets my gaze to ensure I know he means it.

"Thank you." Even as I say it, I know I can't do it. Rémy may be able to hold the line while also holding my hand. I don't think I can. I'm not ambidextrous, people. "Any other lines?"

"Yeah," he says, relaxing a bit and sitting back with his arms crossed. "No laughing."

I raise my brows.

His mouth curls up at the side. "Your laugh is . . . well, it just makes it harder for me. So if you could just, you know, *not*." He tries to control his amusement by pulling his lips between his teeth. Then he wets his lips again.

"That." I point to his lips. "That's a line."

He stops mid lip-rubbing. "Um, okay. I'll . . . do what I can."

"Me too."

THIRTY-FOUR

MADI

OPERATION: JUST FRIENDS GOES MORE SMOOTHLY THAN I had anticipated. Overall, at least. There are . . . moments, though, when failure looms on the horizon.

It is a frigid day, first of all, which makes snuggling up to someone all the more tempting.

Secondly, four or five times, one or the other of us says "Line!" seemingly out of nowhere to signal that something is making it harder to keep the boundaries we've set. In retrospect, I'm not sure calling attention to those things is actually serving our best interests, since whenever Rémy says it, I just want to do the thing more.

Thirdly, I do *not* manage to keep from laughing. Far from it. But I don't feel too bad about it because it's Rémy's fault I'm laughing so much and also, friends laugh together. Otherwise, what is even the point?

Our day consists of a visit to Luxembourg Gardens and the Jardin des Plantes. They're not as vibrant as they'd be in summer, according to Rémy, but I love them all the same. After that, we've had enough of the cold to opt for an indoor activity, which takes us (via metro with *no hand holding*, I might add) to see the Sainte

Chapelle and the Conciergerie, which are an absolute feast for the eyes.

When Rémy takes my camera in hand and insists on taking some photos of me inside with super tricky lighting, I almost jump off the friend ship altogether.

We're warm enough—and hungry enough—after that to make our way to the Christmas market at Notre Dame.

"What sounds good?" Rémy asks as we stroll past the offerings.

"Raclette again," I say. "And another crepe."

He looks over at me with a smile that's made me consider yelling out, "Line!" about seventy times today. It doesn't seem fair to tell him he can't smile, though, so I've refrained.

"You are a creature of habit, aren't you?" he says.

"What?!" I pretend to be offended. "I'm the very definition of spontaneous and adventu—okay, what gave me away? Is it the baguette and Camembert for breakfast every day? That's *your* fault, you know. I was perfectly content with my Kraft singles and Wonder Bread."

"Kraft singles?" he asks with a furrowed brow.

"Don't ask. They'd obliterate your opinion of America. Same with Cheese Whiz. Though, if you like Finger Lickin' Chicken . . ."

He bumps me with his arm, making me stumble a bit to the side.

"Line," we say simultaneously.

I laugh, and he says, "Line" again, but I can tell he's half-teasing, and that makes me blush. This is one of those moments where I think we're not doing nearly as well at this mission as we had hoped. Once you've crossed a bridge like this with someone, it's really hard to walk backwards over it and pretend it doesn't exist. You can ignore it, sure, but you find yourself using stepping stones to get you right back to the other side.

My phone buzzes with a notification—a private message on Instagram from a name I don't recognize. I scan it quickly, expecting one of the spam messages I get. But it's not. It's a girl named Linnae asking if I'm available to take pictures for her in a few days. She's offering $500, which is quite a bit more than I charge for a couples' session. It's simultaneously flattering and unfortunate, since I could sure use $500.

Madi: I'm actually in Paris right now, or else I would love to! If you still need someone when I get back, I'd be more than happy to schedule something with you.

I start to exit the app, but she's already typing back.

Linnae: I'm in Paris too! I was hoping you'd be able to do it here. Like you did for Laura.

"What is it?" Rémy asks, watching my reaction.

"Someone saw the picture I took of Laura and Luke, and she wants me to take pictures of her and her boyfriend. Here in Paris. For $500."

"That's amazing," Rémy says. "I mean, it's no surprise . . ."

"It is to *me*." I twist my mouth to the side, looking at Linnae's message. "I feel like I should decline. Anyone offering that much money is expecting more than I can safely promise."

Rémy takes me by the shoulders and looks straight into my eyes. "I've seen the pictures you take, Madi. You are worth every penny of that and more. If you don't want to do it, don't. But if all that's keeping you from saying yes is fear? You've shown that you're more than capable of conquering those over the last few days."

Keeping my eyes on him, I nod silently. He believes in me more than I believe in myself, and it makes me want to see myself as he sees me.

I message back and forth with Linnae a bit more, and we settle on a time to meet. She wants to do the pictures in Montmartre, and Rémy offers to take me there beforehand so we can scope out the location and find the best spots.

Once we've got full bellies and hot chocolates in hand, we decide to brave the elements for a river cruise.

"It's a great way to see the city," Rémy says. "But it'll be . . ."

"Frigid? I know. But we can take the metro back home, right? And then we can recover in the warmth of the apartment, so I can survive until then."

THERE IS a reason weathermen talk about the "wind chill factor." This is what I have learned since boarding this Seine River cruise. It's not like we're on a speedboat or anything, but we *are* moving, and it's fast enough that there's a definite wind chill to add to the low temperatures. It's probably why we are two of twelve people on this cruise. The empty seats contain the ghosts of those wiser than us, taunting us for our bad judgment.

If I didn't have some distractions—the tour guide's heavily accented information, for one, and the views of the city, for another—I would be shivering uncontrollably. Rémy has offered me his coat twice, but there's no way I'm depriving him of it. It's not like *he's* working up a sweat. In fact, I could swear there was one point where he looked longingly at the river, like maybe it would be warmer to swim than continue on the boat, and we all know how Rémy feels about swimming in the Seine.

We settle for sitting as close as possible to one another to share some arm heat, if nothing else. I can think of a few ways to generate more heat, but not only are they in blatant violation of our rules, but I'm not big on PDA.

All I want is to sit right next to Rémy, warm from my shoulder to my elbow, but the sites are calling to me, so I reluctantly stand up and head to the side of the boat. I try to operate my camera, but my fingers are completely useless.

Rémy joins me and gives it a shot. He manages a couple of

hard-won pictures that are actually really well done. Sure, I helped him get settings right—night photography is a whole different beast—but his composition ain't too shabby.

"You're doing me proud," I say, teeth chattering. "A straight-A student."

"Too bad I make a living as a teacher," he replies, pressing the shutter again like all of our fingers aren't about to snap off.

It's so frigid, I feel guilty for leaving my bra outside Rémy's window in weather like this.

"Thankfully, I can now also vouch for your teaching skills." He hands the camera back to me, and I handle it clumsily because my fingers have the same grasping capabilities as my toes right now—if I even have toes anymore. I haven't felt them for a while.

"After one French lesson?" he asks.

"*Mais oui,*" I say. "It doesn't take long to know a good teacher."

"I can't just be good, though. I've got to be the best."

"Rémy," I say, leaning an elbow on the side rail and looking up at him. "Anybody who has talked to you for ten seconds couldn't doubt you are the best person for that job at Bellevue. Have a little faith in yourself." Look at me, giving pep talks about things I personally struggle with. Why is it so much easier to believe in others than it is to believe in myself?

He stares at me silently for a second, and the way he does it has a red, flashing LINE sign going off in my head.

"Besides," I say, turning my gaze back to the city in an effort Hercules would appreciate, "if you don't get the job, you can always come teach French in the States—fulfill your dream of living in America." I shoot him a glance from the corner of my eye, and he's got that lopsided smile it feels like my life mission to produce.

"Is that right, Stars and Stripes?"

"Firstly, major *line.* You know how it makes me feel when you talk about Old Glory. Secondly, yes, it *is* right. You would do a much better job than a lot of the English teachers I had. And then there's always the option of being an assistant in my rapidly growing photography empire." I tap through the photos Rémy has taken from the riverboat.

"Oh yeah?"

I stop on a shot of Pont Neuf and stare at it for a second. "Actually, job offer retracted. You're on pace to eclipse me, and I have a very fragile ego."

He looks at me with eyes that twinkle more captivatingly than the Eiffel Tower. If I were confident my lips were at more than 20% functioning capacity in this cold, I would kiss him right here and now. And I could swear he's having the same thoughts.

It's probably for the best that I pre-fired him. If Rémy was my assistant, I don't think we would get much photography done.

THIRTY-FIVE

RÉMY

ONCE THE CRUISE ENDS, WE HURRY OFF THE BOAT AS fast as our frozen legs will carry us and head straight for the metro, which is surprisingly busy for a Monday night. I glance at Madi as we near the entrance to the station, where the stairs are jammed with incoming and outgoing passengers. Given that she's making a bee-line down the stairs already, she doesn't seem to mind.

It's significantly warmer once we get out of the stairway, and she rubs her hands together like we're standing in front of a fire as we line up for the machines. I'm just waiting for her to realize how crowded it is, but she slips through the turnstile like a pro. I don't even know if she remembers I'm here behind her, honestly, and while that's no self-esteem boost, I'm also happy for her. It's a lot of progress in a short amount of time.

We get to the fork in the path where we have to choose which direction of train to take, and she turns around, looking to me for guidance. I'm not mad about it; it's nice to know she still needs me a bit.

When we get to the platform, it's a zoo. An announcement comes on informing us that there are delays on this line. Bad timing. It only takes a bit of eavesdropping on nearby conversations to understand that there are bigger crowds than usual at this station tonight.

"Sounds like there was a big Christmas concert nearby," I explain to Madi. The platform is chock-full as people wait for the next train. Someone brushes past, and I stabilize Madi with a hand on her arm as she gets bumped and jostled. "You sure you're okay with this?"

"Okay with it?" she asks. "If you try to take me back outside again, you will have to pull me kicking and screaming."

I smile. "Just checking."

By the time the train slows to a stop in front of the full platform, there are people lined up all the way from the hall, just waiting to squeeze onto the platform. The subtle but continuous tug on my coat tells me Madi's keeping a hold on me that way. I don't blame her. It would be pretty easy to lose each other in this crush.

The train cars are already pretty full, which means there's no way in Hades that even half the people waiting can fit on board. Thankfully, Madi and I are close enough that we end up inside the nearest train car. It's not like we had much choice in the matter. The herd dictated our movements, and I kept my arm around her because it was clear that her hold on my jacket might not be sufficient. Yeah, it's a line, but I'm more worried about getting separated from her right now than I am about following the rules.

And now we are sardines, packing as many of us as possible inside while people search for the nearest bar or seat to hold onto. Madi and I find ourselves pushed right up against the one floor-to-ceiling bar in this area of the car. It's already covered in hands except for a space at the top and one a bit lower down. I have easier access to it, so I slip my hand into the lower space before it gets taken, just as someone takes the upper one.

The train car jerks forward, and I grab Madi around the waist to keep her from falling into those behind her. That would start a game of dominoes nobody wants to play. Her feet shuffle a bit as she tries to find her equilibrium, just like everyone else is doing, and she holds onto me because it's either that or grabbing a stranger. Lines and rules are out the window right now. We couldn't be much closer than we are. If hugging like Americans greet each other is considered the second base of intimate greetings, being in this metro car is a home run.

I try to draw the boundaries in my mind that are nonexistent for my body, ignoring the slope of Madi's waist under my hand and the press of her body against mine.

The train car is swimming with scents—perfume, food, body odor, and minty gum, to name a few I recognize. The body odor is winning out, though, and Madi's nose wrinkles as she looks at me to see if I'm smelling it too.

I am. Very much.

I grimace. The Paris metro in the summer is body odor central, but the winter months are usually a bit of a respite. Not today. Somebody must have gotten too close to the chestnuts roasting on an open fire.

It's already toasty in here, and it's no wonder. Everyone is dressed for freezing temperatures rather than this sudden oven on train tracks. Keeping his hold of the bar, the man next to me starts shrugging out of his coat, as if there's plenty of room for everyone to be shimmying and wriggling like fish on hooks.

And then it hits me: a giant whiff of BO. I know it hits Madi, too, because she freezes against me, her nostrils flared, and her eyes alert. Her wide gaze shifts up to me, then to the guy next to us, whose sweat-darkened armpit is hovering directly above us as he holds tight to the bar.

Madi covers a cough with her hand, ducking her head closer to me, right up against my chest. Suddenly, she grabs the lapels of my coat, using them to pull her up and me down. Oh my gosh, she's going to kiss me to distract herself from the—

"I'm just going to be smelling your cologne for the foreseeable future," she whispers in my ear. "Lemme know when it's safe to come up for air." And then she disappears again, holding my lapels and using them as insulators around her head to keep the stench out.

And all I can do is smile. And then try not to reel as the train slows and the man switches hands, offering up a fresh batch of re-odorant.

My options are limited, but they aren't non-existent. So I nestle my face into Madi's hair and inhale. It's bliss. I will write an ode to Madi's shampoo. She can even throw it at my head like the first time we met.

I can't believe how much has happened since then. I can't believe I'm holding Madi right now, even if it *is* just because a guy can't figure out how to operate in modern society. To everyone else on the train, we probably just look like a young, in love couple. And suddenly I'm wishing that appearances were correct and that I didn't have to fight myself to stop feeling more and more for Madi. I'm absolutely losing that fight.

THE CONTRAST from the metro to outside for our walk home couldn't be starker. It feels like relief for all of ten seconds, and then the sharp wind finds its way through every crevice and pore, making its way down to our bones and chilling the sweat we worked up in the train, pressed against each other and half of Paris.

I fumble with the keys as I open the door from the street and then the one into the building, my hands already struggling to function again.

"Almost there," Madi says, her teeth chattering.

Once inside, we both hesitate in front of the elevator. We look at each other, and I can tell that, for Madi too, the decision being made isn't between the stairs and the elevator; it's between repeating last night's *events* and keeping our boundaries.

In other words, it's temptation at its finest.

"We'd better take the stairs," Madi says.

"Agreed," I say with a quick but longing glance at the elevator. The exercise required of us going up a few flights of narrow stairs gets our bodies a fair bit warmer. I guess that's our reward for choosing to be rulekeepers.

Yay.

Madi juggles her camera bag as she takes off her coat while I unlock the door. "Home sweet home," she says with unveiled relief. I love that she thinks of this place that we've been sharing as home.

She steps inside, and I follow behind. She hasn't taken more than five steps when she stops, shudders, drops her camera bag, and throws her coat back on.

I haven't taken my coat off yet, but by the way my skin prickles, I know Madi's not just being dramatic. Far from being the cozy sanctuary we were hoping for, it's frigid in here.

I go over to the nearest radiator and put a hand to it. The metal is cold to the touch. I check the dial on the bottom, which is set to about the middle. I turn it all the way to the highest setting.

I make my way to the one in my room, and Madi follows behind me. The radiator in here is ice cold too. In fact, it's even colder than the one in the living room. I just don't understand how, even if the radiators aren't working, it could be THIS cold inside. It's like they've gone rogue and transformed into air conditioners. Or icebergs.

"Um, Rémy?"

I glance up at Madi. She's got her lips tucked in as she points above my head.

Wow. My window is open. I must have forgotten to shut it properly after Madi retrieved her bra this morning.

I swear in French and hurry to shut it. "On the coldest day of the year!"

"In history," Madi says, folding her arms tightly and hunching her shoulders. "I'm so sorry. It's my fault for not shutting the window."

"I'm the one who opened it."

"And I'm the one whose bra started all this." She shivers again. "I'm going to put more clothes on."

Ah, the seven words every guy loves to hear a woman say.

While she's upstairs, I compose and then delete a text to André. I don't want to bother him with this stuff. It's the last thing he needs right now. It'll just stress him out.

When Madi comes downstairs five minutes later, she's still wearing her coat, but she looks like a sad puppy. "I did my laundry this morning. None of it's dry yet."

I bust up laughing. I can't help it. "I'm sorry. It's just so ridiculous."

"*Now* do you believe your city hates me?"

"No, and neither should you. Maybe you just have Paris Syndrome."

"Come again?"

"Paris Syndrome. It's when foreigners come here and are so overwhelmed by disappointment—the gap between expectation and reality—that it affects them physically."

Madi stares at me. "You're joking."

"Nope. Look it up. People are hospitalized for it and everything." I head to my dresser and open the top drawer. "You can wear some of my clothes. I don't have many clean ones—most of my stuff is still at home—but you're welcome to whatever strikes your fancy."

"A blazer and slacks?"

"Sure. Slip on three blazers under that coat, and you'll be set."

Madi opts for my gray sweats, though—the ones she wore the first night here—and it's all I can do not to call out *line* when she comes down in them a few minutes later while I'm heating up water in the kettle.

She chafes at her arms. "Isn't heat supposed to rise?"

"That's assuming there's any heat *to* rise. Also, that room is probably the worst insulated one in the entire building."

"It's cute, though," she says with that smile that gets me every time.

"True. A fair trade." I turn and lean against the counter, folding my arms and clenching my teeth. "So . . . I called the heating company, and—"

She puts up a hand to stop me, then tucks it right back into its spot under her arm. "Good news first."

I hesitate, looking at her for clarification. "Good news?"

"You look like you've got bad news, but bad news should always be prefaced with good news."

"Right . . . um, okay. Good news, good news . . ." The kettle starts making a racket behind me. "We may not have hot water for the radiators, but we've got hot water in the kettle."

"Can't we just pour it into the radiators?"

"Um, no."

"Ugh. So this is still bad news. Do we at least have hot chocolate mix?"

I nod, and she smiles. "Okay, I'm ready for the bad news now."

"Bad news is they say it's probably the boiler, but they can't get anyone out here until late tomorrow morning to look at it. Apparently, we are not the only ones dealing with this issue tonight. Old pipes love to crack in the cold."

She sighs, and the end of it turns into a teeth chatter.

"All right," I say. "Let's get some hot chocolate in you, *mademoiselle*. I'll mix it for you while you go snuggle up on the couch under that new blanket we bought."

"Rémy Scott. You are the best." She starts moving toward the couch. "Make it with a lot of chocolate, okay?"

"I know how to make a hot chocolate, Madi."

"Okay," she says doubtfully as she disappears from view, "but if I take a sip and it tastes like the hot chocolate version of LaCroix"—she says it with an overdramatized French accent—"I'm not gonna be happy."

"You know LaCroix isn't a French company, right?"

Silence.

"Right, Madi?"

She still doesn't bother answering, but when I peek my head around the corner of the kitchen, she's smiling like a sly little fox who loves pushing my buttons.

Once I've made two cups of hot cocoa, I find Madi cocooned in the blanket. She has no arms, no legs. She's a mound of blanket with a hooded head sticking out.

She looks at me with brows raised. "What? You think you're getting some blanket too?"

I set the mugs and a couple of napkins down. "No, no, it's fine. Take *all* the clothes and *all* the blankets." I put a hand to the bottom hem of my hooded sweatshirt. "Did you want this too?"

She glances at my stomach and hesitates before responding. "Yes. I mean no. I mean—*line*."

I laugh and take a seat next to her as she unwraps herself from her blanket fortress.

She shivers and shakes her head. "The things I do for you . . ."

I accept the end of the blanket she offers me. It reaches about two-thirds of the way across me.

She stares at me like she's waiting. "You're gonna have to scoot closer than that."

"I'll be fine with this much." Any closer and I'll be in trouble.

"I'm not worried about *you*. You've compromised the integrity of the heating system." She points to three gaps where the blanket is letting cold air through.

I scoot closer, muttering in French under my breath like I'm mad about it.

"What was that?" she asks.

"Nothing," I say with false innocence as she helps drape the blanket over me. "Nothing at all."

She gives me the evil eye as she scoots closer. "You know, one day I'm going to speak fluent French, and you won't be able to pull moves like that." Our bodies touch, and her eyes widen a bit.

"What?"

"Who are you? Jacob Black?" She puts a hand to my arm, which is covered by my sweatshirt, then moves it to my hand, like she needs to check my skin temperature. After a day of avoiding contact with her, the touch trips up my heart.

"How are you possibly *that* warm, Rémy?"

"I may *seem* warm, but I don't *feel* warm. Who's Jacob Black?"

She shuts her eyes, as though pleading with the heavens to grant her serenity. "That's it." She reaches for the remote on the coffee table. "We are drinking our hot chocolate while we watch Twilight. And if you want to know who Jacob Black is, we have to watch the first *and* second movies, so get comfortable."

I protest, but Madi will hear none of it, and since I'm only doing it because I feel like it's my duty as a man to pretend I'm not interested in watching, my protests are half-hearted. I'm preoccupied with how close we are, despite the rules we set in place this morning. The way my body is feeling, I won't be needing this blanket for long, and yet, I can feel Madi's body tremble every ten or fifteen seconds, so I grit my teeth.

Her phone vibrates next to her, and she extracts an arm to pick it up. Her brow furrows then rises. "I got another request for a session! Through my website!"

How does it surprise her that people want her to take photos of them? I put up my hand and give her an all-American high-five. "When is it for?"

Her eyes scan her phone screen. "Oof. Christmas Day." She reads on. "Sounds like it's an important anniversary for"—she glances at the end of the email—"Ashleigh Jo Wrutton and her boyfriend."

"Are you going to do it?"

She considers it for a minute. "I don't see why not. I need the money, and it's not like I won't be enjoying myself." She taps to respond to the email, and I keep quiet. I hadn't really considered what Christmas will be like for Madi here, but I'm pretty sure there's a hard line right next to "inviting a girl to spend Christmas with you and your mom."

When Madi spills hot chocolate during the opening credits, she goes quiet for a few seconds, sighs, then starts pressing a napkin to the wet spot on our laps. "On the new blanket."

"That's why we went with black. It'll come out in the wash."

"Still. Today is not our day."

"No. But I had a really good time."

She looks at me for a second, her smile softening and her eyes searching mine. "Same here."

Warning bells are going off in my brain. What I'm feeling right now is too close to what I felt last night, and this time, there's no jolting elevator to stop me. "Who knew being miserable could be so much fun?" It's my weak attempt at shifting the trajectory we're on, and I can see by the change in Madi's eyes that she understands that.

She gives me a smile and picks up the remote again. "The perfect segue for *Twilight*."

Her shivering seems to calm as she drinks the hot chocolate. It warms me up, too, but it's only temporary. The air in the room isn't much warmer than the air outside, and it's not long before I feel her tremble again.

"Want more hot cocoa?"

She groans. "My body says yes—you make a fine hot chocolate, by the way—but my stomach says absolutely not. Is there a way to give it to me intravenously?"

"I think the prevailing medical wisdom says not to inject boiling liquid into human veins. And the last thing we need is to add a hospital to the day we've had."

She straightens suddenly, her hand grabbing mine. "Rémy, you're a genius. The hospital. It's *just* what we need. They'd have heating *there* for sure. You could take me there and pretend I fainted from that Paris Syndrome thing!"

I laugh because Madi is so ridiculous—and so ridiculously

lovable. And also, her icy hand is still holding my hand. "So you *don't* want to watch *Twilight* . . . ."

The movie has been going during our conversation, which she had clearly forgotten about until I mentioned it. She releases my hand and settles back into place, fixing the blanket so that it's pulled all the way up to her neck. She extracts one arm to handle the remote, rewinding a couple of minutes. "This plot moves lightning fast, so we better go back to make sure you can keep up. American young adult cinema is notoriously high-brow." Her nose is pink from the cold, and was that her breath I just saw?

I can't handle it anymore. "Come here." I lift my arm, inviting her to snuggle up next to me.

She looks at the space I'm offering, and I can see the longing there like she's wearing heat vision goggles and I'm glowing red and orange. Her gaze travels back up to me. "What about the lines?"

I take in a breath and let it out slowly. "We're going to have to blur them a bit in the interest of fending off hypothermia. Besides, I don't think the lines are doing as much for me as I hoped they would."

She doesn't answer for a second, like she's considering what I just said. "I don't want to make things more difficult for you."

"I'll be fine." I probably won't. But I wrap my arm around her and pull her toward me, trying to convince myself it doesn't feel like locking two puzzle pieces together to have her there. "I promise to keep inside all the other lines."

"Me too."

So I watch Edward Cullen sparkle (gosh, it's painful) with Madi snuggled up next to me, no longer shivering. It's not long before she's warm enough to fall asleep, and it's even *less* long before I'm struggling to pay any attention to the movie. My body isn't crossing lines, but my brain and my heart have sprinted past so far, they can't even *see* the lines anymore.

I don't even care about kissing her right now. Okay, that's a stretch. I would absolutely love to kiss her right now—if she weren't unconscious. But what I'm feeling as I hold her against me and try to shift so that her head doesn't roll off my shoulder? It goes so far beyond mere physical attraction.

It's crazy to care this much about Madi after how short a time she's been here—I get that—but knowing that doesn't change how I feel.

When my dad would leave on business trips when I was a kid, it didn't matter that I knew I'd see him again in a few days. It was hard every. single. time. And I *won't* be seeing Madi again. Maybe if she left tomorrow, I would be okay. Maybe? I don't know. But she's here for almost two more weeks. If I feel this way about her right now, how will I feel *then*?

I take another look at her—or as much of her as I can see from this angle—trying to gauge whether it's possible for me to keep doing this, to compartmentalize. They do it on TV shows, right? If a covert agent can kill druglords at midnight and kiss his kindergartener at school drop-off the next morning, can't I manage to separate being Madi's host for the holidays from my desire to spend every second of every day as close to her as possible?

I sigh and let my head drop onto the back of the couch. Pretending we can just be friends *isn't* working for me. Not at all. Not even after one measly day. And I have a suspicion it's not working for Madi, either, which means things are bound to turn sour for both of us—just like André feared.

But even though there's no doubt in my mind that spending a frigid night without radiators is a solid 1-star Airbnb experience, this isn't even about the 5-star rating. It's about doing the responsible thing. It's about not hurting Madi when she's already experienced major career and relationship disappointments this week.

And yes, it's about protecting myself, too, because I can't pretend I don't see the oncoming train wreck. I can't sit and do nothing to stop it, no matter how fun playing on the tracks is.

THIRTY-SIX

MADI

I force my eyelids to open, but all they'll do is flutter like a fledgling bird. I'm covered by a layer of blankets, while Rémy's body makes my left side cozy and warm. It takes me a second to realize that I'm slumped over onto him with my head on his lap. He's shifting under my weight, probably trying to get more comfortable.

I push myself up sleepily. "Sorry." My voice comes out weak and crackly. "Here, there's space for you." I lie down, inviting him into the place directly in front of me. "I'll be the big spoon." My eyes are already closing again.

He moves so that he's sitting on the very edge of the couch. "I think I'm just gonna go to my room."

My eyes open a bit more. "Oh." I can't tell what's in his voice, but it's *something*. He sounds more serious than usual. He's probably been super uncomfortable for the past—I check the TV screen and see the rolling credits—hour and a half.

"I'll bring you the blanket from your bed to make sure you stay warm," he says.

It's really generous of him, and yet the thought of swapping out Rémy for a blanket—however new and cute that blanket is— is depressing. Depressing but smart. We promised to keep inside the other lines, and I think spooning all night falls squarely on the wrong side. I'm going to chalk the suggestion up to fatigue.

He leaves for a couple minutes, then returns with my blanket, which he drapes over me, spending time making sure every part of me is covered.

"Goodnight, Madi," he says, and then he's gone.

I hover between consciousness and sleep for a few minutes, vaguely aware of the sound of running water as Rémy brushes his teeth (kudos to him for braving the elements for his dental hygiene), and a couple of minutes later, the shutting of his bedroom door.

⚓

WHEN I WAKE up in the morning, I have the same sensation I did camping as a little girl. I'm a hot pocket in the middle of the arctic tundra, and any movement of mine risks introducing sub-zero temperatures into the delicate crust that is my blankets.

It takes me a full half an hour to persuade myself to heed the demands of my bladder and stomach, and I do so wrapped in one of the blankets, cursing as my feet hit the tile floor. Maneuvering a bathroom experience in my state gives me a new respect for women in the ages of massive skirts. They are the real MVPs.

While I'm up, I heat some water and glance at Rémy's door as I wait for the kettle, trying to remember how everything played out last night.

I don't think the lines are doing as much for me as I hoped they would.

My skin prickles as I remember those words. I wanted to kiss him so badly right then. And about a hundred other times throughout the day. I could see how hard he was trying, though, so I stuffed little temptress Madi back into her box and matched his efforts with my own. And pretty soon, warmth and contentment put me to sleep.

Rémy still hasn't emerged by the time I've finished my hot

chocolate. He's never slept this late, which makes me worry that having my dead weight on him kept him up last night.

I'm anxious for him to wake up, to get the day started and see what it holds. I'm counting on something warmer than yesterday. Preferably with less body odor.

My pulse quickens at the memory of taking refuge in Rémy's cologne and having his face nestled next to my ear.

Friends don't fantasize about friends, Madi.

I wake my phone, which displays a few different notifications. One is Siena requesting a daily update, the other tells me I have photo memories waiting. I'm a sucker for these ridiculous methods apps find to make you open them when you otherwise wouldn't, so I tap on it.

The photo is from two years ago. It's Josh and me on our first real date—his work Christmas party. I'm all dolled up in an ice blue dress, while Josh is wearing a slim, gray suit. His arm is around my waist, and he's pulling me close and smiling big.

It's weird to see it. Like a vestige of a different life. Not that my relationship with Josh was so long ago, but *this* phase of it— the exciting part, before he kind of stopped trying—was brand new. He had just told me he wanted to date me the night before, and I had rushed around all morning to find a dress for the party.

I stare at my face in the photo, so happy and full of hope. Little did I know, two years later, everything would have fizzled out, like room temperature, day-old soda.

My thumb hovers over the trash icon, but I have a phobia of deleting photos. It's punishable under International Photographer Statute 11.542.43, which is something I just made up but feels real.

Rémy's door opens, and I turn off my phone screen, eager to leave those kill-joy thoughts behind. But Rémy's mood seems a little low, too, as we talk. I'm hoping I can help him feel better throughout the day, wherever we end up going.

"Any thoughts on where to go today? Should we scope out Montmartre?"

Rémy glances at me as he grabs two eggs from the fridge. "Um, maybe I can meet you there for a half hour or something. I need to make up some sample lesson plans to give to Monsieur Garnier—he's the one in charge at Bellevue—and I have an errand to run for my mom's Christmas Eve dinner."

"Oh! That's great about the lesson plans." I can't very well plan Rémy's English lessons for him, but it doesn't escape me that he isn't inviting me to run the errand with him. "We could go later. Around dinner?"

He shuts the fridge door and looks at me, apology in his eyes. "Actually, I have plans with friends tonight."

"Oh!" Why is my voice so high? I sound like I'm auditioning for the part of Mickey Mouse. "That sounds great. No worries. I can scope things out on my own. You've trained me up well." I laugh, and it sounds every bit as unnatural as my Mickey voice.

Rémy looks a little hesitant. "I think it's for the best. And you'll do just fine." The ghost of a smile touches the corner of his mouth. "If you need the help number for Paris Syndrome, I can give it to you."

"There's a *help number*?" I gladly latch onto that part because inside I'm feeling the tiniest bit sick to my stomach, and I don't want him to know that.

"So I've heard."

I opt to leave sooner than later to Montmartre because I'm afraid if I stick around, I'm going to say or do something stupid—like ask Rémy why he needs friends or plans that don't involve me.

I make it successfully to Sacré Coeur and Montmartre—a definite personal victory part of me wishes I could rub in Josh's face. The views of the city are beautiful from the basilica, and I can pinpoint a number of monuments and sites we saw on our Antarctic river cruise last night. It feels like I'm getting to know the city, finding my bearings, and I love that feeling. But I wish Rémy was here to share in it with me.

I wander around the streets, taking pictures of places that would be a good fit for the photo session. There are plenty of locations I'm just itching to shoot with a beautiful couple in front of my lens.

I grab a bite to eat at a little cafe not far from Place du Tertre. As I sit on the heater-warmed terrace, I fluctuate between feeling proud, independent, and Wonder Womany for eating lunch by myself, and staving off a bit of loneliness that's trying to creep in.

Distraction arrives in the form of a street performer using sticks, ropes, and dish soap to make bubbles for the children passing by. The joy on their faces is indescribable as they jump and chase them, so I do the only thing I know how to do when that happens: pull out my camera to snap a few shots.

But mostly I just watch as the bubbles sail through the air, perfect blobs of iridescence, floating off until they inevitably pop. It's kind of how I feel. This time right now in Paris with Rémy is my bubble. It's beautiful, it's magical, it defies gravity. But inevitably, it will pop, leaving me splattered with dish soap.

When my phone buzzes around two and I see Rémy's name on my screen, my heart does a little hopeful dance. Hoping for what? I'm not sure.

Rémy: The radiators are working again, so you are safe to come back whenever.

I read the message a couple of times. Is there an implied wish for me to come home in that text, or am I reading into things?

Madi: Hallelujah! Have a good time tonight *smiley face emoji*

When I get back to the apartment around 5, it's already dark. I stare at the elevator button for a few seconds, deciding whether I'm feeling brave enough to go it alone. But on top of the idea of it breaking while I'm inside by myself, the thought of trying to communicate with the elevator technician is enough to scare me away. I head up the stairs instead.

As I turn the key in the lock, I hear the muffled sound of keys jingling on the other side of the door. It opens, and Rémy's there. When I saw him this morning, he was still wearing what he wore to bed. Now he's got on dark jeans, a white t-shirt, and a leather jacket. It's a killer ensemble, and suddenly I'm assaulted by questions about exactly *who* these friends are. And was it *friends* plural?

"Hey," he says with a little smile.

"Hey," I say, still standing in the doorway. I have the strongest desire to hug him; this was the longest I've gone without seeing him since we met, and I'm about to not see him all night. "On your way out?"

He nods. "Did you have a good day?"

"Yeah." It doesn't sound as convincing as I had hoped. I *did* have a good day, though. On paper, it looks a lot better than yesterday. But it wasn't. "I found some really pretty locations for the photoshoot."

"I bet you did. You've got the eye for it."

"Well, it's not hard in Paris."

There's a short silence.

Rémy fiddles with the keys he's holding. "Will you be going back out?"

I wrinkle my nose. "I think I'll just stay in and watch a movie or something. Go to bed early." I hadn't really planned on that, but suddenly it's how I'm feeling. It sounds a little pathetic, I realize, and I can see in Rémy's expression that he's not sure what to think of it. "I love movies," I say like it's some odd quirk I have that he should be aware of.

"Just don't watch *New Moon* without me."

I smile big, happy he even remembers the name. "I'll try, but I can't make any promises."

I wish Rémy a good night, and he shuts the door behind him.

I look around the empty apartment, coaching myself to look at it as a cool, freedom thing rather than a slightly depressing thing. I probably should have thought far enough ahead to bring home some dinner for myself, but I kind of hurried back, hoping to see Rémy before he left.

I know. I'm pathetic. And I'm going to embrace that tonight. I finished the last of my Camembert this morning, but the orange cheese I bought when I first arrived is still sitting in the fridge, calling out to me in a strong American accent, "Eat me!"

I wrinkle my nose. Orange as a cheese color *does* feel a bit suspect now, but hey, beggars can't be choosers.

I head to the kitchen and crouch down to open the small fridge. There's a new Camembert sitting on the top shelf. The yellow sticky note on top says, "For Madi." I smile, feeling a bit better about my night. We might not have spent the day together, but he *did* think of me during it.

Standing up straight, I look around until I spot it: a baguette. Rémy would never buy me cheese without a fresh baguette to pair it with. It's still in the brown bakery paper, and there's another sticky note on top. "Supposedly the best baguette in Paris."

I do my best cutting it, but I'm not blessed with Rémy's biceps *or* a lifetime of practicing exactly how thick to cut the slices, so it's not pretty. It'll do, though.

Armed with my plate of bread and cheese, I head over to the couch and start flipping through Netflix, trying to decide what movie will pair best with my bread, cheese, and mood.

My phone vibrates on the coffee table, and I grab it, hoping for a particular name and notification. But it's Siena.

Siena: Looking at the evidence, you clearly made the right decision, Mads.

Madi: Wait, what are you talking about?

Siena: Oh.
Siena: Thought you'd have seen it already.

She sends me an Instagram link, and I click on it with a little foreboding in my stomach since I can see Brianne's handle on the preview. The foreboding turns into something sick and hollow as my gaze settles on the picture.

It's Josh and Brianne. Well, it's them and others, but they're right next to each other. He's wearing his usual business attire, while she's got on a slinky red dress with a generous sprinkling of sexy shoulders and a dash of cleavage. They're. . . cozy. It looks like they're at some swanky work party. And in the background? A view of the Eiffel Tower and the city through tall glass windows.

I stare at it. And then I stare some more. It's so weird that Josh and I are in the same city right now but not together. Last year, I really thought he'd invite me to come along on his business trip here—enough that I made a spreadsheet of places I wanted to go together, complete with prices and opening times. He never asked me, never acknowledged the hints.

I suspect he wasn't planning on asking me this year, either, until I started telling him I didn't know if we should stay together anymore. He begged me not to give up on us, dangling Paris in front of me, complete with an implied proposal. It was everything I had wanted the year before, so of course I said I'd come.

That was how things with Josh had gotten. We'd gone from that starry-eyed couple in the picture that came up in my photo memories this morning to the one where the only way he would show some commitment was the moment he sensed me teetering. He's great at big promises, but the delivery never really lived up to them. He couldn't even make it to the Eiffel Tower with me—not even to walk somewhere close enough to just see it from afar. But there he is with Brianne.

I tap away from the picture, hoping it'll rid me of the tingling at the back of my eyes. It's not even jealousy. It's that I put up with being such a low priority for him for so long.

I scroll through photo after photo to distract myself. It's just a few days before Christmas, which means most of the posts I see are of people at work parties, family parties, ugly sweater parties. All the holiday parties.

And then it hits me. Christmas is in just a few days. And I'll be here. On Christmas. Alone. I've had a couple of rough Christmases—the one when we had no presents right after my dad died being at the top of that list—but at least then I had my family. Here, I have no one. Rémy's going to be at his mom's house for Christmas Eve dinner and sleep there, I assume, because that's what normal people do on Christmas. They spend it with their families, not thousands of miles away in a foreign country by themselves after they just broke up with their boyfriend.

The beginnings of panic—or maybe it's homesickness—start to creep into my stomach. My mom is on a cruise, so there's no reaching her. I shoot a text to my brother, Jack. Dire straits, people.

Madi: Greetings, big bro. Remind me where you are again?

He's a busy guy, so I don't expect to hear from him for 10-12 business days, but I happen to be wrong tonight.

Jack: I'm in Aspen with Paul's family. They invited me to spend Christmas with them. I've been wondering how you were doing over there. How's Paris? Is this THE TEXT?

I sigh.

Madi: If by THE TEXT you mean the text informing you that Josh and I broke up, then yes. Consider yourself informed.

The three dots appear, disappear, reappear, disappear. It's really awkward for people to express sympathy for a relationship they never really wanted to work out. I get it.

Madi: You don't have to pretend to be crushed, Jack.

Jack: *thankful hands emoji x 5* Are you flying home, then?

Staying with the Sheppards for Christmas? Tell Siena I say hi.
wink face emoji

Madi: You're so not funny. I'll break you. But I haven't decided my plans yet.
Madi: PS Merry Christmas and I love you

Jack: Merry Christmas. Love you more.

I click out of my texts and stare blankly at my phone. Suddenly, this whole thing feels stupid. So. Stupid. I came to Paris to get a job and get engaged. Spending Christmas with my new fiancé in the City of Love sounded like the best thing in the world a couple weeks ago.

Well, I'm in Paris now with no job and no fiancé. All I'm doing here is skirting the line between friendship and . . . what? I don't even know. Nothing can happen with Rémy.

This game we're playing is for people with hearts less weathered than mine. If I'm trying to convince myself that I'm successfully staying on the side of friendship with him, I'm only fooling myself. And I've been the fool enough recently to last me a lifetime.

So why am I still here?

THIRTY-SEVEN

RÉMY

"RÉMY. RÉMY."

I blink, and four people, all looking at me, come into focus.

"You still with us?" Guillaume asks, waving a hand in front of my face to check my awareness.

"Yeah, sorry." For someone who spends a lot of my time trying to redirect young, wandering brains to the present, my more seasoned brain is frustratingly similar. I refocus it on the conversation.

The bar we're at is a mishmash of smells: cigarettes, marijuana, alcohol, and the sweet scent of vape pens. It's not my favorite environment, but when I texted Guillaume to see if he wanted to hang out, he already had plans to come here. We went to university together, but it's been a while since I've seen him. He teaches at a lycée in Lille, but he's visiting his parents during the holiday break. I was desperate enough for something to do that I actually took him up on what was probably just a polite invitation to join him and his friends.

One of those friends, Marion, has her eye on me across the table. It's been like that since I arrived. She's nice and everything, but, not only am I not interested, I'm terrible company tonight.

287

I've had Madi on my mind all day, which is frustrating since I've made a point of keeping busy to avoid that.

For some reason, along with Madi have come thoughts of my dad. Maybe it's the prospect of her leaving—and back to the U.S., no less—that's rustling up old baggage. Sure, I could leave it zipped and contained all neatly, but instead I pull out my phone and start unzipping. I don't even bother with the usual hellos or polite chitchat.

Rémy: Why don't we ever talk?

I set my phone aside and try to pretend I'm not impatient or curious about what's spilling out of the baggage I just opened. Guillaume is talking about politics, though, and since I missed the first part of the conversation, I don't even attempt to chime in.

My phone lights up, but instead of the text I was expecting, it's a call. I stand up and excuse myself, my heart thrumming.

"Hey, Dad," I say as I make my way out of the bar to where it's not so loud.

"Rémy," he says, and I can hear in his voice that this contact was unexpected. I don't blame him. We're not really in the habit of deep talk. Or much talk at all. "How are you?"

"I'm . . ." I press my lips together. I don't even know how I am, and I definitely don't feel like my dad and I are in a place where I could freely explain that, even if I *could* verbalize it.

"Right," he says, apparently understanding that it's complicated. "Listen, I got your message, and I . . . well, I thought it might be easier to talk than text."

I nod as though he can see me.

There's silence for a few more seconds, but it's not because he's waiting for me to answer. I can hear him clicking a pen in the background. I had forgotten that sound, but it's one that takes me back to my childhood—a nervous habit of his.

"To answer your question"—he sighs— "I guess we don't talk much mostly because I didn't know you *wanted* to talk more."

I'm still quiet because *what*? "You're my dad."

"Believe me, I know that. I think about it all the time, Rémy. More than you realize. But both of us know your mom doesn't particularly welcome my influence in your life."

I don't respond because he's right. Whenever he comes up in conversation, she gets this look on her face—it's the same one she gets when we talk about my career teaching English. She won't outright say what she's thinking, but her opinion comes through loud and clear in the way she talks about Americans and in the way she refuses to speak English at all.

"Anyway," he continues, "I guess I got it into my head that you felt the same way as she does. So I've tried to let you set the pace and depth of our relationship."

"How could you think that I feel the same way?"

If you look back at my text conversations with my dad, I'm always the first one to text. I feel like I've spent my whole life trying to impress him, trying to do things that would make him more interested in me, more proud of me.

"Do you remember when I left, Rémy?"

"Yes." I couldn't forget that day if I tried. And I've tried hard. I held out hope until the very end that he'd change his mind and stay. He didn't.

"I told you what time I would be leaving so we could say goodbye after you were done at school for the day. And I waited —almost missed my flight because of it—but you didn't come."

I swallow, memories from all those years ago flooding me. "I said goodbye to you every other week for most of my life, Dad. That was hard enough. I didn't want to say goodbye again, this time for real. I was young and mad and hurt. I thought you were leaving because—" I can't even say it. I breathe deeply, trying to rein in my emotions, but they're chasing me like a swarm of bees whose hive I just knocked down. "Why do you think I've focused so hard on English all my life, Dad? I just wanted you to be proud of me, to"—I lift my shoulders—"notice me."

He clears his throat, and I could swear I hear a sniffle. "I *have*,

Rémy. I couldn't be more proud of you. Ask anyone who works with me. I talk about you all the time. I check your school's website for news on you and your students every week. I printed out a picture of you holding that award you got last month. The one where you're standing with your students? It's sitting right next to my desk. Right here."

I'm silent. I had no idea. And it makes no sense. Why is he going on the lycée website and cyberstalking his own son when he could text me? Call me? "Why haven't you said anything? Why not just ask *me*?"

"I'm not there, Rémy. And I haven't *been* there. In a lot of ways, it feels like I don't have a right to know what's happening in your life." He sighs. "But I probably should have told you. I shouldn't have assumed you knew I wanted to be in your life more. I'm your dad, Rémy. Of course I want to be in your life." The pen clicks more. "I just worry that encouraging you in your teaching and in your English will hurt your mother, that she'll feel I'm trying to . . . I don't know, drive a wedge between the two of you."

We're both quiet because, once again, I can see why he would think that. It's a distinct possibility.

He continues. "I haven't handled all of this well, as you see. The point is, I *do* want to talk to you more, Rémy. I've thought a hundred times about coming there or flying you here. But I should have told you that myself, and that's on me."

My voice is shaking like it's trying to set a record on the Richter scale. "It's not just on you, Dad. It's on both of us."

We sit in silence for a few seconds, and I watch my breath come out in a puff, then disperse and disappear.

"Well," he finally says, "tonight is as good a night as any to change things. So . . ." I hear the muffled squeaking of a chair, like he's getting comfortable. "Why don't you tell me about life, son?"

I clear my throat. "Aren't you at work right now?"

"It can wait."

THIRTY-EIGHT

RÉMY

Pure adrenaline takes me up the flights of stairs at André's apartment building, but adrenaline cannot make up for the fact that my lungs are not used to this type of exercise. I rest a hand against the door frame for a second before pulling out the keys.

If Marion had any shred of interest left in me before I took the call from my dad, it was shot to heck when I came back only to inform the group that I was leaving. But I had to.

Talking to my dad made it clear how much regret both of us had. So many years where both of us wanted more but felt *un*wanted. All of it could have been solved with some honesty, some vulnerability. And I don't want any more unnecessary regret like that.

I unlock the door and open it, not even sure yet what exactly I'm going to say to Madi. I just think it's best if we can be clear with each other. I should have been more upfront with her about why I chose to spend the day away from her instead of letting her draw her own conclusions. Once she knows how I feel, if she prefers, I'll go and stay at my mom's. I just want to be forthcoming.

She's sitting on the couch, her cell phone to her ear, but the

TV is on. She obviously heard the key in the lock, so she's already looking at me. It's only seven-thirty, so I'm sure she's surprised to see me home so early.

I close the door quietly, not wanting to disturb her call. For some reason, my heart feels a little sick, wondering if this is Josh calling her, begging her to take him back. He seems like the sort of guy to mess up bigtime and try to patch things up later. And probably succeed, honestly.

"You don't have to be quiet," Madi says. "I'm on hold."

"Oh." I walk over and glance at the TV, where I recognize Cameron Diaz and Jude Law on the screen. It's not a movie I've seen, but I can already tell it's a romance based on the pregnant pause while they look at one another. I look to Madi, and my brows pull together. She looks . . . different.

And then it hits me. Her eyes are a little puffy underneath. Her cheeks are red.

"Are you okay?"

"Yeah, yeah," she says. "Just been on hold forever."

"On hold with whom?"

She smiles. "*With whom*. You speak way better English than me." Her eyes narrow. "Than I?"

"Both are accepted," I say with an attempt at a smile. Why do I feel like she's avoiding my question? I sit down on the couch, my gaze still on her. "Are you really okay, though?"

Her smile weakens, and the way she draws in a breath has me preparing myself.

"I'm going home," she says. "Changing my flight."

My stomach ties into a thousand pretzels. "When?"

She sighs, her shoulders slumping. "Tomorrow maybe? Or never, I guess, if I can't get a hold of the airline."

"How long have you been waiting?"

She takes the phone from her ear, showing me the screen. Seventy-one minutes.

I chew my lip for a minute, trying to ignore the aching in my chest and focus on Madi—what got her to this point. "You could set it down and put it on speaker, you know."

"I have been." She puts it on speaker and sets it down on the coffee table with a smile that rips my heart out. "The hold music changed right before you came in, and I thought it was someone answering."

I nod, and the upbeat hold music feels gratingly dissonant with the mood in the room. "What made you decide to change your flight?" Those words are dead words. They don't mean anything. I can't comprehend that Madi might be leaving tomorrow. That she's choosing to leave tomorrow.

She lifts her shoulders. "I dunno. A lot of things."

"Things you want to talk about?" I want to understand this. I *need* to understand it. But I'm not going to press Madi if she doesn't want to talk.

"I think the day just started off weird. There was this photo memory from when Josh and I started dating two years ago, and that was . . . well, it was just not the way I wanted to begin the day. And then later, Siena told me his coworker posted a photo of them, and I've always kind of felt weird about her and her intentions. And then I saw all the pictures of people at their Christmas parties with their families and friends, and then you were with *your* friends— which is great, really, I'm not saying that to make you feel bad at all. But I *love* Christmas, and I guess I hadn't really thought about how it will be to spend it alone in a foreign country. I feel awful canceling the photoshoots, but I just don't think I can stay. Maybe I've been in denial or something, but I'm just feeling things more tonight."

Feeling things more. Things about Josh, it sounds like.

Any thought I had of telling her what I came to talk to her about disintegrates faster than cotton candy in front of a fire hose. She's got enough to process as is. Saddling her with my overeager feelings for her would be selfish.

"You've had a lot to deal with since coming here," I say. "And this apartment has only added to that."

She shakes her head. "It's not about that at all. Trust me. Staying here has been the best part of all of this. You've been *so* good to me, Rémy. So good. Which, by the way, if you wanted any of that baguette you bought . . ." She clenches her teeth.

I raise my brows. "You ate the entire thing?"

She rolls her lips between her teeth, looking at me guiltily. "I'm not proud of it, okay?"

"No, I'm not judging. I'm . . . impressed. And really glad you liked it."

"I did," she says, her expression turning almost pathetic. "So so much. But I feel so so sick."

I laugh, and the hold music changes, making our ears perk up for a second. But it's just a new song.

Madi sighs and leans against the back of the couch. I wish I had a better sense for how much of what she's feeling is centered around Josh. She said she thinks she's been in denial or something. Is she regretting the breakup?

Just the thought makes me ill—not just because I'm selfish enough to want Madi to want *me*, but also because I genuinely want her to be happy, and I don't trust Josh to make that happen.

"I didn't expect to see you until a lot later," she says. "Did you have a good time?"

I think for a minute before responding. I don't really know how to describe the evening.

"Yeah. I mean, it didn't start out great, but . . ." I fiddle with the button on my coat. "I actually talked to my dad."

Her eyes light up. "Really? And?"

"It was good. I just wish it had happened a long time ago." I meet her eyes. "Thanks for pushing me to do it." We finally talked. *Really* talked. He asked me about my job, about my mom, about dating, which included a short discussion about Madi. It's not like it fixed the years of surface-level contact we've had, but it feels like a good start.

She smiles at me, and there's a tinge of bittersweet in it. "I can't imagine anyone not wanting to know you better."

Except you. You're leaving.

The music softens briefly. "Your expected hold time is"—the voice shifts to become more robot-like—"two hundred minutes."

Madi's eyes widen. "What?! No! How is that possible? The last time it said thirty!"

I grimace my sympathy. "Maybe you should try in the morning. The time of day can make a big difference." Am I saying that partially because I hope maybe she'll have rethought things by then?

No comment.

She lets out a huge sigh that sounds like it's about a lot more than just the hold time—like maybe it's about her entire day, or this entire trip. I know it's not my fault she and Josh broke up or that he didn't come through on the whole job thing, but somehow I feel responsible for the fact that Madi's looking like a deflated balloon. A really beautiful one, but still . . .

"Yeah," she says, her voice more tired than I'm used to hearing. "You're probably right. I'll set my alarm for early and see if I have any luck then." She grabs the remote and proceeds to rewind the movie. I had figured she would go to sleep, but apparently not.

She rewinds it all the way until the beginning, then glances at me. "I wasn't really watching before, and *The Holiday* deserves my full attention."

I hesitate for a second and then, even though it makes my stomach clench with nerves, I say, "Care for some company?"

There's a bit of hesitation in her eyes that makes me immediately regret asking. Whatever happened today, it changed something for her. For us. She wants to watch this movie by herself.

My stomach feels sicker than ever. "You know, I should probably get to bed anyw—"

"I'd love some company," she says at the same time.

There's an awkward moment where we both pause, then laugh. And because I want to believe she wants my company, I take a seat on the couch. She's got the blanket from last night on her lap, but she doesn't offer it to me, and I don't ask to share it.

I watch the movie—it's about two women down on their luck in love who swap houses for the holidays. I don't know how much thought went into choosing this movie for Madi, but I'd be lying if I said I didn't see some of Madi and me in Cameron Diaz and Jude Law. That's how gone I am over Madi.

And all I can think as we watch together is how this might be the last night I have with her.

THIRTY-NINE

RÉMY

Spoiler alert: I didn't sleep well. Between the talk with my dad and Madi's sudden decision to leave, my brain is in overdrive. Even when I do fall asleep, it's the kind of sleep that leaves you feeling even more tired than before. It's been hours when I realize how hot I am, too. I forgot to adjust the radiator dial back to its usual position once the boiler was fixed.

My real downfall, though, is checking my phone at one point and seeing that it's 5:30—a great time to be up for the day, apparently. Madi said she'd be getting up early to try calling the airline again, and my brain assures me this task requires my attendance as well.

Only, she's not even awake yet. Too frustrated to try to sleep anymore, I head to the kitchen to make the earliest breakfast any human on Christmas break has ever eaten.

I've got a lot of nervous energy, like I had too much caffeine, except that I didn't have *any*. I direct my fidgets into making a more elaborate breakfast than usual. A ham and cheese omelet, berries and cream, and hot chocolate—with extra chocolate powder.

Madi makes an appearance just as I'm finishing the omelet, the hold music alerting me to her approach.

Gut punch. It's safe to say she didn't change her mind.

"Only a fifteen-minute wait," she says.

I smile even though I want to sabotage the phones at the call center. I hadn't realized how diabolical I was until this exact moment, but my TV villain impulses are apparently all talk, because I settle for offering Madi some breakfast instead.

"You're up early," she comments as I serve her half of the omelet.

"Yeah. I"—*thought about you for the past eight hours*—"was too hot to sleep." Partially true.

She's eaten about half of her omelet when an agent with an incredibly thick French accent picks up. The woman asks Madi a question, and Madi's expression turns into one I know all too well. I see it on my students' faces on the first day of class when I start speaking to them exclusively in English. It is utter bafflement. Complete lack of comprehension.

Madi asks the woman to repeat herself, but ultimately, I have to step in and explain that the woman just needs Madi's name. Next she wants Madi's booking number, and as Madi repeats it back to her, I already know it's going to be an ordeal. The woman is parroting it back, but she's almost unintelligible. The only reason I can understand her is because of the practice I've had with my students' attempts at speaking English.

Ten minutes later, I find myself pacing the front room, speaking French with Jacqueline from the airline, which is definitely a more efficient option than whatever botched communication was happening between her and Madi. I've turned into an interpreting service, explaining the situation to her and relaying her responses to Madi, who's standing still and watching me intently as she waits for me to feed her hope.

Enter Villain Rémy from stage left, whispering in my ear. I could tell Madi there are zero flights departing from France between now and the New Year, and she would never know the truth.

Okay, that might be a hard sell. But I do have some power here.

I shove the villain back where he came from and listen to what Jacqueline is saying about changing the flight. I glance at Madi, feeling a bit sick on her behalf.

"There's a 250 euro fee to change your flight," I say. Madi's hurting for money, and that fee is a pretty penny.

She nods, her jaw setting determinedly. "I'm gonna pay Siena back for it."

Siena's a good friend, but I kind of wish she hadn't offered to do that. I get that Madi being *forced* to stay here isn't exactly what I want. I want her to *want* to stay, but I guess part of me is hoping that, in time, she'll change her mind.

But I do my job, conveying the information that Madi is aware of the change fee. I hate that I'm the one arranging for her to leave when I really really really want her to stay.

Jacqueline asks what date Madi wants to fly out.

I stop my pacing and ask Madi the question, even though she answered it last night. Better to check.

Madi looks at me for a second, her eyes scanning my face, like maybe the answer is there. "Today?"

Curse words.

She keeps her eyes on me, biting the edge of her lip. "Or maybe tomorrow would be better?"

I hold her gaze, trying to understand whether it's my imagination or if she's waffling a little bit now that the moment to change her flight is here.

I keep my gaze locked on her as I ask Jacqueline to look at tomorrow's flights, trying to communicate telepathically to Madi that it's okay if she doesn't go. No. Not just okay. I don't *want* her to go.

She knows that, right? I mean, I've spent pretty much every possible waking moment with her. Some non-waking moments, too. And there's no way in heck she hasn't noticed me checking her out. Or that I kissed her like she was the only thing keeping me alive.

But I could swear there's a question in her eyes as she looks at me. And yeah, maybe it's just because I want her to ask me that question, but I can't help but think of my conversation with my dad last night. How quickly things changed with a bit of honesty.

"*Monsieur?*"

I blink, realizing Jacqueline is waiting for a response from me, for some sign of life on the other end of the line.

My gaze never leaves Madi's as I ask Jacqueline to hold, my heart thrumming in my ears. I bring the phone down, and Madi's brow furrows a bit.

"Everything okay?" she asks.

"No. I mean, yeah. I mean . . ." I suck in a huge breath. "Madi, I don't want you to leave."

FORTY

MADI

THEY SAY BREATHING IS SOMETHING YOUR BODY DOES on its own. If that's true, my body is the worst. Essential respiratory processes are down for maintenance.

I don't want you to leave. Those words. They have me feeling . . . a lot.

Rémy runs his teeth over his lower lip—*line*, my brain squeaks in weak protest—his eyes on me, just like they have been for the past minute and more. "And I don't want you to get back together with Josh."

At that comment, something inside me gives, and I manage to get out a single, raspy, "What?" There's no way I haven't misunderstood what Rémy's saying. Does he think I'm going home to beg Josh to take me back? "I'm not going home to get back together with Josh, Rémy."

"Then why?" he asks. "Is it because you don't want to be alone for Christmas? Because if that's it, you *won't* be, Madi. I'll be here." There's a pause. "If you want me here." He rubs his head like he's frustrated with himself and can't get things out the way he wants. "Look, I know it sounds crazy—we've only known each other a little over a week, and I have no idea what's going to happen. I just know I don't want you to go. For whatever that's worth. I needed you to know."

This isn't real. This is what happens when you watch *The Holiday* until your eyes won't stay open. Your brain starts making up scenarios that only happen in chick flicks.

I take a step closer to Rémy, noting the morning stubble on his jaw and the tiny movements of his eyes as he looks at me, waiting for me to say something.

"But . . . you left yesterday," I say. "You said it was . . .best. I thought . . ." Those half-baked phrases are an accurate reflection of my brain function right now.

"I left because I knew I couldn't stay within the lines if I spent the day with you again. I don't know how to keep things light between us, Madi. I don't know how to be just friends with you. I just"—he lifts his shoulders—"I want more. I thought maybe some distance would change that, I guess. But it didn't. I spent the whole day thinking about you, and I came home early last night because I wanted to be with you. Because I had to know if it's just me who feels this way."

My heart is playing a raging game of pinball in my chest. Rémy wants me to stay. He doesn't want lines. He doesn't want to be just friends.

He's watching me, his brow creased as his eyes search my face. His Adam's apple bobs. "*Is* it? Is it just me?"

Everything is moving so fast inside me. My breathing has caught up to my heart, and my thoughts are all over the place. But slowly, I shake my head twice.

Rémy's gaze intensifies as we stare at each other, the implication of my response settling over us.

And then we're kissing, his hands on my hips, mine clasped behind his neck, our lips locked together. It's full of pent-up want, of palpable relief, and the mixture of the two is the best thing I've ever tasted. It's been a long time since I kissed anyone like this, and by a long time, I mean my entire life. I was made to kiss Rémy Scott, and by the way he's holding me, the way his lips are coming back for more, again and again, it feels like he was made to kiss me, too.

His hands slide up from my hips, and my hips miss them, but my back is more than ready for their hold, like it's been waiting for its turn.

"*Monsieur*?!" Jacqueline's annoyed, muffled voice comes through the speaker, which is pressed against my back now as Rémy holds me close.

We break apart like she's in the room with us.

Rémy looks at me, and a guilty smile tugs at his lip. "Whoops."

I shake my head. "Not whoops."

Rémy smiles. "So . . . what do I tell Jacqueline?"

I rub my lips together, holding his gaze. "Tell her I'm keeping my two hundred and fifty euros. Or Siena is. Whatever. We don't want the flight." I pause. "Right?" If I misread this situation and we hang up on her only to call back in five minutes and wait on hold again, I will be incredibly embarrassed and more than a little annoyed.

Rémy looks at me for a second, then puts his hand to my cheek and comes in for another kiss, this one soft and slow. Then he pulls back just enough to put his lips out of reach. "Right."

I take in a shaky breath. My body doesn't know how to function in such prolonged proximity to Rémy. And yet, it refuses to move, so I guess I'll just try to learn how to breathe again. Seems easier than leaving his arms.

He brings the phone back to his ear, holding me against him as he speaks to Jacqueline. As always, I'm starstruck listening to his smooth French, trying to pick out familiar words and smiling a bit every time I find success. But mostly, I'm relishing the feel of being held by him.

He sets the phone down and tucks my hair behind my ear. "You are officially the happy owner of the same flight you had before you spent hours on hold. And, not to hold you hostage or anything, but Jacqueline says it's for the best that you changed your mind since you'd have to pay the difference between your fare and the current fare *on top* of the two hundred and fifty euro change fee. Given that it's only a couple days before Christmas, that fare difference is close to fifteen hundred dollars."

"Fifteen hundred dollars?!"

He nods, a rueful smile on his face. "For the cheapest option —three layovers." His expression grows softer. "You sure you're okay with this?"

I look him in the eye. "Are *you*?"

His eyebrows rise. "Okay with getting another eleven days with you?"

I lick my lips nervously. Eleven days with Rémy sounds like heaven. "It's what happens *after* the eleven days that I'm worried about."

His expression gets more serious. "Yeah, of course. Look, I don't know what's going to happen, Madi. I just . . . if you went home and we had spent all our time together trying to be just friends when it's not what I want, I'd always wonder."

"Me too."

The corner of his lip tips up like he's happy to hear me agree with him. "I know nothing's changed. You just got out of a relationship, and I'm not trying to rush you into anything before you're ready."

"I don't feel rushed."

His brow pulls together a little. "But you've still got feelings for Josh to work through. Which is fine—and totally normal."

I shake my head. "I probably seem heartless to you, but . . ." I press my lips together, trying to think how to explain this to him. "Remember when you said I was a creature of habit?"

He nods.

"I am. Absolutely. And my relationship with Josh was a lot like that." I clench my eyes shut and shake my head. "Ugh, that sounds bad. I care about Josh, and I want him to be happy. And maybe I'm wrong. Maybe it's all gonna hit me suddenly, but . . . I've been going through the motions for a long time. My family and friends never really liked Josh, even in the days where he hadn't given them reason not to—from my perspective, at least—so I've always been defensive about the relationship. That just became so ingrained in me that it took me a long time to see that I was defending things I didn't need or even want to defend. So me being sad about the photo memory this morning or about the picture of him and Brianne . . . that's my frustration that it took so long for me to figure things out."

Rémy looks down and grabs my hand, rubbing his thumb along it. "Okay, as long as you know you can tell me if you change your mind." He looks up at me. "I really like you, Madi. *Really*. I'd be lying if I said I wasn't nervous about how things will play out—nervous about getting hurt or causing hurt. But it's a risk I want to take because . . . you're worth it."

There goes my breathing again. Rémy's saying everything I'm thinking. Maybe we'll figure out that this has all been an exciting but short-lived romance—like those bubbles at Montmartre. Beautiful and captivating, but not made to last.

Or maybe, just maybe, this is the start of something more.

SIENA'S still asleep when I text her to update her on the fact that I'm *not* coming home after all. Rémy invited me to Christmas Eve dinner—they call it *le Réveillon*—at his mom's house, which simultaneously makes me feel like a million bucks and like I might throw up from sheer nerves.

When Siena responds, I'm lying on the couch next to Rémy, watching *New Moon*. Okay, "watching" might be a generous term, but what woman wants to watch Taylor Lautner hold Kristen Stewart when she's got Rémy Scott on offer?

Siena: Wait, what?
Siena: Explain yourself, missy.

But she doesn't give me the opportunity. She video calls me because Siena has the patience of a two-year-old.

Rémy and I sit up, hoping to give the impression of respectable behavior, but Siena sees right past it within seconds, immediately accusing us of making out instead of texting her back.

Her enthusiasm for the turn of events makes me look at Rémy to check whether she's driving him away with how gung-ho she is, but he just wraps his arm around me like he's happy he doesn't have to pretend we are just host and guest watching a movie together, and then he kisses me on the cheek. Kissing Rémy on the lips is a whole-body experience, but being kissed by him on the cheek is a whole-heart experience, and I melt right into him.

How is he so perfect? How does he make me feel so valued with everything he does?

When we get off the call with Siena, I've got a text waiting for me.

Josh: Hey, Madi. How are you?

I glance at Rémy, and he raises his brows. "What?"
"It's Josh."
"Oh."
I wish I knew what he was thinking. I don't know why Josh is texting me—maybe to him, "space" is a couple of days. Either way, I feel in no hurry to respond. *If* I decide to respond.

I turn off my screen, but it lights up right after with another notification.

Josh: Can you send me the link to the pictures you took of our holiday essential oils line?

I sigh—mostly with relief, but there's a little disappointment mixed in there. Not because I want anything from Josh but because it's so par for the course. He needs something from me. That's why he's texting.

"Classic," I say, showing it to Rémy.

He gives something between a smile and a grimace. "Maybe you shouldn't take such amazing photos."

I chuckle, navigate to the app I use to deliver clients their photos, and copy the gallery link.

Madi: Sure thing. Here you go.

I paste the link in and hit send.

He's already typing back before I can turn off the screen. It's weird texting with Josh. What's weirder is how I'm not feeling much about it.

Josh: Thanks. You're the best. I hope you're doing well. *heart emoji*

Madi: Hope you're doing well too

I leave off any punctuation because an exclamation point seems overeager but a period is just as weird. I turn off my phone and set it on the table, grabbing Rémy by the hand and pulling him back down onto the couch. But instead of picking up where we left off, I thread my fingers through his and look into his eyes.

"Siena is obsessed with you."

"Is she?"

I nod.

"I couldn't tell if she just has the type of personality to make everyone feel special."

"Um, no," I say with a laugh. "She speaks her mind, for better or for worse. But she's been Team Rémy from the beginning."

The corner of his mouth pulls up in a smile. "Really?"

"Dyed in the wool."

He looks a little too pleased with himself. "I'm happy to hear that. But there's really only one person I need on Team Rémy."

I pull his face toward me. "I'm not only on that team, I'm coach, captain, and cheerleader."

He brushes my lips with his, and I'm glad we're lying down because it means it's fine that my knees are completely useless right now.

RÉMY COMES with me to the photoshoot in Montmartre. He holds my bag and lenses the entire time, he smiles at me in a way that seriously undermines my ability to act professional, and he holds my hand on the way there and on the way home.

But the part that makes me so happy I want to cry is how he wants to go through all the photos from the session with me when we get home. He flips through them slowly, taking them in like he's really paying attention. "Madi, these are . . . unbelievably good."

I smile like a fool because he's making me feel like a million bucks *and* because I'm really happy with the photos. The session was nothing short of magical—the perfect combination of likable, photogenic clients, amazing lighting, and a gorgeous location: the trifecta. I thought maybe it was just a result of me pirouetting all over cloud nine given the situation with Rémy, but looking through these photos assures me that it wasn't just me. Linnae is going to be really pleased with these.

Rémy wants to see the whole process—from shooting to delivering the photos—so we sit together on the couch all night, culling the photos (such a tedious and torturous part of my job, made so much easier having a second opinion), making the edits, and uploading them to a gallery.

"We are definitely setting the record for the quickest ever delivery," I say as I press the send button. Linnae deserves it after insisting on paying me twice as much as my normal session fee. I almost cried when she sent the money. It feels like a crime getting paid for something I enjoy so much—and in a place like Paris.

"We're a good team." Rémy takes my computer, sets it on the coffee table, and pulls me over onto his lap so that I'm facing him and looking down into his eyes.

"I should be helping you with *your* work now," I say.

"Okay," he says. "Maybe you can solve my dilemma."

"Chances are good. It's always easier to solve other people's dilemmas."

He smiles, then sighs. "My mom really wants this position at Bellevue for me."

"But you *don't* want it . . . ."

He tips his head from side to side. "I'm not sure. It's an objectively good career move. A more established and prestigious school. Better job security."

"But . . ."

"But I really like where I am. I was telling my dad about work when we talked on the phone last night, and it made me realize just how much I like it. There's a lot of freedom working for a private *lycée*. And then I like my students a lot. The administration really values my input, and they give me a lot of flexibility with my methods as long as I'm getting results. It's a very good fit for me."

I chew my lip. "Have you talked to your mom about it?"

"I'm not sure how to. When it comes to my career, things are . . . touchy. She's taken my interest in English as me choosing sides with my dad or something. And because the Bellevue position was her idea, it feels like she sees this as . . ."

"More than just the job."

He nods. "She's been texting me to send my material to Monsieur Garnier, but I keep putting it off."

I run my thumb along Rémy's jaw, thinking. "If you don't want the job, there's got to be a different way to help calm those insecurities she has without sacrificing your career. I'm sure she wouldn't really want you to choose less happiness, Rémy. But if you're not sure whether you want the job or not, if this might just be nerves about making a change from what you're used to"—I shrug and drop my hand to my lap—"you can always send him the material while you're figuring out what you want for sure. Keep both doors open until you know which one you want to go through."

Rémy takes my hand and threads his fingers through mine, his eyes still on me.

"*Or*," I say, "you can just tell me to stuff it because I have no idea what I'm talking about and have no career to speak of."

He shakes his head and pulls me down for a kiss. We've kissed a dozen times today, but every one has been different, unique, its own brand of intimate. This one is slow—so slow, so unhurried, so deliberate that it has time to travel down into my body and through my extremities before our lips shift. It's almost painful in its perfection.

If this is what the next eleven days are going to be like with Rémy, I might need to scrounge up a thousand dollars so that Jacqueline can change my flight to 2030.

FORTY-ONE

RÉMY

"I'VE ONLY PLANNED FOR FIVE, RÉMY." MY MOM IS LESS than thrilled that I've added Madi to the guests for her *Réveillon*.

I'm treading tricky ground here. Just like the position at Bellevue, this is about a lot more than the invitation, and both of us know it. "I know. It's rude of me to spring this on you, but, Mom, Madi was going to be alone on Christmas. She really wants to experience France, and I can't think of anyone better than you to show her what a real *Réveillon* should be like."

She sighs audibly. "The turkey I bought is small, Rémy, and she's American, isn't she?"

I laugh. "Yes, Mom. She's American; she's not a horse." *She did eat an entire baguette the other night, though.*

"She'll be expecting a super-sized meal."

Okay, now she's just being ridiculous. "She's not expecting McDonald's, Mom. If you're really worried about not having enough food, I can bring a baguette and some cheese. Madi would be content with that, honestly. I just want her there." I pause, holding my breath a bit. "Mom, I really like her. I'd like you to meet her because you're the most important woman in my life."

There's a pause, but I wait. My mom has a crusty exterior, but like any baguette worth its salt, once you break through, she's soft.

311

"Five o'clock," she finally says. "You'll have to bring extra foie gras. Have you sent your lesson plans to Monsieur Garnier?"

I suppress a sigh. One dicey subject at a time, right? "I sent them this morning. Love you, Mom."

TOMORROW IS CHRISTMAS EVE, which means today is the last day for me to get more of the foie gras I'm taking to my mom's—slightly annoying since I only bought it yesterday. But since Madi is completely on board to come with me on the errand, I don't even mind.

On the way there, I hear from André for the first time since we sent him the new pictures.

André: Rémy, I'm so sorry for not getting back to you sooner. Things have been so crazy, I didn't even see your email until this morning. I don't even know what to say. The place looks incredible. I'm uploading the new photos to the listing right now, and I feel like we should give Madison a major discount for her help—at the very least.

I read the text with a smile. Technically, she's already had a serious discount, but André has no idea I paid part of her stay. Neither does Madi, for that matter.

I hesitate before responding, trying to decide whether I should tell him about the change in Madi's and my relationship. But there's nothing really official to tell—we're just seeing where things go. Besides, I know Madi well enough now to feel confident she wouldn't 2-star the Airbnb even if things *did* turn sour between us. Telling André would just be causing him unnecessary stress.

Rémy: I'm glad you like it. I hope it takes some of your stress away and helps get you more bookings. How's your mom?

We text back and forth a bit as he gives me updates on his mom's treatments. Things are starting to look up—and I'm really hoping they continue to do so. André deserves the merriest Christmas he can get.

After picking up the foie gras, we stop in at IKEA for some string lights and a miniature Christmas tree, which Madi is totally on board with, despite the fact that it's only two feet tall.

It takes all of five minutes to set it up, but it's surprising how much joy it brings to the main room of André's apartment. The string lights on the windows really bring it all together.

"We should have grabbed some dinner while we were out," I say as we gather up the garbage from our decorating endeavors.

"Oh," she says, "I actually already ordered some food to be delivered. Should be here any—"

The doorbell rings, and I give her a look like she might have some supernatural powers I was hitherto unaware of. I press the button to ring the delivery guy in, and a couple minutes later, I open the door to the smell of Finger Lickin' Chicken on the welcome mat.

I pick it up and glance at Madi, who smiles and stands there, encapsulating everything I ever wanted in a woman.

Our fingers are greasy, and we're halfway through the food when my phone rings with a video call. My heart stutters at the name on the screen. It's my dad.

I don't remember the last time he video called me, which is crazy now that I think about it, but we've mostly texted. I hurry to wipe my hands clean, then swipe open the call.

It's weird having Madi meet my dad. Weird in a good way. I don't know what to expect from him meeting a girl I care about, but he's surprisingly cool as he talks to her. He doesn't say anything embarrassing or overeager, but I can tell he likes her. That makes one of my parents, at least.

"Well," he says after a few minutes, "I won't keep you two any longer. I figured you'd be busy tomorrow, though—I know how your mom feels about doing a proper *Réveillon*, so I wanted to call and wish you a Merry Christmas."

"It's so nice to meet you, Mr. Scott," Madi says. "Merry Christmas to you."

"Nice to meet you too, Madison. Take care of Rémy, will you?"

"I'll do my best, but he's really the one taking care of me."

My dad smiles. "That's my boy."

FORTY-TWO

MADI

We're technically still in Paris, but this is suburban Paris, and it's completely different from the city. Hedges line either side of the street, punctuated at regular intervals to make space for driveways. It's not that different from an American suburb for the most part, but there's still something foreign about it. Maybe it's the narrower driveways and garages, or maybe it's the look of the windows. It's just different enough to make a few nerves pop their heads out of hiding like ground squirrels.

This is Rémy's domain, so I let him set the pace. I don't really know what he's told his mom about us. He keeps my hand in his and squeezes it as we walk up to the door. He coached me a bit on the way here about what to expect.

The Garnier family is already there, and Rémy has to let go of my hand and set down the baguettes and *foie gras* in order to greet them, including Élise. I wasn't sure how to feel about the fact that she was going to be here, but it's actually nice to see a familiar face amongst all the unfamiliar ones.

Rémy introduces me in French, putting his arm around my waist. Having him act so confident, so . . . *possessive*, for lack of a better word, calms my nerves a bit. It makes me feel a bit more like I belong, which is a good thing because I stick out like a sore thumb. Everyone else looks so effortlessly chic, while I'm regretting my decision to dress in bright and festive red and green. I look like I'm crying out for attention. If anyone needs me, I'll just be over here confirming stereotypes about Americans.

Rémy's mom is a petite woman with short, brown hair and dark-framed glasses. The way she looks at me makes me feel like I've unknowingly stepped in front of a panel of judges at a Miss America pageant. Or a Miss France pageant. Either way, I don't want to see the score cards. Her stern expression coupled with her extra tidy appearance gives me the urge to fiddle with my clothes and hair.

"*Maman*," Rémy says softly. He lets go of me and steps over to her, pulling her into his arms. She only comes up to his shoulder, and he leans his head over to press a kiss into her hair.

That sight shifts something in me. I don't know Madame Fortin, but I'm ready to like her for the sole fact that she raised Rémy. So when the two of them separate, I step toward her.

"*Bonsoir, madame*," I say, hoping more than ever that Madame Wilson wasn't just trying to boost the bottomless pit of adolescent self-esteem when she told me I had a good accent.

Even if it's a bit tight, Madame Fortin's smile lightens her expression a bit. "Hello, Madison. We are glad you could come." Her accent is much stronger than Rémy's, but it makes her sound elegant. I don't know that I believe her about being glad I could come, but I'm going to pretend I do because otherwise, I'll spend the rest of the night extra self-conscious, and those levels are already dangerously high.

She ushers us over to the living room, where there's a spread of drinks and little snacks.

"*Amuse-bouches*," Rémy whispers in my ear as we sit down. "That's what we call appetizers."

The conversation starts in English, which makes me feel guilty because it's obvious that it's a struggle, and if I weren't here, everyone would be completely at ease, speaking French.

"You don't have to speak English on my account," I say after a couple of minutes. "Hearing you all speak will help me with my French." *My French.* That makes it sound like I have any grasp whatsoever of the language. These people all speak much better English than I do French.

They take me at my word, though, and I immediately lose track of the conversation as it bounces around the room in the fastest French I've ever heard. Rémy leans over to translate for me as they discuss the improvements André's mom is making. I could kiss him right here for being so sweet, but I also feel guilty for being a burden on him. It makes it hard for him to participate in the conversation when he's busy trying to keep me up to speed while I occupy my hands and mouth with the delicious *amuse-bouches.*

"They're talking about Christmas traditions," Rémy says to me in a low voice. "The Garniers usually attend a midnight service after the *Réveillon.* My mom and I have always gone on Christmas Day."

"What do you do for Christmas Eve at home, Madison?" Rémy's mom asks me in English.

I try to quickly chew the food in my mouth. "Oh, um, our Christmas Eves have always been kind of mellow."

Her brow furrows, and I realize she might not know what that last word means.

"Low-key," I try. It doesn't help. I look at Rémy for assistance because every synonym for *mellow* has completely disappeared from my personal thesaurus.

"*Discret,*" Rémy offers, squeezing my hand. "*Calme.*"

I smile my gratitude at him. "Yes. Those things. My mom usually works, so the past few years we've just done take-out." I may as well have just told her I use a baguette as a curling iron.

"Oh," says Madame Garnier. She's trying. I'll give her that. But she just can't figure out what to say.

"It would be nice to have a break from all the preparation and cleaning, wouldn't it?" Rémy says with a smile.

That earns a laugh, and then Rémy's mom invites us all to

move to the dining table while I let out a breath that's half-relief half-bracing myself for the next time I have to open my mouth and inevitably betray how culturally depraved I am.

Rémy's mom asks for his help bringing things in from the kitchen, leaving me on my own with the Garniers. Élise smiles at me from across the table. Her hair is pulled back in a smooth chignon, revealing pearls in her ears and a long, feminine neck. I can't say I've ever noticed a neck before today, but immediately I know Élise has the neck I should want.

"It is good to see you again, Madi," she says. "When Rémy's mother told me you were coming to dinner tonight, I said, 'How quickly things change!' I have known you almost as long as Rémy has."

I try for a laugh, even though her words feel a bit . . . pointed. "I guess that's true." Strictly, it may be. But I met Élise for all of five minutes when she came to the apartment. I've barely spent five minutes *away* from Rémy in the past few days.

Despite that, her comment can't help but lodge itself inside my brain like a catchy but annoying-as-all-get-out song.

"When did you meet Rémy?" Madame Garnier asks politely.

I take a drink. "A little less than two weeks ago." Okay, a week and a half ago, but everyone knows you round up. I'm trying to be a glass-half-full woman.

She blinks. I've surprised her again. Oh joy.

"And how long do you stay in France?" Monsieur Garnier asks.

"I fly home January 2nd." I can't decide if this conversation would be better or worse with Rémy here. I'm not loving the focus on how short a time I've known Rémy or how the clock is ticking on our time together. I'm kind of wishing Christmas Eve was *just* Rémy and me.

Everything feels so easy when it's just the two of us, but here . . . I'm getting overwhelmed with how utterly out of place I am, how little I know of Rémy, and how much separates us. I hate the feeling.

Monsieur Garnier's phone dings, and he pulls it out, then confers with his wife beside him.

Élise leans toward me. "Would you like some advice, Madi?"

Can I say no to that? I don't think I can. It doesn't matter, though. Élise doesn't wait for an answer.

"Rémy tends to forget how he feels about women who stay away too long." She raises her brows. "Take it from someone who knows. One day you are kissing him, and the next time you see him, he is with somebody new."

Okay, there's a definite message in there. I just can't decide if it's a warning with a dash of resentment or an actual threat.

Rémy and his mom enter with two platters—one of *foie gras* with freshly sliced baguettes, the other with oysters. I look at him, and he catches eyes with me as he sets down the plate. His lip curls up at the edge in a little smile meant just for me.

It makes my heart race, and I smile right back at him as he comes over to sit next to me, even though my stomach is unsettled.

The conversation takes off in French again, and I'm left on the tarmac, observing as it goes places I can't follow. Élise directs her conversation at Rémy, which means he can't translate for me like he was before. The feeling at the table is one of cheer and sociability, and I try not to detract from that, keeping what I hope is a generally pleasant expression on my face.

Rémy glances at me at one point, confirming my suspicions that I'm the subject of conversation between him and Élise. Under the table, he puts a hand on my thigh. He keeps his eyes on me as he talks. They're soft and warm, and the whole thing is just . . . sweet—and it'd be even better if I could understand what he's saying.

I swallow, suddenly overwhelmed with how bittersweet this all is. It's a little bit like hiking. You get to a place where you can see the most amazing views—and then you turn back to the trail ahead and realize you're nowhere near the top. You're not even sure what getting to the top will entail or if you've got it in you to make it there.

I wait for a lull in the conversation between Rémy and Élise. "Hey, where's the bathroom?"

"Down the hall and to the right." Rémy's eyes scan mine. "Are you okay?"

I nod. "I'll be right back."

I excuse myself from the table, hoping it's not a solecism to leave during the meal for the bathroom. It's hard to imagine someone like Élise or Madame Fortin having anything as primal as bodily functions.

I make it to the bathroom and shut the door behind me, then close my eyes and lean against the sink. It's blessedly quiet in here, giving my brain a rest from trying to parse out words from a foreign language. And this isn't Madame Wilson's slow, clear French. This is Busta Rhymes-speed talking.

I pull out my phone, hungry for something familiar—and also because it's impulse at this point to pull it out in the bathroom, which is really gross, now that I'm thinking about it. What is wrong with humans? Or maybe it's just Americans.

I open social media because that's what my fingers are programmed to do. A couple of notifications pop up, and I tap on them because, using the bathroom may be primal, but no instinct is more urgent or constant for my generation than the one to get rid of pesky notification badges.

It's Linnae from the photoshoot yesterday. She posted a bunch of the photos and tagged me in the photos *and* the caption. The post has—what?!—five hundred likes. I look at the timestamp on it. It's only been up for twenty minutes. Who *is* this woman?!

I click on her profile, and my eyes bulge. She has two hundred and eighty thousand followers.

There's a soft knock on the door, and I tense. Is this Madame Fortin, coming to inform me that she can't have the equivalent of Tarzan ruining her Christmas Eve dinner?

"Madi?"

I let out a relieved breath. It's Rémy.

I open the door, and Rémy looks back at me, concern in his eyes. "I came to check on you."

"I haven't been in here *that* long, have I?"

He shakes his head. "I just . . . felt like something might be off."

How can he read me so well after such a short time knowing me?

He takes my hand. "Is it?"

I don't answer right away because I'm not sure what to say. I don't want to ruin Christmas Eve for Rémy. In fact, that's the *last* thing I want to do. It was *really* nice of him to invite me in the first place.

But I also don't know how to go back out there. I don't know what I'm doing or how to behave. I'm flying in the dark.

"Come here." Rémy pulls me by the hand and into the hallway. We walk a bit farther, away from the dining area, then go through a door on the left. It takes us into a bedroom. It smells like Rémy, which makes it feel familiar. Besides the tidy bed, bedside table, and a dresser, it has two tall bookcases against one wall. They're full of books mostly in English.

Rémy leads me over to the bed. He sits down and tugs on my hand to pull me next to him.

I resist. "I don't wanna take you away from dinner."

He tugs more insistently. "Don't worry about that. *I'm* not worried about that."

"Yeah, but you're not the one trying to make a good impression out there." I surrender to his pulling and take a seat next to him.

"Neither should you be. You're perfect the way you are."

"What? Christmas Eve takeout Madi?"

He smiles and puts a hand on my cheek. "Are we talking FLC takeout?"

I chuckle softly and shake my head, leaning into his hand

because it feels good to connect with him after feeling so disconnected from everything and everyone.

"Will you tell me what's bothering you?"

I breathe out slowly. "I just feel a little one-of-these-things-is-not-like-the-other-y, you know? And by a little, I mean majorly. That and the fact that everyone thinks it's crazy for me to be here when we've known each other such a short time . . . it's just a lot. I can't blame anyone for thinking that. I mean, a week ago, I was in a relationship with Josh."

He nods. "It's moved quickly."

"And I don't even know what *it* is," I say. "I mean, my flight leaves in nine days."

"I know," he says, resting his forehead against mine. "Believe me, I know."

I shut my eyes and swallow. "I came here tonight hoping to feel closer to you—getting to know your mom, seeing your home, participating in your traditions—but now I'm realizing how much of it feels out of reach. I don't speak French, I'm not scoring any points with your mom, I'm pretty sure Élise has it out for me, and there's just no time."

He pulls back to look at me. "No, you don't speak French fluently. And I don't expect you to, Madi. I'm here to help if you want to learn. That's all. As for my mom . . . she's intimidating, I know. She's had to be tough to make it through. It's a façade she puts on until she knows people better, and I have no doubt at all she'll love you if you just *be you*." He sighs. "And Élise . . . if she wants to get to you, she'll have to go through me first."

I laugh. "Um, pretty sure that's *exactly* what she's hoping for. She basically said if I stay away too long, she'll steal you back."

"Well, first of all, you can't steal something back you never had."

I cock a brow. "She told me last time she saw you, you kissed her."

He tips his head from side to side. "That's wording it differently than I would. We kissed, yes. I felt like I owed it to her or *something.* It was my attempt to resurrect feelings I'd had for her in the past. And it didn't work. She knows it, too, because I told her I didn't want anything with her. She's just seeing if you'll scare off easily."

He looks at me intently, his gaze running all over my face. When he talks, his voice is so soft, it's almost a whisper. "Please don't scare off, Madi."

"Rémy?" His mom's voice sounds somewhere down the hall.

He looks at me, and taking my face in his hands, he kisses me soft and slow, a seal to his plea, an assurance that nothing has changed for him. I'm powerless against his sweetness. If he is at the top of the peak I've been staring at all evening, his kiss makes me want to sprint up there.

But I'm not a sprinter—not even on flat surfaces—so I guess that means a long, trudging hike to the top. It feels well worth it for Rémy, and I return his kiss, hoping it tells him what I need him to know: we may only have nine days to decide what happens next, but I want to give it what I've got.

"Rémy?"

We break apart reluctantly as his mom knocks on the door, opening it slowly.

"*Ça va?*" she asks. For the first time this evening, I understand something someone's saying—she wants to know if things are okay. Her gaze shifts between us.

"*Ça va,*" I reassure her. My French might be terrible, but I'm not going to worry about that. I want her to see me trying, however pathetic my efforts might be.

"Ready for the main course?" she asks.

I nod and stand up. Rémy follows suit, then leads the way out, while his mom lets us pass in front of her.

I slow as we near the dining area. "Can I help you bring things out, Madame Fortin?"

She hesitates for a second with a quick glance at Rémy. "Of course. Thank you."

I follow her into the kitchen. Dirty dishes are stacked in and next to the sink. On the counter, there's a pile of the plates we used for the *foie gras* and oysters. In short, it looks like the kitchen of a woman who's been working all day to feed a complicated meal to guests. It's relatable. And, boy, have I needed some relatable tonight.

Madame Fortin moves around the kitchen with confidence, giving me a stack of plates to hold while she transfers meat to them from a covered casserole. Then we work side by side, adding a little garnish to the plates to make them look more finished.

She glances at my work and, to my pleasure, looks almost impressed. Not all of my ventures into product and food photography were wasted, then!

She adds a final sprig of parsley to the plate in front of her, then uses a nearby dish towel to dab at the beads of sweat on her brow. "*Voilà*. We can take them in now."

I nod and take two dishes in hand, starting to walk toward the door. I pause halfway there, then turn. "Madame Fortin?"

She's taking the other plates in hand, but she looks up at me, her brows raised. It's a look that I could easily choose to be intimidated by, but I let Rémy's words replay in my mind. *She's had to be tough to make it through.*

"I just wanted to tell you how much I appreciate the wonderful son you've raised." I feel a little emotion rising in my throat and swallow it back down before it can commandeer this moment. "I grew up without a dad for most of my life, so I know some of the sacrifices it takes to do what you've done for Rémy. And I know how instrumental my mom has been in the person I've become. So I guess I just wanted to say thank you. Or maybe congratulations."

It's not my best work. I'd say six out of ten for eloquency, but ten out of ten for sincerity.

Madame Fortin blinks a couple of times, her hands still poised under the plates, ready to pick them up. She clears her throat. "*Merci*, Madi."

I give a little smile and turn to take the plates to the table.

FORTY-THREE

RÉMY

I WAS HESITANT WHEN MADI OFFERED MY MOM HELP IN the kitchen. No one loves my mom more than I do, but no one knows her better, either, and she can be . . . difficult. But when they emerge a few minutes later, Madi seems fine. In fact, she seems better than when I found her in the bathroom.

As for my mom . . . it's hard to tell what she's feeling or thinking because it's always hard to tell with her.

Madi continues to seem better, despite the fact that *le Réveillon* is one of the longest (and most delicious) meals in history. My mom likes to do it "right," which means it lasts at least four hours. More than once during those hours, she looks at me, then shifts her eyes in a very not-inconspicuous way toward Monsieur Garnier.

It's out of character for her, actually. She is a subscriber to the notion that work should not be discussed at the dinner table, and it seems Monsieur Garnier is, too, because he doesn't bring up my email or the position.

Or maybe he saw my lesson plans and thought they were garbage, and he's hoping the subject is never brought up so he doesn't have to let me down. While the second option doesn't appeal to my pride, it *does* appeal to the part of me that wants an easy way out of the situation a.k.a. not telling my mom I don't actually want the job at Bellevue. Because I'm quickly coming to the conclusion that I don't. I want to stay at Lycée Michel Gontier.

I realize it's a lot to bring an American girl home with me *and* destroy my mom's career hopes for me all on a holiday, though, so I'd like to avoid that. I'm hoping Monsieur Garnier will hold off until after the Christmas break if he wants to discuss things.

When ten o'clock rolls around and things wrap up, I keep my eye on Madi while she and Élise say goodbye. They exchange *bises* —Madi's got it down now—and Élise pulls away and says, "Don't stay away too long, Madi."

Madi glances at me, but my mom pulls me with her to walk Monsieur and Madame Garnier to the door.

"We hope you have a very enjoyable time at midnight mass," my mom says as they step outside. "Oh, Monsieur Garnier, I meant to ask . . . did you receive Rémy's email?"

I clench my jaw and stand aside to allow Élise to step out with her parents. Madi's disappeared, and I'm *really* hoping Élise didn't say anything else to scare her off.

"I did receive it," Monsieur Garnier responds. "You're a very promising candidate, Rémy, and I will certainly be in touch about the position once I'm back in the office."

My mom recognizes the hint that he doesn't want to discuss this on Christmas Eve, and with more thanks, holiday wishes, and a lingering kiss on the cheek from Élise, we send them off into the crisp night.

"How can you expect to be given the position if you don't show any interest in it, Rémy?" my mom asks as I shut the door.

"I didn't think he'd want to discuss it here." *I* sure didn't want to.

"Well, it sounds like we should feel encouraged, at least." She folds her arms across her chest and looks at me. "Élise was looking very beautiful."

I shoot my mom a look. For someone who can insult people

with such impressive passive aggression, she is terrible at subtlety in other areas.

She sighs. "Madi looks beautiful too."

"She does. But she's a lot more than just beautiful, Mom. Thank you for letting me bring her."

She doesn't say anything, just nods. But a nod from my mom isn't too shabby.

"I'm going to take her to midnight mass," I say. "Would you like to come?"

She targets me with a brow. "I attend mass on Christmas Day, Rémy." She starts walking back toward the dining room. "Besides, I have a mountain of dishes to do."

To be honest, I'm relieved she doesn't plan to come. I want some alone time with Madi. I think we need it. We turn out of the entryway, and I look for Madi, but she's nowhere to be seen, and my heart drops. Is she in the bathroom again? Did she leave?

"Madi," my mom says, stopping on the threshold of the kitchen. "You are a guest. You should not be doing the dishes."

My shoulders relax, and the fear disintegrates that Madi decided this was all too much for her and just left.

"Madame Fortin," Madi says as she scours a casserole dish, her sleeves rolled up and her hair tied back in a scrunchie, "I *insist* on doing the dishes. I have never had such an amazing meal. I can't imagine how much time you spent on it today. Why don't you go relax with Rémy for a bit?"

My mom isn't one to back down easily, but after a bit of coaxing from Madi and me, she gives in and makes her way to the couch. The way she drops down onto it speaks volumes about how tired she is. She's getting older.

I watch Madi from the doorway for another few seconds, hyperaware of the way my chest feels almost painful at the sight of her. And it hits me right there and then: I'm in love with her. After ten days of knowing her. It's insane. But it's also true.

When we start our walk to the nearest train station half an hour later, it's cold and quiet outside. No more silverware and dishes clanging, no more convivial conversation. Just me, Madi, and the street lamps and Christmas lights.

I feel . . . strange. Nervous, maybe. After acknowledging to myself that I'm in love with Madi, I face a conundrum. Now more than ever I want her close, to hold her hand. But now more than ever, the thought that she's not in the same place as I am, that she might never *be* in that same place—it's scary.

"We didn't really get to finish our conversation from earlier," I say. "Do you want to talk about it?"

She shakes her head, but she grabs my hand and looks up at me with a soft smile.

You'd think I'd just dropped out of an airplane for the way my heart responds to that combination of gestures.

"Let's just enjoy Christmas," she says.

I hold her hand tighter and nod.

IT'S NOT the most comfortable Christmas Eve I've spent, sleeping on the couch next to Madi after midnight mass, but it's the best one I can remember.

It feels slightly shifty of me, though. This—waking up next to Madi—is what I want more and more, and the fact that she doesn't know just how fast or hard I've fallen for her makes it almost feel like I'm taking something that's not rightfully mine.

But what's new? I've been ahead of Madi in my attraction to her and my feelings for her since the beginning, so I guess this is just who I am now.

Madi has her photoshoot today, and I'll attend mass with my mom. Knowing I won't be with her for those hours makes me impatient for her to wake up. But since attending midnight mass kept us up until 1:30, I resist waking her.

It's past nine o'clock when she starts to stir. It's normal for her to be this exhausted. Listening to a foreign language for hours on end is the mental equivalent of running a marathon.

Madi shifts, her head turning from side to side as her lids start to flutter. I hold my breath, waiting for the moment she realizes she's next to me. She stills, her eyes suddenly growing alert as she looks up at me.

And then she smiles sleepily and snuggles her face into my chest. I wish I could bottle this feeling and sell it to myself for the rest of my life. It gives me some hope that maybe she can feel for me what I feel for her.

"What are you doing?" I ask as she burrows even further into me.

"I've got morning breath," comes her muffled response.

I chuckle. "Me too." I try to sit up.

"Where are you going?"

"To get us some gum."

"Not yet." She pulls me back down and puts her head back in the hollow of my chest. "Christmas morning snuggles take precedence over good breath. I'll just keep my head like this."

I relax back down and wrap my arms around her, content to lay like this all day. I can't think of a way I'd rather spend Christmas morning.

It's a slow day—a leisurely breakfast followed by watching *It's a Wonderful Life*. Madi gets a Merry Christmas text from Josh (eye roll), and because the movie has me feeling very charitable and Christmassy, I urge her to throw him a bone and wish him a Merry Christmas too.

Way too soon, both of us are getting ready for our separate Christmas Day activities. I come out of my room, adjusting the collar above my sweater. "Are you sure you don't want to come to mass with my mom and me?"

Madi's got her gear laid out on the table and is changing out SD cards in her camera. "I mean, of course I'd love to. But I think it's best if I don't. That way, you can have some good mother-son time. Plus, it won't really work with the photoshoot, and I would hate to let Ashleigh Jo down by canceling. Especially on Christmas. Also, I need the money."

She rubs her thumb against her fingers and wags her eyebrows.

"That hand gesture means something else here, you know."

Her eyes widen. "Oh my gosh. Is it crude? Super offensive?"

I smile. "No, it just means you're afraid."

She lets out a huge sigh of relief. "*You're* the only thing making me afraid. Don't scare me like that."

"Just helping prevent future miscommunication. Your photoshoot is at the Champs de Mars?"

She grabs her phone and swipes and taps a few times, then reads something. "No, it's at the . . . Trocadéro?"

I nod. "Opposite side of the tower from the Champs de Mars. It's a great view of the Eiffel Tower, but it's a busy place. It might be hard to get photos without people in them. But maybe it'll be calmer today. People will be busy with Christmas activities and all."

"If it's crowded, I'll work my magic and move us elsewhere. A key skill as a photographer is the art of convincing people to accept my vision of their session rather than theirs." Her mouth draws up in an evil smile, like she's about to skin a hundred and one dalmatians rather than ensure her clients are happy with the photos she's going to take of them.

I can tell by the way she's obsessing over the cleaning of her equipment that she's excited for this session. Only Madi can spend Christmas day taking photos of strangers and be thrilled about it.

We agree to meet afterward, and I make my way to meet my mom for mass. We'll be catching the last of the day's services.

I STAND OUTSIDE of the church, saying hi to familiar faces from the neighborhood until my mom walks up. Her eyes scan the area around us, which is full of bare bushes, and I raise my brows.

"I thought Madi would come," she explains.

"And that she'd be hiding in a bush? She thought you and I could use some time together."

My mom doesn't say anything, but I can tell she's secretly impressed. She should be. Madi is thoughtful and kind and fun and all the best things. I'm confident my mom will see that with time.

"I really like her, Mom."

"You barely know her."

"I know it seems like that. We've spent a lot of time together, though. And I want to keep spending more time with her."

"And how do you plan to do that? She's leaving."

I stuff my hands in my pockets. "I don't know yet."

I've got to find a way, though.

My mom says nothing, and I glance over at her as we walk inside the church. She's not the type of woman who lets her face betray her, but I can see by the tilt of her chin that she's fighting some emotion. I think I know what it is.

We sit down, and after a few seconds, I put my hand over hers. She looks over at me, eyes alert. She's not the touchy-feely type.

"Mom, you know I'll always be here, right?"

Her eyes stare into mine, and behind the strong, determined woman, I see a wisp of vulnerability peek through.

"I owe everything to you. And I promise I won't forget that." I take in a deep breath. I wasn't really planning on doing this right now, but maybe it's a good time. Maybe saying what I need to say before the service starts will give my mom some time to let it settle in. "Sometimes I get the sense that you're disappointed in me— whether that's my interest in English, my job teaching it, my lack of motivation to try for the position at Monsieur Garnier's school, or my dating Madi. Maybe I'm wrong, but if it *is* because you feel like you might lose me, that I might choose those things over you, I promise you I won't.

"I don't know what'll happen with Madi and me. I know

what I *want* to happen, but I don't know what *will* happen. And if I'm being completely honest, I also don't know that I'll take the position at Bellevue even if it's offered to me. I love where I am now, and I don't really want to leave. But none of that has any bearing on you and me." My mouth tugs up at the corner. "You're stuck with me forever."

She squeezes my hand, which, for my mom, is the equivalent of running at me full speed and hug-tackling me. "I just want you to be happy, Rémy. I don't want you to go through what I went through."

"I know, Mom."

She looks down at our hands for a minute while we both let things sink in. She starts to fiddle with my hand in hers. "Madison cleaned my dishes perfectly." She looks up at me and smiles softly.

My mouth pulls up in a grin because that is a major compliment from Sylvie Fortin—and I know what it means, even if she's still a bit too proud to say it: she likes Madi a little bit already.

I take my hand from hers and wrap my arm around her shoulders, pulling her into me and kissing her hair.

"She leaves in a week?" she asks.

"Eight days." I'm like a kid who insists on correcting people who say it's 2:30 when it's really 2:29. But that one extra day is important.

"Then what are you doing here, Rémy?"

I pause, trying to make sure I heard her right, then I pull away enough that I can look at her.

"Go," she says with a teasing glint in her eye. "I've seen enough of you today."

FORTY-FOUR

MADI

I'M NOT USUALLY ONE TO GO FOR LONG PERIODS OF time without looking at my phone, but since coming to Paris, I've become that kind of person. And I don't think Paris has much to do with it. It's Rémy. I couldn't care less about scrolling through social media apps when I could be talking with him. It's not even that I'm resisting; I just forget social media exists when we're together.

But now that he's gone to mass, instinct is back in full force, so I navigate to social media like the tech zombie I am.

Whoa.

This tech zombie has a ridiculous number of notifications. I tap on them—an endless line of likes and comments from usernames I don't recognize, and a *ton* of new followers. Some are liking the picture Linnae tagged me in, while others are apparently going back through my entire feed and liking my old posts. I scroll and scroll and scroll, stopping when I notice a tag.

It's a repost of the same picture Linnae posted, and the account tagged both of us in it. I tap on the account, and my eyes bug out of my head. One million followers. It's a massive photography account with a feed featuring shots from destinations around the world. And the photo I took is right there at the top of them all.

Heart racing, I tap on my own profile and stare at the number of followers. Between the post from Linnae and the one from the massive photography account, I have four thousand new followers. Four thousand. That's four times more than I had to begin with. Not to mention my inbox has a bunch of unread messages.

I start reading. Every single one is a request for a session, most of them in Paris. One asks if I would be interested in coming to Bruges and another to Barcelona. There's a request for a date next week, one for a Valentine's couple's session, and one all the way out in summer. And that's just three of the ten.

My phone buzzes in my hands, startling me out of my dazed state. It's my mom video calling.

I hurry to accept it; I didn't think I'd hear from her at all today. It's her last cruise day, and I figured she'd have no service.

"Mom!"

"Hi, honey! Merry Christmas." She's got sunkissed skin and messy, beach hair. It's very unChristmassy of her. I haven't seen her glow like this in years, though, and it warms my heart like the end of a cheesy Hallmark movie. So cheesy that my eyes are actually prickling. She deserves this break more than anyone.

"So?" she says with a huge smile and an enigmatic look. "Do you have some news for me?"

Oh dear. How many times will this happen? A lot has gone on since I last talked to her.

"Um . . . yes? But maybe not the news you're expecting."

I regale my mom with a Reader's Digest version of what's happened over the past couple of weeks—the rough arrival, the unmet expectations once I was here, the lead-up to the breakup between Josh and me, and finally, the actual breakup. Even after that, she's still *way* behind.

I don't know exactly how to catch her up on the rest. Things have happened at warp speed, and telling it all in this way only highlights that. How exactly do I explain that, since we last saw each other, I've ended the relationship I staunchly defended for two years *and* started falling for someone new? It makes me sound like a complete loon—more unstable than a French elevator.

So I hold off on all the Rémy stuff. A few minutes can go a long way to space out all the action.

"Wow, Madi," she says softly. "I feel awful."

"Why?"

"Because I haven't been there for any of it! All these huge things happening in your life . . ."

"Mom," I say, "first of all, it's expressly forbidden for you to feel awful on a cruise—unless it's the result of overeating. Secondly, you have been here for the entirety of my relationship with Josh. Despite the fact that you never really liked him, you've been patient with me as I figured things out for myself."

She straightens, looking mildly offended. "I *did* like Josh, I just—"

"Mom."

Her shoulders drop, and she relaxes. "Okay. I didn't like him. At least not for you. But I tried, Madi."

I laugh softly. "I know you did."

"Tried what?" Jack's face pops up on the screen as he joins the call. He's in a living room I've never seen before. Behind him is a fireplace with a pine garland draped artistically across the top, two red bows, and a half dozen stockings.

"There you are!" Mom says. "I sent Jack a text invitation since he never answers FaceTime calls right away," she explains to me.

"Never answers them at all, more like," I say.

"Hey, I'm here, aren't I?"

I pull my clasped hands to my chest and bat my eyes. "Our very own Christmas miracle."

Jack shoots me a look—at least I assume it's for me. "Not all of us want to be at the beck and call of our phones twenty-four hours a day, seven days a week."

"No," I say, "but five minutes a day, one day a week wouldn't kill you."

"What did Mom try?" Jack asks, ignoring my dig at his lack of connectedness.

"Liking Josh," Mom says.

"Hardest thing I've ever done," Jack says without missing a beat.

I tip my head to the side and plaster a fake smile on my face. "Aw. Poor Jack. And here I thought being a terrible brother came naturally to you." I don't really have a spicy side, but Jack sure brings it out of me.

He smiles widely, scrunching up his nose in the most annoying older brother expression I can think of. "I'm sorry you haven't had as much success in romance as I've had, Mads. But hey, I can't take all the credit for my success. You've got *great* friends."

There is so much history implicit in those stupid words that I want to use the garland behind Jack to strangle him.

"Enough of that," Mom breaks in. "Madi already has someone new, and she was going to tell me about him before you joined us."

I blink. I kept my references to Rémy as bland and relevant as possible, only mentioning him when it was pertinent to the story of Josh and me. I certainly didn't tell her I *have someone*.

Mom smiles at my reaction. "Motherly intuition—isn't it a glorious thing? Now, was it Rémy? Did I catch his name right? It's a great name."

"Wait, you're serious?" Jack asks, looking back and forth between us. "Didn't you break up with Josh like a week ago?"

It's not meant to be judgmental, but given that I'm already worried about how this whole situation sounds, it hits that way. So I snap back, "Oh, because *you're* the model of careful deliberation when it comes to relationships?"

He puts up his hands defensively. "Hey! You won't ever hear me complaining that you gave the boot to Josh. I just don't wanna be on this same phone call in two more years because you've jumped headfirst into something with an equally dumb dude."

"Jack," Mom says in a warning tone.

"Don't worry," I say sweetly. "I didn't call you today, Jack, and you wouldn't be the one I'd call in two years."

He laughs. "Fair enough."

That's one good thing about Jack. He can take what he dishes out. That's the only reason I get snippy with him—I know it won't hurt his feelings.

"If this is about to become girl talk," he says, "I'll leave the two of you to it. I just wanted to jump on to say Merry Christmas."

"Thank you, Jack," Mom says, looking at him like he's the sweetest thing in the world for spending two minutes on a video call with his family on Christmas. "I love you, sweetie."

"I love you, too, Mom. And you, Mads."

"Love you, Jack," I say with a hint of annoyance. "Merry Christmas."

"Merry Christmas. Oh, and Mads? Make sure Ratatouille is better than the last guy."

And then he's gone. How he manages to balance the protective brother vibe with the couldn't-care-less-about-your-love-life vibe is truly impressive.

My mom shakes her head with a smile. "Okay, sweetie. Now tell me about Rémy."

So I do. And whether it's because of Jack's comments or because I need someone besides Siena to reassure me that I'm not crazy, I don't hold back—not about how amazing Rémy has been, not about how fast my feelings have developed, not about how scared I am beneath it all.

"Oh, Mads," Mom says after I've dumped all my words onto her. "He sounds perfect for you."

I swallow. He does. Rémy *feels* perfect for me. Not perfect. But perfect for *me*. "But, Mom, what if Jack's right? What if I'm right back here in two months? Or in two years?"

"Impossible."

"Mom . . ."

"I mean it, Madison. Even if things ended between you and Rémy, you wouldn't *be* right back here. You'd have learned and grown. You'd be in a new place. Life's a journey, and sometimes all we get to decide is who we take with us and for how long. But we're never back at square one, even if it seems like it."

I let that sink in. "I just don't see a clear path forward for us, though. We live in different countries, for heaven's sake."

"Who said the path has to be clear, sweetie? You think your father and I were skipping along the yellow brick road together? We cleared away our fair share of bushes and debris. It's not what the path looks like. It's having someone who's willing to do the work to clear it *with* you. Better a dedicated partner on a rough road than someone sleeping at the wheel on a straight stretch."

My mom is right. I know she is—she and her Chicken Soup for the Soul wisdom.

FORTY-FIVE

MADI

I'M GOING THROUGH MY MENTAL SHOT LIST AS I GET off the metro at the Trocadéro stop. Not only did I come here on my own, I had to make a metro line change to do it.

It's wild how far I've come in my comfort level on the metro since first arriving. There's a powerful sense of satisfaction that comes with being able to navigate the system and get where I need to, all on my own. Sure, it took a little (literal) handholding to get me here, but I've done a lot of things in Paris that scared me, and it's shown me that many of my fears are conquerable with the right support and the right mindset.

Which brings me to Rémy. Every time. Always to Rémy. And to what my mom said about him. We haven't known each other very long, but Rémy has shown in every way possible that he will stick with things—with *me*, especially when I need him most.

I wish he was with me right now. I'm glad he's with his mom, though. As easy as it would be for me to monopolize him all day, there's a special bond between a single mom and her child.

The weather is overcast, which makes it a bit warmer than usual. I'm not complaining. It sure makes my job easier. I'm always a bit jittery before a shoot—you never know what clients will be like—but today even more so. Since talking to my mom, I've been thinking about changing my flight. Again.

But this time, I'm thinking about pushing it back, and the money from these shoots might just make that possible.

I reach the corner of a wide, open area set between two tall, columned, symmetrical buildings. This is the Trocadéro, and I pause to admire the view. It's a straight shot ahead to the Eiffel Tower, and I can absolutely understand why Ashleigh Jo would want this location. There are people here, sure, but if I get creative, I can keep most of them out of my shots. Any of the pesky ones I can't keep out of the frame can be forced out with Photoshop if needed.

I pull out my camera and take some test shots, using a suit-clad gentleman with his back to me as my involuntary test subject until I'm satisfied with my settings.

"Madi."

I whirl around, sure I'm hearing things. But Rémy's jogging toward me. My heart does a wacky little dance at the sight of him there, wearing his Christmas mass sweater in a way that, quite frankly, makes it hard to remember the reason for the season.

"What're you doing here? I thought mass didn't start until three." I pull out my phone and check the time. It's only 3:30, and it takes about thirty minutes just to get to his mom's.

It also means Ashleigh Jo and her fiancé should be here any minute. I try to give my clients a thirty-minute grace window to show up before I call it and leave. I'll probably give them more today because it's a lot less skin off my back to hang out by the Eiffel Tower than it is in a studio back at home. Also, I need their money.

"It didn't," he says, a little breathless as he stops a couple feet away from me. "I just . . . I wanted to come help with the session." He holds my gaze. "I wanted to be with you."

Mom said she and Dad cleared away a lot of bushes and debris from their path. As I stare back at Rémy, trying to breathe, I realize I will wield a flipping machete if that's what it takes to see where the road with Rémy takes me. I'm hoping the road doesn't require that, though, because the thought of me with a machete is frightening.

"What about your mom?"

He smiles slightly. "She's the one who told me to come."

I have no response for that because, even though Madame Fortin and I had that little moment of connection in the kitchen last night, I was under no impression that she was over the moon about my presence at her special dinner—to say nothing of my presence in her son's life.

But maybe I did better than I thought I had.

Somewhere nearby, a violin starts playing. Gosh, I love Paris. It's as close as real life gets to a musical, with street performers starting up songs worthy of a life soundtrack all over the place.

"Madi?"

I whirl around to the sound of the new voice, expecting Ashleigh Jo and her boyfriend.

It is not Ashleigh Jo and her boyfriend.

It's the man in the suit whose back I used as a test subject walking toward me. That suit is a tux, and that man is Josh.

"Josh." My voice comes out like a croak.

He smiles big, and I'm mentally shaking my fist at both Paris and fate who have teamed up to make it so that Josh would have a business function—or maybe it's a date with Brianne—right here at the same time that I have a photography session. It's unreal.

"Merry Christmas," he says.

"Merry Christmas to you, too." I glance at Rémy, who's taken a step back. I turn back to Josh. "Um, it's good to see you. I'm actually here for a photoshoot, and it's supposed to start right now, so I should probably go look for my clients."

His smile widens. "Your photoshoot is right here." He looks over his shoulder and makes a jerking motion with his head. The violinist starts moving toward us, his bow sliding over the strings as he walks, chin to violin.

Josh puts his hands out and smiles widely. "I'm Ashleigh Jo."

I open my mouth, but no words come out. I have never been this confused in my life, and the confusion emoji is one of my top five most used, so that's saying something.

"Ashleigh Jo Wrutton," he repeats like it should mean something to me. "It's an anagram for my name. Joshua Elton Wright."

My mouth plops closed, and I blink a thousand times. "Like Tom Marvolo Riddle and *I am Lord Voldemort*?" Harry Potter is the strongest mental association I have with anagrams, and I am mystified that Josh would follow Voldemort's lead.

He looks a bit miffed. "I mean, no. Not like that. I wanted to surprise you, but I thought I might leave you a little clue. For fun."

I have no words. I'm trying to process the fact that I'm evidently *not* here to take beautiful pictures of Ashleigh Jo and her fiancé in front of the Eiffel Tower on Christmas Day. I will *not* be pocketing a few hundred dollars tonight to help me pay for a flight change. But what I don't understand yet is *what in the heck is happening?*

"I have a lot to say, Mads," Josh says, the violin accompanying him from a few feet behind. "I'm really *really* sorry for what happened at lunch last week. I royally screwed things up, and you had every right to be angry with me. I've been spending my time since trying to figure out how to make up for it. I've shown the company your portfolio, though, and"—he takes in a breath and spreads his mouth wide in that charming smile—"they want to hire you on. As an in-house photographer for the brand."

People are starting to look, and a few are indulging their inner Curious George enough that they've stopped to watch. I don't know if they're here for the violin music or . . . oh gosh. Do they think that—

"But that's not all," Josh continues, taking a step closer and reaching for my hand.

More people stop, and even though there's an abundance of space at the Trocadéro, I start to feel claustrophobic. I'm frozen, my brain completely disconnected from my body as I process what's happening.

"We've been through a lot together, Mads. Two years worth of stuff. *Two years.* I've spent the last week since I saw you thinking about it, and guess what? Two years isn't enough. I want more— and I'm not gonna give up on things. When I look at our future together, you know what I see?" He twists and gestures to the scene lying before us—the Trocadéro, the Eiffel Tower, Paris. "I see a vision as beautiful as this one. And I want to give all of it to you—I *will* give it all to you, Madi." He reaches into his pocket and pulls out two small, rectangular papers. "These are Eiffel Tower tickets. I have reservations for the restaurant at the top at 5:30."

The audience we've acquired breaks into little *ahhh*s.

"But before that . . ." Josh reaches into his pocket again (how many pockets does this man have?) and pulls out a sleek, black velvet box.

This moment is perhaps the strangest of my life, and it's happening in slow motion. Slow, painful motion. Everything he's saying is what I would have given anything to hear a few weeks ago. But right now? It's like reading an old journal entry— familiar but distant.

I look at Josh, at the way he's waiting for me to react some-how. This is what he does. He sells a product, a vision, and right now he's selling himself. All he can point to to get me on board is the future. He came in with the big guns, too: a job, a romantic evening with the entirety of Paris in view, promises of a better future than the past, and that ring I waited so long for.

He couldn't even propose to me without telling me what he had planned for us afterward—dinner at the top of the tower— like that should factor into my answer.

But as I look at the Eiffel Tower, and as my gaze takes in a city shifting from afternoon to twilight, all I see is Rémy.

Rémy took me out for groceries my first night in Paris. Rémy took me to my first museum. Rémy took me to the top of the

Eiffel Tower and held my hand the whole time. Rémy showed me how to get around on the metro—again, holding my hand the whole time.

Josh is promising me Paris, but Rémy already gave me Paris. And without Rémy, Paris is just a pretty city that very possibly used to hate my guts. He showed me how to love it until it loved me back.

Josh takes in a deep breath and starts to go down on one knee.

"Josh Josh Josh," I say, looking at all the people who've gathered around us. Some even have their phones out. "Can I talk to you for a second?"

He pauses on the way down, glancing at the people all around and coming back up every bit as slowly as he descended. The man's quads must be burning.

I look around for a place where we could be private for a minute, but we are essentially on an enormous stage, except all hell has broken loose at this theater because, not only am I an unwilling participant, the audience has stormed the stage and is blocking the exits. They demand a performance. But I can't give it to them.

"What is it?" Josh asks.

I swallow, accepting that there is no way out of this that is not humiliating for Josh and does not make me look heartless. Could he not have at least chosen to do this on some small, cobbled side street?

No. Because he's Josh, and he goes big. But he's missed his mark this time. By a lot.

I take in a breath and look at him, hoping he can see how badly I feel about this. "I'm sorry, Josh. I . . . I just can't. It's not what I want anymore. And I don't think it's what you want, either. Not really."

There's a collective *aww*. It's like we're on an episode of *Full House*.

Josh doesn't talk. He can't. His face says, *I don't believe this.*

I wonder for a second if I should tell him about Rémy, be

completely upfront with him, help him accept how serious I am. Given this audience, though, I don't know that it's a merciful choice to reject him and throw another man in his face.

I glance over at Rémy.

Except not, because he's not there.

FORTY-SIX

RÉMY

I couldn't watch.

Maybe that makes me a coward. There were twenty-five other people watching, after all. But I'm not a tourist watching a romantic engagement in front of the Eiffel Tower with no skin in the game.

I'm in love with Madi, and the moment Josh took her by the hand, I realized that I didn't know what was going to happen. I know Madi cares about me. I don't doubt that at all. But I also know a couple of other things.

I met Madi less than two weeks ago. She and Josh were together for two *years*. She came to Paris hoping to get engaged to him. And now she has that chance.

She told me her relationship with Josh is like a habit. Humans are terrible at breaking habits. We do things all the time that aren't healthy for the simple fact that it's what we're used to doing. And Madi would hardly be the first person to get back into a bad relationship because she hoped it would be different this time.

And Josh? He came prepared to get a *yes*, with a slick sales pitch and a violinist and everything. Every woman's dream proposal.

And I? I couldn't bring myself to wait and see what she

decided. It's like when my dad left; I stayed away because watching the act of him actually leaving was too much for me to handle. I think some part of me hoped that when I went home afterward, he wouldn't be gone, that he'd have stayed.

But he didn't. And what if Madi doesn't either?

I stop just shy of the crosswalk and shut my eyes.

I assumed you knew.

That's what my dad said when we talked the other night. And because of that assumption, I spent the last few years thinking my dad didn't care about me, that I had to prove myself to him and earn his love. We both could have avoided all that if one of us had been brave enough to just say what we wanted and what we felt.

And yet here I am, doing the same thing with Madi, waiting to see if she leaves without making sure she knows exactly where I stand.

I turn back toward the Trocadéro, my heart picking up speed. If she chooses Josh after I say my piece, so be it. At least I won't have to live my life wondering what might have been different if I'd had the courage to tell her. At least my pain will have a foundation in reality rather than assumption.

I start jogging back toward the esplanade, my eyes searching for the group of people congregated to watch. It's getting darker, making it harder to see. I slow down because I don't spot anyone where it was all happening.

And then I see her, slowing from a jog, just like me, her camera bag bumping against her hip.

She stops, her gaze on me, her chest rising and falling, and we both stand there, ten feet between us.

"You left," she said, and I can see the uncertainty in her face. She doesn't know what to make of me abandoning ship.

"I came back."

She takes a few steps toward me. "Came back for what?"

I breathe in deeply. The fact that she's here right now and I can't see Josh anywhere around is a good sign, but I'm not here to make assumptions. I'm here to make it 100% clear to Madi what I want and to let her do the same. "I came back to convince you to choose me, Madi. I know we haven't known each other very long —not nearly as long as you've known Josh, but . . ."

She steps up right in front of me and looks up into my face. "What makes you think I need to be convinced?"

I swallow, then gesture vaguely toward the esplanade. "You just got the most amazing sales pitch I've ever seen. Everything you've been wanting."

She shakes her head. "I don't want a sales pitch, Rémy. It's not the grand gesture I'm interested in. I want the little stuff." She looks down at my hand and takes it, pulling it up to chest level and threading her fingers through mine. "I want sticky notes left on my cheese and baguette. I want gentle urges to face my fears and support to give me the courage." She looks up and into my eyes. "I want someone who pays for a stranger's Airbnb because she's an absolute disaster, melting into a pool of puddle iron."

I open my mouth, then shut it. "Josh told you?"

Her mouth turns into a lopsided smile. "I told him I'd reimburse him, and he got confused. He assumed I had paid for the remaining balance." Her expression grows more serious, and she tightens her hold on my hand. "*You* are everything I've been wanting. I don't know what happens in eight days, Rémy. I have no clue how we're going to make this work. But I want to give things a real shot. I will fly here every weekend, lose my luggage, and get stuck in every elevator in Paris if it means I get to be with you."

I pull our clasped hands to my lips and kiss her knuckles. "Why do you get to give your sales pitch, but I don't get to give mine?"

She smiles as I wrap an arm around her waist. "Every second I've spent with you has sold me on you, Rémy." She holds my gaze, soft and intent. "I want you. All of you."

"You've got it, Stars and Stripes." I press my lips to hers, and a hushed *ooh* sounds. We break apart at the reaction, unaware we had an audience.

But we don't, and the sound effect is not for us. The Eiffel Tower just started sparkling.

We look at each other and laugh softly.

"Little do they know," I say, "the real show's back here."

"Such a shame," she says, reaching up and moving a piece of hair out of my eyes. "Guess we should make it a regular performance, then. For their sakes."

I laugh and take her face in my hands, looking into her eyes. She may not let me give her my full pitch, but she can't stop me from the condensed version. "I love you, Madi."

She shuts her eyes and smiles, waiting for me to kiss her. "*Je t'aime*, Rémy."

EPILOGUE

MADI

I'M RUNNING ON VERY LITTLE SLEEP, BUT I'M *WIRED*. I'M looking out the taxi windows like I've never seen Paris before. And it's true in a way; I've never seen Paris like this. It's autumn, and it's . . . different. The light, the smell in the air, the energy.

I grin like a fool because I'm *thrilled* to be back. It's September and, even though I was here as recently as the end of May, it feels too long.

I actually look much better than I should after such a long day and night of travel, but Siena forced me to change and freshen up before we left the airport. We'll be going directly to surprise Rémy.

Siena's sitting opposite me in the taxi, looking out her window. She's been helping me with this surprise for Rémy, and when I invited her to come stay for a week, she jumped at the chance.

She shoots me a glance through narrowed eyes that say *I could kill you*. "Your life is a joke. You know that, right? Moving to Paris to be with your hot boyfriend and take pictures for a job?"

When she puts it like that, it does sound pretty great. "Hey, it hasn't exactly been smooth sailing."

351

Figuring out how to legally work in France has been a headache. Despite all the requests for sessions I've gotten, I haven't been able to formally charge for them during the months I've spent in Paris. All I've been able to do is accept "donations," which, to be fair, most people have been generous with.

In the meantime, I worked on and finished up the city guide and also let my social media followers know I was available to do shoots anywhere within a couple hours of home during the months I spent in California. Surprisingly, a lot of people reached out to me. Since then, my following has continued to grow, and I've been earning actual money. Enough to live off of. *Cue happy tears.*

But today is different. As of now, I'm officially a French long-stay visa holder. Rémy thinks I'm just coming for another three-month stint like the last time. Ninety days is as long as I can stay in a six-month period as a tourist, so Rémy and I have traded off spending time in France and the States. I did three months in the spring; he spent his summer holidays with me. Now it's my turn again. But this time, I'm back for a year, at least.

Siena scoffs. "Who cares whether the sailing is smooth? You've got the hottest co-captain to hold onto, and you're 'sailing'"—she does air quotes—"on the equivalent of a yacht."

"The yacht being . . ."

"Paris. Duh." She pulls out her phone and freezes. "Oh my gosh! Can we make a quick stop?"

"Do you need the bathroom? It can be tough to find one in the city, Siena—at least one you'll feel comfortable using. Can you wait—"

She brushes my words aside. "No. It's not the bathroom. There's this street I saw on a Pinterest post, and we're right by it, and I *really* wanna get a picture there."

"Siena. We have all week to see Paris. I'll bring you back here tomorrow."

"*Please*, Madi! Rémy isn't even gonna be home for another three hours. What's the rush?"

"Well, we have FIVE huge suitcases to get up to his apartment." Rémy found a place back in March right by Lycée Michel Gontier, and, like any good French apartment, it's up on the highest floor. It also has a lovely birdcage elevator not unlike the one from André's apartment. It's really grown on me. Nostalgia and all that. But it's broken twice while we've been in it.

We managed just fine.

Anyway, I actually tried to book André's apartment for Siena's visit, but the place is booked out for months, which makes me pretty dang happy. André is living with his mom now since her cancer is in remission, so he's renting out both rooms.

"I will carry all five of the suitcases myself," Siena promises. "Just this quick stop?"

I sigh. I get it—the excitement of being in Paris and wanting to experience it immediately. Heck, *I'm* feeling it myself.

I scoot to the edge of my seat and talk to the driver in French, doing my best to explain what we're requesting. I've been taking French lessons from an amazing tutor (Rémy), and, while I've still got a ton of work, I've made a lot of progress. Staying with Rémy's mom during the spring sure didn't hurt, either. She takes my goal of learning French so seriously that she hasn't spoken a word to me in anything but French in months. It's freaking hard, but it's pushed me to learn faster than I otherwise would have.

Siena hands me her phone, and I convey the address to the driver, then sit back in my seat and shake my head. "You're lucky I love you so much. This taxi ride is going to cost a small fortune." It was really the only option if we wanted to fit all of our luggage, though. Moving to a different country requires a lot of bags. And Siena isn't the lightest traveler, either.

"I thought you said we were right by the place," I say after we've been driving for a few minutes.

"I mean, we *are*. Much closer than we were back at home."

I shoot her an unamused look. "By that logic, we should be asking the driver to take us to Rome."

Siena looks mildly intrigued. "Think he would?"

She's ridiculous.

The taxi driver pulls over to the curb on a street in the 19th arrondissement. It's lined on one side by the Haussmannian buildings that make Parisian architecture so recognizable, and on the other side, there's a long, green iron fence that extends the length of the street. What lies beyond it isn't visible, as trees just beginning to change yellow and orange block the view.

I recognize one of the signs by the nearest entrance gate, though. Parc des Buttes-Chaumont. I smile. Siena has good taste in location; this is one of the happiest places in Paris for me. It's where Rémy and I came on New Year's Day when we decided I would come back for the spring.

Siena asks me to tell the driver to wait for us, which I do, assuring him we will be back soon and will pay him well for his time. I'm not trying to have him drive off with everything I own in the back of his car. I'd rather not make a habit of getting scammed by Parisian taxi drivers, but this guy seems nice.

"You realize this park is huge, right?" I say to Siena. "Do you know where you're going?"

But she's got her phone out as she leads the way into the park, confident in her steps. This girl does her research. "It's close."

"Close like Rome close?"

We walk for a minute, then round a familiar bend and stop.

"This is it," Siena says loudly enough for everyone in the park to know she's here and she's American. But I don't even care that she's being embarrassing.

"Seriously?" This is the exact spot Rémy brought me that freezing day in January. It's just off the main park path, but it feels like a different world: a waterfall pouring into a stream, lined on either side by stone paths. A peaceful oasis in the city.

"This is it," Siena repeats, even louder this time. If there were anyone in sight, I would definitely be shushing her right now, but mostly I just want to know why she's acting so weird.

Up ahead, Rémy steps out from a small alcove by the waterfall. He's wearing a slim-fit gray suit and a blue tie.

I look at Siena, who just smiles like she's part of *Ocean's Ten* and has just pulled off an amazing heist. "Surprise," she says.

"Rémy!" I run to him because I haven't seen him on anything but video chats in a whole month. When you spent almost every second together from the get-go, that's a lifetime.

He smiles and jogs over to meet me—is it just me, or has he become ten times more attractive since I last saw him?—and I barrel into him, burying my face in his shoulder and inhaling because unfortunately, the geniuses that run the tech world have not figured out how to let me smell my boyfriend through the phone. Truly a modern travesty.

It's a tad dramatic to arrange a meeting here when I'd be seeing Rémy in three hours anyway, but I love it all the same.

He holds me close. "Gosh, I missed you," he whispers into my ear.

"You have no idea."

When we pull away, I turn to Siena. "You planned this together?"

She just grins and taps her fingertips together like Mr. Burns from *The Simpsons*. I laugh and turn back to Rémy. "I can't believe she went behind *my* back. She loves you way too much if she's conspiring with you."

Rémy looks at me kind of funny. "You think this is what we conspired together about? Tricking you into meeting me here earlier than planned?"

"I mean, you *did* conspire to do that."

He takes a step back, keeping his eyes on me. "Yeah, but we conspired about a lot *more* than just that." He drops to one knee.

I stop breathing. He does this to me a lot—makes my body forget basic physiological processes—and I wonder if my first to-do list item as a resident of Paris should be to see my doctor about it. There's gotta be a prescription for it. Or an essential oil.

Rémy takes my hand in his free one. "Madi, the first time we met, you threw a shampoo bottle at my head. And you missed *pretty bad*."

I cover my mouth with a hand because the sounds coming out are in a very gray area between a laugh and a cry.

"But you knocked me down anyway, and I have been absolutely crazy about you ever since. I know you aren't big on sales pitches, and I'm too impatient to give one. So"—he pulls out a gold band with a glimmering diamond in the middle—"will you marry me?"

Can't breathe, can't speak, can't laugh, can't even cry properly. So I just nod and pull him up from his knee and into a kiss to make up for the last month of missed ones. It actually can't make up for those, but . . . we've got time.

When we pull away, he takes my left hand and slips the ring onto my finger. We both look at it for a few seconds, then Rémy puts his palm against my palm and threads our fingers together.

"I really do hate to interrupt this excruciatingly adorable moment," Siena says, "but I just have to draw attention to the masterful way I made *both* of you believe I was your secret keeper, while really, I had my own game the whole time."

Rémy and I look at each other, but neither of us has any idea what she's talking about.

"Gah! The two of you are so slow. Allow me to spell it out for you. Rémy, Madi isn't here on a tourist visa." She looks way too satisfied with herself. "They approved her long-stay visa application, which, if my research is correct— and it is, but please don't be mad at me if it's not—will be turned into a residency card after the wedding, making your path forward"—she does a showy gesture with her hands—"seamless."

Rémy looks at me, eyes wide. "You got the visa?"

I smile and nod. "And I have four heavy suitcases—and the airport receipt for the excess fees—in the taxi to prove it."

He pulls me in for another hug, pressing his mouth to the spot just behind my ear. We sit like that, holding each other (with a very willing and self-satisfied audience of one) until Rémy whispers, "Then let's go home."

Home. I smile, because with Rémy, I really am home.

THE END

Read the rest of the *Christmas Escape* series

Christmas Baggage
by Deborah M. Hathaway

Host for the Holidays
by Martha Keyes

Faking Christmas
by Cindy Steel

A Newport Christmess
by Jess Heileman

A Not-So Holiday Paradise
by Gracie Ruth Mitchell

Later On We'll Conspire
by Kortney Keisel

Cotswolds Holiday
by Kasey Stockton

AUTHOR NOTE

When I was seventeen, I was an exchange student in France. Before leaving, I had a vision of sitting at the foot of a tree on the grounds of a castle, sketching as the tall grass around me waved in the breeze.

Martha, meet reality.

My time in France was . . . tumultuous, from beginning to end. My first day, I was picked up from the airport and driven around Paris, where I was in severe language shock, not to mention having my first experience with 8-hour jetlag. We got into a fender bender in the humongous and infamous traffic circle around the Arc de Triomphe. Afterward, we went to eat at a restaurant. Having no appetite, I barely touched my steak and fries, so I tried to ask for a doggy bag, only to be laughed at—the first of many faux-pas.

And that was just my first day. I've traveled *a lot* since then—I'm traveling as I write this, in fact—and those travels have given me a plethora of embarrassing and incredible experiences to pull from.

Though I didn't set out intending to write Madi as me, that's what I ended up doing, in a way. Despite my first experience in Paris being jarring, I have returned many times since then, including a 3-month internship (during that internship, I was in an unfulfilling and very unhealthy relationship, just like Madi). Paris is one of those cities people either hate or love. I love it. Unabashedly.

If you've never been, I hope reading this book gave you a taste for Paris—and I hope your real experience starts out better than mine and Madi's.

If you've already been, I hope the book took you back.

More than anything, though, I hope you enjoyed watching Madi and Rémy fall in love.

OTHER TITLES BY MARTHA KEYES

The Donovans

Unrequited (Book .5)

The Art of Victory (Book 1)

A Confirmed Rake (Book 2)

Battling the Bluestocking (Book 3)

Families of Dorset Series

Wyndcross: A Regency Romance (Book 1)

Isabel: A Regency Romance (Book 2)

Cecilia: A Regency Romance (Book 3)

Hazelhurst: A Regency Romance (Book 4)

Regency Shakespeare Series

A Foolish Heart (Book 1)

My Wild Heart (Book 2)

True of Heart (Book 3)

Tales from the Highlands Series

The Widow and the Highlander (Book 1)

The Enemy and Miss Innes (Book 2)

The Innkeeper and the Fugitive (Book 3)

The Gentleman and the Maid (Book 4)

Standalone Titles

Host for the Holidays (Christmas Escape Series)

Goodwill for the Gentleman (Belles of Christmas Book 2)

The Christmas Foundling (Belles of Christmas: Frost Fair Book 5)

The Highwayman's Letter (Sons of Somerset Book 5)

Of Lands High and Low

A Seaside Summer (Timeless Regency Collection)

The Road through Rushbury (Seasons of Change Book 1)

Eleanor: A Regency Romance

If you would like to stay in touch, please sign up for my newsletter. If you just want updates on new releases, you can follow me on BookBub or Amazon. You can also connect with me on Facebook and Instagram. I would love to hear from you!

ACKNOWLEDGMENTS

Diving into a new genre is a scary experience as an author. I can honestly say, though, that the actual writing of this book was loads of fun! I wrote the entirety of it while we've been traveling full-time, and I release it two days after we return to the States, so it marks a milestone for our family.

My husband was an even more essential part of my process this time around (didn't even know that was possible!). He not only helped me work through plot and character snags, he held the family together during our travels.

My kids are ever-patient with me, even though they can't wrap their heads around how long my books are and how I'm never done writing "my book."

To my critique group—Kasey, Jess, Deborah—you are my people, and your friendship is the best part of this gig by far!

To my beta readers—Mom, Anna, Maren, Nancy, Brooke, Cindy—thank you for reading the first version of this and for making it better than it ever would have been without your careful eyes and feedback.

Thank you to my editors, Jacque and Emily, for cleaning up the messes I made.

Thank you to my Review Team for your amazing help and support. Thank you for believing in me as an author, even in a new genre.

And thank you, finally and most importantly, to God, for blessing me with everything I have, including the travels that have shaped me as a human.

ABOUT THE AUTHOR

Whitney Award-winning Martha Keyes was born, raised, and educated in Utah—a home she loves dearly but also dearly loves to escape to travel the world. She received a BA in French Studies and a Master of Public Health, both from Brigham Young University.

Her route to becoming an author has been full of twists and turns, but she's finally settled into something she loves. Research, daydreaming, and snacking have become full-time jobs, and she couldn't be happier about it. When she isn't writing, she is honing her photography skills, looking for travel deals, and spending time with her family. She is currently traveling the world full time with her husband and twin boys.

Made in the USA
Coppell, TX
27 December 2022

90840765R00219